# Amelia's Hope

Plain Paths, Book Two

## SUSAN LANTZ SIMPSON

# Praise for Amelia's Hope

"Dive into the captivating world of this Old Order Mennonite novel, where a satisfying romance blossoms between a widow and widower who belong to different groups of Mennonites. The narrative weaves in the tension of a local thief, adding an intriguing layer as stolen moments intertwine with stolen possessions. The story promises a delightful blend of love, mystery, and the charm of Plain life, leaving readers smiling and yearning for more." ~ Suzanne Woods Fisher, bestselling author of *Lost and Found*

"Susan Lantz Simpson spins a gentle mystery wrapped around the sweetest of romances. The result is a satisfying read that will leave you smiling. With an Old Order Mennonite community, two lonesome souls who have lost their spouses, and a combined total of five little girls in need of love, you can't help but sink into this story. In the midst of all the chaos of the world around you, give yourself this treat. You won't regret it!" ~ Patricia Johns, *Publishers Weekly* Bestselling Author, Most recent releases: *An Amish Mother for His Child, Murder of an Amish Bridegroom*

"*Amelia's Hope* is a must-read for lovers of Amish fiction. The main themes of faith, forgiveness, and new friendships weave together all throughout Simpson's sweet and captivating romance between Ryan and Amelia. I liked the secondary characters and found them helpful as the couple navigated their growing attraction." ~ Diane Craver, author of Amish Adoption Series

"Simpson has done it again, bringing us an endearing romance filled with strong community bonds and the importance of family. Then she tosses in a mystery that had me struggling to find out who-did-it! *Amelia's Hope* will check all the boxes." ~ Mindy Steele, author of *The Flower Quilter* and *An Amish Flower Farm*.

"If you have a soft spot for blended family stories, *Amelia's Hope* is the book for you. The novel takes the reader on an adventure as widow Amelia Stauffer and widower Ryan Miller learn to love again, while caring for five little girls. The story has all the warmth you'd expect, along with a mystery that adds to the fun. Find a quilt to snuggle under and get ready to enjoy *Amelia's Hope*." ~ USA TODAY bestselling author Dana Mentink

"*Amelia's Hope* is a story full of matchmaking and mystery. Readers will root for Simpson's selfless characters, a loving mother and father who want the best for their children and for each other." ~ Laurie Stroup Smith, author of The Pocket Quilt Series

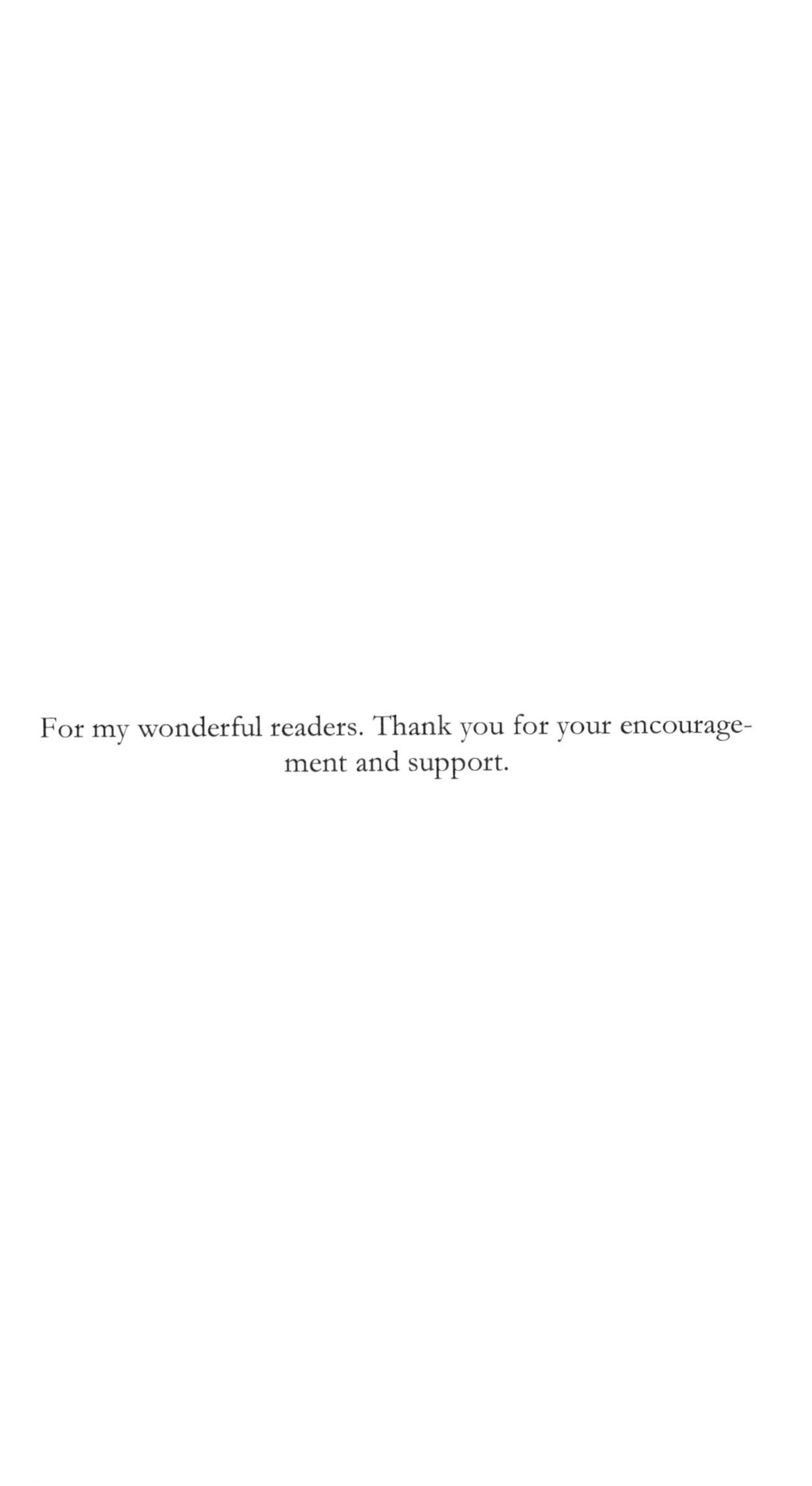

For my wonderful readers. Thank you for your encouragement and support.

"For I know the plans I have for you," declares the Lord, "plans to prosper you and not to harm you, plans to give you hope and a future." ~ *Jeremiah 29:11*

And we know that all things work together for good to them that love God, to them who are the called according to his purpose. ~ *Romans 8:28*

# Glossary

The German dialect used by Amish and Old Order Mennonites is a spoken, rather than a written, language and varies from one community or location to another. The spellings are approximate.

| | |
|---|---|
| *Ach* | Oh |
| *Aenti* | Aunt |
| *Applendisch* | Delicious |
| *Ausbund* | Amish/Mennonite Hymnal |
| *Boppli; bopplin* | Baby, babies |
| *Bruder* | Brother |
| *Bu; buwe* | Boy, boys |
| *Daed* | Dad |
| *Danki* | Thank you |
| *Dochder* | Daughter |
| *Englisch, Englischer* | English or non-Plain |
| *Fraa* | Wife |
| *Freind(en)* | Friend(s) |
| *Gott* | God |
| *Grossmammi* | Grandmother |
| *Gut* | Good |
| *Jah* | Yes |
| *Kaffi* | Coffee |
| *Kapp* | Prayer cap/women's head covering |
| *Kinner* | Children |
| *Kumm(s)/Kumming* | Come(s)/coming |
| *Lieb* | Love |
| *Maedel* | Girl, young woman |
| *Mamm* | Mom |
| *Mariye* | Morning |
| *Mudder* | Mother |
| *Nacht* | Night |

| | |
|---|---|
| *Narrisch* | Crazy |
| *Nee* | No |
| *Onkle* | Uncle |
| *Ordnung* | Set of rules for Plain living |
| *Rumspringa* | Period of "running around" before joining the church |
| *Schweschder* | Sister |
| *Wilkom* | Welcome |
| *Wunderbaar* | Wonderful |

# Chapter One

The quilt had to be there. She had left it right on the buggy seat. Amelia Stauffer bent to search beneath the seat and reached her arm as far as she could until her fingertips brushed the back of the buggy. She knew the quilt wouldn't be all the way in the back but checked anyway. Where could it have gone? It certainly didn't hop from the buggy and run off.

"Where is it?"

She pulled out a nursery rhyme book, a couple of tissues—unused, thank goodness—and a child's sock. Just one? The neatly folded buggy blanket remained in its place. Amelia dragged it out and unfolded it even though she knew the quilt couldn't have gotten folded up inside of it.

This did not make any sense. "I am absolutely certain that I left the quilt on the seat."

Suddenly, her vision blurred. *Amelia, you are a twenty-eight-year-old widow with three* dochders. *You will not cry over a missing quilt.*

The quilt would only be a bed covering to anyone else, but it was special to her and her girls. Amelia had lovingly stitched scraps from all their old dresses into a patchwork quilt and had embroidered a different animal in each corner. The brown-and-white dog was for Rhonda. The tabby cat was for Judith. The bluebird was for Joanna. And the black-faced sheep was for her. If she arranged the quilt just so, she could cover all three little girls with their favorite animal.

"I don't understand this."

"What is it, Mamm?" Six-year-old Rhonda poked her head through the opening on the opposite side of the buggy.

Amelia quickly swiped a hand across her eyes and sniffed. "I was looking for something."

"We'll help." Four-year-old Judith leaned against her older *schweschder* to peek at her *mamm*.

"Help." Two-year-old Joanna tugged at the back of Amelia's skirt.

"*Danki*, girls." Amelia suppressed a groan as she straightened from her cramped position. "Let's go back inside The Green Thumb for a minute."

She must have grabbed the quilt when she gathered up the items she had carried inside the store. That had to be the explanation for the missing quilt. The girls would be heartbroken if it was truly gone. To be honest, she would be upset herself.

Amelia reached down and swung Joanna onto one hip. "You're getting big, my *boppli*." The two older girls pranced along on either side of their *mudder*. At least she only had her own three to keep track of today since it was Saturday. Five days a week, she babysat widower Ryan Miller's two little girls. She loved them as her own, but right now three *kinner* were all she could handle.

"Is something wrong?" Christina Brubacher, owner of The Green Thumb, looked up from the display she had been arranging.

"Is my quilt mixed in with the things I brought?" Amelia spoke in *Englisch* so the girls wouldn't understand everything. Little ones usually learned *Englisch* when they started school. They spoke Pennsylvania Deutsch until then.

Rhonda had begun learning *Englisch* since she now attended school, and Amelia had been teaching a little of the language at home so it would be familiar to them. But she didn't believe they would get the gist of her conversation with Christina. There wasn't any need to upset them just yet. Maybe not at all, *Gott* willing.

"I just started unpacking your items. These pot holders, place mats, baby bibs, and wall hangings are so pretty. You do *wunderbaar* work, Amelia."

"*Danki.* And I appreciate your taking them to sell. I know you aren't running a consignment store, and you're busy with your nursery and garden supplies."

"But my customers love all the sweet treats you and Marjorie bring to sell, and many of my *Englisch* customers have been begging me to sell more handmade items. I think my *grossmammi* would be pleased that her store has become an outlet for ladies of our community to share the fruits of their labors."

"Well, I, for one, am grateful to you. I earn a little money from babysitting and my basket making, but with these growing girls, every little bit helps."

Christina fished around in the bag Amelia had brought into the store. "You know, this bag doesn't feel heavy enough to contain a quilt, but let me pull the rest of the things out to make sure."

"I'm almost completely sure that I did not put the quilt in that bag. Why would I? I certainly don't intend on selling it. Besides, I would have needed it for the ride home, which is why I am certain I left it right on the buggy seat like I always do."

"*Nee*, it's not in here." Christina gently laid each hand-stitched item aside and showed her *freind* the empty bag. "Would you like me to help search your buggy?"

"I've searched. It's really hard to hide a full-size quilt, but I did check beneath the seats anyway. It couldn't have walked off on its own steam. Do we have a quilt thief around here?"

"I hope not, but I'd take that over a murderer." Christina shivered and briskly rubbed her hands up and down her arms.

"For sure."

Only a few months earlier, Christina had discovered an *Englisch* man's body in her shed. Originally, his death had been ruled a drug overdose, but his *schweschder* had persuaded Christina and Noah Zimmerman to help her prove otherwise. Christina had quite a scare when the man's killers showed up at The Green Thumb threatening her with harm. She cleverly thwarted them, and the two men were now serving life sentences in prison. Jill, the deceased man's *schweschder*, had become a *freind* and a regular visitor to The Green Thumb and the Mennonite community in general.

"I'll keep a lookout for your quilt. Maybe it will turn up unexpectedly. I'd also better keep an eye on these lovely things you brought so they don't wander off as well."

"*Danki*, Christina. I suppose I will need to get busy stitching another quilt. I probably still have scraps from most of the fabrics I used before. Finding the time for such a big undertaking might be a challenge since I have little Gabby and Jessie five days a week. They are *gut* girls though, and I can usually get the four younger ones down for a nap at the same time. That should give me a couple of hours to stitch if I get my chores done early."

"Four?" Christina counted to herself. "*Ach!* Silly me! Rhonda is a big girl now and goes to school."

"*Jah*, she does, and she loves it. I'm sure the transition was harder for me than it was for her."

"You're a *gut mudder*, Amelia."

"I try."

"I hope Mr. Miller knows what a great caregiver he chose for his *dochders*."

Amelia's cheeks burned. She'd rather not talk about Ryan Miller. She still cringed when she remembered the little trip to town that she and the girls took with him during the summer. The Millers were Mennonite but belonged to a more modern community. They used electricity in their homes and drove dark-colored vehicles. As far as Amelia could tell, their basic beliefs were quite similar. She had only allowed him to drive them that evening because he needed her help making a purchase.

"I didn't mean to embarrass you." Christina patted the slightly older woman's arm. "I only meant you are such a caring person. I'm sure you are just right for his poor *mudderless* girls."

"They are such *gut* little ones. It is sad they won't have any memories of their *mamm*."

"It must be very difficult for their *daed* to be both parents to them and work full time too, just as it must be difficult for you."

"I'm sure it's harder for a man, but he's doing a fine job from what I can tell." Why did heat flood her cheeks again? Her comment sounded like a perfectly normal, natural observation to her.

"As are you."

Amelia needed to steer the conversation in a different direction, or maybe she should simply leave. Christina had been a *gut freind* and would never deliberately make her squirm, but Amelia found herself doing exactly that. She shifted Joanna in her arms and prepared to go.

Christina held out her arms. "Let me see how big this girl has gotten."

The two-year-old willingly leaned over for Christina to take her. She giggled when Christina raised her high.

"My, you will be as big as your *schweschders* before we know it. Then I won't be able to lift you so high." She set Joanna on her feet and turned her attention to Rhonda and Judith.

"You will make a great *mudder* one day. Any chance that will be soon?"

This time Christina's cheeks reddened. She shrugged. "One day."

"I thought you and Noah would be ready to make an announcement."

Christina's flush deepened. "I, uh, well…"

Amelia squeezed her *freind's* arm. "I'm teasing. You take your time making such an important decision. But I am looking forward to a wedding."

"Whose wedding?" Annie Wenger shot through the door, gasping for breath, her white *kapp* strings swirling around her face.

Amelia laughed. Not much occurred in their community that Annie didn't know about *and* talk about. She might be Christina's best *freind*, but the two young women were as different as night and day. "Your wedding!" Amelia couldn't resist teasing the red-haired girl.

"*Ach!* You will have a long wait, then. In fact, Rhonda might even get married before I do."

The little girl giggled. "I'm only six."

"And she had better not think of marriage for a very long time." Amelia gave her oldest *dochder* a brief hug.

"Whose wedding were we discussing?"

Leave it to Annie to latch onto a topic like a dog latched onto a bone and refused to release it. Amelia glanced at Christina and rolled her eyes. "*We* weren't discussing anyone's wedding. I don't know anybody getting married soon. Do you, Christina?"

"*Nee*, I can't say that I do."

"Oh. I thought…Well, never mind." Annie looked from one woman to the other as if she wasn't quite sure she believed them. "Wedding season is upon us. I'm sure we'll all witness someone's marriage in the upcoming weeks."

"For sure. I need to get these little ones home and get some work done. And I guess I will have to start cutting out quilt blocks."

"I'll keep a look out!" Christina called.

Amelia heard Annie ask what that was all about. She would let Christina explain that if she chose to do so. But she didn't particularly want rumors of a quilt thief in their midst to spread far and wide.

"Let's get in girls. Brrr! The wind is brisk." Amelia lifted each one into the buggy before hopping in herself.

"I'm cold, *Mamm*. Where is the quilt?" Rhonda's gaze traveled from the seat to the floor to her *mudder's* face.

Amelia reached for the folded blanket beneath the seat.

"I want our quilt, Mamm." Judith tried to hop off the seat, but Amelia's hand stopped her.

"The blanket will keep you plenty warm. The quilt is, uh, missing."

"Where is it?" Rhonda always needed answers.

"I'm not sure. Perhaps it went visiting."

Judith burst out in a fit of giggles. "Quilts can't go visiting." Joanna joined in on the laughter even though she didn't understand what was so funny.

"Really, *Mamm*. What happened to the quilt?" Without a doubt, Rhonda would keep her on her toes over the years.

"I'm not sure, dear. It was here when we went inside The Green Thumb, but it wasn't here when we came out. It vanished."

"Someone took it?"

"I suppose so. Maybe they will return it to Christina."

Rhonda slumped back in the seat. "Someone took *our* quilt."

"It's gone, *Mamm*?" Judith's big, blue eyes filled with tears.

"Gone?" Joanna echoed.

Amelia had to think of something fast before she had a three-way wailing session in the confines of the buggy.

"Let's look at the bright side." She forced a big smile. "We can all pick out the fabrics we want to use for a new quilt."

"You'll make us a new one?" Judith's lip still trembled.

"We will make it together."

"We can't sew," ever-practical Rhonda stated.

"Maybe it's time you learned. And you can all help select the fabrics."

"I want it to look like the old one." Rhonda's voice ended in a wail.

*Keep calm, Amelia.* "Did you know that I still have a lot of the material from that quilt? And we can add new colors too."

"What about the animals?" Judith loved animals, especially cats.

"I can embroider animals in the corner just like before, unless you want different ones."

"I want my kitty."

"Then you shall have your kitty, Judith."

"I want my dog. My brown-and-white dog."

"You shall have him, Rhonda."

"Her."

"Sorry. Her. And Joanna and I will have our bird and sheep. So, is everyone ready to start the adventure of designing a new quilt?" Amelia infused all the enthusiasm she could muster into her question.

"*Jah!*" three small voices cried in unison.

*Thank you, Lord Gott.* A would-be tragedy had been averted. Amelia hoped so anyway.

"We can start this afternoon."

She managed to hold in the huge sigh that threatened to escape. She had so many things she needed to do this afternoon, but she could not go back on her promise. The quilt was important to her little girls. They would only be small once, so their needs would take precedence over chores. Besides, the quilt held a special place in her heart too. She shook her head. Who would take a well-used quilt?

~

Ryan Miller buckled his small girls into their car seats in the back of his black SUV. Baby Jessie still faced rearward, but Gabby kept a running stream of conversation going that greatly entertained her little sister. They looked so much alike that they could have passed for twins if they'd been the same size. They had his dark hair and eyes, which had been a blessing. If they'd had Marian's light brown hair and green eyes, the pain of her death would have stabbed him anew each time he gazed at them.

Thank the good Lord that grief and pain had eased considerably. The loneliness, though, was another beast altogether. As long as the girls were awake, his mind and hands stayed busy. In the stillness of the night, that old monster crept in. He had begun his own personal Bible study, and that helped immensely.

With the weekly grocery shopping done—no small feat for a Saturday afternoon—he now needed to get the girls home, put groceries away, finish cleaning the house and washing clothes, and come up with a dinner menu. At the same time, he would have to entertain two little ones. How did mothers do it?

Ryan glanced at The Green Thumb as they whizzed by. When alone, he often stopped in for a quick homemade treat on his way home from work. He would definitely forego that side trip today. No way was he going to haul the children out of the vehicle again. Besides, he had way too much to do. Several black buggies sat outside the store. Could one of them be hers?

# Chapter Two

"I hear your quilt got stolen." Marjorie Gehman elbowed Amelia after church on Sunday. She shook her head and clucked her tongue.

Amelia cringed, even though the older woman had whispered. How had Margorie gotten wind of the "occurrence," as Amelia dubbed it in her own mind, already? She had to invent a nonthreatening name since she couldn't bear to think that there was a thief in their midst. She truly doubted that Christina had shouted the news from the rooftop. That left only one other person who could possibly be the talebearer: Annie.

"I ran into Annie Wenger when I first arrived and—"

"I do hope that Annie isn't making a big deal of this and telling everyone in the world."

"There wasn't anyone else nearby at the time."

"That's *gut*. I truly don't believe Annie means to gossip, but she does like to talk. I'd prefer to simply let the matter drop."

"But it's terrible to think that someone would reach into your buggy and take the quilt that you and your girls loved. I-It's a violation." Marjorie's voice rose, and she gave an exaggerated shudder.

"Shhh! Let's keep this between us."

"Amelia, dear, even if you don't say a word to a living soul, and if Annie, Christina, and I keep mum, word will get out and spread faster than a fire in a haystack."

Amelia nodded. She did know that. Somehow news spread faster along the Mennonite grapevine than an *Englisch* telephone line. Probably even faster than the speediest computer or cell phone. "Maybe it will all blow over soon."

"How are the girls taking the loss of their beloved quilt?"

Since little ears were listening, Amelia forced a cheerfulness that she didn't feel into her voice. "We're making a new quilt. The girls are helping with this one, so it will be extra special."

"How *wunderbaar*!" Marjorie switched to *Englisch*. "You'd better nail this one down every time you get out of the buggy or else leave it at home. *Ach!* Let me get next door into the kitchen. I've run my mouth, and I need to help Nora Weaver serve the noon meal."

Amelia stared after her *freind*. Tears filled her eyes for some unexplained reason. It was only a quilt for Pete's sake. Fabric. It was silly to cry over it. She wouldn't. That's all there was to it. Before she could usher the girls to the house so that she, too, could help with the meal, Marjorie rushed back and shook her arm. "Maybe Christina can help solve this mystery. She sure helped put the clues together for the mur—" Marjorie looked down at the girls and smiled. "For the *mishap* at her store."

She bustled off before Amelia could reply. Mishap? That word didn't begin to describe what had happened at The Green Thumb. A missing quilt couldn't begin to compare to a dead man. Amelia shivered as if a curtain covered the sun and blocked every speck of warmth. "Let's go inside, girls. I'm cold."

"Are we going to eat, *Mamm*?" Rhonda tugged on her arm. "My tummy is rumbling."

"Mine too," Judith echoed.

Amelia would much rather go home where she could stoke up the fire, brew a mug of hot tea, and try to dispel the chill that gripped her heart and body. But her *kinner* were hungry, and she had promised to help. Besides, if she simply disappeared, she would create a bigger mystery than the missing quilt.

She forced a smile. "Well, we can't have rumbling tummies, can we?"

~

She stayed only long enough to be polite and to feed the girls. Amelia wanted to reach her home and complete outside chores well before darkness fell. A strange uneasiness overtook her and swallowed up her usual sense of well-being. She couldn't put her finger on a specific reason—other than the runaway quilt—but something made her wary. She felt a need to be extra cautious, extra protective, maybe even extra vigilant.

Perhaps the unaccustomed nervousness had to do with Marjorie's words. Unknown hands reaching into her buggy was a violation, even if the person who had stolen the quilt only needed it for warmth. If that was the case, he or she only needed to ask. She would gladly have offered warmth to a freezing person.

Amelia shivered as she tucked the buggy blanket around her girls for the trip home.

"I miss our quilt." Rhonda's lower lip poked out in a pout.

"I know, dear one." Amelia patted her *dochder's* leg. "But think how pretty our new one will be. And we will have all made it together."

Rhonda nodded. "Can we work on it today?"

"Not on the Lord's Day, but tomorrow."

"I have to go to school tomorrow."

"When you get home, we will at least choose our fabrics. How's that?"

"Okay."

Two wee voices echoed their older *schweschder*.

Amelia let the girls run off some energy in the cool breeze after they arrived home while she cared for the horse. Then she snatched up Joanna in her arms and raced Rhonda and Judith to the house. They reached the front porch giggling and gasping.

"Where's your basket, *Mamm*?" Judith pointed to the spot where Amelia's big handmade basket sat ever since she'd woven it six months ago. Now only a faint circle outlined the spot the basket had occupied until today. The umbrellas that had been nestled inside lay in a heap next to the vacant circle.

Amelia's wariness blossomed into concern, which threatened to be usurped by fear. She could not give in to the rising panic that whispered, "Grab the *kinner* and run!" Why would someone take the basket off her porch? Was that person inside her house at this very moment? She needed to find out, but she couldn't drag the girls into possible danger. Amelia's eyes darted from one end of the porch to the other. The rocking chairs and porch swing looked the same as always. Terra-cotta flowerpots holding the brave little geraniums that still dared to bloom in the chilly weather sat in their same spots. How very strange. Why had the basket been taken?

She gasped at the sound of tires crunching on the gravel driveway. A car engine purred. Her visitor wasn't someone from her community. Should she snatch up her girls and run? Where would she hide? The driver of the car had most likely already seen them. Should she rush inside and risk interrupting an intruder or face whoever dared to disturb her on the Lord's Day?

The car stopped. Amelia had hesitated too long. She reached out to pull her *kinner* close to her. She would protect them however she could.

"Amelia? Are you all right?"

Her knees turned into jelly. If she hadn't been holding onto the girls, she would have sunk to the ground. Tears of relief blurred her vision. She heard footsteps running toward her but had to blink several times to bring the person into focus.

He leaped up the steps two at a time. "What is it?"

"*Ach!* Mr. Miller."

"Ryan. Remember?"

She nodded. "*Jah.* I-I was frightened for a moment. What are you doing here?"

"I saw you all standing on the porch but not going inside. He laid a tentative hand on her arm as if unsure how she would react to his touch. "Are you sure you're all right? You're as white as new snow."

"I...oh, it's—"

"Our basket is gone. Just like our quilt," Rhonda answered before Amelia could organize her thoughts and send a message to her tongue.

"Your basket?"

Rhonda pointed to the vacant spot. Amelia clarified. "I've always kept one of my baskets beside the door."

"I remember. A big basket. Those umbrellas were in it."

"That's right."

"When did it go missing?"

"It disappeared while we were at church."

"A basket can't simply walk away." His gaze took in the immediate area.

Rhonda giggled. "Baskets don't have legs. Neither did our quilt." Judith and Joanna laughed along with her.

"You are exactly right, Rhonda." Ryan smiled at the girls, but Amelia noted the concern in his eyes. "What's that about a quilt?"

"Our special quilt got tooked yesterday." A frown replaced Rhonda's smile.

"Taken, dear. The quilt was taken."

"Taken."

"From your house?" An expression akin to fear crossed Ryan's face.

"*Nee.* We had gone inside The Green Thumb. When we got back in the buggy, we discovered my quilt was missing."

"The one with the animals in the corners?"

Amelia couldn't help but smile. Her girls had made that quilt famous by dragging it with them on outings and by talking about their favorite animals. "That's the one."

"Who on earth would take a quilt or a basket?"

"It's a mystery to me, for sure and for certain."

"You haven't been inside the house yet, have you?"

"*Nee*. We arrived home only a few minutes before you got here. I tended to the horse and put the buggy away while the girls played. We had just started up the steps when I noticed the basket was gone."

"Let me go inside and check things out for you."

Amelia gasped. Her heart thudded so hard it stole her breath. She glanced at the girls and lowered her voice to a whisper. "Do you think someone is inside?"

Ryan's expression softened. His brow smoothed. Only his eyes held evidence of his concern. "I doubt it, but let me check around. Please?"

Amelia nodded.

"Would you mind standing near my car in case the girls wake up and start wondering where they are?"

"Not at all." Amelia hustled Rhonda, Joanna, and Judith across the yard. She knew Ryan wanted them out of the way in case some unsavory character flew out of the house. Such a thoughtful man.

"Wait!"

Amelia whirled around as Ryan jogged close. He held out his cell phone. "Take this. If I'm not out in ten minutes, call 9-1-1."

Her hand shook as she took the tiny phone from his big, rough hand. The mere thought that she might have to call for help turned her blood to ice water. *Please, Lord, let everything be all right.* "*Kumm* girls, let's make sure Jessie and Gabby are still sleeping." If the little girls focused on the black SUV, perhaps they wouldn't see if anything bad happened at the house.

How would she know when ten minutes had passed? Every second seemed an eternity. She looked at the phone in her hand. Was it working? The screen was dark. She tried pressing a little button at the bottom to see what would happen. Maybe it would make a light flash or something. Immediately, the screen lit up with the date and time. Thank goodness. Now she could keep track of how long Ryan was gone.

"*Mamm!*" Judith tugged at her cloak. "Gabby's waking up."

"Okay."

"Can she get out?"

Amelia certainly didn't want Ryan's little girl endangered. Actually, she would feel better if her own *dochders* climbed into the vehicle to wait. But that might be too confusing for all of them. She hoped Gabby slept a little longer. The little girl wiggled in her booster seat, but her eyes remained closed. Amelia patted Judith's shoulder. "Let's give her a few more minutes. She might not be finished napping."

She stole another quick peek at the phone. Seven minutes had passed since Ryan dashed up the porch steps and into the house. Three more minutes. What was taking him so long? She hated that the kind man could be in danger because of her. As frightened as she was for his safety, relief that another adult—a man—had arrived to help flooded her entire being. But she certainly didn't want any harm to *kumm* to him. He was a single parent, and his little girls needed him. *Please protect him, Lord Gott.*

Amelia held her breath and silently counted the seconds. When she got to sixty, she would double-check that another minute had passed. Why didn't he return to the porch? What if he needed help? What should she do? Fear wrapped its tentacles around her and threatened to squeeze the life right out of her.

She pressed the button to make the time pop up on the phone. Ninety seconds had passed. In another minute and a half, she would have to place that emergency call. Her little ones jabbered and played, totally oblivious to their *mudder's* turmoil and terror. Amelia wanted to gather them into her arms to shield them, but she didn't want to transfer her fear to them. A voice from inside the vehicle grabbed her attention. Gabby, Ryan's four-year-old, had fully awakened and fumbled with the straps on her booster seat.

"Wait, Gabby." Amelia hoped to keep the little girl in the vehicle for as long as possible. "Your *daed* will be right out." *Please let him walk out the door now.* Surely, the time was up, and she would need to place that call. She fumbled with the buttons on the phone to access the dial screen.

"Amelia! Everything is all right."

She nearly dropped the phone. Her knees wobbled. She leaned against the SUV for support. Never had she experienced such relief. *Danki, Lord Gott, for keeping Ryan safe.* She couldn't bear it if something happened to him—for his girls' sakes, of course.

Amelia watched the tall, broad-shouldered man jog down the steps and sprint across the yard. He stopped right beside her. Close.

He grasped the arm she had glued to the SUV and gently pulled her away from the vehicle. "Are you okay?" His brown eyes registered concern beneath knit brows.

"*Jah.* I was worried. You took so very long." At least the ten minutes had seemed like an eternity for her.

"I'm sorry. I wanted to be thorough. I wouldn't want you to run into any problems later. Are you sure you're all right? You're so pale that your little freckles are practically glowing."

She attempted a smile. Gauging by the warmth, her face had now flushed bright red. "I'm fine now that I know you are."

"I believe everything is in its proper place inside, but you would know that better than I. Why don't you take a look while I'm here?"

"Daed! Daed! I want out!"

"Looks like they're both awake now." Ryan shook the index finger of the hand that was not holding Amelia's arm at his four-year-old. "Patience, Gabby."

"Why don't you bring them inside? They are probably hungry after a long morning at church."

"You have to put up with them five days every week. You need a break on Sunday."

"I do not *put up* with them. Your girls are a joy. They have become like my own." Amelia bit her bottom lip. Perhaps she shouldn't have said that. Would he read something into those words that she hadn't intended?

He gave her arm a gentle squeeze that sent an unexpected little shock wave along her nerves. "I'm glad you feel that way. I know they love being here with you and your girls."

For some reason, Amelia had trouble catching her breath. She needed to step away, but how could she do that without appearing rude? "Well, get them out and let them stretch their legs a bit if you have time."

"I have plenty of time. Sundays can sometimes stretch on endlessly."

Didn't she know it! The hours often dragged by, especially on no-church Sundays. That was one more thing she had in common with Ryan Miller, besides the fact they were both single parents of little girls. *Ach!* She shouldn't be thinking of things they had in common at all.

# Chapter Three

Ryan Miller sank into the comfortable, old recliner with a sigh. Both girls had been fed, bathed, and tucked into bed for the night. At least, he hoped it was for the night and that Gabby didn't ask for another drink of water or that Jessie didn't develop some teething issue. He loved his daughters, but raising them alone was mighty difficult. Some days he didn't know if he was coming or going. He knew life couldn't be easy for Amelia either, but she sure appeared to have a handle on things.

Amelia. Simply picturing her pale hair, blue eyes, and tiny freckles brought a smile to his lips. She had such a sweet nature. Angelic. His girls adored the woman who had unwittingly become their surrogate mother. They would never remember their real mother. Sometimes he even had difficulty conjuring up Marian's image, and it hadn't been quite a year since she passed.

He hadn't been able to bear living in the house in their Pennsylvania town without her. When news that Norman Hoover needed a top-notch engine mechanic trickled along the grapevine, Ryan pulled up stakes and relocated to Southern Maryland. He had not regretted his decision one bit.

In fact, he enjoyed the small community of more modern Mennonites surrounded by Old Order Mennonite farms and businesses. Work had been steady, the community welcoming, and the area beautiful. And he could drive to Pennsylvania in a few hours should he get the urge to visit.

What a blessing that the young widow, Amelia Stauffer, had been referred to him as a caregiver for his girls. And what an answer to prayer that she eagerly welcomed Gabby and Jessie into her home and her life. Ryan's heart had warmed when she'd said she thought of them as her own earlier in the day. He couldn't have asked for a more caring, tender woman to entrust with the care of his children. Her affection and concern for them couldn't be missed. Did those feelings possibly extend to him as well?

Ryan rubbed a hand across his stubbly jaw. *You are members of different communities. Similar in some ways but drastically different in others.* He drove a dark SUV. She drove a horse and buggy. His house was lit with electric lights. She used kerosene or propane lanterns and lamps. But their basic beliefs and style of dress, though not identical, were close. Very close.

He shouldn't be thinking of her. But he saw her twice every weekday when he dropped off and picked up his daughters for all the months he'd lived in Maryland. Something odd had recently happened. Somehow, his thoughts of Amelia had begun to change in ever so subtle ways.

His heart had wrenched when he spied Amelia and her girls staring at their house earlier. One look at her ashen face after he pulled into the driveway told him the situation was grave. Fear had made his heart pound. He had the insane desire to scoop up the tiny woman and her children and whisk them away to safety. That would have been highly improper.

He knew Amelia had tried to don a brave face for her girls, but he didn't miss the fear shimmering in her eyes when she told him of the newest theft. Who would take a basket and a quilt? Nothing else in the whole house had been touched. Everything had been in place in the barns and sheds too. He had checked those while his little ones enjoyed a homemade chocolate chip cookie. Why had Amelia been targeted?

Ryan couldn't come up with any possible reason. The woman was goodness personified. She wouldn't hurt a fly and had probably never uttered a harsh word to a soul. And why take items that had sentimental value but little monetary value? True, handmade items could bring in a tidy little sum if they were sold in town, but more valuable items in the house had been ignored. It didn't make sense unless...

He sat up straighter in the chair. Could someone be taking handmade goods to sell somewhere in town or on the internet? Was someone trying to turn a profit from Amelia's handiwork? Or worse, was someone trying to frighten her?

~

Amelia had never been jumpy in her own home before, but tonight, every nerve was on edge. She managed to maintain some semblance of calm while the girls were awake, and they hadn't seemed to pick up on her discomfort. Now that they were tucked into bed though, her imagination ran wild. Every little creak of the house made her jump. Every branch that scraped a window caused her breath to catch, even though she had checked the locks on every door and window twice.

She poured a second cup of chamomile tea and perched on the edge of the rocking chair next to the woodstove. She sighed and prayed the herb and the warmth would make her drowsy enough to go to bed or at least calm her jitters. But her mind refused to shut down. Who would take an ordinary basket off someone's porch? It was one of a kind because it had been handmade, but it certainly was not an item of great value. Some of the tools in the shed and barn would bring a much higher price if they were sold. Amelia sipped her tea. It just didn't make sense. Who would want a basket and a quilt?

The warmth from the fire and the tea gradually spread throughout her body, easing a bit of her tension. She slid back in the chair and closed her eyes for a moment. Five little faces stared into her thoughts, bringing a smile to her lips. Her *dochders* were so precious. And as she had told Ryan, she often thought of his girls as her own.

What would she have done today if he hadn't driven by at the exact moment that he did? She would have had to leave the *kinner* outside alone while she investigated, or she would have had to drag them inside with her to face whatever might be in there. Ryan had truly been an answer to a prayer.

He was such a nice man. A *gut*, caring *daed*. And pleasant to gaze upon too with that brown hair and those big, chocolate eyes. Her cheeks warmed at the thought—a thought she should not have. *Ach, Amelia! Pull yourself together. You are the man's babysitter. Nothing more. Never could she be anything more than that.*

She had been on her own with the girls ever since Jeremiah had passed over two years ago. She would continue to be on her own even though *freinden* urged her to consider the few men who had shown an interest in her. It would need to be a very special man to take on three little girls.

*Ryan Miller is special.* Amelia jerked upright, nearly sloshing tea all over herself. The words had been so clear that she was almost sure someone had spoken them aloud. She set her mug on a side table and glanced around the dimly lit room. She was alone. The voice whispering in her brain had been her own, and she needed to squelch it immediately. But would she be so determined to ignore that voice if Ryan was a member of her own community?

He wasn't, though. His group of Mennonites was slightly more worldly. Their basic tenets of faith were similar, but folks didn't simply cross over from one group to the other.

Amelia couldn't imagine living in a house where she flipped a wall switch to turn on lights or air conditioning. She couldn't picture hopping behind the wheel of a car and driving. She chuckled at that idea. She would probably flatten every mailbox lining the side of the road if she tried to operate a vehicle.

Likewise, Ryan would probably never want to abandon the luxuries he was used to. Did he know how to hitch a horse to a buggy? Did he know how to plow without using a tractor? Did he even know the Pennsylvania Deutsch language they spoke? Most of the members she knew in his community spoke only *Englisch*.

She smacked the chair arm. What was wrong with her? It made no difference what the man did or did not know. There would never be a need for him to learn her way of life. There couldn't be.

~

Amelia moaned when she attempted to move her head. Her stiff neck allowed only the most minimal alteration in position. How long had she been dozing, and how did slumping in such a cramped position not awaken her? She shivered as much as a half-paralyzed person could. The room had grown so chilly. Had the fire gone out?

She pushed against the chair arm with one hand in an effort to straighten up. She needed to support her aching neck with the other hand. She hadn't slept in this chair since right after Jeremiah passed, and she couldn't bear going to bed alone. She shrugged several times to loosen her tense shoulder muscles. If she didn't get herself out of the chair and add wood to the stove, the whole house would sprout icicles. Would it even be worthwhile to go upstairs to bed? Or was it almost time to get the day started?

She got to her feet with a groan and stamped several times to rid her toes of that tingling sensation. Amelia hoped the creaking noise came from the rocking chair and not her knees. At twenty-eight, her bones should not yet be popping and cracking. Twenty-eight. Some days she felt much older.

Amelia shuffled to the stove to toss a couple pieces of wood on top of the embers. The fire had almost gone out, but she thought she could coax it back to life. She grabbed her half-full mug of tea and the small lamp and stumbled into the kitchen. She squinted at the battery-operated wall clock. Four-thirty. Her body urged her to go to bed for thirty or forty minutes, but her brain deemed that idea useless.

She set the mug in the sink. She would change out of her wrinkled dress and try to modify her bedraggled appearance. Then she'd whip up some muffins for breakfast. Ryan would be here with his girls before she knew it.

~

"Hello!"

"*Kumm* in. It's open."

Ryan nudged Gabby inside with the diaper bag he clutched in one hand. Jessie wiggled in his other arm as she reached out for Amelia. "You really should lock your doors, don't you think? You know, in light of yesterday and all."

"I only unlocked it a few minutes ago for you to enter. Otherwise, all the doors and windows have been locked tight. I checked them." Under her breath, she added, "More than once." She glanced up from the oven at his chuckle. The poor man looked as tired as she felt. "Did someone keep you up all night?" She set the muffin pans on hot pads and lifted Jessie from his grip.

"You can tell, huh? I guess the raccoon eyes are a dead giveaway. I probably look like I crawled out from under a rock."

Amelia laughed. "*Nee*, you look fine. Tired but fine." She jostled the little girl in her arms. "Did you keep your *daed* awake last night?"

"She didn't. I just had trouble sleeping."

"Oh." She didn't mention her own rough night in the rocking chair, but it probably showed.

"Something sure smells good." Ryan peeked over Amelia's head. "Cinnamon?"

"And apples." How was she able to detect the scent of his soap and aftershave with cinnamon permeating the air? Amelia took a tiny step backward. "Sit down, girls. The muffins are ready."

"Gabby and Jessie have had breakfast."

"There's always room for a muffin though."

"I only had cereal," Gabby said.

Ryan patted his older daughter's head. "I know. I'm sorry I don't have a lot of time to cook eggs or pancakes when I need to get all three of us dressed and out the door, especially when two of us like to dawdle."

"That's okay, Daddy. I like cereal."

He smiled. "That's a relief since you have to eat it every morning."

Amelia wanted to erase the apologetic expression from his face. His mornings must be pretty hectic, and his girls always arrived neat and clean. As far as she was concerned, he was a great *daed*. "Cereal is a fine breakfast, Ryan. There are a lot of *gut* ones." She smiled at Gabby. "But there is always room for a muffin, isn't there?"

The little girl nodded and climbed onto a kitchen chair. "I still have an empty spot." She patted her belly.

Amelia chuckled. "I'm sure the muffin will fill that right up." She settled Jessie in the high chair while her own three girls gathered around the table.

"I'd better get to work." Ryan set the diaper bag on the counter. "Be good, girls."

"Wait!" All eyes stared at her. Her cheeks grew warm. She hadn't meant to startle everyone. This was one of those times she wished her long hair hung free to hide her face. "Let me give you some muffins to take with you." She bit her lip. She had never sent food with him before but suspected he never took time to eat breakfast himself. Would he think her forward? "Y-you didn't eat, did you?"

His smile put her at ease. "Actually, I didn't, but I don't want to take your food. It's bad enough my girls mooch off you."

"I have plenty to share. The girls and you are *wilkom* to whatever I have. Truly."

"Hmm. If you're sure. A muffin would be mighty tasty. But go ahead and feed your girls."

"I'll give them a muffin to tide them over for a few minutes while I wrap one for you." Or two or three. A big man like Ryan Miller couldn't subsist on a single muffin. It was a *gut* thing she had stirred up enough batter for two pans. She quickly set a muffin on a napkin in front of each of the older girls and then broke one into pieces, which she laid on Jessie's high chair tray. "I'll get your milk and oatmeal in just a minute."

She scooted over to the counter to lift three muffins from one of the pans. As she wrapped them in foil, she sensed his presence. She whirled around, nearly ramming her head into Ryan's broad chest. "Oh my!" His hand on her arm steadied her but also sent heat surging up to her face. "H-here." She held the package out to him.

"Thank you, Amelia. I appreciate your looking out for me, uh, us." His smile lit the room.

"I-I'm happy to help." And she was. She couldn't explain why, but a sudden warmth enfolded her in a hug simply because she could do something nice for him. His smile had nothing to do with that. Much!

# Chapter Four

Ryan's feet didn't touch the ground on the way to his black SUV. He clutched the muffins to his chest as if guarding a treasure. The muffins really were special. Sure, he'd snatched a cookie or two if Amelia had a fresh batch cooling on racks, and he'd certainly purchased more of her treats from The Green Thumb than he could count. But the muffins were completely different.

She *offered* them to him. Out of the blue. He hadn't had to look longingly at them. She *wanted* him to take them to work and seemed worried that he hadn't eaten breakfast yet again. If he read her expression correctly, her eyes registered concern. Of course, that could have been his own wishful thinking, but he didn't believe so. Wishful thinking? Really? Hmm. That might be something to ponder later, maybe while savoring a muffin.

The gift, small and simple though it was, touched him so much that he hated to eat a single bite of a muffin because then the gift would be gone. A loud rumble practically echoed throughout the vehicle. He patted his flat, empty belly. Well, maybe he could eat one muffin to appease that monster growling in his stomach.

Ryan whistled some nonsensical tune as he drove. He paused to consider where he'd heard it but then remembered the silly song Gabby had sung to Jessie earlier. Such good little girls. He smiled, remembering their big, bright eyes when Amelia set homemade muffins in front of them. *They needed a mother.*

His whistling died. He'd heard those very words last night in the dream he had nearly once a week. How could a dream be so like reality? His last conversation with Marian must have been etched in his subconscious mind.

Dear Marian. What if they had known about her illness before her last pregnancy? Could she have received treatment, recovered, and then had Jessie? What if the birth had been easier, if she hadn't bled so much? Would she have lived, or would the disease have claimed her anyway?

Ryan groaned. All the what-ifs in the world wouldn't change a thing. Nothing would bring her back. It was God's will. He had accepted that, but it had been hard to live with. Lately, he felt like he was fighting his way out of the fog that had enveloped him.

Marian wanted that for him. She had made him promise not to grieve. She even squeezed his hand, stared right into his eyes, and told him he had to move on. The girls would need a mother, she'd said. At her pleading, he had to promise her he would move forward. He would have promised to snatch the moon and planets from the sky if she had requested it. She hadn't been sad when she repeated her request more firmly and made him promise again. "Make sure the girls have a mother and you have a wife. It's important."

He had nearly wept like a baby, but he gave her his word. He never believed he would be able to fulfill that promise and hadn't even considered it until lately. The dreams kept nudging him. Marian's words kept haunting him. He touched the muffin bag and smiled.

～

Amelia couldn't fathom what possessed her to fuss over Ryan Miller like she had. She'd been about to feed the girls, so wasn't it only polite to offer Ryan muffins as well? After all, he did admit that he hadn't eaten breakfast. Anyone would have acted as she had, wouldn't they? It would have been terribly ill-mannered to do otherwise.

Having justified her actions, at least somewhat, Amelia focused her attention on her tiny charges. She ladled oatmeal into five small bowls and set them on the table before pulling a chair close to the *boppli*. She didn't dare set Jessie's bowl within reach. The little girl would be finger painting with the gooey mixture in a matter of seconds.

Since they had given silent thanks for the meal earlier, Amelia encouraged the girls to eat without dawdling. "The bus will be here soon, Rhonda." She hated putting the little girl on the bus all alone, but she was grateful St. Mary's County provided transportation for the Mennonite school. It saved her from hitching up and hauling all the children out twice a day, five days a week. Thankfully, Rhonda had adjusted well and happily boarded the bus every day.

Banging on the high chair tray drew her gaze away from the older girls. "All right, Miss Impatience. Here's a bite for you." Amelia spooned oatmeal into Jessie's open mouth. "You look like a little bird waiting for a fat, juicy worm."

The other girls burst into fits of giggles. Amelia had to grab Joanna's cup of milk before it flooded the table.

"We could call her Birdie," Rhonda choked out in between hiccups and giggles.

"And we can call you Late for School if you don't eat a bit faster." Amelia shot her best stern look at her firstborn.

"I'm almost finished." Rhonda scraped her bowl with her spoon.

Amelia scooped up the last bite of oatmeal for Jessie and wiped her messy face. "If the rest of you are finished, please set your dishes in the sink. Judith, can you help Joanna?"

~

With the last load of laundry flapping on the clothesline, the kitchen swept, the dishes washed, and the girls happily playing, Amelia checked her basket-making materials. She would like to replace her missing basket, but she had several orders to fill before she could construct anything for herself. She'd start on the baskets later while the girls napped, but she wanted to make sure she had everything she needed. She was glad to have resumed the basket-making business she'd put aside after her husband passed. She enjoyed the craft, and the extra money was a plus.

Amelia liked creating things, be it treats for Christina to sell at The Green Thumb, a new quilt or afghan for a wedding gift, or a basket for an *Englisch* or Plain customer. Her *daed* had owned a chair-caning business, and she'd spent hours watching him and learning the craft. It had seemed only natural to move on to basket weaving. She secretly enjoyed constructing fancier, more decorative baskets for her *Englisch* customers, which allowed her to give in to her creative flair.

She whipped around at a dark flash outside the window. Was it a buggy? Did one of the ladies in the community decide to visit on this busy Monday morning? Maybe someone wanted to purchase a basket. After all, she did have signs tacked up in The Green Thumb and in the general store. She returned her supplies to the storage containers and hurried to look outside. It was not one of her *freinden* or a customer who hopped out of the black buggy. Amelia gasped. Her heart pounded. Why had Bishop Micah *kumm* here now?

She watched a moment longer. The bishop's *fraa* did not exit behind him. He came alone, and she seriously doubted he wanted to buy a basket. She couldn't recall a single infraction she had committed. What could he want?

She tried to moisten her dry lips, but her tongue had already stuck to the roof of her mouth. She ran her hands down her dress to smooth out any wrinkles and tucked a loose strand of hair beneath her *kapp*. There was nothing to do except go to the door and learn the reason for his visit.

"*Gut mariye*, Amelia," the bishop called before she had even opened the door all the way.

"Hello, Bishop Micah." She tried not to fidget. She didn't have any reason to be nervous. "D-do you want to *kumm* in for a cup of *kaffi*?"

"*Nee*. I won't stay long. I know how busy you are."

Amelia nodded and waited for the man to state his business. She wished she had grabbed a shawl off the hook near the door. The wind had a definite bite. She resisted the urge to tap her foot. It wouldn't do to show impatience with the bishop.

"Several of the men will be by tomorrow with wood for you."

"*Danki*." The bishop didn't normally stop by to inform her of such a thing. The men simply showed up and stacked the wood for her. Something else was brewing. Why didn't he just spit it out instead of beating around the bush, which was totally uncharacteristic of him? Her anxiety heightened.

"You weren't working yesterday, were you?" The bishop's gaze wandered around the yard before settling on Amelia's face, almost as if he had been reluctant to ask the question.

Amelia's hand flew to her chest to pat her galloping heart. "Of course not. Yesterday was the Lord's Day. I came home after church."

"I was told you had an *Englisch* visitor." The man's small, brown eyes bored into hers.

She hadn't had any *Englisch* visitors. She frowned. The bishop spoke again before she could even respond to his previous comment.

"A black vehicle was observed in your driveway."

"Oh. Ryan Miller stopped by. He—"

"He didn't expect you to care for his *kinner* on a Sunday, did he?"

Who could have seen Ryan at her house? She didn't remember seeing any buggies pass by. Someone must have driven past her house after they had all gone inside. "*Nee*, he did not bring his girls here for me to watch."

"It was a social call, then?"

"Not exactly. I'm sure he hadn't planned to visit at all. He happened to drive by while I was standing outside with the girls."

"And you all went inside together?"

"Not at first." She felt as if she was digging a deeper and deeper pit for herself. "Did you hear about the quilt that was taken from my buggy while I was inside The Green Thumb?"

"I did." Now, it was his turn to appear confused.

"Yesterday, when I arrived home from church, I found that my basket had been taken from the front porch. I was standing outside debating about going inside. I knew I needed to check the house, but I didn't want to take my girls inside in case someone was in there. Ryan Miller was driving home from his church service and noticed us. He stopped and checked out the place for me. His little ones wanted a snack, so I took them inside for a cookie."

"I see. It's a blessing he was able to help."

"I thought so too."

"I haven't heard of anyone else having items stolen from them." Bishop Micah stroked his long, gray-speckled, brown beard as he often did when in deep thought. "Do you have any idea who could be taking your belongings?"

"None whatsoever."

"Hmm. And they aren't taking things of great value. I don't mean to imply your belongings aren't important to you."

"I know what you mean. I thought the same thing. If someone needed a quilt to keep warm, then I'm happy to help, but stealing is the wrong way to gain assistance. I can't imagine why someone would take the big basket though."

"We will all have to be a little more vigilant. Are you afraid to be alone here with the *kinner*? Would you like someone to stay with you, at least at night?"

"I'll admit I was a little uneasy last night, but I will be fine. I wouldn't want to inconvenience anyone. I already feel like a bother since the men bring me wood and perform many of my outside chores."

"It is never a bother. We work together. We help each other. That's our way."

"I know. I appreciate the hard work, for sure and for certain. I only wish I could return the favors."

"You do. You help with work frolics. Those are important."

"I suppose so." Amelia suppressed a shiver. She would either have to convince the bishop to go in the house or else reach inside for a shawl.

"I will let you get back to your little ones. Don't hesitate to let me know if you need help."

"*Danki*, Bishop Micah."

With that, the man turned and loped off toward his buggy. Amelia wanted to ask how she was supposed to ask for help in the middle of the night, but she held her tongue. She would trust the Lord *Gott* as she'd always done.

She stepped back inside and made sure she locked the door. She didn't used to worry about locks or intruders. Now she double- and triple-checked every door and window before going to bed at night.

As she peeled and chopped vegetables for the stew she would put on to simmer all afternoon, she pondered Bishop

Micah's strange visit. Who could have seen Ryan Miller's car in her driveway yesterday? And why did they report their observation to the bishop? She felt like a naughty scholar whom a classmate had tattled on. At twenty-eight and the *mudder* of three, she should be considered old enough to make her own decisions. She had never been promiscuous and had never committed any infractions against the *Ordnung*. People should have more faith in her. That's all there was to it!

# Chapter Five

Ryan couldn't get Amelia and her girls out of his mind all day long. He'd been so concerned about her. Yesterday, she had looked like a scared little girl who tried to cover her fear with a brave mask. He wanted to erase that fear for good. He wanted to hold her close and tell her everything would be all right. He wanted to take care of her.

What was he thinking? He mentally slapped himself. He couldn't do any of those things and should wipe those thoughts right out of his mind the way the teacher used to erase the blackboard at school. If only it could be that easy.

Ryan knew he was setting himself up for heartache, and his poor heart had only recently begun to mend. He sighed. He tried to concentrate on his work but couldn't focus. *Snap out of it, man. Nothing can come of an interest in Amelia Stauffer. She is Old Order Mennonite and would never forsake her commitment to her faith.*

Could he change though? He tried to picture himself exchanging his SUV for a horse and buggy. He could probably do that, but it would take some getting used to. He'd need help learning the language, but that would be the least of his worries. Living without electricity could prove to be much more challenging.

Ryan didn't care about powering a computer, television, or radio. His community did not use those either. But having lights and heat come on with the flick of a switch was awfully nice. Old Order Mennonites used propane or oil lamps and woodstoves for heat. He would need to toughen up!

"Ouch!" The screwdriver slipped and dug into the flesh between his thumb and index finger. He dropped the tool to the workbench and rubbed his hand. He needed to stop daydreaming and pay attention to what he was doing. Norman would be sorry he ever hired him if Ryan broke up something he was supposed to be repairing.

Crazy, that's what he was. What made him think Amelia would ever think of him as anything other than the father of the children she babysat? Ryan frowned, shook his head to clear away the ridiculous notions, and retrieved the screwdriver. *Repair, don't break.*

~

Amelia dumped two quarts of home-canned tomatoes into the big soup pot and peeled the remaining two potatoes. As soon as she chopped them, she would prepare the girls' noon meal.

"Yoo-hoo! Amelia!"

She jumped and gasped. A potato shot off the cutting board and rolled across the kitchen counter. Heavy pounding on the back door followed the loud voice. Now who interrupted her task? This must be the day for visitors. She wiped her hands on a checked dish towel and scooted across the room to open the door far enough to peek out to identify the person on the other side. "Annie."

"*Gut mariye*, Amelia." The younger woman pushed the door wide open and sashayed inside.

"Your door was locked, so I couldn't get in without interrupting your work." She tucked a loose orange-red curl beneath her *kapp*.

"I'm keeping the doors locked now."

"I know about your quilt. That's so awful. I know it was special to you and your girls. I thought I heard about something else missing too."

Amelia grew breathless simply listening to the nonstop chatter. Annie Wenger was a talker, for sure and for certain. Amelia squeezed the redhead's arm. She needed to change the subject. She did not want to be the topic of the latest gossip. "What brings you by today, dear? I mean, it's always great to see you, but I wondered if you had a special reason to visit." *Other than to wheedle information out of me.*

"Oh." Annie paused a moment as if she needed to adjust her thoughts. "I was on my way to The Green Thumb, so I figured I'd stop and see if you had something to send along."

Amelia knew Annie must have some ulterior motive. She rarely stopped to pick up items for the store. "I didn't get to bake much this morning. I do have some muffins I can send." Thank goodness she had baked a couple more batches of them.

"I'm sure that would be fine. Your muffins are always delicious. I almost always grab one if I spy them on the shelf."

"Let me put them in individual baggies for you."

"Where are the *kinner*?"

"They're playing in the living room."

Annie lowered her voice. "Are you scared? I probably would be."

"We haven't been threatened or anything."

"But someone was right here. They took a basket off your porch. That's creepy."

So, Annie had heard the details. The grapevine must have quivered all morning. Amelia didn't want to resurrect the fears she had worked so hard to calm. She shrugged and snatched a box of small plastic bags from the cupboard. The sooner she packaged the muffins, the sooner Annie would leave. *Ach!* That wasn't nice! Amelia liked Annie very much. It was just that the girl could beat a topic to death and couldn't seem to pick up on clues that the person she conversed with didn't want to talk.

"You know, Amelia, my cousin Elam from Pennsylvania is visiting for a while. I'm sure he wouldn't mind stopping by your house a couple times a day to check on you."

Aha! Now Amelia knew the motivation behind Annie's visit. The girl wanted to play matchmaker. Exactly what Amelia did not want or need. "That won't be necessary. The girls and I are fine. Let your cousin enjoy his visit with you."

"He'll be here for a while. I'm sure he'd be happy to visit."

From the blatant stares she'd received at the church service or the few times they'd crossed paths, she guessed Elam wouldn't mind dropping in at all. Amelia suppressed a shiver. For some reason, the man's watchful eyes gave her the heebie-jeebies. "That won't be necessary at all."

"Don't you think he's handsome?"

Amelia's thumb punched smack through the muffin she'd been trying to wrestle into the bag. Well, she couldn't send that one now. She slid it aside and lifted the next one with a gentler touch. "I haven't paid much attention to tell you the truth."

"Amelia! How could you not notice that red-brown hair and green eyes? I wish my hair was that color instead of this red-orange mop I got stuck with."

"I guess I don't pay a lot of attention to men's appearances." Except for a particular brown-haired, brown-eyed one. Heat rushed into her cheeks. She'd better not face Annie, or the girl would falsely assume her flush had something to do with Elam.

"*Ach*, Amelia, you need to pay attention. Don't you want to get married again?"

Did she? Sometimes she missed having an adult to talk to at night, a shoulder to lay her head on, a hug when she was weary, a companion to share the load. But she'd adjusted to single parenthood and had been content—for the most part. She needed to be careful how she responded to Annie lest some rumor ignite and spread like wildfire. "I really haven't entertained that notion very much."

"Really? I want to get married."

"I'm sure you will one day."

"Soon, I hope."

"Does that mean you have a fellow in mind?" Amelia hoped Annie hadn't developed some new irrational crush like she'd done in the past.

Annie heaved an exaggerated sigh. "*Nee*, but I wish I did."

"Don't worry. I'm sure the right *bu* will *kumm* along."

"That could be a problem. There haven't been any new faces here for a long time, and all the fellows I grew up with think I talk too much."

"I'm sure none of them have ever told you that."

"They haven't had to tell me. I can see it in their expressions. And the fact that they try to hurry away whenever I approach is a dead giveaway."

Amelia tried not to smile but couldn't hold back a little giggle. She squeezed the younger girl's arm. "You're only twenty or so like Christina, ain't so? You have plenty of time to find someone. Who knows? One of the fellows you've always known might wake up and see what a *gut* person you are."

"I don't know. I am twenty, but sometimes I feel like life is passing me by."

She rolled her eyes and sighed again.

Amelia laughed at the girl's dramatics. "It will probably happen when you least expect it."

"That had better be soon, or I'll be the old *maedel* of the community."

"I hardly think being twenty years old qualifies you for that title."

"Look at you. You're only six years older and you have three *kinner*."

Amelia shrugged. "Everyone is different. The bishop's *schweschder*, Eleanore, is older than you and not married."

"That's true. I guess she and I can form a spinsters club."

"Don't be too quick to establish that group. I believe there is someone out there who is just right for you and for Eleanore."

"And you?"

"I'm not looking."

"Don't you think your girls need a *daed?*"

"We're doing fine as we are."

"Why don't you think about getting to know Elam better?"

*I'd rather take a beating.* "I'm sure he has someone special back home who wouldn't appreciate you trying to match him up with another woman."

"He doesn't have anyone. He told me. I think he's hoping to meet someone here."

*I am not that someone!* How was she going to squelch Annie's matchmaking attempt? "Maybe you should make sure he's met Eleanore." Immediately, Amelia regretted siccing the man on someone else, but she had to get Annie's focus off her.

"Maybe, but I get the impression he's interested in you."

Just what Amelia was afraid of. She needed to nip this whole thing in the bud right away. "You should let him know I'm not ready to make any changes at this time."

"It's been more than two years."

"I know, but the girls and I are fine as we are. I wouldn't want Elam to waste any time pursuing a woman who is not ready to start a relationship."

"But as you said, things can change when you least expect it."

Amelia ground her teeth. She placed the muffins in a large plastic bag she'd saved from the grocery store and held it out to Annie. "Tell Christina I'll try to bake later so she'll have more of a variety tomorrow."

Annie looped the bag around her wrist. "I believe Marjorie was bringing some treats by this morning, so she should be set for today."

"*Gut. Danki* for stopping by." Amelia hoped she didn't sound rude, but she also hoped Annie took the hint and left.

"I'm glad I could help out a little. I'll see you soon." Annie trotted toward the door. She paused to fling a parting shot over her shoulder. "Think about what I've said, Amelia. Elam is a nice fellow. Don't let someone else snap him up."

Grrr! Amelia apparently didn't dissuade the girl one bit. She did not need to think about Annie's words. Elam Wenger was not the man for her. And the man who continued to occupy her thoughts *could not* be for her.

~

How did a person go about banishing someone from his thoughts? Especially someone with hair like corn silk and eyes the color of a cloudless May sky. Someone gentle and kind. Someone whose love for children—even those who were not her own—bubbled out of every pore of her petite body.

Ryan groaned silently. It had been a tough day to say the least. Every undertaking had been challenging. He wasn't certain if each of his projects had been fraught with problems or if his distraction made every task more difficult. He prayed Norman hadn't noticed all his fumbles throughout the day. His hand still smarted from the screwdriver attack, and now he had a sore knee from whacking it against the leg of the workbench. Quitting time couldn't come soon enough.

Relief shot through Ryan's weary mind and body when Norman called out that the workday was done. Now he could collect his children and maybe his thoughts. The only drawback would be seeing the very person he struggled not to think about.

Should he find another caregiver for his girls? He'd never find a better person for the job. And he knew Amelia could use the money he paid her, even though it wasn't an exorbitant sum. But if he took Gabby and Jessie somewhere else, he wouldn't be able to see Amelia every day.

Exactly! That was the whole point, wasn't it? To put some distance between them. Out of sight, out of mind. Right? No! Even if he went for days without seeing her, Amelia would invade his thoughts. Previously, caring for and playing with his girls had filled his mind and his days. Recently, Amelia and her little ones crowded in. It was a hopeless situation. He was hopeless!

Norman clapped him on the shoulder on his way out the door. Did the older man have any inkling of the battle going on in his brain? Would his boss and friend be a good person to confide in? After all, Norman had remarried after the loss of his wife. He might be able to shed some light on the jumbled-up mess Ryan wallowed in. But Norman married a widow from their own community, not someone of a different sect altogether.

"Coming?" Norman called.

"Sure." Ryan stowed his tools and straightened his workbench. He wanted to walk into a tidy work area in the morning. If he couldn't unclutter his mind, he could at least have a neat space to do the work he'd been struggling to do.

# Chapter Six

"Amelia! It's *gut* to see you and the girls. I didn't expect you today." Christina hurried around the front counter of The Green Thumb to relieve her *freind* of some of the bags she had hooked around a slim wrist. Her other arm clutched Jessie tightly to her. The two four-year-olds and a two-year-old trailed behind her holding hands.

"I felt bad that I only had a few muffins to send yesterday, so I baked early this morning before the Miller girls arrived."

"You didn't have to do that, but I certainly appreciate it." Christina leaned over a bag and sniffed. "Something in here smells *wunderbaar*. What did you bring?"

"Apple cinnamon popovers, marble brownies, peanut butter cookies, and snickerdoodles."

"I don't think you got up early. I think you stayed up all night."

Amelia shrugged. "Not really." Truth be told, she had been awake most of the night but hadn't started baking until shortly before three in the morning. She would have a very hard time not napping when the girls did later.

"Did you have trouble sleeping? I imagine you've had a lot on your mind the past few days."

"*Jah.*" Amelia knew Christina alluded to the missing quilt and basket. Those incidents did weigh heavily on her mind, but images of a certain tall, handsome man were the real cause of her inability to sleep.

Christina glanced at the little girls before mouthing, "You aren't afraid or nervous, are you? I mean, especially alone there at night?"

"Not really. I'm keeping all the doors and windows locked though."

"*Gut.*" Christina set the bags on the counter and began removing items. "Girls, would you like to help me?"

Three heads bobbed.

"I'll hand you the treats and you can lay them on that empty shelf." She pointed at a low shelf only a few steps away from the counter. Obviously eager to help, Judith, Joanna, and Gabby left Amelia's side to lend a hand. While the girls stayed busy carrying items one by one to the shelf, Christina took the opportunity to study Amelia's face. "Do you want to talk about whatever is troubling you?"

Amelia jumped. Her cheeks grew warm. "I-I'm fine."

"And I'm ten feet tall."

Amelia giggled. She and Christina were nearly the same height—about five feet nothing. She would like to confide in her *freind.* She needed someone to help her think rationally, sanely, since she seemed incapable of talking sense into herself. But Amelia wasn't ready yet and probably never would be. Any interest, however slight, in a non-Old Order Mennonite man would be frowned upon. And that was putting it mildly. Unfortunately, her interest must not be slight if it kept her awake all night.

She had been concerned by Ryan's fidgeting and general discomfort when he picked up the girls the previous evening. She had feared he would twist his hat in half. He hadn't been much calmer this morning. She couldn't figure out what she might have done to upset him, but she couldn't *kumm* right out and ask. That would be too forward, too embarrassing.

"Amelia?"

"Huh?"

"Where did you go?"

"I'm right here, silly." Amelia pasted on a half-smile.

"*Nee*, you were a million miles away. Are you worried about something other than the thefts?"

"Not really."

"Nothing else is missing, is it?"

"Not as far as I can tell. I suppose I should check the barns every day, though, since they aren't locked."

"You could always ask the men who stop by to help out to keep an eye on things in the barns for you."

"They do enough as it is. I don't like being a burden to anyone."

"You shouldn't feel that way. We all help each other out, ain't so?"

"True. On a brighter note, I'm hoping to start selling more baskets. I do have some orders to fill."

"I'm so glad you've gotten back into basket weaving. You do such lovely work. You can always display baskets in here. I keep your sign posted, so I'm sure you will be bombarded with orders soon with the holidays approaching in a few months."

"I've been trying to keep a few baskets on hand for samples or to sell if I don't get new ones made. The big one on my porch was my sample big basket."

"It's such a shame that someone would take it. I've been considering possibilities but haven't thought of any logical explanations yet. I'll keep investigating."

"You got plenty of practice with investigating with the death of that poor *Englisch* man."

"I didn't really investigate. It was more like putting pieces of the puzzle together."

"How is the man's *schweschder* doing?"

"Jill has coped quite well with his death. She was so relieved he was cleared of any wrongdoing. She stops in here to visit now and again." Christina lowered her voice to a whisper. "I've also been on the lookout for your quilt."

Amelia laughed. "You sound as if you've been reading Annie's suspense novels. I do appreciate your help, but I've pretty much resigned myself to starting over with a new quilt—and a new basket too."

Christina nodded. "Just the same, I did ask Jill to stop in different craft and consignment stores around to make sure your things don't show up there." She handed the last of the treats to Judith and Gabby. Joanna had long since given up the effort of stocking the shelf and sat on the floor playing with a small rubber ball. "You've done a fine job, girls. *Danki.*"

Amelia smiled. "They are all excellent helpers."

Three little faces beamed.

"I should get home to feed these hard workers." Amelia shifted Jessie on her hip. "This one is getting heavy." Before she could gather the girls, who now all sat rolling the ball back and forth to each other, the front door creaked open and the little bell above it clanged, drawing her attention.

Christina whipped around to face the door. "Jill! We were just talking about you."

"Really? Good things, I hope." The dark-haired *Englisch* girl laughed as she closed the door behind her. Long, spiral curls fell over her shoulders. "Hi, Amelia. How are you doing?"

"Fine. It's *gut* to see you."

"I took an early lunch break and decided to stop in." She threw a glance at the fully stocked treat shelf. "It looks like I picked the perfect time. I'll never be able to decide on just one treat."

"They're all freshly baked by Amelia," Christina offered. "So I'm sure they are all delicious."

"You don't have to sell me on her baking. I've sampled as many of her goodies as possible." Jill scooted closer to the shelf. "I've got to have one of these." She plucked a popover from the pile. "And cookies for an afternoon snack." She bent down to speak to the little girls before turning back to the women. "I wanted to let you know that I've been checking any store in the area that might sell quilts or baskets. I've even gone to pawn shops. No luck."

"I didn't expect them to be found in another store." Amelia shifted the *boppli* again. "I can't imagine anyone stealing them to sell. They wouldn't have brought that much money."

"Oh, you'd be surprised. Some people will pay lots for handmade items. And unfortunately, some people will steal anything to make money." Jill fumbled with her purse. "Speaking of money, let me pay you and get back to work. Lunchtime is never long enough." She handed Christina a five-dollar bill, deposited her change in her purse, and scurried out the door. "I'll keep a look out for your things," she called over her shoulder.

"I didn't realize the morning had slipped away. I'm sure I must have some very hungry *kinner* here, ain't so, girls?" Amelia looked down at the little ones. Joanna had lost interest in rolling the ball and merely watched Gabby and Judith play.

"I'm hungry, *Mamm*." Judith set the ball on a shelf and scrambled to her feet. She reached out a hand to help Joanna up.

"Me too." Gabby jumped up beside Judith.

"I guess that settles it. I'm sure you are hungry too, little one." Amelia kissed Jessie's cheek.

"I appreciate all the treats you brought." Christina laid down her pencil. I've recorded everything so I can pay you next time."

"I'm not worried about that. We'll see you later." Amelia herded her charges toward the door but stopped abruptly when it flew open right in front of her. The three little girls crashed into each other. They cried out and all rubbed their heads.

"Oops! I'm sorry!" Annie poked her head inside the store. "I wasn't expecting anyone to be on the other side. Is everyone all right?"

Amelia quickly examined each girl. They all sported a red spot on a cheek or forehead, but nobody shed tears. "They're fine." She directed the girls to step out of the way so Annie could enter.

Annie reached back to pull in a young man whose red hair almost matched her own. He wasn't much taller than Annie and had a solid, almost stocky, build. He stumbled inside and stared at the women and children. "I'm sure you all met my cousin Elam at church. In case you don't remember, Elam, this is Amelia, the woman we were just talking about."

Amelia wished the floor would swallow her. Of course she knew who Elam was, and she had absolutely no doubt he remembered her. What was Annie trying to do? Hadn't Amelia made it clear to the girl that she had no interest whatsoever in her cousin? "Hello, Elam." Her voice sounded strained and not very friendly, even to her own ears. She had to get out of the store right away.

"What brings you by, Annie? This isn't your usual day to help me out." Christina edged closer to Amelia and the girls.

*Bless you, Christina, for trying to help me out of this awkward situation.*

"Can't I come by on other days?"

"Sure." Christina turned to Amelia. "I know you need to get home. *Danki* again for bringing the treats." She wrapped an arm around the nearest little girl and inched toward the door.

"You're leaving already?" Annie elbowed Elam. "Why don't you help her get the *kinner* in the buggy?"

"That isn't necessary, Annie." Amelia forced out a little laugh. "I've been getting them in and out of the buggy forever."

"But a little help is always nice, ain't so?" Annie nudged her mute cousin again.

Amelia ground her teeth so hard that she expected them to chip. "Please go ahead with your visit. I can handle this." She didn't dare glance in Elam's direction. She could feel that his gaze was fixed on her. Every nerve in her body sensed that. Her goal became to get the *kinner* inside the buggy and race away before Elam spoke or moved.

The girls must have picked up on her unspoken cues. They hustled out the door right on her heels and practically ran for the buggy. Amelia reached inside to fasten Jessie in her carrier. She called out to the older girls to hop inside while she raced to untie the horse.

"I can help."

Amelia gasped and jumped at the deep voice behind her, cracking her elbow on the side of the buggy. "Ow!" She backed up, rubbing her arm, and stepped on toes that were much too close to her. "I'm so sorry. I didn't know you were right there." Why had he planted himself in her space? She'd almost gotten the horse untied and made her escape.

"It's okay. A little bitty thing like you couldn't hurt my foot."

Since he obviously did not plan to step away, Amelia sidestepped to put as much distance as possible between them. She couldn't bring herself to look up into his face. Instead, she made sure the girls had climbed into the buggy and could have cried with relief to find them seated and waiting for her. "It looks like we're all set. I appreciate your offer to help though."

Amelia hurried to untie the horse. A big hand clamped down over both of her fumbling smaller ones.

"Let me help. I don't bite."

She forced a little giggle. Why did this man make her feel nervous? He'd never said or done anything inappropriate. They'd scarcely communicated at all since she scurried away after church services. But she always got the impression that he watched her every move. She got goose bumps even now just thinking about his watchful eyes. She wiggled her hands out from under his and let him untie the horse so she could climb into the buggy and get away from him.

Amelia chewed her lower lip to keep from mumbling. If only she'd gotten Jessie buckled in her seat a mere two minutes sooner, she could have avoided this whole uncomfortable scene.

"Here you go." Elam handed her the reins.

"*Danki.*" Since he still held onto the buggy, she couldn't very well cluck to the horse to get him moving. Was she going to have to ask the man to step back?

"I heard about your, uh, losses."

"Oh." Amelia really didn't want to keep rehashing everything, especially with the girls listening. She didn't want them to be fearful.

"I would be happy to drop by your place, you know, to keep an eye on things."

"I'm sure there is nothing to worry about."

"You never can tell if something else might happen. Maybe something more serious, even."

Amelia fought off a shiver. She would not let this man add fears to the apprehension she had worked hard to tamp down. "I appreciate the offer, but we are fine. You should enjoy your visit."

"I might be here for a while." He chuckled. "I might even decide to move here, especially if I had a *gut* reason." He patted her arm.

It took every ounce of her self-control not to flinch and shake his hand off. "I-I need to get the girls home for lunch and naps." Surely, he'd take the hint and step back. She pretended to adjust Jessie's carrier so she could slide out of the man's reach. When she straightened up. She found that Elam had stepped back ever so slightly. She used the opportunity to escape. She clucked to the horse to get him moving.

"I'll be seeing you, Amelia."

She cringed. *Not if I see you first and can duck out of sight.*

# Chapter Seven

Ryan groaned softly as he removed a machine part he'd put in backward. If he didn't get a handle on his thoughts and emotions, he was going to ruin everything he touched. At least he'd caught this mistake before any harm had been done. But what if he hadn't? He shook his head to clear the cobwebs. *Get a grip on yourself, man.*

"Is everything okay?" Norman Hoover's face showed concern. He ran a hand through his gray-streaked brown hair and clamped the other hand on Ryan's shoulder.

"I seem to be all thumbs today. I think I need to get more sleep." *Or something.*

"Do you have a load on your mind?"

That was an understatement! Could he talk to Norman about his concerns? "I suppose there's always a lot going on in my head."

"I'm a good listener and not a blabber. Anything you want to talk about would stay between us."

"I appreciate that." Ryan wanted to share his disturbing thoughts. He wanted another opinion. He'd like to get someone else's input. He needed to know he wasn't losing his mind.

"Do you need help with anything?"

Ryan glanced at the engine in front of him and then at his boss. "I've got this straight now."

"Oh, I have no doubt about your ability with engines or machinery. I meant do you need help with whatever is going on in here?" He tapped Ryan's head.

Ryan chuckled. "It would take about a week to sort out the mess in there."

"It's almost quitting time. I'll flip the sign, and you can tell me what's eating at you. Sometimes just voicing your problems gives you the answers you need." The older man loped off to lock the door.

Ryan nodded. What else could he do? If he refused the man's help, he'd look like the most ungrateful human alive. Who knows? Maybe Norman could help him sort things out. He put his tools away and wiped his hands on a nongreasy corner of the rag lying on the workbench.

Norman returned, pulled up a stool, and perched atop it. He waited in silence as if he had all the time in the world.

Ryan couldn't seem to get his thoughts in order. He drummed his fingers on the workbench until the sound echoed in his head like a drill. "Tell me, Norman, how long was it after your first wife passed until you married Sarah?" He wanted to kick himself at his bluntness. He should have eased into the subject. But no, he had to dive right in. Now he felt like he was flailing about in a deep river with no life jacket and no way to swim out.

Norman's hand raking across his stubbly jaw sounded like fingernails scratching a blackboard. Ryan summoned every ounce of willpower to avoid cringing or to keep from slapping Norman's hand away from his face.

"Well, let's see." Norman wiggled on the stool as if settling in for a long haul. He closed his eyes for a second and whispered numbers as if counting weeks or days or years. "Two years and three months." He opened his eyes, blinked, and focused on Ryan's face. "Are you thinking of remarrying?"

Ryan coughed. He suddenly had difficulty catching his breath. "It hasn't quite been a year."

"There's no set waiting period. Some folks are ready sooner than others. And some folks never remarry."

Ryan shrugged. His thoughts swirled around in his brain, but he couldn't seem to nail one down to focus on.

"You know, someone—I forget who it was now—once told me that the happier a person was in his marriage, the sooner he remarried. I guess that makes sense. I mean, if you were happy once, you'd want to recreate that."

"Maybe." Ryan had been happy with Marian. They hadn't had many years together, but the few they'd had were good ones.

"And you have those little girls to think about. It can't be easy for you to juggle everything."

"No. I've gotten into a pretty good routine though. And I have an excellent caregiver for them."

"I know Amelia Stauffer. She's a very nice lady. And a widow too." Norman cocked an eyebrow.

Ryan pretended he didn't catch the older man's hint. "How did you know you were ready?"

"Ready?"

"To move on. To start seeing someone else."

"I realized I was tired of talking to myself and rattling around in that big house all alone. My children are grown, of course. They would come by to visit or to bring dinner, but then the silence tried to eat me alive after they left. I knew I needed someone to share the rest of my life with."

"Sarah had been alone too?"

"She'd been widowed a year before me. She was one of the ladies who brought me food from time to time. Naturally, different ones brought casseroles or desserts, but Sarah makes the best chicken casserole and peach pie I've ever tasted." Norman licked his lips and patted his round belly.

Ryan chuckled. "It must be true that the way to a man's heart is through his stomach, huh?"

"Not entirely, but being a good cook helps. Sarah fattened me right up."

Ryan thought of the delicious muffins and other sweet treats Amelia baked. If the rest of her cooking was half as tasty as her baking, he'd probably put on weight too. What was he thinking? His cheeks burned. Maybe Norman had fallen too deeply into a well of memories to notice.

"Do you have somebody in mind?"

Ryan almost swallowed his tongue. "Huh?"

"A lady. Do you have a lady that you're interested in?"

"It's too soon...isn't it? I didn't think I'd ever want to look at another woman, but lately my Marian's words keep coming back to me."

"What were her words?"

"She told me to go on with life and to provide a mother for our children."

"That sounds like wise advice."

"The girls have all the ladies at church fawning over them. And I couldn't ask for a better babysitter than Amelia."

"Yeah, but they need more than that. They need a woman around full time, especially as they get bigger and need to discuss, uh, things. They need a mama."

Ryan shrugged.

"Are you thinking Amelia might be more than a babysitter?"

Ryan jerked so hard he almost overturned the stool he was perched on. He gripped the edges to hold the thing in place. "I, uh...She's Old Order."

This time Norman shrugged. "You got a problem with that?"

"Well, not personally, but we, uh...we're different. We do things differently. We have different lifestyles."

"How many *differents* are you going to throw in there? We believe in the same God and the same Lord and Savior, don't we?"

"Yes, but..."

"But you can't see her driving a car or yourself plowing with horses. Is that it?" The older man chuckled and ran a hand through his hair, so it stuck out in several directions.

"I think our differences are a bit more involved than that."

"Every couple has differences. We are individuals who are trying to combine our lives into one. If you care about each other, you work things out to suit you."

Ryan sighed. His next thought slipped out before he could stop it. "Easy for you to say. You married someone from your own community." He bit his tongue and wished he hadn't spoken. Had he offended Norman? The man was not only his boss but also his friend. To his surprise, Norman slapped his knee and laughed.

"You're right about that, my friend. Sarah has been a member of the community forever, so that made things a little easier for us."

"And you didn't have young children who would need to adjust to a new situation."

"Right again. But sometimes young ones are more accepting than grown ones."

"Did your children or hers oppose your marriage?"

"No, I can't say they opposed it. I think my youngest two did have a little trouble seeing me with someone other than their mother, even though they said they wanted me to be happy."

"But they eventually came around?"

"Sure. They realized that just because I love someone else, that didn't mean I didn't still love their mother. A person's heart can hold love for a lot of people."

"I believe that too. I'm sure the church leaders had no problem with your remarriage since you were both members."

"Nope. No problems this time."

"This time?"

"Linda, my first wife, was *Englisch*."

"What?" Ryan's jaw dropped. How had he not known this? "How in the world did you ever get involved with her?"

Norman's features softened, and his smile broadened. His travel back in time was obviously a pleasant trip. "She was young and searching for acceptance. Her growing-up years had been tough. She'd visited different churches and said she felt like she'd come home when she stepped inside our little church. I hadn't been serious about any girls in our group, but once I laid eyes on Linda, I got serious real quick." He chuckled.

"It must have been a big change for Linda to completely change her life."

"Not as bad as you might think. She'd grown up in the foster care system so she really didn't have a family to dissuade her. She didn't care much about computers and television. Back then, we didn't have as many electronic gizmos. She could still drive a car and have a house with electricity, so the change wasn't so terribly drastic. Linda didn't mind adopting our style of dress, and the ladies all took her under their wings and taught her whatever she needed to know."

"Brave lady. I guess she loved you more than she loved any of her modern ways."

"I like to think so. We had a good life and raised four children." Norman sighed and gave his head a little shake. "I have a good life now too. Sarah is a special woman. I thank the Lord for her every day." He tapped Ryan's arm. "You can have a good life again as well."

"My life is good."

"All right. You can have another good marriage, then. How's that? Just open yourself up to the Lord's leading, and don't be afraid of change."

"Change for whom?"

"You or your lady, whoever she might be. Or both of you. Maybe all of you since children are involved too." He winked.

Change for either him or Amelia would mean leaving their church and community. Sure, they all lived in close proximity to each other and often formed friendships, but one or the other of them would have to sacrifice their way of life. Could he ask her to do that? Could he do that? "What if the change is too great to even consider it?"

"Nothing is impossible with God. Remember that."

~

Norman's words rattled around in Ryan's head all evening. He'd been a little late picking up the girls, but Amelia had taken it all in stride. She said she hadn't even looked at the clock and didn't know he was late.

Jessie and Joanna had been rolling a little, red rubber ball back and forth on the linoleum floor in one corner of the kitchen. Rhonda, Judith, and Gabby stood at the table squishing dough through their fingers as Amelia instructed them in the fine art of biscuit making. A cloud of flour swirled around them.

Amelia didn't seem to mind that her usually immaculate kitchen looked as if a tornado had roared through. She patiently offered advice in her calm, gentle voice. Ryan was sure she had no idea how adorable she looked with a smudge of flour on her nose. He'd been inclined to wipe it off but didn't yield to that temptation. She invited them to stay for supper, but he declined. He had some serious thinking to do after he got his children to bed.

He stayed lost in his thoughts the whole way home. He couldn't get the image of Amelia tending his children with all the love she showed her own girls out of his mind. Gabby and Jessie adored the woman. That fact would be plain to a blind man. All the children would no doubt adapt to a change in their living situation with relative ease. The adults, however, might be an entirely different story.

Somehow, Ryan got the girls fed, bathed, and tucked into bed. He should crawl into his own bed, but any attempt at sleep would probably prove futile. He had to get a grip on himself. He wandered the house, putting away stray toys and riffling through the junk mail. He stopped and smacked his forehead. *Stop the madness right now. You don't even know how the woman feels about you. Most likely you are simply the father of the children she babysits.*

Ryan didn't think that was the case though. He was pretty sure he hadn't imagined the light in Amelia's lovely blue eyes when he arrived at her door or her welcoming smile or her strict attention to his every word. But he couldn't come right out and ask her how she felt about him. How would he ever resolve his dilemma? Was his hope for a relationship with Amelia merely wishful thinking?

"Nothing is impossible with God." Ryan spoke to the silent room. Weren't those Norman's words? He did believe that, didn't he? If he answered affirmatively, he needed to leave everything in God's hands and trust Him to work things out for good.

*So stop this ridiculous pacing and go to sleep.*

# Chapter Eight

Amelia thought Ryan had seemed a bit more relaxed, more like himself, when he picked the girls up after work. He had laughed at their lopsided biscuits but promised to eat one later. She had taken note of which ones Gabby had made and sent them home with her. Ryan praised her efforts and thanked Amelia for her time and patience. He had seemed genuinely happy and at peace.

She roamed the house checking windows and doors yet again. She extinguished the last lamp and headed through the darkness to her room, following the flashlight's beam. She couldn't stop thinking about Ryan. She had expected him to smile when he saw Gabby's biscuits, but as usual, she was amazed at how that smile affected her. It always warmed her heart and all the way down to her toes. And those chocolate eyes could see into her soul. *Ach!* She had to stop thinking such things. There was no use in setting herself up for heartache.

A sudden loud noise outside stopped her thoughts, her heart, and her breath.

Amelia's first inclination was to switch off the light and hide, but that would definitely not be a mature, responsible reaction. Times like this made her wish a man was around to take care of things. She should force herself to investigate. She'd wait a minute to see if she heard the noise again. Her imagination might be playing a mean trick on her.

She gulped in a breath before she passed out from lack of oxygen. She held the flashlight against her body so it gave only enough light to keep her from tripping over furniture. She crept to the window and immediately jumped back with a gasp.

A light bobbed near the barn as someone circled the structure. Who was out there and what did they want? She would have to check. It was up to her to take care of her place and to keep her girls safe. She couldn't dive under her bed and pretend everything was fine and dandy.

Whoever was out there must have been closer to the house when she heard that noise a few minutes ago or she would not have known he was out there. She shivered. What did he want? After the basket incident, she had moved portable items from the porch and yard, but she couldn't very well stash the farm and garden tools someplace else. If that was what the person was after, he would need a vehicle or wagon to cart the things off.

A flash of anger spurred Amelia into action. How dare someone waltz onto her property and steal her things! Did he know a woman lived here alone with her *kinner*? Well, she would stand up for herself. She marched to the back door, snatched a shawl off the hook, and yanked open the door.

Now what? She hadn't figured out what to say or do beyond this point, but she vowed not to let this person intimidate her. She refused to listen to that nagging little voice in her brain that hurled question after question at her. *What if he was an escaped criminal? What if he had a gun? What if he kidnapped you? What if he hurt the girls?*

That last question brought her up short. But it was too late. The person spotted her and shone his light right at her, blinding her. She threw an arm over her eyes to shield them.

"Who's there?" Her heartbeat roared in her ears. How would she even be able to hear if the person answered her?

"It's me, Amelia. Elam Wenger."

She almost crumpled in relief. Not that she was at all thrilled to see Elam at her house at night, but at least the person wasn't a complete stranger who was up to some mischief. "What are you doing here?" She probably sounded rude, but the man didn't have any business nosing around her place in the dark of night—or any other time either, for that matter.

Even squinting into the bright light, Amelia couldn't determine his expression, and she liked to read people's faces to get a handle on their feelings. "Could you lower that beam, please?"

"*Ach!* Sorry."

She blinked a few times as she approached her intruder. And she did think of him as an intruder rather than a visitor. A guest would not prowl around in the dark.

He hadn't answered her question, so she repeated it. "What are you doing here so late at night, Elam?" She stopped two feet away from him and stared into his face. The flashlight provided just enough illumination for her to determine he had difficulty looking her in the eye. What had he been up to?

"I, um, wanted to make sure you and your girls were all right."

"By sneaking around my house in the dark and scaring me half to death?"

"I didn't mean to scare you."

"How did you think I would react?"

"I didn't expect you to see me."

The remark took her aback. So he intended to be sneaky? "Why didn't you simply knock at the door?"

"I didn't want to wake you or your girls."

Amelia sighed. What was she supposed to say? What was she supposed to do? "I appreciate your concern, Elam, but you really don't need to worry about us. We are fine."

"There isn't any harm in checking, is there?"

*There is when you sneak around in the dark without my knowledge.* "To tell you the truth, it was a little scary to find someone outside in the dark when I wasn't expecting it. Were you on the front porch too?" She might as well say everything on her mind and get it over with. Well, not everything. She couldn't find a polite way to tell him to go away because he caused her stomach to get all queasy.

"I, uh, I..."

The question shouldn't be so difficult to answer. Either he was or he wasn't. She barely resisted the urge to tap her foot.

"I wanted to make sure nothing was missing from your porch."

How would he know if it was? As far as she knew, he'd never been on her front porch before. "Really?"

"*Jah.*"

"I had already moved anything lying loose in my yard and on the porch lest they be a temptation if my basket thief returned."

"That was a *gut* idea. I saw that the porch was empty except for the swing."

"Everything was all right in the barns and shed when I was out earlier. Was there anything amiss now?"

"Of course, I don't know what all you had out there, but everything appears neat and orderly."

"Great. Now I guess we can both get some sleep." She couldn't be more obvious unless she bodily removed him from the property—a physical impossibility, for sure and for certain. "*Danki* for checking on us, but please don't disrupt your plans or your sleep on our account. I truly don't think anyone will bother us. I'm sure the basket theft was a random act."

"And the quilt?"

"Perhaps someone who was cold or homeless needed it. I can certainly sew another quilt."

"Maybe the two things are connected."

Amelia shrugged, feigning nonchalance. She would not allow herself to dwell on that possibility. "I doubt it. And as you can see, all is well here."

"For now. Maybe you should be a bit more wary."

"I'm fine." How many times had she said those words to him? Certainly he didn't plan future nocturnal visits to check on her welfare. That thought chilled her more than the breeze. "I-I need to get inside. Morning *kumms* fast, and I wouldn't want anyone to get the wrong idea if they saw us out here."

"It's late and dark. There's little danger of that."

"*Gut nacht*, Elam." Amelia spun around and forced her feet to take their normal strides instead of running like they wanted to do.

"I'm happy to keep a watch on your place," he called.

She stopped in mid-stride. "Please don't bother. Please enjoy your visit with your family."

"I have plenty of time with them." He chuckled. "I need to give them a break from me sometimes."

She resisted the urge to groan. "I'm certain they don't look at things that way."

"I wouldn't be too sure about that. They are forced to tolerate Annie's nonstop talking and crazy ideas. I'm sure they could use some peace and quiet. Sometimes I need a break from Annie myself."

"Annie is a nice girl." Amelia knew the young woman talked a lot, but she was a *gut* person.

"I didn't say she wasn't nice, but she is incessant."

*Like you!* "I need to get inside." Amelia hated to be so abrupt, but she did want to check on her girls. What if one awoke after a bad dream and couldn't find her? What if one suddenly got sick and called out to her only to be met with silence? She didn't think she had been outside for too long, but any time alone with Elam was too long. Annie needed to sic him on someone else. "Please don't give us another thought." With that, she sped toward the house, not even pausing to hear his reply.

Amelia locked the back door behind her and hung the shawl on a hook. Goose bumps broke out all over her body, and she rubbed her hands to generate heat. She didn't think her chill came entirely from the breeze. She would add wood to the stove as soon as she checked something else.

She crept to the window and peered into the blackness. Had he left? Or did he still lurk about somewhere? She strained to detect any movement. Right before she turned away, she caught sight of the thin beam from the flashlight. He must be retrieving his horse and buggy. How had she not heard or seen him arrive? She ducked out of sight, in case he glanced at the house, and tiptoed forward again in time to watch him disappear from view on a bicycle, of all things. How safe was that in the dark?

Amelia knew she should be grateful for Elam's concern, but for some unexplainable reason, she felt uneasy instead. He had never said anything to frighten her or to upset her, so it was probably her own silliness or overactive imagination that made her edgy around him.

She rubbed her arms again and shuffled to the stove. She grabbed a piece of oak to throw inside but found a roaring fire still blazing. She tossed the log back into the box beside the stove. Her nerves were playing tricks on her. She needed to go to bed to grab a few winks of sleep before the new day began—if it hadn't already arrived.

~

"My, you're out and about early." Amelia closed and locked the door after Christina entered. Had she become too obsessive about securing her house? "Where is your buggy?"

"I rode my trusty bicycle. I want to get to The Green Thumb a little early since I'm expecting a delivery."

"Isn't it getting a bit nippy for the bike?"

Christina shrugged. "It's cool early in the morning, but by afternoon, it's not so bad. Something sure smells yummy."

"I've been baking."

"You must have gotten up extra early, too, if you've baked before the Miller girls arrived. I saw Ryan leaving his house."

"I've been up for a while." *Most of the night!*

"As soon as I clean up some of my mess, I'll dish up some oatmeal for the girls. Would you like some?"

"*Nee*, but I can help you get theirs ready."

"I can take care of it. You need to get to the store for your delivery. Let me package up my treats for you."

"What did you bake this morning?"

"Brownies and cookies again. But I also made a marble pound cake if you want to slice and bag that."

"Yum! That might be my morning snack." Christina pulled plastic baggies from the box on the kitchen counter and grabbed a knife.

Amelia dropped chocolate chip cookies into a bag. Before she could stop herself, she blurted out her concern. "What do you know about Elam Wenger?" She kept her eyes focused on her hands so Christina wouldn't be able to read her expression.

At the dead silence that followed her outburst, Amelia dared a peek at her *freind*. Christina couldn't have looked more surprised if Amelia had asked her if she'd booked a flight on a spaceship. "I'm sorry. I probably shouldn't have asked that. I didn't mean to put you on the spot." She grabbed another baggie from the box and stuffed cookies into it.

"That's all right. You took me by surprise. Are you interested in Elam?"

"I'm interested in keeping him at bay." Amelia slapped a hand across her mouth, horrified that she'd revealed that thought.

Christina broke out into a fit of giggles. She shuffled close to give Amelia a hug. "You are so funny."

"I'm sorry. I shouldn't have said that."

"We're *freinden*, ain't so?"

"Of course."

"*Freinden* can tell each other anything. If it makes you feel any better, I'd want Elam to keep his distance too."

This time, Amelia laughed. "Oh my, we're quite a pair. I'm not sure what it is about the man that puts me off, but I thought it was just me."

"I figured it was just me because I already have, um—"

"You have Noah."

Christina nodded. Her cheeks turned crimson.

Amelia patted the younger woman's arm. "I am very happy for you. You and Noah make such a nice couple. Do you have any idea why Annie keeps trying to throw her cousin at me?"

"I think it's because she cares about you and wants to see you happy. Since Elam is her cousin, she probably wants to see him find a special person too."

"He seems older than us. Older than you and Annie, for sure, but older than me too."

Christina laughed. "You aren't so ancient at twenty-six, you know. But I believe Elam is in his early thirties, maybe thirty-four."

"And he's never been married?"

"Not to my knowledge."

"Doesn't he have someone special back home?"

"Apparently not if Annie is trying to play matchmaker."

"I am not in the market for a match."

"You could be. You've been a widow for quite a while. I'm certainly not saying you should consider Elam if he doesn't interest you." Christina giggled at Amelia's expression. "But don't you think you'd like to marry again?"

Amelia shrugged. "Perhaps one day, but I am perfectly capable of choosing the person myself." Her face burned. She hoped Christina didn't notice. Thank goodness her *freind* couldn't read minds. Christina would be horrified at the man who claimed Amelia's thoughts.

"I'm sure you can do just that whenever you're ready."

"How do I get Elam to stop visiting my house in the dark of night?"

Christina gasped. "He did what?"

Amelia explained the previous night's adventure. "I know I should be grateful for his concern, but truth be told, I was so unnerved by the whole thing that I probably showed little, if any, gratitude. It was all so strange. He poked around with that flashlight like he expected to find someone hiding in my barn." Amelia shivered. "I had never thought of that possibility. Except for my new obsession with locking everything and checking those locks twice before going to bed, I have been feeling rather brave and comfortable. After he left last night, I jumped at every little creak the house made."

"I'm sorry he frightened you. I don't believe you have anything to worry about though. I'm sure the two thefts were random occurrences."

"I hope so." Amelia smiled. "In the light of day, I can be quite brave, huh?"

Christina gave her *freind* a hug. "I think you are very brave all the time." She tucked the last slice of pound cake into a bag and sealed it. "Who can we steer Elam toward so he forgets about you?"

# Chapter Nine

"Shame on you, Christina. Now you're playing match-maker."

"You want him to focus his attention elsewhere, ain't so?"

"Definitely, but I figure he'll soon change his mind when he realizes how much is involved in caring for three *kinner*. And if I do nothing to encourage him, he should abandon his effort, don't you think?"

"Hmm. Have you done anything to encourage him thus far?"

"Absolutely not!"

"That hasn't worked out so well, then, has it?"

"If you mean has he been discouraged yet, I would have to say I don't believe so. Even though I told him several times not to bother checking on us, he insisted it wasn't any trouble for him. I'm afraid if I look out the window tonight, I'll find him prowling about with his flashlight."

"He wasn't shining it into your bedroom window and tossing pebbles, was he?"

"*Ach*, Christina! We aren't young folks in our *rumspringa*." Amelia gave her *freind* a playful little shove. "He'd better not do that. I would jump into my bed, cover up my head, and pray for him to go away."

Christina laughed. "I'm only teasing, but I can see you are troubled by Elam's actions."

"I simply think he could put his time to better use pursuing a woman who might be receptive or merely visiting with his family."

"And then returning home."

Amelia smiled. "Have you taken up mind reading?"

"I don't have to be too bright to decipher the meaning behind your words. Your wrinkled nose screams volumes."

Amelia reached up to touch her nose. "I hope I didn't do that while talking to Elam. That would be so mean, not to mention rude."

"I doubt you did that. Besides, everyone knows you wouldn't be mean to a single soul."

"Not intentionally."

"At least it was dark, so he couldn't have seen your expression too clearly."

"Thank goodness for that." Amelia packaged the remaining cookies on the cooling rack. She jerked and broke a cookie in half when Christina snapped her fingers.

"My, you are jumpy. Here, I'll relieve you of these." Christina plucked the cookie pieces from Amelia's hands and popped one into her mouth. "Yummy as always." She licked the crumbs from her lips. "I had a brilliant idea." She held the remaining cookie fragment out to Amelia.

"I'm almost afraid to ask about your idea." Amelia nibbled at the proffered treat.

"Eleanore is single. And she's close to Elam's age."

Amelia coughed and patted her chest. "The bishop's *schweschder?*" Her voice squeaked, and her eyes watered. She coughed again. "You'd pawn Elam off on Bishop Micah's *schweschder?*" Never mind that she'd had the same thought.

"Well, it isn't like Eleanore would be forced to accept his attention, but she might be lonely and ready for a new *freind.*"

"I seriously doubt she's that lonely. Oh, I'm so bad. I didn't mean that."

Christina laughed so hard that tears trickled from her eyes. "Eleanore was sick recently and in the hospital. Maybe she'd like some company."

"Physically sick, *jah*, but there isn't anything wrong with her mind."

Christina laughed again and swiped at her eyes. "My belly hurts from laughing. Just because Elam doesn't appeal to you, doesn't mean he isn't perfect for someone else."

"True enough, but I'm sure Elam has seen Eleanore at church and social gatherings. As far as I know, he has never approached her."

"You know how Eleanore is, though. She tends to hide in the shadows. She thinks fellows will run the other direction because of her diabetes."

"She has that under control now after her hospital stay, doesn't she?"

"I hope so. I believe her condition can fluctuate, but she's really been trying to stick to her diet."

"*Gut.* She's such a lovely person. She's pretty for sure with that chestnut hair and those big, green eyes, but she has a heart of gold as well." Amelia paused, not sure if she should voice the rest of her thought, but then threw caution to the wind and continued. "I wouldn't want to see her hurt or taken advantage of."

"I agree. Maybe we can simply make sure she has an opportunity to talk to Elam. If sparks fly, fine. If not, that's fine too."

"I guess that would be all right, especially since she is older and doesn't attend singings. I don't believe she's stepping out with anyone, but of course, I wouldn't know that for sure and for certain."

Christina winked. "Oh, of course not. It isn't like we don't all know each other's business."

Amelia gasped. "Oh my!" She clapped her hands to her cheeks. "Do you think everyone knows Elam was here last night? I wouldn't want rumors to spread." The bishop certainly knew Ryan Miller had been at her house on a Sunday, but that had been an accidental meeting in broad daylight.

"I don't think anyone would know unless Elam mentioned it. Most of us are tucked into our beds shortly after sunset. And you can trust me not to breathe a word to anyone."

"You don't think Elam is the type of person who lets people know he's done a *gut* deed, do you?"

"I don't really know the man, but I would hope not. Bragging and pridefulness are frowned on by all of us."

"If he let it slip to Annie..."

Christina laughed. "Then he might as well have taken out an ad in the *Budget.*"

Amelia's cheeks flamed. "Don't get me wrong. Annie is a nice girl, but she does tend to talk a bit."

"A bit? Annie has been my *freind* forever, but I'm well aware of how much she likes to gab. She doesn't mean any harm, but she often speaks without thinking. After the problems we had regarding Noah, I don't confide in her as much as I used to do."

"I'm sorry about all that heartache. I'm glad you forgave her and the two of you are still *freinden.*"

"We're supposed to forgive, ain't so? Annie was going through a rough patch then. I guess she thought it would boost her self-confidence if she could gain the attention of the fellow I had my eye on. Anyway, that's over." Christina packed all the treats in a sturdy canvas bag. "Look at the time! I won't be early getting to The Green Thumb if I don't stop talking and start pedaling."

"I'm sorry. I held you up with my tales of woe."

"You didn't do any such thing, Amelia. I enjoy talking to you."

"The feeling is likewise. Are you going to be able to transport all this stuff on your bike? I got a little carried away with my baking."

Christina laughed. "You did, just a bit. It should all fit in the basket attached to my bike's handlebars. And I'm sure it will sell lickety-split." She started for the door but paused with one hand on the knob. "Did you know Ryan Miller often stops in to buy your cookies and brownies or whatever you've baked?"

~

Amelia didn't know why, but Christina's words put a bounce in her step. She fairly floated across the linoleum floor to the wood-burning cookstove. A smile that began in her heart tugged her lips upward. It was a *gut* thing Christina hadn't turned around after making her last comment or she would surely have noticed Amelia's flushed cheeks.

She lifted the lid from the pot on the back burner of the stove and stirred the thickened oatmeal. She decided to add a little milk, so the stuff didn't have the consistency of paste. But if she added brown sugar, the girls would eat it regardless of how thick or thin it was.

Amelia peeked over her shoulder at the battery-operated wall clock. She would need to hurry to throw the morning meal together or Rhonda would be late to school. The girls needed something besides oatmeal. She debated her options. She could scramble some eggs quickly but wouldn't have time to fry bacon or make pancakes.

"*Mamm*, we're hungry." Rhonda ran into the kitchen and stood beside Amelia. She raised up on tiptoes to peer into the pot.

Amelia hugged her oldest *dochder* with her free arm. "Well, you've *kumm* to the right place. Christina came by to pick up items for her store and visited longer than I thought.

I don't have time to cook anything besides the oatmeal. We could have zucchini bread to go with it though."

"Mmm. That sounds yummy. I'll set the table."

"*Danki*, dear one." How grown-up Rhonda seemed! Only six but taking on responsibility like a much older girl. The Lord *Gott* had certainly blessed her with three *wunderbaar dochders*. Five, if she counted Gabby and Jessie, whom she loved as much as if she had given birth to them.

~

Amelia sighed as she pulled out her basket materials. The morning had been full, but most mornings were. She had managed to get breakfast into all five girls and to get Rhonda out in time to catch the school bus. She'd hung out two loads of laundry that should dry quickly in the brisk breeze. She had played with the four younger girls in between mopping and dusting, fed them a hot meal, and tucked them beneath quilts for a nap. Now she could get to work on her basket orders. She had a few special orders, and she wanted to make some holiday baskets for Christina to sell in her store.

The morning conversation with Christina echoed in her mind. Did she want to marry again? Amelia's fingers expertly wove the fiber while her mind meandered. *Jah*, she would like to be married again. She would like a complete family for her girls. She didn't realize how much she had missed having a partner in life until recently. She'd been too busy dealing with grief, caring for her family, and keeping up with chores.

But ever so gradually, that black cloud of grief lifted. She had found joy in life and embraced hope for the future.

Sometimes in the quiet hours before bedtime, she allowed herself to consider remarriage. The man would have to be someone she respected, who loved her and her girls, and who was willing to take on the challenge of raising *kinner* who weren't his. Could very many men do that? She knew other widows and widowers who remarried and had seemed quite happy, but was she ready to travel down that road? Perhaps.

Amelia dredged up and discarded images of unmarried men in her community. None of them sparked the slightest interest. She supposed *freinden* could introduce her to relatives or acquaintances who lived in other areas, but that seemed unnatural, like a business arrangement. The only face that came to mind, that she couldn't banish even when she tried, was the one man she needed to forget about.

~

Ryan congratulated himself for making it thus far through the workday without any serious mishaps. His butterfingers only dropped the screwdriver twice, and he managed to remain focused on each task—most of the time.

Norman had entered the shop with a knowing smile and a friendly pat on the shoulder as if to say he was there for moral support or for another heart-to-heart chat. Ryan planned to avoid that. He wasn't accustomed to wearing his heart on his sleeve and didn't plan to start doing so now. He'd been kicking himself for divulging some of his secrets ever since they slipped out of his mouth. Norman was discreet though. He wouldn't blab. At least, Ryan hoped he wouldn't.

Somehow, he had remained calm when he dropped Gabby and Jessie off that morning. Even though Amelia's eyes shone brighter with the reflection of her blue dress, she still looked tired. Had she wrestled with her thoughts as he had? His attraction or interest or concern or whatever it was he felt for her had not dimmed after his prayers. Did that mean it was the Lord's will for him and Amelia to forge a relationship? *Patience, man. There's no rush.*

Ryan whistled softly as he worked on his last project of the day. He was determined to get this engine running before he headed home. He could probably work a lot faster if he could stop daydreaming, but how did a person dictate his thoughts?

Too many sweet images crowded into his brain: Amelia's smile when she opened the door. Her tender expression when she greeted his children. The sparkle in her blue eyes. The little, brown freckles that dotted her slightly upturned nose. Her laugh, which reminded him of a robin's song on a bright spring morning. *Hopeless! I am absolutely hopeless and need to stop this schoolboy dreaming immediately!*

"Did you say something?" Norman called from his workbench across the shop.

Had he spoken aloud? Ryan didn't think so. "No, I'm just mumbling. I'm bound and determined to get this job done."

"I heard you whistling earlier. You must be feeling better."

"I'm fine."

"Any more thoughts about our last conversation?"

*Only constantly.* "Nothing specific." Ryan resumed whistling. Maybe Norman would let this conversation die.

"It's probably good to let things simmer for a while, but don't wait too long. Those little girls of yours need a mother. And it's not good to be alone for too long. It makes you get set in your ways. Besides, you aren't getting any younger."

*Who is?* Ryan didn't think thirty was over the hill, but Norman was right about the girls needing a mother. He never knew how to fix their hair properly. He wasn't a great cook, so they tended to eat the same few things he could prepare over and over. He didn't know how to talk to them about female things when that time came. The very idea of that made his heart pound and his cheeks flush. And, worst of all, loneliness had begun to creep in. "I'll keep that in mind, Norman."

Twenty minutes later, Ryan uttered a sigh of relief. The engine purred like a kitten with a belly full of cream. His gargantuan effort to focus paid off. Now he could go home without feeling like a failure.

"Ready to call it a day?" Norman pushed his own project aside. "I'm not making much headway here, so I think I'll start afresh in the morning."

"I'm ready." Boy, was he glad to hear he wasn't the only one with concentration issues today.

Ryan bade the older man good evening and bolted for his SUV. He glanced at the dashboard clock as soon as he cranked the engine. Good. He was a few minutes early so he'd have time for a quick stop before picking up the girls. He adjusted the thermostat so the vehicle would be toasty for the girls. He wished he could protect them from every hardship or hurt in life as easily as he protected them from the cold.

He swung into the parking lot of The Green Thumb and hopped out of the SUV as soon as he cut the engine. Thank goodness the place stayed open later than Norman's shop. "Hi, Christina," he called out as he swung the door open.

"Hello there, Ryan. Hmm, I wonder what you might be searching for today."

His face must be glowing if the heat in his cheeks was any indication. "Just looking for a treat to tide me over."

"It just so happens one of my fantastic bakers provided some yummy cookies and other baked goods today."

"Do you have some left?"

"Indeed, I do. And they're all made by your favorite baker." Christina swept her arm toward the shelf holding the treats.

"Great!" Ryan shuffled over and selected a package of cookies and a piece of pound cake. He'd share the cookies with the girls, but the cake was all his.

"Tell Amelia I'll see her soon." Christina grinned as she tallied up the purchases.

Ryan felt like a young boy with his first crush. How mortifying. Yet, he smiled in anticipation of seeing the object of that crush.

# Chapter Ten

A chicken noodle casserole bubbled in the oven, its savory fragrance wafting throughout the kitchen and beyond. Rhonda arrived home from school, ate a snack with the other girls, and completed her smattering of homework. Amelia gathered up her laundry basket and clothespin bag. As soon as the girls licked the last oatmeal cookie crumbs from their lips, she'd take them outside to play while she removed clothes from the line.

With winter approaching, they had better take advantage of whatever pleasant weather the Lord *Gott* sent their way. One could never accurately predict Southern Maryland's fickle weather. One winter could be mild with a sixty-five-degree Christmas. The very next winter could have snowstorm after snowstorm. Amelia figured the Lord liked to surprise them.

The wind had been blowing off and on throughout the day, so Amelia helped the little ones into jackets that should keep them plenty warm, especially once they started running around the backyard. Thankfully, the yard was fenced, so she wouldn't have to worry about Jessie toddling or crawling off somewhere.

Shrieks and giggles filled the air as soon as the girls tumbled out the back door. Amelia smiled at their antics. They made her want to run and leap along with them. Once she had the clothes off the line, she'd push them on the big wooden swing hanging by a rope from a thick, oak limb. She might even sneak in a turn herself. There was nothing like soaring to the sky to make a person forget her cares.

Amelia sat Jessie down near the clothesline and talked or sang to her to keep her happy. She hung the clothespin bag on the line, unclipped clothes, tossed the pens into the bag, and folded each item before laying it in the basket.

"What happened?" She abruptly stopped singing the silly song that made Jessie giggle. There was a gap between the dresses. She hadn't left a big, open space, had she? She always pinned things close together. What was missing, and where did it go?

She searched her memory and then counted small and large dresses. The shawl. She had washed a black, knitted shawl and hung it between the dresses. It wasn't on the ground where it would be if it had blown off the line.

She checked the back line in case she'd been mistaken about where she had pinned it and scanned the yard. What had happened to it? The wind hadn't been strong enough to blow away a heavy shawl. The clothespins that had fastened it to the line were still in place. Amelia's breath caught. Her knees grew rubbery. Someone had yanked the shawl off the line and run off with it. She and the girls had never been aware of a thing. The culprit had walked right past the house and into her yard without her even knowing it. How brazen!

How frightening! What would have happened if she or one of the *kinner* had stepped outside while the thief was at the clothesline? Could they have been hurt? Why was someone taking her things? Amelia rubbed her hands up and down her arms repeatedly. Her sudden chill did not arise from the wind

She whipped around every which way, straining to see beyond the edges of the yard, still rubbing her arms. Nothing looked amiss. No one stared at her from the shadows as far as she could tell. This was getting ridiculous. *Nee*, it was frustrating. It was downright scary. She willed herself to calm down so she wouldn't alarm the girls.

"Amelia, are you all right?"

She yelped and jumped. So much for calming down. "I-I... oh my." She patted her chest and gasped.

Ryan rushed forward. He reached out to steady her as if he expected her to collapse. "I'm so sorry I frightened you."

"I-it's okay. I was distracted and didn't hear you approach."

"Is anything wrong?"

She looked from the empty spot on the clothesline to the girls happily chasing each other to the giggling *boppli* and finally into Ryan's brown eyes. "I'm not sure."

"Are you sick?"

She shook her head. "I'm fine, I think."

"The girls seem all right." He turned away from Amelia for a few seconds to check on them.

"They are."

"Tell me what's troubling you, then."

"It's probably nothing." Amelia tried to smile but knew her effort fell short.

"Tell me anyway."

She pointed to the space between the dresses on the clothesline. "It's gone. The shawl. It was right there."

"Someone took clothes off the line? Do you think one of the girls yanked it down?"

"They haven't been near the clothesline at all."

"That's very strange. I don't suppose it blew away."

"I don't believe it's been that windy today. And even if a gust did kick up, it would have blown away the lighter-weight clothes."

"That's true. I can check the nearby woods to see if it's there. Maybe someone was pulling a prank and dropped the shawl out there."

"I wouldn't want you to waste your time. My quilt and basket haven't shown up anywhere, so I doubt the shawl will either." She shook her head and reached up to unpin the next item from the clothesline. "I don't understand it," she mumbled as she folded the dress and laid it atop the pile already filling the basket.

"I don't either." Ryan wrapped a hand around her arm when she reached for the next little dress. "Are you sure you're all right? You're awfully pale."

Amelia shrugged and tried to smile. "I'm always pale. It's a consequence of having a fair complexion."

"You are more pale than usual. Your cheeks are the color of fresh-fallen snow."

"It's only the shock of discovering someone has once again approached my house and taken a personal item." She pulled her arm away with reluctance. She liked the warmth and strength his hand offered and the concern his eyes conveyed. She liked them entirely too much.

"I'm sure you must be frightened."

"I can't dwell on that. There haven't been any threats or attempts to harm us. Like you said, someone is probably playing tricks." But she couldn't imagine who would do such a thing.

"Has anyone else in your community mentioned something similar happening?"

Amelia thought for a moment. "I haven't heard of anything."

"I haven't heard of such things either." Ryan laid a hand on her shoulder. "Are you afraid to stay here?"

She gave a slight shrug. "This is my home."

"Do you have someone you could stay with for a few days?"

"I wouldn't want to intrude on anyone."

"Could someone stay with you?"

"Again, I wouldn't want to disrupt someone else's routine."

"I'm pretty sure they wouldn't see it that way."

"But *I* would see it that way. I'm enough of a bother as it is with the men taking turns bringing me wood and doing heavy outdoor chores. We will be just fine." If she said that enough times, it would be true, wouldn't it?

~

In the stillness of the long, dark night, Amelia almost wished she had asked someone to stay with her. As had become her custom, she'd checked every door and window more than once. She had maintained some semblance of composure around the girls and had even laughed and played with them after supper.

Now, only the crackling of the fire broke the silence, and Amelia was alone with her thoughts. She glanced out the window from time to time to make sure no flashlight beams bobbed around her barn. She hoped she had finally gotten through to Elam. She pulled the afghan tighter around her shoulders and laid her head against the back of the rocking chair. She should go upstairs to bed, but weariness had claimed her.

A flash registered in her brain, instantly alerting her. Had blinking her eyes caused that quick glimmer of light, or was it something else? She stared at the dark window until her eyes watered. Nothing. Her imagination must be working overtime. Now that she was wide awake, she should drag herself upstairs. She added another log to the fire and turned toward the stairway when she saw another flash.

Anger usurped alarm. How could she convince Elam to leave her alone? She snatched up a flashlight and yanked an old shawl off the hook. She hadn't yet figured out what to say, but she would somehow get through to the man and demand that he stop the night visits. If someone saw him, she would be mortified.

Amelia slipped out the back door and waited for another flash of light to determine which direction to take. No flash appeared. Had he gone home? "Elam?" Silence answered her. "Elam?" She called louder but still got no reply. Could he have cleared the area so quickly? She hadn't detected the sound of a buggy or bicycle or even running feet. Strange indeed.

She took two steps toward the barn and barely stifled a scream at a shuffling sound. "Elam?" An owl shrieked and swooped down after some poor, unsuspecting little creature. Why didn't Elam answer her? She knew that light had not been a figment of her imagination. "Is anyone here?"

Her body shook with a mighty shiver. This whole situation was too bizarre. Someone was here or had been here. Who was it, and where had they gone? "*Ach*! My *bopplin*!" Amelia ran like she'd never run before. She shouldn't have left the girls alone in the house. What had she been thinking?

She flew into the house and slammed the door behind her. Her fingers fumbled with the lock but finally turned it. Her lungs burned. Her legs throbbed. She took the stairs two at a time and only slowed when she reached the girls' bedroom. She paused to catch her breath and eased the door open. She switched on the flashlight but held a hand over it to dim the brightness.

"*Danki*, Lord *Gott*." All three girls lay unmoving in their beds. One day, she would move them into their own rooms. She had plenty of space, and there would be no more little ones. But for now, they were happy to be together.

She tiptoed across the room to lay a hand on each little chest. Assured they breathed normally and slept peacefully, she slipped back out of the room but left the door ajar so she could hear if one of them called out to her.

Alone in her own room, Amelia questioned her sanity. Had she drifted off to sleep in the rocking chair and only dreamed of a light outside? Had she imagined someone prowled around her property? She quickly exchanged her dress for a nightgown and dove beneath the covers. Sleep would not likely be on her agenda tonight.

~

Before daylight even thought to hint at the sky, Amelia abandoned even the hope of a catnap. She dragged herself out of her warm bed and hopped across the cold wood floor. *Kaffi*. She needed *kaffi*. Strong *kaffi*. And lots of it. Ordinarily, she preferred tea to the bitter taste of *kaffi*, but she didn't think tea would pack a powerful enough punch this morning. She needed energy and alertness to care for five active little girls, and both of those were in short supply.

Amelia dressed by rote and crept down the hall and stairs. The girls didn't need to get up this early. And she needed a few minutes to herself to think and to sip that nasty brew. She planned to venture outside as soon as the inky sky turned gray. She would check on the animals and make sure everything was in its proper place.

After mulling it over all night, she was convinced someone had been outside before she went to bed. And that person either ran off with a quickness or deliberately kept silent when she called out. Either option gave her the heebie-jeebies. She owned nothing special, nothing of great value, so why would someone be interested in her possessions? Why had she been singled out?

Christina hadn't mentioned that items had gone missing from her home or store. The other women she'd spoken to at church hadn't reported any thefts either. So why her? Was it because she was a widow and was alone with her young *dochders*? Did someone consider her easy prey since she didn't have a man in the house?

That idea stirred her anger. She'd always been the independent sort. Of course, her husband had been the head of the family, as he should have been, but he was far from a tyrant. He respected her intelligence, her skills, her opinions. They'd had a partnership, unlike many other marriages.

In the years he had been gone, Amelia had grown used to making all the decisions regarding her family and her household. She might be a small woman, but what she lacked in size, she made up for in determination. "Well, Miss Independent Woman," she whispered as she glanced out the kitchen window at the awakening world, "are you ready to go out there and investigate?"

# Chapter Eleven

Amelia pulled on a heavier jacket since a light layer of frost glistened in the dim light of dawn. Scarlet and purple streaks crisscrossed the sky. She shoved her hands into the jacket pockets as soon as she pulled the door closed behind her. Mornings had been chillier each day. Winter's approach couldn't be denied any longer.

She strode toward the barn first since that's where she'd noticed the intruder last night. She stepped inside, leaving the door open to allow the faint early morning light to filter in. She inhaled the blended scents of fresh hay and horses. A soft whinny broke the silence. Amelia patted each horse and promised to return soon to let them out. She glanced around the barn but didn't notice anything out of place. Last night's visitor must not have *kumm* in here.

Amelia studied the ground outside the building, looking for footprints or any obvious disturbance of nature. If it had been Elam, wouldn't he have answered her? He had hesitated to speak right up the previous night he was here. She bent further to examine the footprints in the dirt. They were too big to be hers, but she didn't know if they had been made last night or at some earlier time. They could have been left by the men who came to help her out.

She sighed as she straightened up. She was not a *gut* detective. Or maybe she simply didn't have enough evidence. This little venture turned out to be a waste of time, so she'd better get inside to start breakfast.

Amelia threw out her hands to steady herself as she stumbled over a stick. She looked down to kick it out of the way. "What is that?" Something white caught her eye. She squatted down to check out the foreign object. "*Ach*! A cigarette." She didn't know of any Mennonite men who smoked. That nasty habit was frowned upon. Did Elam smoke? Surely not. She had never smelled smoke on him. Did that mean last night's trespasser had been *Englisch*?

She hopped up and sprinted for the house. Why did it seem worse that her interloper might be *Englisch*? Maybe because she didn't know very many of them. But all the ones she had met were extremely nice. She couldn't imagine any of them stealing her belongings. She remembered that the men who had been responsible for the death of Jill's *bruder* were *Englischers*, but they were in jail. Did they have *freinden* who would prey on the Plain community? Such an unsettling thought!

Amelia stopped to catch her breath at the back door and surveyed her property one more time. She didn't know what she expected to see but simply wanted reassurance that all was well in her little corner of the world. She hurried inside and locked the door behind her. Were she and her girls in any danger?

Maybe she should move back to Pennsylvania where she grew up. Her parents would take her in. She really didn't want to do that though. She had become too independent to live under her parents' authority again. Some of her *freinden* had recently moved to Virginia to establish a new Mennonite community. They had encouraged her to accompany them. Should she reconsider, pack up her belongings, and join them? She really didn't want to do that either.

Amelia had moved to Maryland as a bride and had lived here for eight years. She had put down roots and considered this home. She liked the quiet, rural atmosphere where the tourist attractions found in many other Plain communities were nonexistent. She had grown to love Southern Maryland, and she wouldn't let some pranks drive her away. She stomped a foot for emphasis.

The three thefts were pranks, weren't they? Surely, no one meant any harm. Usually, pranksters tired of their antics and moved on to some other mischief if their acts didn't cause a stir. If she didn't react, would they leave her alone?

Amelia hurried to wash her hands. Time was slipping away, and she had breakfast to prepare. Ryan would soon arrive with his little ones, and she wanted to have the meal ready. She also needed to get her own girls up and dressed. She'd love to sip a cup of tea and think things through, but she didn't have time right now.

She filled a pan with water and set it on the back burner to heat. Even though Jessie had some teeth now, she still liked oatmeal. The other girls would eat it too. She should have time to prepare French toast. She would slice some of the whole grain bread she had made and let the girls sprinkle powdered sugar on the finished slices.

She cracked an egg into a large ceramic mixing bowl and stirred in milk. She paused only long enough to pour oats into the boiling water and to plop a pat of butter into the center of the big cast-iron skillet.

"Can I help, *Mamm*?"

Amelia looked over her shoulder at her oldest. "You're up early, Rhonda."

"Judith rolled over and thumped me on the head. I saw the sky turning purple, so I figured it was time to get up."

"Almost. You could have slept a little longer, but I'm glad for the company."

"French toast!" she squealed. "Can I dip the bread in the bowl?"

"Sure." The kitchen would be a mess, but if the little girl wanted to help, Amelia would deal with that later. It was a *gut* thing that Rhonda showed an interest in cooking. Amelia pulled a chair close to the counter so Rhonda could kneel on it and better reach the counter. "Are your *schweschders* still asleep?"

"*Jah*, but Joanna was tossing and turning."

"I suspect she'll be up soon, then. Let's get the French toast cooked, and then I'll check on them."

"I can help Joanna and Judith get dressed."

"*Danki*, dear. You are a very *gut* helper, but I'll tend to them. You can set the table for me though."

"Okay."

Amelia's thoughts kept drifting to the strange occurrences. Whenever fear tried to creep in, she countered it with logic. She had been through much worse and survived. She would get through this as well.

"They're done, ain't so?"

"Huh?" Amelia looked at the golden-brown bread slices in the skillet. Another minute or two and she would have had to scrape off char. "They certainly are." She lifted out the last slices and added them to the plate already piled with French toast. She checked the oatmeal and removed the pan from the burner. "If you will go ahead and set the table, I will get your *schweschders* ready for the day."

Rhonda scampered over to the silverware drawer. "Gabby and Jessie will eat with us, won't they?"

"I expect so." Amelia smiled as she watched her *dochder* count out enough utensils for everyone. Such a smart girl! She offered a quick prayer that all the girls would always keep their kind, helpful attitudes.

~

"Good morning, Amelia. How are you this brisk day?" She looked tired, as if she had missed several days of sleep, but she was still as lovely as ever. Ryan bit his tongue to keep the compliment to himself because it wanted to fly right out of his mouth.

"I'm fine, Ryan. You're right about the cool morning. I believe winter is knocking at our door."

"Do you have plenty of firewood?"

"I do. The men take turns bringing me loads, so I should be fine. It's too bad I don't know how to chop down a tree and saw wood. I could save them a lot of trouble."

He laughed until his eyes watered. "I'm sorry, but I can't see you wielding an axe."

She drew herself up as tall as possible, which was no taller than his shoulder, and shot him a serious look. "I'm sure I could with some instruction and practice."

He held up a hand as if to ward off an attack. "I don't have any doubt that you can do anything you set your mind to. I know you're a strong woman and completely capable of taking care of yourself and your family."

"Well, mostly. I admit there are some things I can't do, like shear sheep or shoe horses."

"Or split wood."

"Right. So I'm afraid I must rely on the generosity of others for some things whether I like it or not."

"Most people truly like helping others. Don't deprive them of the opportunity to do good."

"I understand that in here"—she pointed to her chest—"but my brain likes to be in control and be self-sufficient."

Ryan smiled. "I know exactly what you mean. I often have trouble asking for help even though I clearly need all the assistance I can get—especially with the girls."

"You are doing a *wunderbaar* job with them."

"With your help."

"I love the girls."

Ryan's breath caught momentarily when he imagined her saying those words about him. She looked at him like he had sprouted a second nose. Had she read his thoughts? "I know you love them, and they love being here with you." Had he salvaged that situation?

"Here, let me take Jessie. Gabby, you can hang your jacket on the peg and wash your hands. We're having French toast for breakfast."

"Yummy!" The little girl shrugged out of her coat and ran to do as she was told.

"So that's what smells so good. I haven't attempted to make that. I'm afraid my meals are pretty basic."

"Basic is fine. I can make a little plate for you to take with you if you like. Rhonda and I cooked plenty."

Why did her cheeks grow rosy? Was she afraid she had been too forward? She had sent him off with food before. He wished *he* could read *her* thoughts. "Well, I don't want to put you to any trouble."

She pulled off Jessie's coat and carried it to the row of pegs near the door. "It's not a bit of trouble. You haven't eaten yet, have you?"

"No, I didn't take time."

"You certainly can't concentrate on work with an empty stomach growling at you."

"That's true." A little sleep would go a long way too.

Amelia wiped Jessie's hands and sat her in the high chair. She sprinkled a few Cheerios on the tray to keep the little one occupied until her food was ready. The older girls took their places at the table and patiently waited while Amelia pulled out a plastic container to fill for Ryan.

He followed her to the kitchen counter to make sure she really did have plenty of food and hadn't made her offer only to be polite. "If you want to feed the girls first, that's fine."

"They can wait a few minutes. You need to get to work."

"I'm running a little ahead of schedule. Let me help you get food on the table so Rhonda won't be late for school."

Amelia peeked at the clock. "Where did the time go? If you're sure you can wait, I will fix their food first."

"Sure. I'll hold the plates, and you fill them up since you know how much food to put on each one."

"All right."

They worked as a team assembling the meal for the girls. Amelia sat with them for their silent prayer. She made sure they had all sprinkled their French toast with powdered sugar and the bread was cut into bite-sized pieces before returning to the task she had abandoned.

"I'm sorry. I'm keeping you from your breakfast and taking up your time."

"Nonsense. I'm not very hungry, and it doesn't take long to put food in containers for you."

Ryan watched her arrange three slices of French toast in a container and pour powdered sugar into a tiny plastic cup with a lid. Should he ask her why her hands trembled ever so slightly?

"Ryan—"

"Amelia—"

They spoke in unison and halted at the same time. Ryan smiled. "You go first."

She shook her head and acted like she wasn't sure she should speak. "I was wondering if you know any Mennonites who smoke cigarettes."

That certainly was a strange question. He thought for a minute. "I can't think of a single person in my community or yours either. Why do you ask?"

Amelia shrugged but kept silent.

"You must have had a reason for posing that question."

"I had another visitor last night, and I think he dropped a cigarette."

She whispered, but he'd heard every word.

"What? Did he take anything?"

"Not as far as I could tell."

"And it wasn't Elam Wenger again?" Ryan had heard all about Elam's desire to play protector, and though he had no right, he'd been bothered by that. A lot. But if Elam was stalking Amelia, that was an entirely different matter.

"I don't think so. I called out but didn't get an answer."

"You went outside to confront an intruder?" Ryan wasn't sure if he was proud of her courage, even though he was not supposed to show pride, or upset that she could have endangered herself.

"*Jah.*" She hung her head like a reprimanded scholar. "I thought it was Elam, and I wanted to tell him again to please stop prowling around my home at night."

He'd been so afraid she was going to say that she wanted to see Elam that he almost gasped in relief. He certainly had no claims on the beautiful, petite woman packing his breakfast, but he couldn't bear the thought that she might actually *want* to see and talk to Elam Wenger. "Nobody answered you when you called out?"

"*Nee.* I, uh, got a little scared and ran back to the house." She peeked up at him through those thick, dark lashes.

"Good."

"*Gut?*"

"Yes. If someone wanted to remain anonymous, that could mean he was up to no good. I wouldn't want you to get hurt." He would be devastated if she got hurt.

Amelia shivered and rubbed her hands up and down her arms.

Ryan had the sudden urge to hold her close and comfort her. He'd like to shield her from all harm, and now he'd probably scared her. "I didn't mean to upset you."

"You didn't. I had those same thoughts but not until I was already outside. I hate to admit it, but I was quite perturbed when I noticed the light outside after I had specifically told Elam not to trouble himself checking on us. I'm sure I stormed right out of the house last night not even considering it could be someone else nosing around. When the person didn't answer...Well, fear kicked in. I ran back to check on the girls as fast as I could."

Ryan smiled. *I bet she took off like a mother lion running to protect her cubs.* "I'm glad everything turned out all right. When did you find the cigarette?"

Amelia snapped the lid on the plastic container of French toast slices. She placed it and the cup of powdered sugar in a small, brown paper bag. "I went outside as soon as it got light enough to see. I wanted to check on the animals and make sure nothing was missing."

"I assume everything was fine in the barn."

"As far as I could tell. I was on my way back to the house when the cigarette on the ground caught my eye. I don't know any smokers, so I can't imagine where it came from."

"Hmm. That is very strange. I don't know any smokers either, but I guess folks could smoke when they're alone." Ryan was more worried than he let on. Who could be preying on the young widow and her girls? He had half a mind to spend the night in her barn to try to catch the culprit, but that would be out of the question. There must be some way he could offer protection.

"You're probably right, but you can usually smell smoke on a person's clothes."

"True enough. I can have another look around out there when I pick up the girls this evening. I'd do it now, but—"

"You need to get to work. I've delayed you long enough."

Even though she smiled as she held the bag out to him, he could see the concern in her eyes. He had to try to allay that. "I don't think you have anything to be afraid of since no one has tried to get in the house." He took the bag from her hands. "Thank you for feeding me yet again."

She nodded. "I'm happy to help out."

And she was. Ryan knew those weren't simply polite words. Amelia truly did enjoy helping others. A sudden inspiration struck, and he paused at the back door. "Hey! I've got the perfect solution."

She stopped scooping oatmeal into her own bowl and stared at him. "What?"

"A dog. You need a dog."

# Chapter Twelve

Amelia needed another mouth to feed like a picnic needed ants. She had been stunned by Ryan's declaration. He had looked so pleased to have found a solution for her that she hadn't had the heart to protest—yet.

"Are we going to get a dog, *Mamm*?" Rhonda practically jumped up and down in her chair. Why did little ears always hear conversations not intended for them?

"I am not planning to get a dog. Please sit still and finish your breakfast."

"We'll take care of it, won't we, Judith?"

The younger girl's cheeks bulged with several unswallowed bites of French toast. She couldn't speak but nodded so vigorously that Amelia feared she would choke.

"Chew and swallow, Judith. I appreciate the offer, girls, but don't get your hopes up." Suddenly, Amelia's uneaten bowl of oatmeal looked completely unappetizing. She dumped it back into the pot. She'd try to eat later. Unresolved fear and confusion left a bitter taste in her mouth.

"I want a dog too," Gabby whined.

"Maybe we'll all get dogs." Judith finally managed to add her two cents' worth to the conversation.

"Let's not concern ourselves with dogs. Rhonda, you need to get ready to leave." Amelia would have her work cut out for her today trying to keep little minds busy thinking of something other than dogs. She didn't need Judith and Gabby and even Joanna begging for a puppy all day.

After breakfast, she gave the girls dustcloths and sponges so they could help clean. Later, she let them mix dough and help roll out sugar cookies. By the time the cookies had been transferred to cooling racks, tummies grumbled for the noon meal.

Amelia breathed a relieved sigh. She had been successful at keeping thoughts of dogs at bay. At least for the morning.

While the girls napped after scarfing up their macaroni and cheese and green beans, Amelia dragged out her basket-making supplies. Her practiced fingers flew through the weaving of a small Christmas basket an *Englisch* customer had ordered. The tension in her shoulders eased as her creative juices flowed. If only she could calm her troubled mind too.

What should she do if she observed a light outside tonight? Should she try to investigate again? Should she barricade herself in the house, pretend she hadn't seen it, and hope the person went away? If nothing had been stolen last night, what did the person want here?

If he had intended to hurt her or the girls, he certainly could have done so. There wasn't much she could have done to defend them. So harming them must not have been the objective. Perhaps he hadn't stolen anything last night because she had interrupted him and he needed to run off before being discovered. Did that mean he would return tonight to finish his job?

Amelia flexed her fingers for a minute. Maybe she should ask someone to stay with her for moral support. But who? She didn't want to jeopardize anyone else's safety. Ryan's suggestion might not be as preposterous as she originally thought it was.

*Nee*, she did not need a dog. That would mean she'd have to buy dog food regularly and take it to the vet for shots. It would be like having another little one to care for. She told herself the same thing she had been telling everyone else. She would be all right.

Amelia forced herself to think of something different, but her next thoughts were equally as troubling. The image of Ryan's thick, dark hair, kind, smiling eyes, and deep, rich voice should not fill her brain. He was Gabby's and Jessie's *daed*, and that should be the only way she thought of the man. If she couldn't do that, then she should tell him to find another caregiver for his girls.

Tears sprang into her eyes. How could she possibly give up caring for those adorable *kinner*? She loved them as if they were her own. She sighed. If only she didn't have such confusing thoughts and feelings about their *daed*.

The memory of their one outing into town that evening during the summer vied for her attention. Although she had been nervous about someone from the community spotting them and getting the wrong idea, she had fun. The girls had all enjoyed themselves too, especially the ice cream treat after the completion of their errand.

Amelia hadn't been nervous with Ryan at all after the first few awkward minutes. She had almost allowed herself to pretend they were a regular family on an outing. Even now, she smiled, remembering their laughter.

She'd had that moment of panic when Christina Brubacher had spotted them, but she had looked equally as dismayed at having been discovered with Noah Zimmerman. Amelia and Christina had talked later and decided to keep each other's secrets.

Of course, everyone knew that Christina and Noah were now a couple planning to marry. And everyone was happy for them. She couldn't think of a single person who would be delighted about a relationship between her and Ryan, except for two little girls who needed a *mudder* and three little girls who needed a *daed*.

*Nee,* she and Ryan could not have any relationship other than the one they had right now. She simply had to get her heart to agree with her brain. She frowned and bit her lip. *Concentrate on your basket, Amelia, and forget your foolish, impossible notions.*

~

Later, with a big pot of beef stew simmering on a back burner of the stove, Amelia bundled up all the girls and took them outside to play. A cold wind whooshed intermittently, but they all needed some fresh air. While the older girls galloped and shrieked, Amelia entertained Jessie with a bottle of bubbles.

She held the wand to her lips and blew in the *boppli's* direction. The little girl giggled as she waddled on unsteady legs, trying to catch the floating bubbles. Rhonda joined in the fun as soon as she got off the school bus, and all were rosy-cheeked by the time a dark SUV drove up the long driveway.

"Oh my! I didn't know it was so late. Your *daed* is here already, Gabby."

"Can't we play a little longer?" The four-year-old called as soon as her father opened the car door.

"Well hello, Gabby! It's good to see you too." Ryan crossed the driveway and entered the yard in several long strides. He scooped Jessie up and held her high.

"My turn!" Gabby ran to tug at his jacket. He set Jessie down and raised Gabby to the sky.

Amelia caught the longing in her *dochders'* eyes. Yet the little girls did not ask for the man's attention. Her heart melted, though, when Ryan gave each of her girls a turn to reach heavenward. What an observant, tenderhearted man.

"Okay, Gabby and Jessie. Let's get your things and give Amelia a little peace." He gave his girls a stern look.

Amelia chuckled. "How much peace can I have with three lively *kinner* underfoot?"

"If I subtract two from your total, you might be able to squeak out a few more peaceful moments."

"Your *dochders* are never any problem."

"That's music to a parent's ears." He patted Judith's head. The little girl hadn't left his side after he'd set her down a few moments earlier. "Why don't you girls run ahead and let us old, slower folks talk a minute? On your mark, get set, go!"

Gabby, Rhonda, and Judith couldn't pass up the opportunity to race. Joanna tagged along behind them.

Amelia slowed to a shuffle. What on earth did he want to talk about? Had he heard some news about the identity of her intruder? Her heart pounded as she waited for him to speak.

"I wondered if you thought about our earlier discussion."

Amelia searched the file of conversations stored in her brain. They had probably had a zillion discussions. "Which one?"

"The one about having someone stay with you or getting a dog."

"Oh. There wasn't much to consider. I wouldn't want to trouble anyone or involve them in this strange situation."

"If you let Gabby and Jessie sleep here tonight, I'll bunk in your barn and try to nab anyone who might show up to prowl around the premises."

"*Ach*! That would never do!" Her face must have burst into flame as badly as it burned. "I-I mean, the girls are always *wilkom*, but it would be totally inappropriate for you to stay."

"I understand your concern. I only want to look out for your welfare."

"I appreciate that." She almost asked why he was so worried. She was only the babysitter. Yet she couldn't deny the warmth and comfort his offer generated. And happiness, too, if she allowed herself to admit that. Could she possibly be important to him as a woman and not merely as his girls' caregiver?

"I can't stand the thought of you here alone and scared."

Her giggle sounded nervous in her own ears. "I'm hardly alone, and I'm not afraid."

Ryan's hand on her arm was as light as a feather. "I know you are a brave, capable woman, but these are strange circumstances."

"They are indeed." And not only the occurrences with the prowler. Why, this very conversation bordered on strange.

"Isn't there a woman friend you could ask to stay with you tonight? I can stop and inquire for you on my way home. I'd feel better knowing there was another adult here if you needed help."

There it was again—that little ripple of pleasure that raced throughout her body. She had missed feeling important to someone. Ryan's concern made her feel special.

"Most have their own families to care for."

"What about Christina Brubacher? She isn't married, and she's a friend, isn't she?"

"*Jah,* Christina and I are *gut freinden.*"

"Can I stop and ask her to come over tonight?"

"I don't want to disturb her. We have been fine all this time, so I expect we will continue to be fine." She shifted Jessie's weight.

"Here. I'll take her. You've lugged her around all day." He lifted the *boppli* and swung her over onto his own hip. "Let me at least ask Christina. If she's busy, I believe she will say so, but please let me talk to her. Please? For me?"

For him? She shouldn't want to do anything simply to please him, but she did. "Christina works hard all day. She needs her time to relax in the evenings."

"Don't you think she will be honest enough to tell me if she's too tired?"

"She's honest, for sure. She's also too kind to deny anyone's request for help."

"Look at it this way. It might be a fun evening for both of you."

Amelia wavered. She hated to be put on the spot like this. But if she allowed herself to be absolutely truthful, she would be downright relieved to have someone else with her tonight.

"Please?"

"Okay. You can *ask* her but not *badger* her."

"Badger? Me? Never!"

Amelia burst out laughing and nudged the chuckling man with an elbow.

"Now, about the dog."

"Ryan Miller! Who doesn't badger people?"

"I merely asked a question." He looked down at her with wide, innocent eyes, but a smile tugged at his lips.

"Right."

"I'm pretty sure I know someone with puppies they need to find homes for."

"Shh! If the girls hear you, they'll worry me about dogs until bedtime."

"Maybe I should enlist their help."

"Don't you dare!"

~

Ryan continued to smile as he buckled Gabby and Jessie into their car seats. Amelia's reaction to his mention of the puppies amused him. Her voice declared no, but something in her eyes led him to believe she might possibly change her mind. He'd like to think he caused the sparkle he observed in her eyes and the tiny smile on her lips, but she was probably only remembering a pet from her childhood.

He really hoped she would relent and at least let him show her the puppies. He was sure she would fall in love with the little balls of fluff after seeing them and stroking their soft fur. She had such a tender heart. He knew she would be won over immediately. He might even have to take a puppy himself.

Of course, a puppy wouldn't exactly be a guard dog, but it would certainly bark if someone came near the house. And that might be enough to scare off an intruder. At the very least, barking would warn Amelia that something was amiss.

Ryan sang a few stanzas of a silly song with Gabby before his mind raced off again. He wouldn't badger Christina, but he sure hoped he could persuade her to stay with Amelia this evening. There was a chance that almost getting caught last night would deter the trespasser from returning tonight, but one never knew. Amelia must have been so frightened the previous night, yet she'd been brave enough to investigate. Christina could at least provide support and a diversion from troubling thoughts.

He hoped he could catch Christina outside so he wouldn't have to drag both girls out of the car or air his concerns in front of the entire Brubacher family. They would surely question his motives. It was fine for the different groups of Mennonites to work together and to help one another, but any perceived relationship other than friendship would be taboo. He didn't want to get Amelia into hot water with her bishop and ministers.

Ryan clicked on the signal light and turned onto the long gravel driveway leading to the Brubacher home. "Girls, I have one quick stop to make." He glanced into the rearview mirror. Gabby tickled Jessie beneath her chin to elicit giggles and then burst into laughter herself. Such good girls. He was blessed.

He could see a distant figure dismount a bicycle and squinted to try to bring the person into focus. Christina. Thank goodness. He pressed harder on the gas pedal to propel them a little faster. He had to catch her before she went inside.

# Chapter Thirteen

Amelia tried to ignore the goose bumps that skipped up and down her arms as darkness fell. She wandered through the house to check the locks on every door and window a second time. If she didn't calm herself, she would make the girls nervous and scared. She rubbed her arms to dispel the chill and forced a smile. "Who's ready to get supper on the table?"

Three exuberant little voices cried, "Me!" in unison.

"Okay. Let's see who can wash up the cleanest to help me."

All three scampered off toward the bathroom. They had been coloring and gluing and probably had sticky fingers. They giggled as water sloshed from the faucet. "Use soap, and don't make a mess." Most likely those last words were spoken in vain.

Amelia handed Joanna paper napkins and Judith silverware to carry to the table. She entrusted half-full glasses of milk to Rhonda and prayed the little girl wouldn't drop them. She stirred the stew and ladled a spoonful into the first bowl on the counter. She gasped and jumped, sloshing stew everywhere when a knock sounded at the back door. She stood as if frozen and stared.

"*Mamm?* Someone knocked on the door." Rhonda tugged on her skirt. "I'll go see."

That jolted Amelia out of her stupor. "*Nee*, I'll get it." She grabbed a paper towel to wipe stew off her arm and took baby steps toward the door. She wanted to know who was out there but, at the same time, didn't want to know.

"Amelia? It's Christina."

The muffled voice was music to Amelia's ears. She breathed a sigh of relief. "*Danki*, Lord *Gott*," she whispered. She hurried the last few feet and yanked open the door to greet her *freind*."

"Hi, Amelia. Is it okay to visit for a while?" Christina peeked around Amelia as if searching for the girls. She lowered her voice. "I'll stay here tonight if that's okay with you. Are you all right?"

"I'm fine. *Kumm* on inside." Amelia closed and locked the door as soon as Christina crossed the threshold. "I'm sorry Ryan bothered you. I told him I would be fine tonight. I believe he was more concerned than I am."

Christina shrugged out of her cloak. "He's a very nice man."

"*Jah*." Amelia willed herself not to blush.

"There is nothing wrong with having concerned *freinden*."

"I suppose. I don't like to be a bother to anyone."

Christina squeezed Amelia's arm. "Stop saying that. You are not a bother to anyone. We all need a little help now and then, ain't so?"

"Some of us more than others, I'm afraid. I was just dishing up some stew. Please join us. You haven't eaten supper yet, have you?"

"*Nee*, and stew sounds great." She rubbed her hands together. "I do believe winter is upon us. There is quite a nip in the air tonight."

"Rhonda, please put out more silverware and a napkin. Christina is going to eat supper with us."

"Hi, girls." Christina smiled at each one. "Let me wash, and I can help you."

~

Christina kept the girls entertained with stories until their eyelids drooped and then helped Amelia tuck them into bed. "You look tired yourself." She squeezed Amelia's hand as they left the girls' room.

"I'm sure all *mudders* are tired at the end of the day. Would you like to join me in a cup of tea? I usually sip tea after the girls go to bed and the house is quiet. It sort of helps me wind down after a busy day."

"I hope it's herb tea unless you enjoy staring at the ceiling all night."

*That would be preferable to staring out the window, straining to glimpse anything out of the ordinary.* "I usually drink orange or mint tea."

"Maybe you should make it chamomile and crawl into bed when you're finished with it."

"That might be a *gut* idea." If she didn't feel like she had to stand guard all night.

"Are you afraid to go to bed?"

Amelia shrugged. "Not really. I made sure the doors and windows are locked. There isn't much more I can do."

Christina wrapped Amelia in a hug. "You poor dear. I can tell you aren't sleeping much at all. Why don't you and the girls stay with us for a while?"

Amelia laughed. "Wouldn't your *mudder* love having four more people in her house!"

"Mamm would say, 'The more, the merrier.'"

"I'm sure she would be very kind and generous as she always is, but having guests in the house increases everyone's stress level. You know the old saying about fish and company stinking after a few days."

Christina smiled. "Not you and your girls."

"You already have eight people in your house. Four extras would be way too many."

"Then I guess I'll simply have to stay with you."

"It's very sweet of you to offer, Christina, but you have your own life to lead, and I'm sure it does not include babysitting me."

"We're *freinden*, and *freinden* look out for each other."

"Hmm. But they don't sacrifice their lives because one of them is a scaredy-cat."

"You are definitely not that. You are a very brave, capable woman who should not have to face these strange happenings alone. Besides, I hardly think I will be sacrificing my life by staying here."

"I'm hoping and praying there won't be any more odd visitors or missing items."

"Me too."

"Let's get our tea and relax. We can talk about something more pleasant, like Noah Zimmerman and weddings and things like that."

Christina's cheeks flushed. "There's nothing to tell."

"I don't believe that for a minute. I'm pretty sure a wedding would have already occurred if Noah had not been called away for a family illness and death." Amelia tugged the younger woman toward the kitchen. "Let's chat."

A few moments later, they carried their tea into the living room and settled into comfortable chairs. Christina picked up fabric from a basket near her feet. "Are you making a quilt?"

Amelia nodded and swallowed her sip of apple cinnamon tea. "The girls and I are constructing a replacement quilt."

"For the one stolen outside my shop?"

"*Jah*. They want to help, so the quilt will take a lot longer than usual to complete."

"That's very nice they want to help. I can't imagine who took that quilt from your buggy or why. Jill stops by The Green Thumb periodically to give me updates on her search."

"I think it's hopeless at this point. Perhaps some homeless person needed it to keep warm." Christina gave her a questioning look. "Don't you think that could be possible?"

"Anything is possible, but I don't think that is likely. How would a homeless person happen to know you had a quilt in your buggy? Didn't you have a blanket in there too? They didn't take that."

Amelia shrugged. "Who knows why people do the things they do." Elam provided a perfect example of that. The mere thought of the man caused her gaze to wander to the window. She hoped she wouldn't see any lights out there tonight.

"You don't see anyone out there, do you?"

"*Nee.* I'm sorry. It has become a habit to peer into the darkness in search of some wanderer with a flashlight. In times like this, I wish I had heavy curtains to hang at my windows."

"Maybe we could ask Bishop Micah about doing that temporarily."

"I don't want to be different from everyone else, and I wouldn't want the girls to ask me a zillion questions. They don't need to be afraid in their own home."

"I understand." Christina sipped her orange spice tea.

"Let's talk about something more pleasant. When will your wedding take place?"

Christina sputtered and coughed. Tears leaked from her eyes. She quickly set her mug on an end table. With one hand, she patted her chest, and with the other, she swiped the moisture off her cheeks."

Amelia reached over to pat her *freind's* knee. "I'm so sorry. I didn't mean to cause such a reaction. I must have touched on some deep secret, ain't so?" She winked.

"Not really." Christina coughed again and fanned her face. "Is it warm in here or is it just me?"

"It's you, dear. I'm only teasing, you know. I am absolutely thrilled for you and Noah. I know we are supposed to pretend we are in the dark about courting couples, but I, for one, have observed that special look you two have exchanged on numerous occasions."

Christina pressed her hands to her cheeks. "I didn't know we were so obvious, but it is very hard to keep secrets around here."

"That's for sure." With a start, Amelia realized others in the community were probably well aware of the times Ryan Miller had visited her house. They probably noted whenever his car appeared in her driveway. Now her cheeks burned.

"What secrets might you be keeping?"

Amelia's heart skipped several beats before slamming against her ribs. "Me? I don't have secrets. I don't even have time for secrets." She forced a laugh.

"You haven't had any more jaunts into town?"

Amelia gasped. "Christina Brubacher! If you are referring to that one time last summer...well, I've already explained that."

Christina smiled and patted Amelia's knee exactly the way Amelia had done to her a few moments earlier. "I know. It was perfectly innocent. I believed you. It must be very difficult being a single parent. If you and Ryan can help each other out, then that's a *gut* thing."

"It certainly is hard being a single parent. You're right about that."

"I imagine it is doubly hard for a man with little girls. I mean, how many men can cook, clean, fix girls' hair, and do all those other things that women can do blindfolded."

"Probably not many. And there probably aren't many widowed women who can perform their husband's tasks." Amelia took a sip of her tea and searched for a way to change the topic of conversation.

"He is a nice man."

"Who?"

Christina clucked her tongue. "Ryan Miller."

"*Jah.*"

"He seems pretty taken with you."

"Why would you say such a thing?"

"He often stops in The Green Thumb to purchase treats you've made."

"The man has a sweet tooth, I'm thinking."

"He specifically asks which items you've made, and he is clearly disappointed when there aren't any left."

"Oh, he's just used to my baking because I often send food home with his girls."

"I don't think that's all it is. I seriously think he is interested in you."

"Please don't go around repeating that to anyone." Amelia sat forward and looked directly into Christina's eyes. "My life could get considerably harder."

"I would never start rumors. I keep my thoughts to myself, except for here with you. Ryan is a Mennonite though."

"But not one of us. His beliefs are different."

"I thought we shared the same basic beliefs."

"Basic, maybe, but they are more modern, more progressive, though not like the *Englischers.*"

Christina nodded. A frown furrowed her brow as if she considered weighty matters. "A person can change. Maybe he could join our group."

"Wouldn't that be like asking a leopard to give up his spots?"

Christina laughed. "All things are possible. Would you consider joining his group?"

"Absolutely not. I am perfectly happy with the way things are." But was she?

"It's okay to care about someone again, Amelia. Aren't we encouraged to do so?"

"I guess. If it's the right person."

"How will you know if you don't give someone a chance?"

"I certainly hope you aren't referring to Elam Wenger."

Christina laughed again. "*Nee*, I believe we have concluded he is definitely not the man for you."

"Or maybe not for anyone else either." Amelia clapped her hand over her mouth. "Oops!"

"It's all right. I've had the exact same thought."

"Well, you aren't encouraging me to consider someone out of our faith, are you?"

"Not exactly."

"What does that mean? Either you are or you aren't."

"I certainly don't want you to do anything against our teachings, but I do think you and Ryan Miller make a cute couple."

"Cute? Cute is for *kinner*."

"You know what I mean. And I believe in my gut that you harbor an interest in him too."

"Whether I did or didn't is all the same. A relationship between us could never be."

"We never know what the Lord *Gott* has in store for us. We need to listen and obey. That's what my *mamm* says anyway."

"It isn't always easy to know what the Lord's will is and what is our own desire or whim."

"That is very true."

"Like I said before, I am perfectly fine here with my *dochders* and don't need to..." Amelia's mouth opened, but no more words tumbled out. She stared out the window behind Christina.

"Amelia? What is it?"

# Chapter Fourteen

Christina turned and looked behind her. "Oh my!" She leaped from her chair and scurried out of the way. She grabbed Amelia's arm and tugged. "Get out of sight of the window. Who do you suppose that is? You weren't expecting anyone, were you?"

"Absolutely not." Amelia followed Christina to a remote corner of the room. "He's never *kumm* here in a car before." Car lights bobbed along the long, gravel driveway and drew closer and closer to the house.

"He who?"

"The person who has been wandering around my place."

"Trespassing, you mean."

"*Jah*." Amelia wrung her hands. "What should we do? Do you think he saw us sitting there?"

"I don't know." The car stopped, and a door slammed. "Has he been brave enough to knock at your door before?"

"Never. Last night, he ran away when I called out."

"It doesn't look like he will be running away tonight."

Amelia's heart thumped so hard her chest hurt. Surely, she wouldn't have a heart attack cowering in a corner of her living room. Her ears strained to detect any sound. She bit her lip until she tasted blood. Christina grabbed her hand in a bone-crunching grip.

Light footsteps approached the door, not the heavy clumping Amelia would expect from a man wearing work shoes. Seconds stretched into eons. A scream bubbled up in her throat and threatened to escape. She fought hard to tamp it down but nearly lost the battle when knuckles rapped on the front door.

"He wouldn't knock, would he?" Christina whispered. "I mean, a person intent on some sinister deed wouldn't be polite about it, I wouldn't think."

"You're right." Amelia inched closer to the door, towing Christina along with her.

"What are you doing?"

"Your words made sense. It might be someone who needs help."

"Are you going to open the door?"

"Don't you open your door when someone knocks?"

"*Jah*, but I haven't had anyone stalking me."

"I haven't received any threats of bodily harm or anything."

Christina giggled. "It sounds like you must have heard Annie talk about her beloved mystery novels. You've picked up the lingo."

"I've only heard her a few hundred times."

"I don't know about opening the door though, Amelia. That seems kind of risky."

"I'll only open it a crack, just enough to see."

"You're braver than I am."

"I doubt it. You've faced far worse." Amelia didn't know if she could deal with finding a body in her shed the way Christina had. Goose bumps attacked her.

"Amelia?" The rap came again, a bit sharper this time.

Amelia sagged with relief. She squeezed Christina's hand. "It's okay. It's Betty Ann."

"Betty Ann?"

"I'm sure you must know her. Betty Ann Schlabach. She's a Mennonite but not of our community."

"Oh. The same as Ryan Miller?"

"*Jah.*" Amelia dropped her *freind's* hand and turned the lock. She yanked the door open just as the older woman on the front porch raised a hand to knock again.

"Oh!" Betty Ann lowered her arm. "Amelia, dear, I'm so sorry to disturb you. I didn't want to knock hard for fear of waking your precious girls, but I wanted you to hear me. I didn't wake you, did I?"

"Of course not. I was talking with my *freind.* You know Christina Brubacher, don't you?"

"From the Green Thumb."

"That's right." Amelia stepped back. "Please *kumm* in. Is anything wrong?"

"No. Yes. I mean, I guess that depends on how you look at it."

Amelia cocked her head and waited. Past experience assured her Betty Ann would eventually get to the point in some roundabout fashion. "Would you like to have a seat in the living room?" Since this could take a while, they might as well be comfortable.

"Oh no, dear. I can't stay. Gordon is in the car. He has the patience of a two-year-old."

Amelia smiled. The man had to have a great deal more patience than that to live in the same house as Betty Ann for so many years. She hoped he left the car running so he wouldn't freeze waiting for his *fraa.* Amelia would try to speed things up a bit. "You were dropping by tomorrow for your baskets, ain't so?"

"Yes. I had planned to pick them up on our way to Pennsylvania tomorrow. Gordon got the crazy idea to leave tonight so we could avoid some of the traffic. I hope it isn't a problem to get them now. I'm so sorry to disturb your evening, but I couldn't call, you know. If the baskets aren't done yet, that's okay."

Amelia almost panted for breath simply listening to Betty Ann. The woman must drop into bed totally exhausted every evening simply from rambling all day. "It's not any problem at all. The baskets are finished and waiting for you. I'll get them so you can be on your way."

Amelia nearly laughed aloud when Christina rolled her eyes. She hurried from the room to retrieve the three Christmas baskets Betty Ann had ordered. She returned to find the woman chatting nonstop as she fumbled with bills in her wallet. Christina nodded and mumbled an occasional "uh-huh."

"Oh, they are quite lovely. You did a splendid job as always, Amelia," Betty Ann gushed. "My relatives are going to be so pleased."

"I hope so."

"I know so. Here you go." Betty Ann pressed the money into Amelia's hand.

"I can put them in a bag for you to protect them. I wanted you to see them before you paid for them."

"The bag would be great. I really didn't need to see them though. I know the quality of your work. I am never disappointed."

"That's great to know." Amelia asked Christina to hold the bag open so she could ease the baskets inside of it.

"That is wonderful, dear. Thank you so much." Betty Ann took the bag from Amelia. "I'd better get out there before Gordon has a fit."

"Have a safe trip!" Amelia called after the woman. She immediately closed and locked the door.

"I'm exhausted simply listening to her." Christina sighed loud and long.

"I know, but she is a very nice person."

"I'm sure she is. She has always been pleasant when she visited The Green Thumb, but my, can she talk. I thought Annie rambled." Christina shook her head. "I'm relieved it was her at the door."

"That makes two of us." Amelia shuffled to the window and gazed at the darkness. She turned her head from side to side to see as much of her property as possible.

"You don't see any other lights or vehicles, do you?"

"*Nee*. I believe I'm about ready to head to bed."

"Do you think you'll be able to sleep tonight?"

"I certainly hope so. You need some rest, too, so you can get up early for work tomorrow."

"I'll be fine."

Amelia gathered up their mugs. "I'll take the mugs to the kitchen."

She had only left on one lamp in the kitchen, turned down low, after making tea earlier. She started to turn it up but changed her mind. She wanted to take a quick peek out the back window for peace of mind before attempting to sleep.  Dim light would make it easier to see outside.

As Amelia crossed the room, the little hairs on the back of her neck stood at attention. How strange! She rolled her head from side to side to release the tension. She glanced out the window as she set the mugs in the sink. She jumped back with a cry and loosened her hold on the mugs. She barely heard the crash or the thunder of running feet.

"Amelia! What is it? What happened?" Christina skidded to a stop and gasped for breath. She grabbed Amelia's arm and shook it.

"I've got to go outside."

"You'll do nothing of the kind. What is wrong?"

"I thought it was hazy out there, but it isn't. It's smoky. I need to see if there is a fire and check on the animals."

"You can't go out there alone."

"I have to. I need you to stay here with the girls."

A pounding at the front door made both young women shriek. Amelia didn't know whether to slip out the back or see who stood out front.

"Amelia! Amelia! It's me. Betty Ann Schlabach. Can you hear me?" She pounded on the door again.

Amelia grabbed a shawl from the hook before dashing to the front of the house. She yanked open the heavy wood door. "What's wrong?"

Betty Ann dropped the hand that had been about to bang on the door again. "Fire! Something must be burning behind your barn."

Amelia sniffed. The acrid smell of smoke assaulted her nose. "I have to go see."

"Gordon called 9-1-1 on his cell phone."

"*Danki.*" Amelia prepared to push past the older woman, but the hand that shot out and clamped around her arm stopped her.

"I won't let you go out there alone." Christina tightened her grip.

"I'll be fine. Please stay here with the girls."

"I'll stay," Betty Ann offered, batting at the wisps of gray and brown hair that had escaped from her bun and flew about her face. "Go with her, Christina."

"I don't want to hold you up. You're on your way out of town." Amelia broke free from Christina's grasp and pushed past the women.

"Here, Christina. Take my cloak and go with her. I'll stay with the little ones." Betty Ann thrust her cloak into Christina's arms.

"Wait, Amelia!" Christina called.

Amelia didn't slow down. If there was a fire outside of her barn, the horses would be frantic. She heard Christina's footsteps behind her but didn't stop to wait. The smoke grew thicker. She couldn't tell if it was a shed or the woods on fire. She reached for the latch on the barn door.

"Wait!" Christina shot forward and threw her weight, slight as it was, against the door.

"Christina, I've got to get the animals out. It might be too smoky to breathe in there."

"There also might be someone waiting in there, someone who intends to harm you along with the animals."

"I can't worry about that right now. Please move."

"Your *dochders* need you."

"I'll be careful. I can't let the animals die."

Christina relented. "Let's go in together, then." She backed up enough for Amelia to turn the latch. Smoke swirled out when she pulled open the heavy door. "Cover your face with your shawl, Amelia."

Amelia pulled the shawl over her nose and mouth and rushed into the barn. She scanned the entire building but couldn't determine the source of the smoke. It must be drifting in from outside. The horses stamped and snorted. She would have to turn them out into the cold to ensure their safety.

"I'll lead the horses out." Christina's voice was muffled by the cloak pulled across her face.

"Take them out the back door. They should be safe in the back paddock." Amelia was seized by a coughing fit as soon as she choked out the last word. Where was the smoke *kumming* from and where were the fire trucks?

She made her way across the barn to the enclosure where two young female goats paced. Poor babies were probably so scared. Amelia tried to soothe them without coughing again. She didn't want to waste time trying to harness them and prayed they would follow her outside to safety.

The animals must have been eager to breathe in fresh air. They didn't protest or balk when she prodded them outside. Why was the barn so smoky if the fire wasn't inside of it?

"Amelia! Are you all right?" Christina trotted over from the fence where she'd been waiting.

"*Jah.* I don't want to put the goats in with the horses. Where is the fire?"

"I don't know."

"I'm going to put these girls in the backyard for now. It's fenced in so they'll be safe." The wail of a siren grew louder. "I need to hurry, or they might try to get away from the noisy fire trucks."

The fire chief approached the women as they headed toward the barn a few minutes later. "Mrs. Stauffer?" He looked from one woman to the other.

"I'm Amelia Stauffer. Where is the fire?"

"There isn't a fire. At least not now."

"I don't understand. There was a lot of smoke." Amelia coughed again. Her lungs still felt irritated.

"We found evidence of several smoke bombs that we will let the police investigate. One of them outside the barn briefly ignited some leaves, but the recent rain left them too wet to burn for long."

"There was so much smoke." Amelia coughed once again.

"Yes, and smoke from smoke bombs can also be damaging. Why don't you let the EMTs check you out?"

"I'm more concerned about the animals. Should I have the vet look at them?"

"I think we got them out pretty quickly," Christina said. "The horses seemed fine. The goats breathed in the smoke a little longer, so I'm not sure about them."

The fire chief looked thoughtful for a moment. He pushed back his hat and scratched his head. "I guess it wouldn't hurt to have the vet give them a once-over. I'd really like you to get that cough checked out."

"I'm feeling better."

Christina nudged her none too gently. "Let them listen to your lungs. You don't have to go to the hospital."

"What about you? You were in the barn too."

"But not for as long as you were. And my cloak was thicker than your shawl."

Amelia barely suppressed another cough and nodded her assent.

"I'm sure the police will have questions for you too," the fire chief said.

"Can I wait inside? My *kinner* are being watched by someone who needs to leave."

"Sure. Go on in—after you see the EMT."

Christina wrapped an arm around Amelia and steered her toward the ambulance. Amelia attempted to wiggle free. "Christina, I've got to get to the house. Betty Ann needs to be on her way. I don't want to make them any later heading to Pennsylvania."

"I don't believe another minute or two will make a difference."

"Honestly, I'm fine."

"Let the experts determine that." Christina tugged again.

Amelia stumbled along behind her *freind*, mumbling under her breath the whole way.

"I caught that, Amelia Stauffer, and making sure you're all right is not a waste of time." Christina stopped in front of the EMT. "This woman needs to be checked. She's been coughing."

The young man motioned the women over to the waiting vehicle where red and white lights still flashed. "This will only take a minute or two, ma'am. If you'll sit on the stretcher, I can listen to your lungs and take your blood pressure. Do you need help stepping up?"

"I can climb up." Under her breath, she added, "If I have to."

Christina poked her in the back. "You have to."

Amelia perched on the edge of the stretcher and stared at all the gadgets and lights surrounding her. He explained what he was doing as he wrapped a blood pressure cuff around her arm and clipped a little gizmo on her index finger to measure her oxygenation.

"Everything is good," the man announced a few minutes later. "I recommend that you let us take you in for a thorough check, though, since you're still coughing."

"It's improving with the fresh air. I don't think I need to go to the hospital."

"Are you sure?"

Amelia nodded. "I'll see the doctor tomorrow if I am still coughing."

"Okay, but I will need you to sign this release form."

She scrawled her name on the indicated line and hopped out of the ambulance. "Your turn." She gave Christina a little push.

"I'm fine. I don't even have a hint of a cough."

"I've got to check on my girls." Amelia took off in a sprint, coughing as she ran. Her breath came in gasps by the time she reached the back door.

"Maybe you should have gone for that ambulance ride." Christina panted behind her.

"I'm fine." Amelia paused only long enough to grab a deep breath. "Betty Ann!"

"I'm right here." The older woman turned from the kitchen window.

"I'm sorry I held you up. Are the girls okay?"

"I never hear a peep from them. I did tiptoe up to check, and they were sound asleep."

"*Gut. Danki* for staying with them. I'm sorry you're getting a late start."

"I'm glad I was here to help. It was no problem at all." Betty Ann smiled and squeezed Amelia's hand. "Gordon was the one who wanted to leave in the black of night, not me. He searched for the source of the fire once he smelled smoke, but he was asleep before that, so he didn't see how the fire started. That man can sleep through a tornado. When the trucks showed up, he retreated to the car. I'm sure he went right back to sleep despite the commotion. He should be well rested to drive. You take care, dear."

Amelia wished she knew how to do that.

# Chapter Fifteen

"Are you sure you and the girls are all right?" Ryan had a bad feeling the previous night when he'd heard sirens so close by. Some sixth sense told him the commotion somehow involved Amelia. Only the two precious little girls asleep in their beds kept him from dashing out the door to check. If he could have tucked them into the car and been assured of their safety, he would have raced to Amelia's rescue.

"We are all fine. Even the animals seem to be back to normal this morning. The barn is clear of the fog or smoke or whatever that stuff was." Amelia paused to cough.

"You didn't have a cough yesterday."

"It's nothing."

"It's from the smoke or chemicals you breathed in, isn't it?"

Amelia shrugged. "I guess so, but it's better."

"Do you mean it was worse?"

"It was right after I got out of the barn, but it has greatly improved."

"Let me take you to the urgent care center to get checked out."

"Absolutely not. The EMT listened to my lungs last night and said everything sounded okay."

"He probably advised you to see your doctor too, didn't he?"

"He did, and I said I would do so if I felt worse. I do not feel worse. I appreciate your concern though." Amelia quickly dropped her gaze to the floor.

Ryan smiled. It was adorable how she could suddenly become embarrassed and look away from him. The rose blush on her cheeks made the little caramel freckles pop out across her nose. It took all his willpower not to pull her into his arms, but that would never do. In fact, this whole line of thinking needed to stop immediately.

That resolution would have been a lot easier to keep if she hadn't looked up at him with those big, blue eyes. Now he was lost again. "Uh, if you're sure you're all right, I suppose I'd better get to work."

"I am quite sure. Did you eat breakfast?"

"I wolfed down a banana while I gathered up the girls' things."

"Christina and I made enough muffins for the whole community. She took some to sell at The Green Thumb, but I still have plenty."

"I do like muffins. You know, I'm glad you let Christina stay here last night. Will she be back tonight?" Ryan didn't want to come across as overbearing or overprotective, but he needed to know she had some help if she should need it.

"I believe she's planning to return even though I told her she didn't have to."

"Please let her stay." He wasn't sure if he spoke the words or only thought them.

"Pardon me?"

He must have spoken. "I hope you will let her stay again tonight."

"I don't think there will be a need. Christina has her own life and has better things to do than play watchdog for me."

"Didn't you feel better having another adult in the house?"

"I cannot lie. I did feel a bit more at ease, but I will have to deal with my qualms and stop depending on other people. The Lord *Gott* will take care of us."

Ryan wished he could be the one to offer protection. "I believe He will too, but I'm sure Christina would not mind staying another night or two."

"She's too kind to tell me if I'm bothering her." Amelia sidestepped to the kitchen counter. "We made blueberry, strawberry, and apple cinnamon muffins. Do you have a preference, or would you like to take one of each?"

Obviously, she was finished with the conversation. Ryan didn't want to push, but he would try to reason with her again this evening. He followed her to the counter and peered over her shoulder. "You two certainly did do a lot of baking."

"And this is only half of it."

"You must have been up all night."

"We got an early start this morning."

"Or a late start last night."

Amelia's laugh made him smile. It was such a sweet, merry sound. It suited her perfectly. Without waiting for him to answer her question, she plucked several muffins from cooling racks and slid them into a large plastic bag.

"How many are you putting in there?"

"Enough for you to share with Norman or to take home for later or whatever. But I suspect a banana won't hold you for too long. You'll be ravenous by ten o'clock."

He shouldn't take so much pleasure in the notion that she cared about his well-being, but he did. "I appreciate that, Amelia." He even liked saying her name. He needed to have a stern talk with himself later about his silly, boyish attitude, but right now, he wanted to bask in her attention.

"Here you go."

How long had she been holding the bag out to him? He hoped he didn't have some dreamy, dopey expression on his face. "Thank you. You're so good to me."

Her face must have turned ten shades of red. He hadn't meant to embarrass her. The thought had popped out of his mouth before he could catch it. He wished he could do something for her in return. But what he really wanted was to find out who had been hassling her and make them stop. He lowered his voice so little ears wouldn't overhear. "Did the police have any idea who caused last night's ruckus?"

"Ruckus. That's a *gut* word. It might not have been an actual fire, but it was quite a commotion, nonetheless. The police think maybe some wayward teens pulled a prank. I don't believe they are taking the matter any more seriously than that."

Ryan instantly became alarmed. No, he became angry. How could they not take the incident seriously? One of the animals could have been hurt. Amelia could have been hurt. That thought ripped a hole in his heart. He couldn't bear to think of Amelia injured. Her nagging cough was bad enough.

He struggled to calm himself. He certainly didn't want to frighten her any more than she must already be. "I wonder if there have been other pranks in the area to make the police think that. I haven't heard of any or read about any in the county newspaper. But I haven't had a whole lot of time for reading anything other than children's books."

Amelia smiled that smile that warmed his heart. "The officers didn't say if there had been any similar occurrences."

"Did they think the smoke bomb was connected to the thefts?"

"I don't believe they know much about those."

Most likely because she hadn't told them much. Ryan wanted to drive right over to the police station and demand they thoroughly investigate and that they protect Amelia and her girls. He couldn't do that though. He hated to ask his next question but he needed to know. "Did they think you were in any danger?"

"*Nee*. Since I haven't received any specific threats, they didn't think someone wanted to harm us. Christina said there probably wasn't enough evidence for them to do much more." Amelia laughed. "As much as Christina enjoys figuring things out. I wouldn't be surprised if she dug around and fit the pieces of this crazy puzzle together."

Ryan laid a hand on her thin arm. "I think it's a good idea for you to stay vigilant and to continue locking all the doors and windows." He wished he could offer her more than that advice.

"You can be sure I will."

The concern in Ryan's big, brown eyes haunted Amelia all day despite her nonstop activity. She'd had an almost overwhelming urge to throw herself into the tall, handsome man's arms. Only because she craved the comfort and reassurance that everything would be all right. Nothing more. It couldn't be anything more.

What if Ryan Miller was a member of her own community? Would that make a difference? But he wasn't. If she truly believed she was ready for another relationship, she needed to look for someone who shared her beliefs, her way of life, and not someone whose lifestyle was way too modern.

Amelia preferred the old ways. She liked riding in her black buggy and talking to her chocolate-brown horse. She supposed some people talked to their cars, but a vehicle wasn't a living, breathing creature. Sometimes cars wouldn't start. Snickers was always ready for a jaunt.

Electricity and air conditioning would be nice, she supposed, but she actually liked using kerosene or propane lamps. She liked the smell of burning logs and the cozy warmth the woodstove provided. She liked growing and preserving her own food and stitching quilts.

Sure, lots of *Englischers* enjoyed the same activities, but it wasn't a way of life for them. She suspected women in Ryan's community preserved food from their gardens and sewed quilts, but they did so in their air-conditioned houses and used electric appliances.

Could she change? Could she learn to drive a car or use a microwave oven and all those other time-saving gadgets? She liked the slow ways, like baking a ham or turkey for hours and popping popcorn in the big, iron skillet on the stove exactly as her *grossmammi* had done. The old ways suited her.

*Ach, Amelia, where are these thoughts leading you? You'd be better off thinking about a man in your own community if you have the urge to remarry.* The problem was none of the eligible men in her community appealed to her. They were too young, too old, had too many *kinner*, or were too set in their ways. She'd found a reason to discard each one. Not a single one of them made her heart sing.

The only time her heart hummed a happy tune was in the presence of the forbidden candidate for her affection. She had tried to coax her heart to beat normally when he spoke her name and to banish the goose bumps that raced up and down her arms when he smiled at her, but she hadn't been successful at either one.

Ryan was neither too young nor too old, probably only a few years older than she was. He only had two *dochders*, and she already loved them. He did not appear to be set in his ways, stubborn, or demanding. He made her heart sing.

*And he is forbidden to you. The sooner you accept that and move on, the better.*

~

"Ah, it looks like the muffin man is here. Wasn't there a children's rhyme about a muffin man? Reading nursery rhymes was a long time ago for me." Norman chuckled and pointed at Ryan's bag

Heat crept up Ryan's neck and spread across his cheeks. He knew he should have left the bag in his vehicle. He'd been afraid the sun shining through the glass would have made the temperature rise too high. Amelia's muffins were too delicious to be ruined. "I believe there is such a rhyme."

"Miss Amelia sure takes good care of you, doesn't she?"

"She takes good care of my children."

Norman laughed. "And their dad, I'm thinking."

"Don't think too hard. You don't want to blow a gasket." Ryan didn't need the older man jumping to wrong conclusions and sharing erroneous information with the whole world. "Would you like a muffin?"

"Don't mind if I do. I've eaten some of Amelia's goodies from The Green Thumb. The woman can bake up some tasty treats. Let's see here." Norman studied the clear plastic bag with all the attention he'd give to purchasing a new car. "I'll take this one. You can never go wrong with blueberry." He extracted a fat muffin teeming with plump berries. "Thanks for sharing."

"You're welcome. I certainly can't eat all of them."

"It looks like you'll have plenty for later." Norman took a big bite. "Mmm! Scrumptious. Aren't you having one?"

"I ate one on the way here. I'll probably have another one later. They are hard to resist though. I might have to move them somewhere out of sight."

"I could always hold onto them for you."

"No, thanks. If I did that, I'd be taking home an empty bag."

Norman nearly choked as he laughed around the chunk of muffin in his mouth. He coughed and thumped his chest.

"Do you need some water?"

"I-I think I'm good." He wiped his eyes and flicked his tongue across his lips.

"I didn't mean to get you all choked up. Are you okay now?"

"Right as rain."

Ryan sealed the bag and stowed it on a shelf below his workbench. Somewhere outside, a dog yapped. "Hey, Norman, I almost forgot."

"What's that?"

"That hound out there reminded me. Do you know if Levi Wheeler still has pups?"

"Are you thinking of getting your girls a pet?"

"I might." No way was he going to confide he wanted a dog for Amelia. The man would latch onto that bit of information and assume all sorts of things.

"Aren't they a little young for that responsibility?"

"Gabby is four. Jessie will be one soon. They should be fine with a gentle dog. It's important to learn responsibility at a young age, right?"

"I think it will most likely be more responsibility for you. Parents usually end up caring for pets. Trust me. I've been down that road myself."

"I might talk to Levi and see what he thinks."

"Well, as far as I know, he still has pups."

"Maybe you should see about getting one. Sarah might want a puppy to dote on with being alone in that big house all day."

"Oh no you don't! You aren't talking me into getting a critter. And don't go putting a bug in her ear either. We've got grandchildren. They come. We spoil them. We send them home. Works out great."

"Aw, come on. You know you like animals. I heard Levi had a large litter this time."

"You go right ahead and get one for your girls. I like pets best if they belong to someone else."

Ryan pulled out his tools to begin working on his first project of the day. Would Amelia be angry if he happened to have a puppy with him when he picked up the girls this evening? The children would fall in love with a cuddly, furry animal in a heartbeat. He could see it now. They would get a sad, pitiful look if Amelia said they couldn't keep it. She would end up relenting to brighten those little faces.

He could picture her playing with the girls and the dog. She had so much love to share. Anyone who loved children so much would surely love animals too, wouldn't she? He knew she had those two young goats that were supposed to be pets, but a dog was different. Dogs were loyal to their owners, and they barked to warn of visitors or intruders.

Would she bear a grudge against him if she accepted a pet she didn't want though? Ryan couldn't stand to think about that. He never wanted Amelia to be upset or angry with him.

The screwdriver slipped, stabbing his thumb. Subconsciously, he popped the injured digit into his mouth. When he realized he had done what Gabby would have done, he yanked his thumb from his mouth and wiped it on his pants. A sober thought struck him as he bent to retrieve the screwdriver. His own girls would fall in love with a puppy too. Would they be jealous if he brought a pet for Amelia's girls but not for them? "I'll have to get two."

"What's that?" Norman glanced up from his own work.

Ryan hadn't intended to speak aloud. "Just mumbling." His cheeks burned even though he knew Norman wasn't privy to his thoughts. Or was he? The man had an uncanny way of sensing what was on Ryan's mind.

# Chapter Sixteen

Amelia had managed to feed the girls, clean up the kitchen, get Rhonda off to school, and hang out one load of laundry. She'd tackle scrubbing the kitchen floor while the younger girls played. The linoleum should have just enough time to dry before she needed to prepare the noon meal.

She had been scrubbing so hard to banish thoughts of last night's adventure from her mind that she didn't hear someone approach the back door, even though she had opened the window a crack to help the floor dry faster. The knock startled her. She dropped her scrub brush into the pail, splashing soapy water on her green dress. Who would be visiting at this time of day? Most folks were busy with work or chores. Amelia blew a wisp of blonde hair out of her face.

The knock came again, louder and harder.

"Just a minute!" She pushed herself to a standing position and tucked that wayward strand of hair beneath her *kapp*. She hadn't dried her hands, so now her hair was damp as well as messy. She hopped across the floor to the back door. She hoped this would be quick or, better yet, that the person gave up and left.

She unlocked the back door and pulled it open only far enough to peek out. It was a shame she had to take such precautions. She had always opened her door wide to guests, but with all the strange goings-on lately, she had become leery of strange noises, lights, or visits. She had struggled not to let fear rule her life, but she had to be cautious for the sake of her precious girls.

"It's me, Annie!" the girl practically shouted.

"So I see. I'm not deaf, Annie. I can hear even though the door isn't wide open."

"I'm here too!" Elam stepped around the corner of the house.

Amelia's spirits plummeted. She could deal with Annie, despite the fact the girl chattered incessantly. Elam, on the other hand, was a bitter pill to swallow. What had he been doing around the side of her house? *Breathe, Amelia. Stay calm. Be nice.* "Oh. Hello, Elam."

"Aren't you going to let us *kumm* in?" Annie pushed at the door that Amelia still hadn't opened all the way.

"I've been scrubbing the floor, so everything is all wet."

"Including you." Elam nodded at the wet spot on the front of her dress.

Amelia's face burned. Why had he been staring at her dress? She resisted a shiver but couldn't stop the little hairs on the back of her neck from bristling. "Washing floors is not a terribly neat job, I fear. I could step out and talk to you outside, or you can walk around to the front door and we can sit in the living room." She directed her speech to Annie. What she really hoped, though, was that they would divulge their reason for visiting and depart as quickly as they came.

"We'll walk around to the front. I promise we won't stay long." Annie hopped off the back steps.

Amelia wanted to peek around the house to try to figure out what Elam had been doing but figured that would be rather rude.

"I was checking to make sure you had enough wood close to the house," he offered as if reading her mind.

Why did the man fib? "My wood pile is over there." Amelia pointed to the stack of logs within view of the back door. The men of her community saw to the wood like clockwork.

"Right. I was checking to see if you had a second stack somewhere. You never can tell when the weather will turn mean, and you'd need extra wood."

Amelia opened her mouth to question the red-haired man further but clamped her lips together. There wasn't any use making an issue of this. "I'll be right around to open the front door." She closed and locked the back door before skipping across the damp kitchen floor.

Annie and Elam had already reached the front porch by the time Amelia opened the door. She ushered them inside and locked the door behind them.

"Are you scared here, Amelia? You've got the place locked up tighter than a prison, I'm thinking." Annie pointed to the double-locked door.

How would the girl know much about prisons? It must be all the crime novels she read. Amelia ignored the comment and led her guests into the living room where the girls still played. At least they would provide some diversion since lapses in conversation would probably be plentiful and awkward.

Amelia crossed the room to the old, oak rocking chair, leaving the sofa for the cousins to share. She tried to cover the wet spot on her dress with her hands but abandoned the effort. She had been working, and she needed to get back to her chores. She hadn't been planning on entertaining guests, so they would simply have to take her as she was. The chair squeaked softly when she set it into motion. She waited. Were they planning to state the purpose for this visit, or was she going to have to drag it out of them?

Annie perched on the edge of one end of the sofa while Elam settled back against the embroidered pillows at the other end. He surveyed the room as if memorizing its contents. Amelia fidgeted. Why did this man make her nervous? She opened her mouth to ask the reason for their visit, but Annie spoke first.

"We heard about what happened last night. Elam wanted to make sure you were all right, so I said I would bring him. You know, so I could chaperone." She winked.

Amelia gasped. She did not need a chaperone. If Elam had shown up at her door alone, she would not have invited him inside. They could have had whatever conversation he'd wanted to initiate outside, and then she would have sent him on his way. She ignored Annie's embarrassing remark. "As you can see, we are all fine. It was probably some local teens pulling pranks."

"It sounded a little more serious than that." Elam leaned so far forward that Amelia feared he would topple off the sofa. "Are the animals and barn okay? Any damage?"

Amelia coughed. "All is well. The horses and goats were understandably frightened, but they calmed down quickly."

"Do you have a cold?"

Leave it to Annie to comment on every little thing. "*Nee*, only a slight tickle in my throat."

"You might want to get that checked out." Annie did look concerned.

"I'll keep that in mind if the cough continues." She would do everything in her power to avoid coughing again in their presence.

"We could take you to the doctor," Elam offered. "Or Annie could stay with the *kinner* while I take you."

"I appreciate that, Elam, but it's not necessary." She had no intention of going anywhere with the man—ever.

"It could be smoke inhalation." Annie couldn't let a subject die a natural death. "I read—"

"I'm fine. Honest." Amelia hated interrupting, but enough was enough! She rocked harder and faster. "*Danki* for checking on me, but please rest assured that all is well here.”

“Has that *Englischer* been here?” Elam spit the words out as if they had a bitter taste.

Of all the nerve! It was none of his business who did or did not visit her home. She wanted to throw him out but held onto her temper.

Annie reached across the sofa to punch her cousin’s arm. “I told you she babysat for his *dochders*. Of course, the man has been here.”

“He is not *Englisch*. He is Mennonite.” Amelia pushed the words through clenched teeth. She chomped on her tongue to keep other comments from spewing out.

“But not of our—I mean, your—community, ain’t so?” Elam crossed his arms over his chest. “He might as well be *Englisch*.”

Amelia stood. “I really need to see about feeding the girls, so please excuse me.” If they did not take the hint and leave, she wasn’t sure what she would do.

Annie jumped to her feet. “She’s dismissing us, Elam. It’s time to go.”

“*Ach*, Annie. You make me sound so rude.” *And you successfully managed to heap a ton of guilt on me.*

“You could never be rude, Amelia. I know you’re busy, so we will get out of your way. Get up, Elam.”

“Are you helping Christina at The Green Thumb today?”

“Not today. I have some things to do.”

“Oh. Well then, have a nice day.” Amelia’s own day had now been blemished, but she would try to recover for the sake of the *kinner*.

~

Amelia couldn’t close and lock the door fast enough, and it took every ounce of willpower she possessed not to slam the door. Had Annie and Elam traipsed over to her house merely to spy on her? What gave them that right? Did they really think she was doing something improper, or were they simply being nosy? She had the distinct impression the cousins were planning something.

"*Mamm*, we're hungry." Judith served as spokesperson for the group.

Amelia forced a smile. "That must mean it's almost time for the noon meal. Give me a few minutes." Surely, the kitchen floor was dry by this time. She'd have to do the rest of her cleaning later. Her visitors had thrown off her whole schedule.

She hurried to the kitchen before the girls could pick up on her agitation. It wasn't the change in her routine that had her so upset. *Kinner* often threw a monkey wrench into one's plans. *Nee*, she still fumed over Elam's words and attitude. Annie probably was immune to the man's manner since he'd been staying with her family, but he had definitely upset Amelia.

Was she being overly sensitive where Ryan Miller was concerned? She didn't think so. She would have defended any of her other *freinden* or acquaintances who were not Old Order Mennonite. Different didn't mean wrong, and Amelia wouldn't let Elam label them as such. If Christina returned this evening, she might work up the courage to seek the other girl's opinion on today's strange visit.

Amelia retrieved her bucket of water. She strode to the back door and tossed the dirty water outside. She put away her supplies and washed her hands before checking the refrigerator for something quick to prepare for four hungry little girls. She withdrew the big container of chicken noodle soup. The meat, carrots, noodles, and fat egg noodles were all soft enough even for Jessie to eat. While the soup heated, she would prepare grilled cheese sandwiches. All the *kinner* gobbled up cheese like little mice.

She bustled about preparing the meal and forced her thoughts in a different direction. She could not control other people's beliefs and opinions, but she could control her re-action to them. And right now, she chose to be joyful. She hummed a hymn as she browned the sandwiches and stirred the soup. Music had a way of calming her nerves and her soul.

~

Amelia decided to abandon her cleaning regimen altogether and instead worked on a basket order while the girls napped. She had several orders to get out of the way before more holiday orders filtered in. She always had such fun decorating baskets this time of year with bells, balls, and artificial poinsettias and holly. Christmas time was special not only because they celebrated the birth of their Savior but also because of the special appeal to the senses.

She loved the scent of spicy apple cider, snickerdoodles, and gingerbread. She liked hanging boughs of pine, cedar, and holly over doorways and on windowsills. Perhaps this year, she would let the girls help her gather running cedar to wind around wire for wreaths to hang on the doors.

A flicker of light outside drew her attention. She looked out the window in time to see the sunlight glance off an automobile mirror. Another visitor. An *Englisch* one. She certainly hoped this would be a much more pleasant experience.

# Chapter Seventeen

Amelia gathered up her supplies. Basket making was going about as well as the morning cleaning had gone. She resigned herself to accomplishing nothing today other than the muffin-baking marathon with Christina. She peeked out the window in time to see a petite, young woman with long, dark curls hop out of the car. Amelia watched as she struggled to pull something out of the back seat. What in the world?

"Jill!" Amelia flew down the back steps and out to the compact car. "What are you wrestling with?"

"It's, uh, it's..." She paused and yanked so hard that she almost fell backward. "A basket."

Amelia threw out her arms to steady the girl. Why was Jill bringing a basket when Amelia made her own?

Jill turned to face Amelia and burst out laughing. "You look totally bewildered." She gasped between giggles. "I wish you could see your face."

"Apparently, it's hysterical." Amelia couldn't help but smile. Poor Jill had been through so much with the murder of her *bruder* and the aftermath. That she could smile and laugh attested to her faith and resilience. Amelia admired

Jill's strength. But she still didn't understand why Jill waved a big basket in her face.

"Don't you recognize this? Look closely."

"I don't need to examine it closely to determine it's one of mine."

"Oh. But it's not the one you're missing, is it?" Jill's smile evaporated.

Amelia shook her head. "I'm afraid not. That one was a little bigger and a darker brown color."

"Shoot. I thought I was on the trail of the thief."

"Where did you find this basket?"

"It was in that little craft shop on the corner of the town square. Do you know where I mean?"

"I do." Amelia had glanced in the windows of the store when she and the girls had ridden into town with Ryan Miller last summer. What a fun evening that had been walking around the quaint town square, enjoying the slight breeze off the bay, licking ice cream cones. Their mundane errand had turned into a momentous occasion. At least it had for Amelia. She would have liked to reminisce longer but pulled herself out of the past. "Was this basket for sale in the craft shop?"

"It was. That isn't a consignment shop, so I assumed you weren't selling your baskets there."

"You're right. I don't sell baskets there. Perhaps they sell used items, and someone gave the owner that basket to sell."

"I suppose that's possible, but there weren't any signs saying items were used, so customers would naturally assume they were new. That's sort of false advertising in my book."

"Did you buy this basket?"

"I did. I had so hoped it was your missing one, but it might very well be someone else's missing basket. Maybe there is a basket thief on the loose. I wonder if any other things in the shop had been stolen from people."

"I'm not sure you should assume this was stolen." Amelia took the basket and turned it every which way. "It's still in excellent condition as if it had never been used. It could be that someone donated the basket, or maybe it belonged to the owner who decided to resell it."

Jill frowned. "Possibly, but I'm not ready to give up my investigation. I didn't see your quilt or a shawl, but maybe they hadn't been put on display yet."

"Or maybe the owner doesn't have them at all."

"I know." Jill sighed. "And I truly don't want to hurl false accusations. I only want to explain the mystery."

"We might have to accept that the puzzle will never be solved."

"That bugs me. I don't like not being able to figure something out."

Amelia laughed. "You sound like Christina. She's determined to discover what happened to my belongings and who is stalking me too."

Jill gasped and grabbed Amelia's arm. "Someone is stalking you? Oh my goodness, Amelia. That's so scary."

"Maybe I chose the wrong word."

"Tell me more."

"You already know someone has been taking random things, but someone has been outside with a flashlight at night too. One time it was Elam Wenger checking on me, he said. The other time, it wasn't him, I don't believe. And I doubt he was the person who set off the smoke bomb in my barn last night."

"Oh, Amelia! That's awful. Were any people or animals hurt?"

"*Nee*, the animals were only scared. Christina and I got them out okay."

"I bet you were scared too."

Amelia coughed. "Maybe more worried for our safety and anxious over the animals. At first, anyway. Then I felt angry that someone would play such a mean and dangerous trick. I think scared came later after the police and fire truck left."

"You had quite an exciting evening."

"I prefer quiet, boring ones."

"I don't blame you."

"I'm glad Christina was here with you."

"She has been kind enough to spend a couple of nights here. She and another *freind* were concerned about me alone here with three little girls."

"Would that other person be someone I know?"

Amelia's cheeks nearly burst into flame, even though she knew Jill was only teasing her. "You might." She gasped for air when Jill wrapped her in a hug.

"Oh, Amelia, you are so funny. Your face registers your every emotion."

"Somehow, I don't think that is a *gut* thing." She patted Jill's back and pulled away with another little cough. "And you, my *freind*, like to tease!"

"I do, but I don't mean any harm. I wouldn't do anything to hurt you for the world."

"I know, dear. I'm so glad to see you smile."

"It's good to laugh again, and I know Blake wouldn't want me to mourn and be gloomy forever. I'll always miss my wonderful big brother, but he would definitely want me to move forward with my life."

"For sure and for certain."

"You know, I could take turns with Christina staying here with you."

"I wouldn't want to disrupt another person's life. In fact, I plan to persuade Christina to go home tonight."

"You can't!" Jill clapped a hand over her mouth. She softened her tone. "Not after last night, Amelia. In fact, it might be a good idea for both of us to stay here tonight."

"I don't believe that will be necessary."

"This is no time to be stubborn. There's obviously a lunatic out there who is fixated on you."

Amelia couldn't suppress a shiver. "You don't honestly think someone would be foolish enough to return tonight after the police were here and are aware of the strange happenings, do you?"

"I'm not sure what to think, but I do know that crazy people don't use logic. I don't want you and the girls to come to any harm."

"We have not been threatened with harm." Amelia coughed into her arm.

"Did you just develop that cough after last night's drama?"

"*Jah*, but I'm sure it will go away soon."

"Hmm. Let me tell you my idea."

~

It was a good thing he hadn't had any terribly challenging projects so his hands could automatically do what they knew needed to be done. His brain had meandered down so many paths it was a wonder it hadn't worn out from exhaustion. Norman even had to tell him to eat lunch. What a pitiful mess he was!

Ryan rubbed his forehead after setting aside his last job. When had that drumming begun in his head? He wasn't usually prone to having headaches unless he hadn't eaten or hadn't drunk enough water. Norman had reminded him to eat lunch, and he was sure he had, only he couldn't remember a single thing he ate. He glanced at his full water bottle. Aha! There was the problem. He must not have taken a single sip all afternoon.

He twisted the cap and chugged half the bottle without stopping. He couldn't remember when he'd been so thirsty. He paused for a breath before taking another gulp. Every cell in his body must have been dehydrated.

"Are you ready to call it a day, or are you going to inhale the rest of that water? You act like you've been running in the desert." Norman chuckled.

"I didn't realize how thirsty I was. I guess I got too busy to stop for a drink." Ryan wiped his mouth on his sleeve. "I'm ready."

"Too distracted, you mean."

"Hey, I completed all my assignments. I checked each one out to make sure it worked properly."

"I'm not talking about your work. You always do a fine job—even if you have been getting a bit distracted here lately."

"I wasn't distracted." Much.

"Really?" Norman dropped his tools into the box on his workbench. "How come you didn't answer all the times I spoke to you?"

"You're telling tales now. You didn't speak to me. I would have heard you."

"I'm joshing you. You did answer the few times I asked you something. I think my head was off somewhere else today too."

Ryan couldn't decide which was worse, ignoring someone or not remembering the conversations he'd had. He must have given Norman appropriate answers, or the man would have called him on it. "Maybe after a good night's sleep, we'll both be more focused tomorrow." Ryan screwed the cap on the water bottle and cleared his work area.

"Maybe. I'll get a good supper in my belly and try to crawl into bed earlier."

That sounded like a dream to Ryan, one he wasn't likely to experience. By the time he threw together some sort of meal and then got the girls bathed and tucked into bed, early would have turned into late. How did women manage to keep everything running so smoothly? And they made it look so easy too. He now knew taking care of a house and children must be the hardest jobs on earth.

Norman groaned as he locked the door. "Dumb me. I forgot to tell you Sarah made an extra casserole so you can take it home for your supper." He knocked on his head with his fist. "Didn't I tell you my brain had skipped out on me?"

"She did?" Ryan had a sudden urge to run inside the house and give Sarah a great big hug. He wouldn't, of course.

"She told me to tell you when I was in the house earlier, and by the time I got back out to the shop, I had completely forgotten. I hope I'm not losing my mind."

Ryan laughed. "I don't think so, Norman. I sure do appreciate Sarah's thoughtfulness. I was wondering what I had in the refrigerator to feed the girls."

"You eat with them, don't you? Family mealtime is important."

"I sit with them every night, but I'm usually busy feeding Jessie and answering Gabby's thousand-and-one questions. Sometimes I'm too tired to eat after all that."

"It's starting to show."

"What does that mean?"

"It means I'm going to have to find some heavy-duty suspenders for you to hold those pants up. I can't have you losing them in front of customers."

"I don't think there's any danger of that." Ryan tugged at his pants to prove his point. They did seem a bit looser. Maybe Norman was right. "Since I don't have to cook tonight, I'll actually be able to enjoy eating."

"See that you do. Come on. Let's get your casserole so you can pick up your little ones."

*And make one stop along the way.* Ryan followed the older man to the back door of the house.

"Sarah!" Norman hollered before he even got completely through the door. "Ryan is heading out. Do you have his food ready?"

"I sure do."

Ryan stepped inside the warm kitchen. Heavenly scents of beef, tomatoes, and spices enveloped him. Something smelled chocolaty too. His kitchen usually smelled of burned toast or overcooked bacon. The girls never complained though. They ate whatever he fed them. He had been improving a little bit. If he had more time, he could probably prepare a fairly decent meal. Time. That was a precious commodity in very short supply.

Sarah bustled about gathering a casserole dish and plastic containers that she eased into a large paper bag. "I was in a real cooking mood today and prepared way more than we could ever eat. I have casserole, green beans, pickled beets, and coleslaw. Oh, and some zucchini bread and chocolate brownies. I hope the girls will like these things."

Ryan barely kept from chuckling. Sarah didn't fool him one bit. He knew she prepared a lot of food because she felt sorry for him. At first, that bothered him, but he soon realized Sarah truly wanted to help. If he made a fuss, he would hurt her feelings and deny her the opportunity to serve. "My girls aren't picky eaters. They will love your food. And they will be thrilled they won't have to endure my cooking catastrophes."

"Pshaw! I'm sure you manage just fine. Your precious daughters always look happy and healthy. What a blessing they must be."

"They are indeed. I certainly appreciate all the help I get from you and, uh, others." He almost said Amelia but caught himself just in time. He didn't need folks getting any wrong ideas.

A relationship with Amelia wouldn't be wrong in his book. It would be wonderful. But it was not possible. That's why he couldn't say or do anything that might tarnish her reputation. It wasn't her fault he had fallen crazy in love with her. He groaned softly. He had no business thinking about love, especially in connection with Amelia Stauffer.

"Are you all right?" Sarah's eyes were filled with concern.

"Huh?"

"You groaned. Is anything wrong?"

"Uh, no. I was thinking about my cooking and housework inadequacies. That's all." He shook his head. What a flimsy excuse, but it was the best he could manufacture on the spur of the moment. "I'm learning though, and I think I'm improving." He chuckled. "I guess there was no place to go but up. At least none of us has gotten sick from my cooking, and we aren't starving."

Sarah patted his arm. "I'm only a shout away. I would be happy to help out."

"I appreciate that. Truly, I do. You do so much already. We really are getting along much better now that I've realized how important it is to stick to routines."

"That is so true. Children do seem to thrive knowing there is a certain constancy in their lives."

*Don't we all!* Constancy might sound dull to some, but he could use a little boredom in his life about now. As it was, he didn't have time to be bored. He scarcely had time to eat or sleep. "I'll let you and Norman get to your dinner. Thank you again, Sarah."

"My pleasure."

Ryan secured the bag of food in a safe compartment behind the front seat of the SUV. What nice folks. He had been blessed with caring neighbors and friends. He wanted to make one quick stop before retrieving his daughters. The temperature should be plenty cold enough to keep the food from spoiling if he kept his visit brief.

He signaled and turned on a dirt driveway a few miles down the road. He crept along to avoid the assorted dips and holes. He certainly did not want to scrape casserole and pickled beets off the carpet. Was it a mistake to stop at Levi Wheeler's place to look at his dogs? *You don't have to get one, you know.* He had to remember that. No matter how cute the pups might be, he did not have to purchase one today.

Deep barks and high-pitched yips greeted him the minute he pushed open the door. Levi must have a menagerie! The noise increased in volume and intensity as Ryan strolled around the side of the house.

"Hey! Come on over!" Levi waved at him from one of the kennels. "It's feeding time, and they're all excited."

"So I see." Ryan smiled at the boisterous puppies clamoring for attention and a morsel of food. He nodded at their caretaker.

"It's good to see you. What brings you out? Don't tell me you're interested in a puppy."

"I might be."

"You came to the right place, then." Levi chuckled. "I've got plenty of them." He stooped to pour kibble into a huge, metal bowl. "The youngest puppies are still nursing some, but they're taking food too. They'll be ready to go in another week or so." Levi straightened to look Ryan in the eye. "What sort of dog are you looking for? I've got these golden retrievers here and some chocolate labs. I've even got some Pekingese if you're after a lap dog. What's your pleasure?"

# Chapter Eighteen

Without even being aware of it, Amelia's foot tapped on the gravel. What was Jill up to? Amelia could practically see ideas churning in the young woman's mind. She fidgeted with the basket in her hands and shivered when a sudden cool breeze ruffled the little hairs on the back of her neck. She really should get back inside in case the girls were awake and searching for her. "Do you want to *kumm* inside?"

"Let me tell you my plan first." Jill pulled the basket from Amelia's hands. "You're going to reduce this poor thing to shreds and tatters if you keep plucking at it, and it's too pretty to destroy."

"Oh." Amelia dropped her hands to her sides. "What is your idea?"

"I'm going to go home, pick up a few things, and be back here before dark. I can pick up pizzas and snacks, and we'll have a regular ole pajama party."

"A what? I don't party and wouldn't wear pajamas if I did."

Jill hooted. "Oh, Amelia." She paused to wipe the moisture from her eyes. "I'm sorry. We used to call it a pajama party when we spent the night with girlfriends and stayed up all night talking and eating junk food."

"I see...I think. We sometimes spent the night with *freinden*, but we didn't call it a pajama party, and we certainly didn't stay up all night."

"But you talked and had fun, right?"

"We did."

"Okay, so you, Christina, and I can have a grown-up version of a pajama party tonight. We can have a good time, but we'll keep a lookout for any strange happenings outside. I can even bring Casey, the dog I adopted after my own harrowing experiences."

"I-I don't know."

"We don't have to stay up late. In fact, maybe you can go to bed and get a good night's sleep for a change while Christina and I stand watch."

"I don't really think I will need a guard. You and Christina should not worry about me."

"Friends care about each other and want to help each other, don't they?"

"Sure, but—"

"Christina and I care about you and want to help you."

"That's very nice, but I don't think it will be necessary to spoil your evening for me. I believe last night's adventure probably scared off anyone who wants to be mischievous."

"It could have done the exact opposite. The person might figure he got away with his prank so it would be safe to try something else."

Amelia hadn't considered that. She rubbed her hands up and down her arms. Was the sudden chill due to the weather or the conversation?

Jill laid a hand on Amelia's arm. "I didn't mean to upset you or scare you."

"That's all right. It's getting colder, don't you think?"

"Possibly."

"I need to check on the girls. You're *wilkom* to accompany me."

"How about if I go get my things?"

"Oh, Jill, I don't want to cause you any problems."

"You won't be. Besides, I volunteered for this mission. You didn't recruit me. And Casey doesn't have to stay in the house. If you'd prefer, she can sleep in the barn with your animals."

*And bark all night at every strange sight or sound.* "She isn't used to that. She would probably be frightened."

"If she barked, she would scare away intruders. Have you thought about getting a dog? The shelter always has animals that need a home. I could take you to look at them."

"I don't know about that. A dog would be one more responsibility." She already carried a load as it was. Jill was the second person in a matter of hours to suggest she get a dog though. Was the Lord *Gott* trying to tell her something? *Ach! Don't be silly, Amelia. The Lord doesn't care if you get a dog or a pig or a hippopotamus.*

"It's something to think about, Amelia. Casey is a great dog. She's not big, and she's not little. She's a mutt, but she's just right. You go ahead and check on the children. I'll zip home and be back soon."

"You truly don't have to do that. I'm sure we'll be fine. I intend to send Christina home too."

"Good luck with that. You know she wants to solve this mystery."

Amelia sighed. "I just want it all to go away. I want my normal life back. I want my laundry to stay on the line and my belongings to stay where I put them."

"I know you do. Christina and I want to help."

"I appreciate that, but—"

"No 'buts.' I'm coming back. What would you like me to bring for dinner? Pizza? Burgers? Chinese?"

Amelia wrinkled her nose. She rarely ate those foods or fed them to her girls. "I already have supper on the stove."

"Okay. I'll bring some stuff for extra or to snack on later. If you'd rather I didn't bring Casey, please tell me. You won't hurt my feelings."

Amelia shrugged. "I don't suppose she can hurt anything."

"Good. I'll see you in a bit." She held the basket out.

"*Nee*, it's yours. You bought it from the shop in town, ain't so?"

"I did. It's beautiful. I wonder how the store owner got it if she didn't purchase it from you."

"There's another mystery to solve."

"I'll think about it." Jill crammed the basket into the back seat of her car and climbed in behind the wheel. "See you soon."

Amelia waved and hurried to the house, mumbling as she walked. She didn't want to be a bother to people. She didn't like the fact that not one, but two, of her *freinden* were sacrificing their evenings for her. And, most of all, she hated that such a thing was even necessary in the first place. She prayed the perpetrator, whoever he might be, had grown tired of harassing her.

"*Mamm!*" The call came from somewhere in the bowels of the house.

"I'm here, Judith." Amelia rushed inside and ran across the kitchen. Judith stood in the living room wearing a panic-stricken expression. Amelia dropped to her knees and opened her arms wide. The little girl flew into them and threw her arms around her *mudder's* neck. "Are you the only one awake?"

Judith nodded against Amelia's shoulder.

"Where were you?" the wee voice trembled.

Amelia stroked her *dochder's* back. Were her girls becoming fearful because of the bizarre happenings of late? Did they sense her own uneasiness that she had tried desperately to hide? "I was outside talking to Jill. You remember her, right? Well, she is going to *kumm* back later and might bring her dog with her."

Judith pulled back to look in her *mamm's* face. "Really? I like dogs."

"I know you do. Let's go see if the others are ready to get up. Everyone slept longer than usual today. Gabby's and Jessie's *daed* will be here before we know it."

~

The golden retriever and chocolate lab puppies sure were cute. Who wouldn't fall in love with the little balls of fur rolling over top of each other in their excitement? He knew Amelia and the girls would. But those tiny puppies wouldn't stay small for long. They would grow into large dogs. Would a big dog frighten the little girls and overwhelm Amelia? And the Pekingese pups were too adorable for words, but they were indoor dogs. Would Amelia allow an animal to share her house? Somehow, he didn't think so.

Ryan debated. He was torn between a yearning to help and a desire to cause as little disruption as possible. Would Amelia consider him a meddler? He only wanted her and her girls to feel safe and secure. A dog that would bark and warn of anything unusual would provide that assurance. At least Ryan thought so. But would one of Levi's dogs be appropriate?

He jerked his hand up when something bumped against it. He looked down into the big doe-like eyes of a brown, curly-haired dog. "Oh hi, fellow." He patted its head.

"Lady."

"Huh?"

"She's a girl."

"Oh. What kind of dog is she? She doesn't look like a retriever or a lab and certainly not like a Pekingese."

Levi chuckled. "No. She's a mixed mutt. Looks like some poodle or spaniel in her and maybe terrier. She showed up here a couple of weeks ago and apparently decided to stay. We tried to find her owner, but no one responded to any of the flyers we posted."

The dog watched Ryan's every move. "She seems to be a friendly sort."

"She's very friendly and very sweet-natured. That's why I couldn't figure out why no one has claimed her."

"Do you think she's full grown?" She was the perfect size—not so small she would be stepped on but not so large that she would be intimidating.

"As near as we can tell, she's full grown. I had the vet check her out since she's around my other dogs. He gave her the necessary shots and a clean bill of health."

The dog bumped Ryan's hand again so he would continue petting her. He laughed. "She looks like a mop with eyes."

"She certainly has taken a liking to you. Hey, if you want her instead of one of the pups, that's fine by me."

Would Amelia be equally enchanted by this funny, affectionate, little dog? "You know, I might just take you up on that. I was actually scouting out possibilities for a friend, but this little girl might fit the bill perfectly."

"Do you want to take her today? I'd like to see her settled in a home where she'll be loved and well taken care of."

"I would be able to guarantee both of those." If Amelia didn't agree, he could keep the dog himself. "I'm not sure my friend is prepared for a dog today though."

"I sell everything you'd need for her. I have bowls, beds, collars, leashes, you name it."

"How much do you want for her?" Ryan hadn't figured out why this little mutt appealed to him so much, but she had captured his heart. She seemed so happy and grateful for attention. She even appeared to smile at him.

"Since she wasn't mine, you can just pay for any of the gear you purchase."

"Let me at least pay whatever the vet charged you."

"If you want." Levi rubbed a hand across his clean-shaven jaw. "I'll tell you what. If you buy one of the other pups, you can have the mop dog *and* all her gear absolutely free."

Now Ryan was in a quandary. He wanted this curly-haired dog for Amelia so she wouldn't have to train a puppy. He'd love to get a pet for his own girls, but where would he find time or energy to work with a pup? He could barely care for his children and the house. By far, the most sensible thing to do would be to wait until his daughters were older so they could help.

He was glad he hadn't brought the girls with him today. Making this decision was hard enough by himself. It would be ten times harder with Gabby begging and tugging on his sleeve.

He glanced at the puppies yipping and playing in their pens. Mistake. Ryan had to look away. He couldn't let their cuteness overrule his common sense. He glanced at Levi, who was patiently awaiting an answer.

The little dog at his side nudged him. Ryan absently reached to pet the curly head. "Those pups are mighty tempting, but my girls are still a bit too small to help out. And it wouldn't be fair to leave a puppy home all alone day after day."

"They are smart dogs. All three breeds. But I do understand your position."

"Maybe when I get Jessie out of diapers, I can tackle a puppy."

Levi nodded. "I'll always have another litter whenever you're ready. What about your little shadow here?" He nodded at the dog that hadn't left Ryan's side.

"I think she will be good for my friend. She seems loyal, I'll give you that." The dog had stuck right beside him and had studied his every move.

"She is. And she's smart too. She's still playful, but she's beyond that hyperactive puppy stage."

"That could be a great selling feature."

"It sounds like you plan to talk your friend into a pet. Maybe he would want to come see the dogs for himself."

"I think—no, I know—my friend likes animals. Her children are a little older than mine and might be able to help more." Oops! Had he just said her? He hadn't meant to divulge that his friend was a woman. He didn't want Levi trying to guess her identity.

"How old are your friend's children?"

"Six, four, and two." That information should clue Levi in on the mystery friend. Most folks knew an Old Order Mennonite woman cared for his children while he worked. If Levi didn't know which woman that was, his wife surely would.

Enough pondering. Ryan needed to decide and be on his way. He had to pick up the girls, get them home and fed, bathe them, clean up the kitchen, and somehow get them all to bed at a halfway decent hour.

"Would you want to bring your friend over to meet this little girl?" Levi reached down to pet the curly-haired dog.

Amelia would probably never go for that. He knew she still beat herself up over their little visit to town a few months ago, even though it had been a perfectly innocent trip. That had been a truly enjoyable experience, but Ryan wouldn't want to compromise Amelia's standing in her community by suggesting another outing, no matter how brief.

"I'll take the dog now. If my friend can't keep her, I will. I'll need to purchase the necessary paraphernalia." There. Decision made, for good or bad.

Levi chuckled. "I'm glad she'll get a good home. Come on. I'll show you what I have."

Ryan didn't have time to dawdle. He was already overdue to collect his children. He had no way to let Amelia know he was running late or to prepare her for his decision. He'd hope and pray everything worked out. "Say, Levi, does the dog have a name?"

Levi shrugged but kept walking. "I don't know. She didn't have any collar or tags when she showed up here. We've been calling her doggie or Brownie. I guess you can name her whatever you want."

Ryan patted the dog's head again. "Don't worry, girl. We'll think of a good name for you. Something more dignified than Brownie." He sure hoped Amelia bonded with the dog as quickly as he had. She would be able to find a spot in her heart and home for this eager-to-please canine, wouldn't she?

# Chapter Nineteen

Worry began to snake its way into her thoughts after Amelia glanced at the battery-operated kitchen wall clock. Ryan occasionally ran a little late, but he'd never been this late before. She prayed he hadn't had an accident. She couldn't keep looking out the window and wringing her hands. The girls would be hungry soon since their snack had been several hours ago. Maybe she should go ahead and feed them supper.

Amelia checked to make sure the girls were still happily playing in the living room before slipping into the kitchen to lift plates from the cupboard. She nearly dropped them all at the sound of a thump at the back door. Her heart lurched, but she told herself it was only Ryan. At least she knew he hadn't been injured in an accident.

She set the plates down and hurried to the door. She opened her mouth to tell him how grateful she was he was safe but caught the words in time. "Christina! It's you!"

"Were you expecting someone else?"

"*Nee. Jah.* I mean, Ryan Miller hasn't picked up the girls yet, so I thought he'd finally arrived."

"I'm sorry to disappoint you."

"I'm not disappointed, only a little surprised."

"Why? I told you I would return after work."

"But I don't want you to keep changing your plans because of me."

"What plans? I would only be going home to do chores and help with supper."

"Your *mudder* probably misses your help."

"Sallie and Grace are big enough to help. It would be *gut* for them to take on more responsibility."

Amelia smiled. "You sound like a *mudder* yourself."

"Sometimes I feel like one. I've helped care for those two as long as they've been on earth."

"They are *gut* girls."

"Sometimes." Christina laughed. "Let me wash up and I'll help you with supper."

"It's ready. I had been debating about eating now or later, but I think I'll go ahead and feed everyone. That will help Ryan out since he's so late getting here."

"You sound worried."

"I, uh, I'm concerned." Amelia's cheeks burned. She hastily averted her gaze.

"It's okay to be concerned for someone you care about."

Amelia's head snapped up. "Care about?"

"Don't look so guilty." Christina smiled and reached to give Amelia a quick hug. "Ryan Miller is a *freinden*, ain't so? We all care about our *freinden*."

"Of course." Was that really all Christina meant, or did the girl have some suspicion about Amelia's true feelings for Ryan? *Ach!* She shouldn't have any feelings about the man at all. She needed to change the topic of conversation. "Is there any way I can convince you to stop worrying about me? It isn't that I don't enjoy your company, you understand."

"I am concerned about you alone here with the *kinner*."

"I've been alone with them for a very long time and will continue to be alone with them."

"Maybe not forever. I'm sure you will marry again."

"I'm not counting on it, and I'm okay with that." Was she though?

"Hmm." Christina snatched up a handful of paper napkins and distributed them around the huge oak table. "At any rate, you haven't had prowlers before."

Amelia shivered. "That sounds so ominous."

"It is. I would be scared."

"You would not."

"I most certainly would. You were awfully brave to try to catch the person."

"Foolish might be a better word since I didn't have any idea what the man might have been up to."

"That's why you need me here."

Amelia laughed. "So there will be two fools instead of one?"

Christina chuckled. "*Nee*, silly. So we can try to figure out this whole mystery. Two heads are better than one, as the saying goes."

"Three."

"What?"

Amelia nodded toward the kitchen window. "Three heads must be great, then."

Christina trotted to the window and raised on tiptoes to peer outside. "Jill? What is she doing here?"

"The same as you. Guarding me. Now I've messed up two people's lives."

Christina elbowed her. "You haven't done any such thing. *Freinden* help each other. You know if the shoe was on the other foot, you would do the very same thing."

Amelia shrugged. "Probably, if I could."

"I *know* you would. I guess we'd better set another place at the table. It looks like she's moving in."

Amelia slid over from the stove to take another peek outside. Sure enough, Jill appeared to have packed enough gear for a week. She hauled out a bulging duffel bag and two overflowing tote bags. "The dog probably wouldn't fit in the car with all that stuff."

"Dog? Had she planned to bring her dog?"

"That's what she said, but I don't see any four-legged critters out there."

"*Gut.* That's one less thing to worry about. Don't get me wrong. I like dogs very much, but Jill hasn't had her dog very long, so an overnight outing might have been trying for all of us."

"If you'll take out another plate, I'll let her in." Amelia scurried to the door to admit the *Englisch* girl. "You're back."

Jill wobbled under the load she juggled. "I told you I would come back. I decided not to bring Casey though."

"You probably wouldn't have been able to stuff her in the car with all that junk," Christina called from the kitchen.

"Was that Christina Brubacher?" Jill grunted as she dropped her bags to the floor.

"It's me!" Christina poked her head around the corner. "Are you moving in for keeps?"

"Very funny. This happens to be my pajamas, a change of clothes, and my necessities."

Christina hooted. "I can hold my necessities in one hand—a comb and a toothbrush."

"That's because you're naturally beautiful. I have to work hard to look this gorgeous." Jill crossed her eyes and scrunched up her nose in a hideous expression. All three women burst out laughing.

"Look at this." Christina tugged on one of Jill's long, dark curls. "It springs into place naturally. You don't have to do a thing to it."

"Okay, you two. We have five hungry *kinner* to feed." Amelia pulled the casserole from the oven. "And supper is ready."

"Five!" Jill looked from one woman to the other.

"Gabby and Jessie are still here." Amelia hoped worry hadn't crept into her voice. What could be keeping Ryan?

"Oh. The more, the merrier, right?" Jill kicked her bags out of the way. "What can I do to help?"

"One of you can pour milk and the other can help the girls wash up."

"Wash or pour, Christina?" Jill asked.

"Since Amelia won't allow you to touch anything in her kitchen until you've washed your hands, you might as well oversee the scrubbing. I'll pour."

Christina set five small plastic cups on the counter and removed a carton of milk from the refrigerator. "Judging by the giggles and splashes, I think they are having way too much fun in there."

Amelia sighed. "It sounds to me like I'm going to have more cleaning to do." She scooped spoonfuls of casserole onto plates.

"Here for inspection, ma'am," Jill announced from the doorway. "Girls, hold out your hands."

Amelia pretended to study each hand. "I believe you all passed inspection. You may sit down."

"Where's Daddy?" Gabby's face puckered.

"I'm sure he got busy and lost track of time. He'll be along soon." Amelia forced a smile and prayed she was right. She set a plate of the hamburger and noodle mixture and vegetables in front of the four-year-old. "He'll probably be here by the time you eat. I know you like this casserole."

Gabby nodded. "I do. Daddy fixes noodles a lot."

Christina set a cup beside each of the older girls' plates, careful to keep the cups well back from the table's edge. She and Jill wiggled into spaces between the girls while Amelia perched on the edge of a chair next to the high chair so she could help Jessie.

Another thump sounded at the door not two minutes after the conclusion of the silent prayer. Forks clattered onto plates and mouths stopped mid-chew.

"Daddy?" Gabby mumbled around her mouthful of noo-dles.

"I'll go see " Amelia left bits of bread on the tray for Jessie to feed herself and slid from her chair. Poor Gabby was as worried about Ryan as Amelia was. She had probably grown very attached to her *daed* since losing her *mudder*.

Amelia resisted the urge to smooth her dress or poke stray strands of hair beneath her *kapp*. The most important thing was to make sure Ryan was all right. She wanted to see his smile and the laugh crinkles fanning out around his dark brown eyes. She pulled open the door and gasped.

Her first instinct was to slam the door and pretend she'd never answered it in the first place. Of course, she couldn't do any such thing. "Elam! What are you doing here?" She cringed. That sounded awfully rude.

The big, red-haired man shuffled his feet as if suddenly nervous. "I just thought I'd check on you and offer again to stay in the barn tonight."

Why was she having such difficulty getting through to him? Wasn't it only this morning he and Annie had shown up at her door? What a long day it had been! How could she politely get it through his thick skull that she did not want or need his protection? He was probably only trying to be neighborly, but something about him annoyed her. "That's kind of you, but as I told you and Annie this morning, that won't be necessary."

"Are you sure? You might feel more comfortable with another adult around."

"I'm not uncomfortable, Elam. Besides, I have *freinden* here with me right now."

He muttered a response, but Amelia understood his words without any problem. She bristled and fought to remain calm.

"Whoever visits me is none of your concern, but so you don't go spreading crazy rumors, my visitors are women." Her outburst set off a coughing fit, just when she thought her lungs had finally cleared.

"Hey, Elam, what's the problem?"

Amelia hadn't heard Christina slip up behind her. The tiny, young woman stared the much larger man down as if challenging him. The Biblical story of David squaring off with the giant popped into Amelia's mind.

"You drive a car? I thought I'd always seen you pedaling a bike to work."

"Elam Wenger, you should know that I do not drive a car, but our *Englisch freind*, Jill, does. By the way, were you here last night?"

Amelia cut her eyes over to the younger woman. What was Christina getting at?

"Of course I wasn't. Why would you ask me that?"

Christina shrugged. "Someone has been messing around Amelia's barn. They could have harmed the animals. Why, this poor woman still has a cough from their foolishness."

"I heard about the disturbance. I can't believe you would think that was me. Are you trying to accuse me of setting off smoke bombs? Why in the world would I do that?"

"How should I know? People do *narrisch* things all the time."

"And now you call me crazy after accusing me of vandalism or destruction of property or whatever? I'm only trying to help."

Christina shook her head. "I did not accuse you of anything. I merely asked questions. But you haven't heard anything Amelia has said. She has been trying to tell you, very nicely, that she doesn't need you to be her bodyguard."

Amelia coughed until her eyes watered, and tears dripped down her cheeks. She could scarcely believe her ears. If Elam didn't get the message this time, nobody would ever be able to get through to him.

"You should see about that cough." Elam turned his back on Christina and focused on Amelia.

"I'm sure I'll be fine." Amelia barely held back another cough. "*Danki* for your concern though. If you'll excuse us, we were in the middle of feeding the *kinner* their supper."

"Okay. Please send one of your *freinden* if you need me to help with anything."

Amelia knew she wouldn't be able to speak without coughing so merely nodded. She closed and locked the door before Elam had hopped off the last step.

"'Send one of your *freinden*,'" Christina mocked. "Fat chance. I can see now why he has not yet married."

# Chapter Twenty

Amelia laughed and coughed at the same time. She scurried back to the kitchen to check on the girls. Christina followed on her heels.

"Psst!" Christina hissed. "Maybe you should get that cough checked out."

Amelia turned and scowled. "Not you too! I really am getting better. At least, I was."

"That man is enough to get anyone choked up."

"*Danki* for rescuing me. He is a determined sort." Amelia smiled at the four messy-faced girls who watched her enter the kitchen. "My, it looks like four little piggies have gobbled up their food."

"And this one has been trying to keep up with them." Jill had moved to Amelia's seat to feed Jessie.

"I was worried Jessie was going to be getting impatient, but now I see why she has been so content. *Danki* for feeding her."

"No problem." Jill laid the spoon in the empty bowl. "You were pretty tough on him, Christina."

"I wasn't trying to be rude, but I guess that's the way my words came out. I should apologize next time I see him."

"I don't think you were rude exactly. I'd call it forceful, which was probably a good thing because he didn't seem to hear Amelia's gentle words."

Amelia lowered her voice and spoke in *Englisch* since the girls wouldn't understand her words quite as well. "Do you really think Elam is behind all the strange happenings around here?"

Christina shrugged. "It's hard to say. I wanted to see his reaction. He got rather defensive, but I'm not sure that means he's guilty. Maybe I should read some of Annie's suspense novels to learn questioning techniques." She slid onto her chair at the table and picked up her fork.

"Your food must be pretty cold. I can heat it in the oven for a few minutes." Amelia reached for her plate.

"That's not necessary. I like lukewarm casserole, hot casserole, cold casserole—it doesn't matter. But you need to sit down and eat too, Amelia. I haven't seen you eat a single bite."

"Here." Jill handed Jessie the empty spoon to play with as she hopped up from the chair. "Sit down, Amelia. I moved your plate back and covered it with a napkin so no flying baby food would land in the middle of it."

"*Danki.*" Amelia sat, suddenly feeling more weary than she'd felt in a long while. Now she had a new concern besides Elam Wenger's unwanted attention and concern for Ryan Miller's safety. Could Elam be connected to the thefts? Surely not.

Jill handed Amelia her fork. "Eat. The food isn't going to jump into your stomach."

Amelia accepted the fork but didn't start eating right away. Too many thoughts swirled in her brain, making her dizzy.

"Where are you, Amelia?" Christina kicked her under the table.

Rhonda giggled. "*Mamm* is right there. Can't you see her?"

Christina tickled the six-year-old. She opened her eyes wide and gasped. "Why, you're right! She is right there in front of me." All the girls giggled.

Amelia lifted a forkful of noodles but then lowered it to her plate. "Has Annie said how long her cousin plans to stay here?"

Christina swallowed. "I don't think she knows, but she seems to be getting a bit tired of her houseguest even though he's family. You know the saying about fish and company stinking after three days."

Jill shook her head sending her dark curls flying around her shoulders. "He is a strange one, isn't he?"

Christina chuckled. "Maybe he's getting as tired of Annie's chatter as she's getting of him and will decide to go home soon."

Ryan opened the rear door of the SUV and patted the floor. The curly-haired dog hopped in, turned around twice, and then dropped down to lay her head on her front paws as if she'd ridden in vehicles all her life. Perhaps she had traveled a lot with her former owner. Why would anyone leave a seemingly docile, well-mannered dog behind? He hoped some unknown problem wouldn't arise later. He thanked Levi and crawled behind the wheel.

*Bad man!* Ryan kicked himself all the way down the road. What kind of person picked out a dog and brought it to someone who might not even like dogs? How could he have done such a ridiculous thing? He was not usually the spur-of-the-moment kind of man. He generally thought things out, weighed the pros and cons, and prayed about his decisions. How would he feel if someone dropped off a dog at his house and said, "Here. I got you a present."?

Ryan banged a fist on the steering wheel and took a quick peek over his shoulder to make sure he hadn't upset the dog.

She hadn't moved a muscle. In fact, he was almost convinced the dog smiled at him.

Something about the young dog spoke to his heart. It was as if he'd been meant to go to Levi's today and see this particular pup. She had certainly sought him out and remained by his side during his entire visit. It was almost as if she said, "You can look at those other animals, but you need to take me!"

He must be losing his mind if he was imagining dog conversations. Amelia would most likely agree with that assessment as soon as she found out what he had done. Well, if the pup could speak to his heart, he hoped she could speak to Amelia's as well.

Even though he drove slowly, the few miles to Amelia's house zipped by. Ryan had tried out first one approach and then another, but nothing sounded quite right. How was he going to rationalize his "gift" and get her to accept it? He should never have given in to the impulse to visit Levi Wheeler.

His stomach rumbled. The scent of Sarah's casserole wafted throughout the vehicle. How could he possibly be hungry when his stomach was tied in knots? He lowered the window a couple of inches to grab a whiff of fresh air and to, hopefully, clear his mind. Well, if Amelia didn't want the dog, he would keep her. Simple as that. Even though he did not need one more responsibility in his overloaded life, his girls would love the puppy.

He clicked on the signal light to turn onto Amelia's driveway and prayed she would fall head over heels in love with the dog. His tension increased the closer he got to the house. Not only was he very late, but he also came bearing a probably unwanted gift.

No one stirred outside the house. No children played in the yard. Ryan glanced at the dashboard clock before shutting off the engine. Supper time. Amelia probably had his girls sitting at her table, feeding them yet another meal he should have prepared for them. He tried to console himself with the thought that he had never been this late picking up the girls.

He hated having her use up her food on his children. He sometimes wondered how she got by as it was. She had told him that some of the men paid to use her fields to grow their corn, hay, or soybeans, and her basket business seemed pretty steady. And, of course, he paid her to watch Gabby and Jessie. Still, it took a lot of money to care for a family and a home. He knew she sewed their clothes and canned much of their food, but supplies weren't cheap. Amelia was resourceful, though, and smart.

He hoped he didn't have to add angry to that description. He turned around to look at the back of the SUV. Only then did the dog raise her head. She cocked it to one side as if asking, "Are we there yet?" as Gabby always did. He smiled. "Okay, puppy dog. We're here. Your new home. Maybe."

Ryan didn't open the door right away. Should he take the dog to the door with him and spring the surprise on Amelia? Or should he greet her and whoever the guest was who drove that little car and try to prepare her? Maybe he should apologize for his tardiness and explain why he was late. He pulled the door handle. "Be right back. Don't you dare move and get into that bag of food." The dog blinked and dropped her head onto her paws. "Good girl."

The door flew open before he could raise a hand to knock. Any ideas for preparing Amelia for his actions evaporated like raindrops on a hot sidewalk when he saw the concern etched on her lovely face.

"Ryan! I was so worried. I mean, uh, the girls and I wondered what happened."

"I'm so sorry, but I couldn't call to tell you I stopped off at Levi Wheeler's place. Time got away from me."

"I'm relieved you are all right. A person's imagination can go a little crazy."

"I didn't mean to cause you to worry." The thought of distressing her pained him. "The girls?"

"They are fine. They're finishing their supper. I hope you don't mind that I fed them."

"No. They were probably starving. Norman's wife sent some food home with me, but I can save that for tomorrow night."

"Would you like a plate? I made plenty. Christina Brubacher and Jill Sheridan are here. You know Jill, don't you?"

That explained the car in the driveway. "I've met her at The Green Thumb. I hope my girls didn't interfere with your plans for the evening."

"I didn't have plans. I couldn't convince Christina and Jill that I was fine alone with the girls. They insisted on staying with us tonight."

"Since they're with the children right now, may I speak with you for a minute?"

"Of course."

"Would you step outside with me?"

A look of surprise crossed her face. What would her face register when he told her about the dog?

Amelia tugged a black knit shawl off the peg beside the door and threw it around her shoulders. Ryan could tell she wanted to ask questions, but she kept silent. She hopped off the last step and stared up at him with her big, blue eyes.

My, but she was a little thing! Her head barely reached his shoulder. Ryan had an almost irresistible urge to wrap his arms around her to protect her from any possible harm. He cleared his throat. How should he begin?

"*Ach*, Ryan! What is in your car?"

He glanced over his shoulder to check his vehicle. Why did the dog have to hop up at that very moment? He whirled around to try to read her expression. "That's my surprise!"

# Chapter Twenty-One

"Surprise?" Amelia inched a bit closer to the SUV. "It looks like a woolly dog."

Ryan laughed. "That's a good description."

"You stopped at Levi's and purchased a dog for your girls? They will be so thrilled."

"Actually, the dog isn't for them."

"It isn't?" She feared his next words. She was tempted to press her hands over her ears so she wouldn't hear them.

"Do you remember we talked about a dog that could alert you to any intruders or problems?"

"As I recall, *you* spoke of getting a dog. I did not concur."

"But you didn't out-and-out refuse to consider the option."

"Is that 'the option' scratching its fleas in your car?"

"She doesn't have fleas."

"How do you know that?"

"Because Levi Wheeler would not let his dogs go unprotected. He has them checked by the vet, and he takes excellent care of them."

"I thought he sold puppies." Amelia took several more baby steps in the dog's direction. "This does not look like a puppy."

"Levi does sell puppies—golden retrievers and chocolate labs. They're very cute and playful now, but they will grow up to be large dogs. I was concerned the girls would be afraid of them. This dog," Ryan paused to nod toward his vehicle, "is a young dog but full grown. She seems very sweet-natured and gentle. Levi said she is great with children and other dogs. She showed up at his house, and he couldn't turn her away. He tried to find her owners, but no one responded to his posters."

"He didn't raise her?"

"No, but he's had enough experience to know a fine dog when he sees one. Like I said before, he had the vet check her out."

Amelia looked from Ryan to the dog. Thank goodness the girls hadn't *kumm* outside with her. They would make her necessary decision ever so much harder. She knew Ryan only wanted to help, that he was concerned about their well-being, but there was simply no way she could take on one more responsibility, one more challenge. She hated to do it. But she would need to send the dog back with Ryan. Maybe he could give her a good home instead. "Ryan, I—"

"Come meet her, Amelia." He took her hand and tugged her forward.

An instant current flowed up her arm and straight into her heart, leaving a tingling sensation in its wake. The intensity almost stole her breath.

"Please. Just say hello and give her a pat."

Amelia couldn't help but smile at his exuberance. He behaved like a little *bu* whose frog had just won the jumping contest. He must have been awfully cute when he was young, judging by his present attractiveness.

"I-I don't know." She wanted to refuse to step any closer or to touch the curly-haired dog in the back of the SUV. She suspected Ryan somehow knew that once she petted the dog, it would be difficult for her not to fall in love with it. She tried to free herself, but his grip tightened. The tingling sensation intensified, and her face burned. He dropped her hand to open the car door.

The excited pup leaped from the back of the SUV, bounded over to Amelia, sat at her feet, and stared at her with huge, beseeching eyes. "Oh my! She's—"

"She's very well-behaved, don't you think? She didn't pounce on you or anything."

"That's true. She isn't as big as I thought she was."

"And she's full grown. She won't get any bigger."

Amelia struggled not to smile. Ryan was working awfully hard to sell her on this dog. Was he afraid he'd be stuck with the animal if Amelia refused to take her? The dog continued to stare up at her as if waiting for some sign. The fuzzy tail softly thumped the ground.

She knew she should not touch or speak to the dog if she wanted to maintain her resistance, but the poor creature looked so lonely that Amelia's heart overruled her head. She reached out to stroke the curly head. So soft. The dog practically melted at her touch.

"I think she likes you."

"You're trying too hard, Ryan."

"Huh?"

"You're trying to sell me on this dog. I feel like I'm at a horse auction where they're trying to pass off a donkey for a workhorse."

Ryan chuckled. "In other words, I'm coming on too strong."

"A tad." She giggled when the dog's long, pink tongue snaked out to lick her wrist.

"I believe she might have taken offense at being compared to a donkey."

"Donkeys are fine animals, but they aren't workhorses."

"What are you trying to say?"

"Our little *freind* here might be a *gut* pet, but that doesn't necessarily make her a *gut* watchdog."

"Would you be willing to give her a chance? She would certainly alert you to any visitors."

"As docile as she seems, she would probably make *freinden* with anyone who paid her a sliver of attention, including intruders." When the pup nudged Amelia's hand to encourage her to keep petting, Amelia's resistance began to slip. "If—and that's a big if—I agree to keep the dog, I don't have anything she might need."

"Have no fear. I picked up bowls, a collar and leash, and even a little bit of food from Levi."

Amelia tapped her foot but continued stroking the dog. "You were awfully confident in your selling abilities, weren't you? You figured that once I saw this pitiful little puppy, I would be filled with compassion and love and immediately embrace her as my own."

Ryan looked contrite for a moment before brightening and smiling. "Was I right? Do you have compassion and love for this fantastic canine specimen?"

Amelia laughed and bent to hug the dog, burying her face in the soft fur.

"Does this mean the answer is yes? You'll accept my gift?"

"What will you do if my answer is *nee?*"

Ryan shrugged. "Is that what you're saying?"

Amelia hesitated. It might be kind of fun to watch him squirm a little. She had actually made up her mind when she first stroked the little dog's head. It had been love at first sight. The mutt reminded her so much of a beloved pet her family had owned during her growing-up years that it would have been impossible to turn her back on her. Besides, those big, brown eyes melted any opposition she tried to muster.

Ryan didn't know any of that, but somehow, he found a dog that truly did tug at her heart. Or maybe the dog found him. Maybe it had been the Lord *Gott's* will for Ryan to stop at Levi Wheeler's place this evening. Amelia believed the Lord cared about all His creatures, so linking her with this animal just might have been His plan. She might have been wrong before. Maybe the Lord did care if she got a dog.

"Amelia?"

"You never answered my earlier question. What was your plan if I said I couldn't accept the dog?"

"I really didn't have a plan, but I suppose I would keep her. I couldn't bear to see her go to the shelter, and I know Levi has his hands full with the two new litters from his dogs. I don't know how I would manage one more thing to do, but I suppose I could figure out something."

"It's a very *gut* thing you won't have to do that."

"What? Do I dare get my hopes up that you will keep this wonderful doggie?"

Amelia laughed. "You don't have to keep pleading her case. I will take her. I'm not sure where I'll keep her though. With winter almost here, she'll need a warm place to sleep."

"What about the barn?"

"If the horses and goats will accept her."

"They probably wouldn't mind sharing their quarters with one more critter. I've been meaning to ask you why you have two small goats."

"Ugh! Me and my too-soft heart. They are pygmy goats that I acquired quite by accident. We were at the produce auction more than a year ago. A man there had the goats and wanted to sell them. Rhonda and Judith were convinced someone would take them and eat them. The girls knew people raised pigs and cows to eat, so they assumed the goats were doomed." Amelia paused to give the dog another pat. "They cried and raised such a ruckus that the man *gave* me the goats to appease them. I was so embarrassed."

Ryan threw back his head and laughed. "I can picture that, only I see Gabby doing the same thing as your girls."

"I didn't have any idea what I was going to do with two little goats, but they trotted home with us, and as you can see, they are still here. They are part of the family now."

"And I've just added another animal to your menagerie."

"*Jah*. I suppose I'm a pushover when it *kumms* right down to it."

Ryan squeezed her arm. "I'd call it sensitive, compassionate, loving—all great qualities."

Heat rushed into Amelia's cheeks. Her heart did a strange little flip-flop. Every nerve from her head to her toes tingled from his compliment and his touch.

"*Mamm!*"

Ryan dropped his hand so fast it slapped against his leg. "It looks like we've been discovered."

Guilt washed over Amelia, even though she didn't have any reason to justify that emotion. She glanced over her shoulder. "What's wrong, Rhonda?" Her slight movement must have given the little girl a clear view of the brown dog sitting at Amelia's feet.

"A dog!" Rhonda flew down the steps with Judith and Gabby on her heels. Joanna brought up the rear calling, "Doggie, doggie!"

"*Kumm* see our new dog, girls."

Ryan lowered his voice. "Are you sure about this?"

"I can't back out now." Amelia smiled, first at Ryan and then at the girls. "Did you all finish your supper?"

Four heads nodded.

"Our dog? Really?" Rhonda's eyes grew as large as saucers. She ran the last few steps and skidded to a stop at Amelia's side. She reached a hand toward the dog but quickly withdrew it. "Can I pet him?"

"Her. And *jah*, you may pet her. She's very friendly."

Rhonda laid a tentative hand on the curly brown head. "She's so soft. See, Judith?"

Judith had held back as if afraid of the dog. At her *schweschder's* encouragement, she stepped forward and received a lick on the hand as she stroked the pup. Gabby and Joanna followed in Judith's footsteps.

Christina hurried over carrying Jessie. She looked from Ryan to the dog to Amelia. She raised her eyebrows but didn't give voice to her question.

Jill ran out the door to catch up with everyone else. "They all ate their supper, Amelia. Oh! What an adorable dog. It's a good thing I didn't bring Casey, after all."

Indeed. The chaos would have been even greater if that was possible. Amelia still couldn't believe she had agreed to take the dog. Like Ryan, she already had more than enough to keep her busy, but her heart wouldn't let her refuse this lovable mutt.

*Good grief, Amelia. First the goats, and now a dog. What's next—an elephant?*

The dog soaked up the attention showered on her by the little girls and the adults. Christina and Jill acted almost as excited as the *kinner*.

"What is her name?" Jill looked at the girls and then at Amelia, who looked at Ryan.

"Levi said the dog didn't have any collar, so I guess you can choose whatever name you like," Ryan answered.

"Meggie." The wee voice was scarcely more than a murmur.

"What did you say, Judith?" Amelia cupped a hand to her ear to let the little girl know to speak louder.

"Meggie. She looks like Meggie."

Rhonda clapped her hands and jumped up from petting the dog. "She does. Remember the book, *Mamm*?"

"I do. And you're right." Amelia laughed at the other adults' puzzled expressions. "I read the girls a library book— over and over again, mind you—about three *schweschders* who had a little brown dog named Meggie."

"Can we call her Meggie?" Rhonda asked.

"Sure. It might take her a while to learn her name since it's new to her." Amelia didn't want the girls to expect the dog to answer to the name right away.

"She's smart. She'll learn fast." Rhonda spoke as if she was an authority on dogs. To prove her point, she trotted off a short distance, stopped, and called out, "Meggie!"

The little dog leaped to her feet and ran to Rhonda with her tail wagging.

"Well, I'll be!" Jill exclaimed. "It looks like Meggie is the perfect name for her."

"Can we get a dog too?" Gabby tugged on Ryan's pant leg.

Amelia chuckled at the helpless glance he threw her. She would try to help him out. "You'll be able to play with Meggie five days a week. That's almost the same as owning your own dog."

"Sure." Ryan hurried to agree, apparently afraid Gabby would whine and pout. "You can play with the dog, brush her, and even help feed her if that's all right with Amelia."

"Okay." Gabby's sad expression turned hopeful. "But can we get a dog one day?"

"Maybe one day." Ryan hugged his daughter. "How about if you go get your things and help clean up any mess you made so we can go home?"

"Since the girls have eaten, would you like to have some supper? Or if you'd prefer, I can send a plate home with you." Amelia chomped on her tongue as soon as the words left her mouth. Would Christina and Jill get the wrong idea? Would they think Ryan often shared meals with her?

"I'm sure I've been more than enough trouble today." Ryan rubbed a hand over his face. "I was so late you probably thought I had abandoned my children. I brought you an unwanted gift that you felt compelled to accept. I've kept you out in the cold for way too long. And I've caused all sorts of bedlam."

Amelia shrugged and smiled. "It's just another day at the Stauffer house."

"Somehow, I think not. You are the most organized person I've ever met. Thank you for your kind offer, but I have the food that Sarah sent home." He winked and whispered, "Don't tell Sarah, but your casserole is ever so much better."

Certainly, the heat that crawled up Amelia's neck and across her cheeks translated into a red stain that Christina and Jill wouldn't be able to miss. And they wouldn't hesitate to ask her about it later either. How would she explain that?

# Chapter Twenty-Two

After much explaining and cajoling, Amelia managed to convince the girls that Meggie would not be happy sleeping with them. They had introduced the little dog to Mimi and Rudy, the two pygmy goats who would be her roommates, but the meeting had not gone as well as Amelia had hoped.

The goats were a bit squeamish about a newcomer invading their territory. Christina, who had more experience with animals, assured them the animals would adjust in due time, but Amelia had qualms about leaving the pup alone with two perturbed goats.

Jill suggested putting the dog's bed in a protected corner on the front porch, which seemed fine until Amelia remembered someone had stolen a large basket from the porch. She wouldn't want anything to happen to the gentle, trusting puppy.

In the end, even though Amelia had previously declared there would be no animals in the house, Meggie's bed and bowls had been tucked into a corner of the mudroom. She hoped the dog did not bark or whine all night and would not make a mess of the place.

With the dog and the girls finally settled, the three young women could sit and chat for a while before they grew too tired. Amelia had a feeling she wouldn't be able to hold her eyes open for very long. They gathered around the kitchen table since that room was still toasty warm.

"I was going to bring a frozen pizza but didn't know if you had a freezer," Jill said. "Then I thought about microwave popcorn, but I knew you didn't have a microwave. So, I settled for..." She paused and reached into a plastic grocery bag. "Ta-da!" She pulled out a bag of potato chips, a bag of pretzels, and a large package of cream-filled chocolate cookies. "No pajama party is complete without junk food. I even brought a liter of soda."

"Ugh! It is junk food. I rarely bring that stuff into the house." Amelia was glad the girls had gone to bed so they wouldn't beg for the treats.

"But you do bake cookies, cakes, and whoopie pies," Jill pointed out. "I've eaten a lot of your baked goods at The Green Thumb."

"True enough. And those things are junk food too, but I know I only used *gut*, fresh ingredients. Somehow it doesn't seem like junk when you make it yourself."

"So, splurge a little. You can pig out tonight and eat healthy tomorrow."

"Pig out?"

Jill laughed. "It's what we non-Amish call gorging on an assortment of food until we think our stomachs will explode."

Amelia shook her head. "That doesn't sound like fun."

Christina reached for the pretzel bag. "I have to confess. I love pretzels."

Jill opened the potato chip bag. "I'll start with the chips. I guess that leaves the cookies for you, Amelia."

"I think I'll get cups and pour the soda. You two are going to get awfully thirsty eating all that salt." Amelia shuffled to the cupboard. A little soda might settle her stomach.

She'd been a bundle of nerves waiting for one of the others to mention her conversation with Ryan.

Amelia carried two cups to the table. "You know, Jill, it seems a little strange."

"What does?" Jill shook dark curls out of her face and licked the salt from an index finger.

"You brought all this high-calorie, high-fat food and diet soda."

Jill laughed. "I have to cut calories somewhere."

"Like you need to do that." Christina reached for another handful of mini pretzels.

"We're all skinny, so we can indulge without guilt." Jill gulped her soda. "Come on, Amelia."

"I need to get my soda. I'm more thirsty than hungry."

"You hardly ate anything for supper," Christina mumbled as she chewed.

Amelia shrugged. "Some days my appetite isn't so great. I was more concerned with getting the girls fed anyway."

"And their dad?" Jill winked and smiled.

*Here it comes!* Amelia poured her own soda and slurped the foam. The bubbles burned her throat and made her eyes water. She took her time returning to the table. "I merely asked if he'd like a plate of food since his girls had already eaten. That way, he wouldn't have to worry about cooking for himself." She reached for the bag of cookies. Not because she wanted one, but because she needed to do something with her hands.

"I'm sure it must be as hard to be a single *daed* as it is to be a single *mudder*. And I'm sure you have been a big help to Ryan Miller." Christina patted Amelia's arm.

"I try. We all need help now and then. Unfortunately, some of us need more than others."

"If you are referring to yourself, my *freind*, people are happy to help you out too."

"I know. It's just that I feel like a bother sometimes. The men have to take turns doing heavy outdoor chores, and—"

Christina held up a hand. "We've been through this before. You are not a bother to anyone. We all help each other."

"Hey! I've got a great idea!" Jill smacked the table with her palm and then had to steady her teetering cup. She looked Amelia straight in the eye. "Why don't you and Ryan get together? You seem to like each other, and you have a lot in common."

Amelia gasped and snapped the cookie in half. "I-I... that's impossible." Heat rushed from her toes to her face. Her heart pounded so hard it made her stomach queasy.

"Why is it impossible? You're both single. You both have girls of about the same age and seem to adore children. You're both Mennonites." Jill reached for the cookie fragments in front of Amelia and popped them into her mouth.

"B-but we-we..." Her brain couldn't seem to give her mouth any messages. Amelia looked to Christina for help.

Christina laid down the pretzel she was about to eat. "We're different kinds of Mennonites. You saw Ryan drive up in his vehicle, ain't so? You know *we* don't own cars. We converse in two languages, while Ryan speaks only *Englisch*. He uses electricity, and we do not."

Jill held up a hand. "Those things aren't big deals. Either he can start driving a horse-drawn buggy and learning your language or Amelia can learn to drive a car and use modern conveniences. If your basic beliefs are the same, love can overcome the other issues."

"L-love?" The room spun. The heat Amelia felt a few minutes ago dissipated. Now, ice flowed through her veins. Was she about to faint?

"Are you all right?" Christina shook Amelia's arm. "You're as white as the cream in that cookie Jill just stole from you."

"I'm sorry, Amelia. I wasn't trying to upset you. Sometimes my mouth runs away with itself." Jill smiled and patted Amelia's other arm.

"I'm fine. You shocked me. That's all."

"I didn't mean to do that. I don't know all the details about your beliefs. It just seemed to me that you and Ryan would make a great couple. You seem fond of each other and could help each other a lot. I didn't intend to be nosy or rude."

Amelia didn't know if she felt more like throwing up or passing out. The conversation had become so much worse than she'd anticipated. She wished she had convinced Jill to stay home, though she knew the girl didn't mean any harm. *Englischers* seemed to speak their minds so freely. She barely noticed Christina's tightened grip on her arm.

"We know you aren't the nosy sort," Christina said. "Your points might be valid in your world, but we Mennonites don't jump from one group to another. There are repercussions for leaving our church."

A faint whimper from the mudroom brought Amelia to her feet. Did the little dog sense Amelia needed a diversion at this very moment? "I'd better see what's wrong with her." She fled the room but still heard snippets of the conversation continuing behind her.

"That sounds rather harsh. Surely some sort of compromise could be reached if two people really cared about each other."

"It's the way things have always been," Christina replied.

"Doesn't anyone protest and try to change things? It would be so sad if two people had to sacrifice their happiness because of some rule."

Amelia wanted to cover her ears with her hands. How had the conversation taken such a turn? Jill was a *gut* person, but she didn't understand. Much of their lives probably made little sense to an *Englischer*.

Amelia closed the mudroom door behind her. The dog wagged her tail in double time. "What's wrong, girl? Why were you crying?"

Amelia wanted to cry too. She slid along the wall until her behind hit the floor. Immediately, the dog sidled up to her and dropped her head onto Amelia's lap. "Were you lonely, Meggie?" Amelia stroked the curly fur. "Life is strange, isn't it?" The pup shook her head as if in agreement.

What had given Jill the idea that she and Ryan cared about each other? Had there been some expression on their faces to give that impression? Amelia tried to replay their encounter in her mind. She and Ryan had been cordial, as always. She did offer to prepare a plate for him, but anyone else would have done the same, wouldn't they? No woman would send a person away hungry.

Amelia stared into the dog's big, brown eyes. "You were there. What did you see?" Her tumbling heart and tingling nerves at Ryan's smile would not have been observable to any bystander. Maybe one or both of them had given some unintentional cue that they were happy to see one another. How embarrassing!

Christina's words left a hollow space in her heart. "That's the way things have always been," she'd said. And what was done in the past would continue to be done forever. Yet, Jill's words stirred a little fire in her soul. Why couldn't two faithful, caring people transcend ancient rules?

"He doesn't love me, does he?" Meggie's ears pricked up at Amelia's whisper. The little dog swiped her tongue across Amelia's bare forearm. "Is that your answer?" She leaned over to press her cheek against the soft fur. "Do I love him?" This time, Meggie gave Amelia a doggie kiss on the cheek. She jerked up and wiped the moisture off with the back of her hand. "Are you smiling at me, Meggie? Are you trying to tell me you're the expert on love?"

"Amelia?"

Yikes! Did anyone hear her whispered questions to her four-legged *freind*? "Jah?"

Christina poked her head into the mudroom. "Are you okay?"

"Sure. This little mutt was lonely in her new home, so I decided to sit with her for a minute."

"You've been in here for fifteen minutes."

"I have? I'm sorry. I lost track of time. What a lousy hostess I am!" She gave the dog a final pat before scrambling to her feet.

"I'm sorry if we upset you with all that talk about Ryan Miller."

Amelia waved a hand in dismissal. She certainly did not want to rehash any of that confusing, embarrassing conversation. "I'm not upset."

"You ran out of the kitchen like your backside was on fire."

Amelia laughed. "I heard the dog whimper and wanted to make sure she hadn't been destroying the place. I know it's silly, but I didn't want her to be lonely or scared."

"It's not silly at all. You are a very caring person. I was afraid you were angry or upset. Jill doesn't understand our ways. I suppose in her world, couples are free to pursue a relationship regardless of their faith or background."

"Maybe. But why assume that Ryan Miller and I even want to pursue a relationship? I watch his girls while he works, and I occasionally send food home to help them out. There isn't anything wrong with that, is there?"

"Of course not. I think Jill wants to play matchmaker."

"Why does everyone want to marry me off? Annie tries to throw her cousin at me every chance she gets. Jill wants to pair me with a man who is clearly off-limits. No one seems to understand that I'm perfectly fine as I am." Amelia bit her tongue. She hadn't meant to vent.

"Of course you are. I don't think anyone means any harm. They imagine how difficult it must be to run a household alone and want to help."

Amelia sighed. "I know. I didn't mean to spout off. I'd better go tend to my guest."

"I'm sure she's happy collecting crumbs from the potato chip bag."

"Crumbs? Is that all that's left of a family-sized bag of chips?"

"I'm afraid so."

"Oh my! Let's go rescue her from herself."

"Are you sure you're all right?"

"I'm sure." Amelia glanced over her shoulder and shook a finger. "You behave, Meggie." She followed Christina back to the kitchen where Jill had, indeed, just polished off the entire bag of chips. "It's empty?"

Jill hung her head. "Guilty. I hope you didn't want any."

# Chapter Twenty-Three

After receiving word from the police that the smoke bomb incident had been instigated by a few rowdy teenagers, Amelia breathed easier. The police officers had even gotten the teens to admit they had previously been on her property so they could smoke and drink without being seen. They had decided to try making a smoke bomb and setting it off at her house because they believed a Mennonite would not press charges against them. According to the officer who had stopped to give her the news, the teens were now in trouble with the law and with their parents.

Amelia was relieved to know the cigarette she had found had probably belonged to the young *Englisch* boys and not to some other intruder intending to harm her or her animals. She hoped their parents would keep a better watch over them from now on. The teens said they had not stolen anything from her, and she no longer believed her family was in any danger. Perhaps her quilt and other items truly had been taken by someone who needed such things. She even managed to convince her *freinden* that she and the girls would be fine so they could all resume their normal lives. Now she needed to establish routines with the newest member of her family and convince her she was an outdoor dog.

It took a few days and a few repeated introductions, but Mimi and Rudy finally accepted Meggie into their little kingdom. Of course, the dog continued to receive lots of attention, including being allowed access to the house on occasion. Gabby and Jessie loved playing with the pup as much as Amelia's own girls did, and Gabby continued to beg for a pet of her own.

Amelia had great difficulty looking Ryan in the eye after Jill's observations. Had he picked up on any unconscious signals she might have sent the way Jill had done? She fidgeted and kept conversations brief and then worried she might have hurt his feelings. She missed the easy camaraderie they had shared, and she accepted full responsibility for the change.

But she didn't like the distance between them one bit. She needed to find a way to put silly notions of romance out of her head. She was too old to entertain any infatuations. There must be a way she and Ryan could simply be *freinden*. Nothing more. Ever. Surely, she could manage that. She resolved to greet him with a smile and cheerful expression this very evening when he picked up his girls. And she would look him in the eye and stop all the nonsense.

~

Ryan almost missed the turn to his own place of work. His mind replayed his latest encounter with Amelia. She was the same kind, lovely woman as always, but somehow, she was different, more aloof. No. Aloof made him think of cold and disinterested, words he would never use to describe Amelia Stauffer. Hesitant might be a better word. Or nervous. But why would she be nervous around him? He thought they had worked through that stage long ago.

He had brought Gabby and Jessie inside her home the same as always. He chatted about his morning and the girls' antics like usual. But her responses had been brief, and she had refused to make eye contact. Ryan shuffled through his file of memories. He couldn't recall any conversation that would have upset her. Yet, he must have done or said something. He missed gazing into her beautiful blue eyes, but she had kept her gaze averted the entire time he stood before her.

Perhaps she hadn't been feeling well. Her face had been rather pale, making her pin-prick freckles stand out. She could have simply been tired. She certainly worked hard enough, caring for the children and the whole place by herself. She most likely was not sleeping well either with thoughts of a mysterious prowler haunting her. He needed to get her to talk to him, to look at him. He'd like to help her, but he needed to know the problem.

"Were you figuring on getting out of the car and working today?" Norman slapped his own leg and hee-hawed.

Ryan could hear his boss even though his window was closed. He hadn't even noticed that Norman had driven up and gotten out of his own vehicle. "I'm fixing to right now." He unfastened his seat belt and had only barely opened the door before Norman spoke again.

"I sure hope you didn't run over anybody on the road."

"Of course I didn't. I didn't hear any thumps anyway."

"I doubt you would have heard it. You must be about a million miles away."

Nope. Only a few miles. "Sometimes I do my best thinking when I drive. You know, no little voices calling from the back seat."

"You must have been considering some mighty weighty matters. I thought you'd decided to work in your car today or catch a little nap before going inside."

"I'm coming."

"Did you at least solve all the problems in the universe?"

"I can't even solve my own problems."

Norman chuckled. "Come have some coffee. I think Sarah miscounted her scoops this morning. This stuff is strong enough to leap over the moon and back."

"Motor oil, huh?"

"Just about. It ought to get you jump-started."

"That or have me too wired to think straight."

"You're already that."

"All right. All right. Let's get to it."

~

Amelia peeked at the kitchen wall clock. Ryan would arrive any minute to retrieve his *kinner*. She had already collected the girls' belongings and had everything ready to go. She wiped her damp palms down the sides of her dress and tried to figure out why she was so nervous. Her goal to act natural was in serious jeopardy. She crossed the room to stir the pot of soup that didn't need stirring, but she couldn't keep still. She had to keep her hands busy. If only she could find something to think about other than Ryan Miller.

If she ladled soup into a container for him to take home, would that give him the wrong impression, like she was chasing after him? She had never questioned her motives before. She had always sent food home because she wanted to make life a little easier for him and the girls. Now she suddenly worried her actions could be misconstrued as chasing after him. She cringed at the thought.

Perhaps Christina had been mistaken. The girl was so besotted with Noah Zimmerman that she probably thought she saw signs of romance everywhere, even between two people who hadn't any romantic notions about each other whatsoever. Did they? Of course they didn't!

A yip and a bark outside drew Amelia from her reverie. Ryan must have arrived. Meggie had proven to be a *gut* informer. Amelia tapped her wooden spoon on the side of the soup pot and laid it on the spoon rest. She peeked outside in time to catch Ryan petting the dog and smiled. What a likable little pup—and man. She shook her head. She needed to think only about the animal, not the human.

Amelia hurried to the back door to open it a crack before he knocked. Meggie had the idea that she should dwell inside the house with the rest of the family and tried to wiggle inside every chance she got. "Can you squeeze past Meggie?"

"I'll try."

"We're still working on the 'doggie stays outside' lesson."

"Aw, but look at that face. She wants to be with you and the girls."

"Trust me, we spend lots of time with her. The girls always want to go out to play with her."

"Is she working out okay?"

"It's only been a couple of days, but I'd say she's already one of the family." If they kept talking about the dog or the weather, she might be able to look at the man and pretend he meant nothing special to her. Wait a minute! He didn't mean anything special to her.

Ryan patted her arm. "I'm glad. And I'm also glad you aren't angry with me for bringing her here."

His light touch undid her resolutions. Her arm tingled from her shoulder to her fingertips. If she looked into those dark brown eyes now, she would be lost. "I'm not angry." How could she be upset with this gentle man, who only thought he was helping her? "I'm sorry if I gave the impression that I was."

"You didn't actually appear angry this morning, but I sensed you were upset. All day I prayed I hadn't done anything to cause you grief."

"You didn't. I was a bit, uh, preoccupied."

"Is something wrong?"

"Everything is fine."

"You haven't had any more nocturnal visitors, have you?"

Amelia laughed and ventured a peek at his face. "Only Christina and Jill. I believe I've convinced them they don't need to babysit us any longer."

Ryan smiled that smile that practically melted her heart. "They care about you and the girls. We all do."

She saw kindness and concern in his eyes. But she glimpsed something else too. Something deeper that touched her soul. She had to look away, walk away, or do something to break the spell he'd cast over her. "Oh! I need to check on my soup."

She rushed to the stove and lifted the lid off the pot. She welcomed the steam that rushed out to sting her eyes. She could attribute her flush to the vapors from the bubbling liquid. "Would you like to take some soup home? I have plenty."

Amelia heard his footsteps and sensed his presence behind her, but she couldn't turn around. Her nerves twitched, and goose bumps raced along her arms. If he touched her again, she might very well jump out of her skin.

"You're always taking care of us, Amelia. You do so much for the girls all day and then try to lighten my load in the evenings. I appreciate all that you do. I only wish I could do something for you."

Amelia stirred the soup so vigorously that it almost splashed out onto the stove. "You allow me the pleasure of caring for your *dochders*. They are delightful, and I enjoy every minute with them."

"Is their father delightful too?"

Had he really asked that? Was he teasing? How should she respond? She turned just enough to glimpse his face and burst out laughing. He had crossed his eyes and stuck out his tongue. "Oh my! That is by far the most delightful face I've ever seen."

Ryan uncrossed his eyes and smiled. "I like to hear you laugh. I—"

"Hi, Daddy." Gabby raced across the room and threw herself at the big man, who was staring at Amelia.

He looked down when the little girl tugged on his pant leg. He scooped her up into his arms. "How is my big girl?" He tickled her until she giggled.

"Do you know what we did today?"

"I do not, but I'm certain you will tell me."

"We played and we helped clean, and we baked pretzels."

"Pretzels?"

"The big, fat, soft ones with salt on them."

Amelia placed the lid on the pot. "It's a *gut* thing you mentioned that, Gabby. The pretzels completely slipped my mind. I would have forgotten to give them to you to take home." A lot of things seemed to slip her mind lately, especially when she was in the presence of Ryan Miller. She had already wrapped the pretzels in plastic wrap and only needed to lay them in a bag. "Would you like some soup too?"

"Can we, Daddy? It smells good."

"It does smell delicious, but we have Sarah's casserole at home."

"I'd rather have soup."

"How about if I ladle soup into a small container for you to take home to eat with your casserole?" Amelia pulled a plastic bowl and lid off the shelf.

"Okay. Can we have our pretzels too, Daddy?"

"Of course, unless your belly is too full after the soup and casserole." He tickled her again, making her giggle and squirm.

"We made one for you too," Gabby said between gasps.

"Here, Gabby. You can put these pretzels in a bag while I get the soup." Amelia held out three big pretzels.

Ryan set the little girl on the floor so she could help.

"See?" Gabby held a pretzel up for her dad to inspect. "They're a little lop-lop...What is the word?"

Amelia smiled. "Lopsided, but they will taste fine anyway."

Gabby gingerly placed each pretzel in the bag Amelia had given her and left the bag on the table. "I'll help Rhonda, Judith, and Joanna pick up the toys." She scampered off to the living room, where she had been playing with the others.

"She's such a *gut* girl. She's always so helpful."

"She certainly tries. Now, what can I do for you?"

Amelia pressed the lid on the container of soup. "I'm fine. Your soup is all ready for you."

"I mean, isn't there something I can do around here to lighten your load a little? You do so much to make my life easier."

"I'm keeping up with things in the house." Amelia gazed around the room. He didn't think she was a poor house-keeper, did he?"

"I don't mean in your house. It's always immaculate."

"With winter approaching, outside work has dwindled, and various men in the community take turns with those chores."

Ryan shifted from foot to foot like a nervous scholar about to recite a lesson. "Okay. It sounds like the work is taken care of, but I'd like to do something special." He placed a hand on her arm.

"That isn't necessary." Her arm tingled at his touch.

"Can we all go to town again and get ice cream? That was fun."

Amelia stepped out of Ryan's reach. When had Gabby returned to the room? Evidently, that trip had been as mem-orable for Gabby as it had been for Amelia. "That was a special occasion, Gabby dear. Your *daed* needed my help with something. That's the real reason we all went to town." She couldn't let the little girl think it was appropriate for them to go on outings together.

"But Gabby has the right idea." Ryan snapped his fingers. His handsome face brightened, and crinkly lines fanned out at the edges of his eyes. "Fun! We all need to have a little fun. What should we do?"

# Chapter Twenty-Four

Amelia's mouth dropped open. She stared at the two excited faces in front of her. What was Ryan thinking? They couldn't go gallivanting around the county like one big, happy family.

That one innocent little jaunt they took last summer had plagued her ever since. True, she only accompanied Ryan because he needed help purchasing the right things for his girls, but she probably should have written down suggestions for him.

It had been a fun evening though. But her mind had played silly tricks on her, encouraging her to fantasize they were a family out for the evening. Thankfully, only Christina, Noah, and Jill had witnessed that little adventure and so far, they had kept mum about it.

Amelia closed her mouth. Ryan and Gabby waited for her to say something. "I-I don't think that will be possible."

"Please?" Gabby jumped up and down.

Amelia's own *kinner* trooped into the kitchen, with Jessie crawling along behind them. Great! The begging and pleading could begin in earnest.

Gabby turned to Rhonda and Judith. "Wasn't it fun when we all went to town?"

Rhonda acted as the spokesperson. "*Jah*, we walked in the shops and got ice cream cones."

"Do you want to do it again?"

"*Jah! Jah!*" Rhonda and Judith cried together.

"Me too!" Joanna jumped up and down.

"Girls!" Amelia used a stern voice. "Calm down. We are not going out for ice cream or anywhere else. We will be having supper very soon, so you need to pick up your toys." She hated being the voice of reason that disappointed them. Their little faces, which had been so hopeful and excited a moment ago, now displayed utter dejection. Maybe she would take them into town one afternoon for ice cream.

"Gabby, go help clean up." Ryan shooed his older daughter off and scooped Jessie into his arms. "I'm so sorry. I didn't mean to get the girls all excited. We can always do something else for fun. I suppose it's too cold for picnics, but we could go for a hike—or wait! I know!" He snapped his fingers. "We could gather greenery to make Christmas wreaths. Do you usually make those?"

"I do. I sometimes make them for Christina's store, but—"

"Why couldn't we make an outing of collecting the materials?"

"I don't think that's a very *gut* idea." It pained Amelia to say those words. In her mind, she saw the girls running around laughing while she and Ryan selected the right plants for the wreaths. They would return home with rosy cheeks and tingling fingers and would enjoy cocoa and oatmeal cookies.

She needed to end that little fantasy right there. An outing with Ryan would not be looked upon favorably. Amelia had been grateful her previous transgression had gone unnoticed by the bishop.

Ryan's hand on her arm brought Amelia back to the present. Did the man have any idea what havoc his touch wreaked on her senses, her emotions, her thoughts? It awakened that part of herself she had buried with Jeremiah, that part that was woman and not *mudder*. She couldn't look up. Instead, she focused on his large, gentle hand.

"Think about doing something fun with the girls. We both work so hard taking care of our homes and families that we don't do anything simply for fun. Fun is okay, you know. We all need to lighten up occasionally."

"I understand that, but it would not be right for us to be together."

Ryan bounced Jessie on his hip. "We'd have plenty of chaperones."

Amelia giggled. "We would indeed, but we aren't the same. It's fine for me to watch your girls, but anything else would be frowned upon." She knew her cheeks must have gone from red to scarlet. A sudden mortifying thought occurred to her. What if he had been talking about an outing for the girls and nothing to do with the two of them? He might not have been hinting at a relationship between the two of them at all.

"Do you mean because you're Old Order Mennonite and I'm not?"

Amelia could only nod. She didn't trust her voice to speak without cracking and giving away her feelings.

He lowered his voice to a whisper. "You know there is something between us too, don't you? I mean, it isn't only me who feels happy when we're in the same room. I'm not the only one who looks forward to our next encounter, am I?"

Amelia stared at her freshly scrubbed linoleum floor. If only the floor would open and swallow her. She tried to hold back her words, but they whooshed out on her next exhalation. "It is not only you." She immediately covered her face with her hands. How could she have admitted such a thing? She sensed he scooted closer, but she was too embarrassed to peek between her fingers.

"Amelia, look at me."

She couldn't. "Forget I said anything. Please."

"Can you forget your feelings?"

"I can try. At least, I can decide not to act on them."

"Perhaps in your head, but what will your heart tell you?"

Amelia stepped back to put a little more space between them. "I have to ignore my heart."

"I'm not so sure I can do that."

"We have to. It's the right thing to do."

"Right for whom? Can't we figure out a way to spend more time together to see if the feelings we have are true?"

"We see each other twice a day five days a week."

"Ten minutes here. Ten minutes there. Can't we add a little to that?"

"I'm afraid that isn't possible." She meant to take only a quick glance at his face but couldn't look away from the tenderness and caring in his eyes.

"Doesn't the Bible say all things are possible with God?"

"*Mamm, Mamm!* We've cleaned up everything. We're ready for supper." Rhonda raced into the kitchen, followed by the three younger girls.

Amelia tore her gaze from Ryan's expressive brown eyes and turned toward the *kinner.* She swallowed the lump that had formed in her throat. "*Danki,* girls. Supper will be ready in a few minutes."

Ryan cleared his throat as if he, too, needed to choke down a boulder. "We need to get home and leave you to your supper."

"Can't we eat here, Daddy?"

"Gabby, it is not polite to invite yourself to someone else's supper."

"I-it's okay. I have plenty." *Please let him say they can't stay.* It wasn't that Amelia didn't want to be with the man and his girls. She did. Too much. That was the problem.

"We need to do some things at home, Gabby."

"What things?"

"I need to wash clothes because I know two little girls who dirty up a lot of dresses. We need to eat supper and take baths, and that takes a long time."

"If we ate here, we wouldn't have to do that at home."

Amelia and Ryan both laughed. Amelia reached to hug the little girl. "You have a very logical mind."

"What?"

Ryan patted his daughter's shoulder. "That means you think things out and come up with solutions."

"Oh. Can we stay?"

"We've already discussed this, Gabby. We've taken up enough of Amelia's time. She has things to do too."

"We can help."

"You can help me tomorrow, dear." Amelia hoped that didn't sound like she was throwing them out.

"Okay."

"Logical and agreeable. Those are *gut* traits." Amelia smiled at the four-year-old. "Do you think you can carry this bag with the soup and pretzels? It's a little heavy."

"*Jah*. I can carry it. I'm strong."

Amelia's gaze shot to Ryan's face. "I'm really not teaching her the language."

"I believe you. She picks things up pretty quickly. I don't mind if you teach them both Pennsylvania Deutsch. Then they can teach me. You never know when I might need to use it." He winked at Amelia, causing her cheeks to heat again. "Let's go, girls." He paused at the door. "Think about what I said, Amelia. God can work wonders."

~

Amelia's hope for a better night's sleep since the smoke bomb incident had been resolved fell by the wayside. Her concern about intruders now took a backseat to her quandary over her conversation with Ryan. She settled into the old, oak rocker near the living room woodstove and pulled a crocheted afghan up to her chin. Maybe the gentle motion of the chair would help her relax.

She should have picked up her knitting bag or grabbed some items from the overflowing mending basket, but she didn't. She closed her eyes and rocked. But squeezing her eyes shut did not obliterate the images burned on her brain or the words that echoed through its chambers. Tears sprang into her eyes at the memory of Ryan's sincerity.

All things are possible with *Gott*. She knew that. But was it the Lord *Gott's* will for them to meet and have these special feelings for each other? If He wanted her to remarry, wouldn't He lead her to one of her own people? How could a relationship with Ryan possibly work out? Although they were similar in many ways, they were far different in others. She almost giggled at the thought of driving a car and taking down every mailbox she passed. *Nee*, riding a bike and driving a horse-drawn buggy were quite enough for her.

She couldn't picture Ryan driving a buggy either. Would he be willing to give up his electric lights, appliances, telephone, and automobile to do things the old way?

That would be asking a lot. But one of them would have to change if they hoped to pursue any relationship other than what they had right now.

*Ach, Amelia, don't be ridiculous. You are behaving like a scholar with a crush on the fellow across the aisle.* She shook her head. Neither needed to change. She would carry on with her *kinner* the same as always. She would clean and cook and make baskets and bake for Christina's store. She had more than enough to occupy her mind and her time. She didn't need to entertain foolish notions about romance, even if the man in question did have the most beautiful brown eyes she'd ever seen.

Amelia leaned her head against the rocker's high back. She should have gone to bed, but she was so cozy beneath the heavy afghan that she didn't want to move. She'd stay another minute or two and then climb the stairs to crawl into her cold bed.

A shrill yap and then continuous barking penetrated Amelia's dream of five little girls running through a field with their *mudder* and *daed*. She bolted upright. Meggie? She should be in the barn with Mimi, Ruby, and the horses. Why did her bark sound as if it came from right outside the house? Of course, the dog had access to the outside via a little swinging door Jeremiah had designed for a dog they'd had years ago, but Meggie always stayed in the warm barn. Did something happen to the door so she couldn't get back inside?

Amelia pushed to her feet and padded through the house to the back door. She stuffed her feet into an old pair of shoes left by the door and yanked a shawl from the hook. She grabbed the big flashlight off the shelf and the house key on a cord she could slip over her head. She wouldn't give some mischievous person a chance to enter her house, where her innocent *kinner* slept.

She yanked open the door to find Meggie running back and forth between the barn and the edge of the woods. What on earth was wrong with her? What was she trying to report in her doggie way?

Amelia turned toward the woods. A light bobbed through the trees as if someone was running away. She raced in that direction. Her fury that someone had come back to bother them again spurred her on. How dare this person think he could frighten her and steal her belongings! She started to call out but assumed the intruder wouldn't answer her, so she might as well save her breath. Who would keep doing this and why?

The light disappeared. Either the person had gotten too far ahead of her, or he'd switched off the light. Amelia bent over to catch her breath. Her heartbeat roared in her ears. Her calves burned, unused to sprinting. Meggie sat at her feet, barely even panting. "Easy. Jaunt. For. You. Huh,

Meggie?" Each word came out as a gasp. She patted her heaving chest. "I think he got away, Meggie. How did you know he was here?" She stared a few more moments into the blackness. "*Kumm* on, pup. Let's go to bed."

She walked this time instead of running at breakneck speed. Meggie trotted along beside her. What would she have done if she'd caught up with the interloper? It could have been some huge man, who towered over her. How would she have stood up to him? *Now is a fine time to think about that, Amelia.* One thing she did know was she was tired of pranks and intimidation.

"You did a fine job, Meggie." Amelia reached down to pet the curly fur. "But if you were sleeping in the barn, how did you know someone was prowling around?" Maybe Ryan had been right to bring her a watchdog after all. Although the gentle dog was not in the least menacing, she could at least warn of possible trouble, as she had done tonight.

"Are you going in through your doggie door or...wait! How did the big barn door get open? Had the intruder been snooping in there? She pushed the door open farther. What if someone was still inside? *Oh, for Pete's sake, Amelia. Use your head. You just ran through the woods after a possible maniac, and you're going to get squeamish about going inside your own barn?*

She swept the flashlight beam back and forth, trying to peer into the far corners of the barn. Meggie entered the barn without a bark or a growl, so everything must be okay. Amelia took her cue from the dog and paced the entire barn, shining her light into every stall and corner. The horses whinnied until she spoke soothing words to them. The goats raised their heads but couldn't be bothered to totally rouse from their slumber. At least the animals were fine.

Amelia couldn't detect anything out of place, nor did she notice anything missing, but she would need to do a more thorough investigation in the morning. "Here you go, Meggie. A few treats for being such a *gut* doggie." The pup happily accepted her treats and trotted to her bed in the corner.

She turned around three times and finally settled on an appropriate spot. Amelia smiled. "*Danki*, girl."

She hurried back to the house. Even though she had locked the door, she needed to assure herself that her girls were fine. She paused before opening the door to listen for any noise not germane to night sounds in the country. Satisfied that only an owl hooted in the distance, she entered the house and locked the door behind her. Who was behind all these strange happenings? Had she unintentionally done something to upset someone?

# Chapter Twenty-Five

"I don't understand it, Christina." Amelia shook her head. She glanced behind the counter at The Green Thumb, where her girls sat on a blanket playing with small wooden toys. She spoke softly even though she didn't believe the little ones would understand her words. The early Saturday morning shoppers had come and gone, so she used the lull to consult her *freind*.

"I can't believe someone dared to trespass again. What a lot of nerve!" Christina helped Amelia arrange the baked goods on the shelf. She stopped to plunk her fists on her thin hips. "What's more, I can't believe you went out there again, in the dark, by yourself. What were you thinking?"

"I wasn't thinking actually. I was reacting. But I had Meggie with me."

"She isn't exactly a ferocious beast. She'd probably shake hands and lick a person to death."

Amelia smiled. "It's true. She isn't a mean-spirited dog at all, but she is loyal and protective. At least her bark alerted me to a problem."

"That's one *gut* thing."

"What could the person be after? I don't have anything of great value. If they wanted a horse, they could have easily taken one the first time they came." Amelia shook her head. "I just don't get it."

"Shh! Customers." Christina stood on tiptoe to see over Amelia's head. "Worse. It's Elam and Annie."

Amelia crossed her eyes and wrinkled her nose, eliciting a giggle from Christina.

"We'll talk more after they leave. I hope this is a quick visit. I'll try to hurry them along."

"Christina!"

"Well, Elam can be annoying."

"That's putting it mildly." Amelia tried to relax so she would at least appear normal.

"Hi, Christina. Hi, Amelia. I told Elam I thought that was your buggy." Annie bounced into the store with her cousin on her heels.

"Hello, ladies." He addressed both but looked at Amelia.

"What can I do for you?" Christina donned her shop-keeper persona.

"Nothing. We were out and about and decided to stop in to say hello." Annie grinned at them.

Amelia suppressed a groan. Would they have stopped if her buggy hadn't been parked outside? She began shuffling the baked items around on the shelf to appear too busy for conversation.

"I understand you got a dog." Elam spoke behind her.

Amelia whirled around to face him. How did he know? She peeked at Christina, who shrugged her shoulders. "I did. She's a nice, little dog."

"Is she a *gut* guard dog?"

"I don't believe I need a guard dog, but I'm sure she will alert me to any trespassers or problems." She had no intention of informing him of last night's intruder.

"If you're still having any problems. I don't mind staying in your barn at night to see if we can catch the person."

"I don't think that will be necessary." Amelia cut her gaze over to where Christina chatted with Annie. She willed her *freind* to rescue her.

"I don't mind," Elam persisted. "You need a man around to deter trespassers."

"I manage fine," Amelia muttered through clenched teeth.

"Hey, Elam!" Christina called. "Could you bring in that crate of pumpkins out by the back greenhouse? It's a bit heavy for me, and I want to see if they are still *gut*."

"Sure."

Amelia sighed in relief when Elam trudged toward the door. She hoped the cousins would leave once he brought in the pumpkins. She scurried to the counter to check on her girls. Rhonda must have convinced her *schweschders* to play school. She smiled. At least something was normal in her life.

"Is everything okay with you?" Annie tapped Amelia's arm.

"Sure."

"Elam only wants to be helpful, you know. He doesn't mean any harm." She dropped her voice. "I know he can be annoying, but he's a decent fellow and wouldn't hurt a fly."

"I'm sure he's a *gut* person, but he needn't worry about us. We're fine."

Annie shrugged. "If you say so." She tapped her foot. "What is taking him so long to get that crate? We need to go."

"Do you have big plans today?" Christina asked.

"If you call running errands big plans, then I guess I do. *Mamm* has a whole list of things for me to do since I'm not working for my *onkle* today."

Christina smiled. "I'm sure you're a big help to her. How much longer does Elam plan to stay? He's been here a while now, ain't so?"

"Who knows how long he will be here? I haven't heard him say." She tapped her foot on the floor. "I wish he would hurry up so we can get these chores done."

Christina started for the door. "Maybe I should tell him to leave that crate if it's too heavy. I don't want him to hurt his back or anything."

Before Christina could make a move, the door opened. But it wasn't Elam who entered. The women halted their conversation and turned toward the newcomer.

"Hi, Naomi." Amelia smiled at the young brunette who was probably her own age but often acted much younger. She was relieved to have a brief reprieve from Elam's offers to help. "How was your trip?"

Naomi Brenneman blew a loose strand of wavy, brown hair off her face and shrugged. "It was okay, I guess. I mean, it was nice to visit cousins in Indiana, but I certainly wouldn't want to live there."

"Oh?" Christina shot Amelia a questioning glance.

"Do tell!" Annie scooted closer to Naomi as if afraid she might miss some juicy morsel of gossip.

Naomi huffed out a long, drawn-out, overly dramatic sigh. "There isn't much to tell, Annie. It was fun catching up with family, but there wasn't any reason for me to extend my visit. Alas, I am back home to my boring life. End of story." She laid the back of her hand against her forehead and pouted. She must have seen an *Englisch* movie somewhere along the line or else had some natural acting ability. She handed Christina several bills. "Here, I had a hankering for some of Amelia's treats to sweeten up my day. I've actually been home for a while, but I didn't make it to the latest church service. I've certainly missed these *wunderbaar* sweets." She plucked a package of oatmeal cookies and a chocolate whoopie pie off the shelf. "I'll talk to you all later." She swept out the door as quickly as she had entered.

Amelia, Christina, and Annie exchanged surprised looks and then stared out the window at Naomi's tall, solid form beating a hasty retreat.

Annie recovered her voice first. "What Naomi meant was she didn't find a husband in Indiana, so she resigned herself to returning to Maryland."

"Annie! Shame on you!" Amelia scolded.

Annie wrinkled her nose. "You two were thinking the very same thing. Don't try to deny it."

Christina burst out laughing. She clapped Annie on the shoulder. "We can always count on you to say whatever enters your mind without mincing any words."

"Well, you both know—everyone knows—that Naomi's goal in life is to snag some poor fellow who she can boss around. The men here are onto her, so she needs to look elsewhere."

"Now, there's the pot calling the kettle black." Christina winked. "You're looking for a husband too, Annie."

"But not to boss around." Annie shook a finger. "You know I'm not the bossy sort. I want a man who will appreciate all my fine qualities, who loves and cherishes me, who values my opinions, who—"

"Who puts up with your nonsense!" Christina interrupted the litany.

Amelia laughed. "You girls are too funny." She squeezed Annie's arm. "I'm sure the perfect man is out there for you, dear."

"And you too?" Annie shot back.

"Leave me out of this. We were talking about you and Naomi. I will say a little prayer for both of you."

"*Danki*, Amelia. I'm sure we both need all the help we can get." She leaned around Amelia to look out the window. "Where is Elam? Our first stop is going to be the bike shop. I'm hoping he will purchase a used bike so I can stop hauling him around everywhere. He's taken the buggy on his own before but doesn't really like that. Maybe he doesn't like our horses or something. So then he takes my bike when I want to use it. If he gets one of his own, he can use it here and take it home with him."

"You make it sound like he's planning to stay here indefinitely." Amelia hoped she didn't sound rude.

Annie shrugged. "It's hard to tell with Elam. Let me go see what happened to him. He couldn't have gotten lost going to your greenhouse." With that, she slipped out the door.

A few seconds later, Annie returned with a can of soda in her hand, scolding Elam. "We send him on an errand, and he walks next door to the convenience store to buy a soda." She wagged her head.

Elam stumbled in, juggling his load. "Leave me alone, Annie. I was thirsty. Where do you want this, Christina?"

"Right over here by the counter will be fine. I'll go through it when I don't have customers. *Danki*, Elam."

He huffed and puffed and plopped the crate where Christina indicated. He brushed off his hands as he straightened up and then rubbed his lower back.

"I hope you didn't strain your back." A concerned look crossed Christina's face.

Annie nudged her cousin. "He's a big, strong fellow. I'm sure he's fine. Are you ready to leave?"

"Well, we could visit—"

"*Mamm* gave me a whole passel of errands to run, and time is slipping away. You can visit another time. Unless you need to buy something, we need to go." Annie hooked her arm through Elam's, passed him the soda can, and tugged him toward the door. "See you later, Stina and Amelia."

Christina groaned. "She still calls me that ridiculous nickname, but at least she got Elam out of here. And she said she wasn't bossy!  At least her bossiness can be useful at times."

"That's for sure." Amelia almost sagged in relief at the cousins' departure. "What *are* you planning to do with all of these pumpkins?"

"Absolutely nothing. Most of them probably need to be thrown away. It's almost time to display poinsettias and wreaths. I only wanted to get Elam's focus off you, and that was the only idea I could manufacture at the spur of the moment."

Amelia laughed. "It worked. I don't know why, but he unnerves me."

"I know why."

Amelia cocked her head and arched her eyebrows.

"He's overbearing, opinionated, and, well, kind of creepy."

Amelia shuddered. "It's a comfort to know I'm not the only one who feels that way. Hmpf! Telling me I need a man around as if he wanted to apply for that position. I don't need anyone, and he'd be my last choice if I did."

Christina laughed. "It's a *gut* thing we didn't sic him on Eleanore. Her *bruder* might have urged her to consider him for a husband just to get her married off."

"Bishop Micah wouldn't do such a thing, would he?"

"It depends on if his *fraa* is tired of having Eleanore around."

Amelia gasped. "I'm sure Eleanore is a big help to Nancy."

"Oh, I'm sure she is too. It's just that Nancy might not see things that way."

"Eleanore is such a sweet girl. I don't know who could find fault with her. Maybe she will find a nice fellow soon."

"Speaking of nice fellows..."

Amelia held her breath. Christina wasn't about to suggest someone for her, was she? Perhaps she planned to talk about Noah. "*Jah?*"

"Noah said Ryan Collins has stopped him to see him several times."

"Oh? I suppose that isn't too unusual since they both work on engines and things."

"True, but Ryan didn't visit him to talk about work. He was asking questions about us."

"Us?"

"Our community. Things like driving a buggy and learning our language. He even asked if Noah thought Henry Weaver would need another worker in his shop in the future. What do you think all that means?"

Amelia's heart pounded, and her breath caught. She could only manage a small shrug in reply.

"I think Ryan might be interested in joining us, maybe to court one of our fair ladies."

"I-I wouldn't know anything about that."

"Amelia, you can tell the man cares for you, can't you?"

"Of course he doesn't!" She struggled to breathe normally before she grew dizzy and fainted.

"Breathe, Amelia. You're as pale as a white-washed fence."

Amelia gulped in a deep breath. "What, uh, how, uh, why would you possibly think he cares for me?"

"For one thing, he stops in here several times a week to buy baked items—only yours, mind you. He usually asks if I've seen you, even if he is on his way to your house to pick up his girls."

"He probably wonders if I've been dragging them all over the place. How would he know which things I baked anyway? I don't put my name on them." Amelia crossed her arms over her chest and tapped her foot on the cement floor. Christina must be teasing. She had to be.

"He doesn't ask if I've seen his *kinner*, but if I've seen *you*. And he asks me which food you brought in."

Amelia gasped. Her face must surely be glowing if the heat served as any indication. "Are you teasing?"

"Not at all. I am telling the truth."

"Oh my! Why does he ask those things?" She uncrossed her arms and covered her flaming cheeks with her hands.

Christina grabbed one of Amelia's hands and pulled it from her face. "The man obviously cares about you. I've seen it in the way he looks at you the few times we've been in the same place at the same time."

Amelia tried to tug her hand free, but Christina held on tightly. She wished she could crawl beneath a shelf and hide. Guilt mingled with embarrassment. Yet her heart soared at the same time. How could so many emotions war inside of her?

"It's okay, Amelia." Christina pulled her into a hug and patted her back. "Don't look so panic-stricken and ashamed. You haven't done anything wrong."

"But it's wrong for him to care about me."

"Can we choose our feelings? It would be like telling your lungs not to breathe or your eyes not to blink. Those things occur on their own. Hearts have their own agendas too."

"I need to discourage him." Amelia drew back to look at her *freind*.

"You can't make a person quit caring."

"I can try."

"How?"

"I'll tell him to find another caregiver for his girls."

"You love those girls, and they love you. They need you."

"Another woman would love them too."

"I don't think so. And imagine how miserable those poor little ones would be."

"They would adjust." Amelia struggled to keep from bursting into tears. Gabby and Jessie had been through so much. She would hate to upset their routine again.

"*You* wouldn't adjust. I see your concern for them in your eyes all the time. You would be heartbroken to give them up to someone else's care."

"But if it's for the best..."

"Who said it would be best?"

"Well, Christina, I can't very well continue to be in their *daed's* presence if what you said is true." Amelia knew in her heart Christina was correct. She had seen the tenderness in Ryan's expressions, no matter how much she tried to deny it.

Christina laughed. "The girls can't drive themselves to your house. Ryan has to bring them."

"I need to sever the entire relationship."

"You can't do that to the girls or to yourself."

"Are you saying I should continue watching the girls and pretend I don't notice his feelings or care?"

"You do care about him, don't you?"

Amelia tried to turn away. She didn't want to admit her feelings to herself, much less to anyone else. Christina's hand on her arm kept her in place.

"There isn't any shame in caring about someone."

"There is if that person is forbidden to you. Things could never work out for us. You know that."

"They could if one of you changed."

"Give up our faith?"

"I believe all Mennonites believe in *Gott*. Our Bibles might even be the same for all I know. But you and Ryan could talk about it."

"And then what?"

"See how you feel. It sounds like Ryan has already been thinking about changes."

"He's probably curious about our ways and wondering what I might be teaching his *dochders*." Amelia chuckled. "But he's too polite to *kumm* right out and ask me."

"I don't think so, dear. I believe you are trying to deny your own feelings."

Amelia wished she could deny them or change them or bury them so deep they couldn't be dredged up. "I think forgetting any feelings I may have would be the best thing to do."

"How do you propose to do that? I know I could never forget my feelings for Noah."

Amelia smiled at the pretty pink bloom on her *freind's* face. "Yet you were willing to sacrifice your feelings when you thought he and Annie wanted to be together."

Christina shook her head. "That was a strange time. Annie created a big stir when she pulled her jealous act and tried to latch onto Noah. I thought if he was truly interested in her, I would need to step aside. But once Noah made it clear that the attraction was only on Annie's side, then—"

"That cleared the way for you and Noah."

"Right. The way can be cleared for you and Ryan too if you care about each other."

"Our situation is different."

"Different, but not impossible. All things are possible with the Lord *Gott*."

"You make it sound like it would be easy for one of us to leave our community and start over."

"Not at all. I'm sure it would be very hard. And let me make it clear. I do not want you to leave us. But I do want you to be happy. I have observed the spark between you and Ryan. I would hate for you to stomp it out before you see if there is a way to fan it into flame."

"Don't you think that would be difficult to determine unless I spent time with a man I'm not supposed to be with? The bishop would be lecturing me up one side and down the other."

"Hmm." Christina scratched her head beneath her *kapp*. "Let me work on that."

# Chapter Twenty-Six

She should have told Christina not to concoct any wild schemes that would get them both into hot water with the bishop and ministers. "It's brisk out here, girls. Climb in and I'll cover you with the blanket." Naomi's buggy was still parked on the opposite side of the store. Maybe she walked to the convenience store to buy a drink to go with her sweets. Amelia shrugged, dismissing her thoughts of the young woman. She hustled her little ones to the waiting black buggy. Rhonda and Judith climbed in on their own. Amelia lifted Joanna up and helped her to the back of the buggy. "Let Joanna sit between you two so she'll stay warm."

All three girls were petite like Amelia, but she always thought Joanna seemed particularly delicate and fussed over her a bit more. The older two slid to each side so Joanna could wiggle into the space between them. Amelia reached for the blanket beneath the seat but found only empty space. She shifted positions and felt again for the blanket and finally leaned down to peer beneath the seat. Then she checked the floor under the front seat. "Not again!"

"Amelia! What's wrong?"

Amelia heard Christina running toward them but couldn't lift her head. Didn't she already have enough on her mind? She fought hard not to cry in front of her *kinner*.

"Tell me what happened." Christina squeezed Amelia's shoulder and spoke soothingly.

Amelia sniffed and straightened up. "My buggy blanket is gone. It was under the seat, and now it's gone." She stared into Christina's shocked face. "Am I going to have to start bringing Snickers inside with me wherever I go in case someone wants to steal my horse, or do I need to hire an *Englisch* driver to take me everywhere?"

"You poor thing!" Christina pulled Amelia to her in a brief hug. "I'm sure you looked under both seats, didn't you?"

"*Jah*. And I'm sure I brought it today because we used it on the way here. I tucked it under the seat for safekeeping. It seems that I didn't outsmart my personal thief."

"The only other people to enter The Green Thumb while you were here were Annie and Elam, Naomi, and two *Englisch* customers that I've known for a long time. None of them would have had any need for your blanket. I suppose anyone could have walked up to your buggy without visiting the store though."

Amelia lowered her voice. "I feel like I'm being watched, like someone is following me and taking things to annoy me or to frighten me. But I can't figure out who or why."

"It's all so strange. Maybe we should booby-trap your buggy and see if we can catch a thief."

Amelia laughed. "I'd probably get caught in my own trap."

"We'll think of something. Would you like me to find a blanket for you to use on your way home?"

"*Nee*. We don't have that far to go. We'll sing to distract ourselves from the cold. We'll be fine." Hadn't she said that a lot lately?

Amelia and Christina turned at the sound of running footsteps.

"What has happened? Are you all right?" Naomi paused for breath.

Amelia tried to brush off the girl's concern. There was no use involving the whole world in her problems. "I'm fine, Naomi."

"Is something wrong with your buggy or the girls?" Naomi stepped closer and tried to peek inside.

"Amelia is missing something, that's all." Christina tried to steer Naomi away.

"Oh dear. Has something else been stolen? I mean, we all know about your precious quilt and the other things." Naomi laid a hand on Amelia's arm. "I do hope no one has bothered your belongings again."

Amelia offered a shaky smile. "It's only a buggy blanket. I was going to cover the girls with it, but we don't have that far to go. They will be okay. *Kinner* don't seem to notice the cold as much as we do. After all, they would stay outside in winter for hours if I let them."

Naomi persisted. "Did you have it when you came here?" She looked under the buggy. "Maybe it got knocked out on the ground."

"I've looked. It's gone. But I'm not worried about it. It was old."

Christina tapped Naomi's arm. "You didn't see anyone messing around Amelia's buggy, did you?"

"*Nee.* I drove straight to the other side when I arrived." She pointed to her buggy. "I went into the convenience store after I left your shop. I was so thirsty that I downed the whole bottle of juice before I left. But if I had seen anyone nosing around, I would have given him a piece of my mind. What nerve! I'm so sorry, Amelia."

Amelia waved her off. "Don't worry about it, dear. At least it wasn't something valuable or sentimental. I need to get the girls home. I'll see you two later."

Naomi gave her a brief hug. "Please take care, Amelia. And be careful. I'll be on my way, too. I'll keep a lookout for anyone looking suspicious."

Amelia smiled. "*Danki.*" When Naomi was out of earshot, she whispered, "How would she know a blanket thief if she saw one?"

Christina giggled. "Will you be all right at home? I can stay with you tonight. Tomorrow is an off Sunday, so we wouldn't have to rush to get to church or anything."

"I appreciate the offer, but that won't be necessary. I think someone simply likes playing silly pranks. Maybe it's the same teenagers who left the smoke bomb in my barn."

"Possibly."

"Or maybe someone truly needed the blanket to stay warm."

"And only your blankets and quilts will do?"

Amelia shrugged. "I'm trying to consider possibilities, even if they are far-fetched. At any rate, I need to get my girls home before they freeze."

"You be careful."

Amelia climbed into the buggy. She thought she had been careful, but evidently, she needed to be even more vigilant. But she would not hide inside her house and be afraid to do ordinary activities. She forced a cheery smile as she looked at the three solemn, little faces behind her. "Let's sing on the way home. Who knows a fun song?"

~

Amelia hated looking over her shoulder every time she stepped out of the house. Her eyes constantly shifted from the yard to the woods to the road whenever she took the girls out to play. Apprehension was rapidly becoming swallowed up by anger. A person should not have to be hesitant to go about daily activities. If only she knew who was behind all the mischief, she would surely give him a piece of her mind.

She liked attending church and talking with everyone afterward, but she was ever so glad today was an off Sunday. She planned to stay home all day. She would play with her girls and read to them and perhaps take them for a walk when the sun warmed the air a bit this afternoon. They could collect leaves or pine cones or greenery and make some sort of craft project out of them.

Right now, she wrapped her hands around her mug of tea and enjoyed a few moments of solitude before wee people vied for her attention. She sipped as she gazed at the awakening world outside her kitchen window. The bright red cardinal danced around the bird feeder while his less colorful mate hopped beneath it. Dew sparkled in the early morning sun. In another week or so, it would be frost coating the ground instead of dew. Amelia shivered. The days had been growing shorter and colder.

She opened the stove and threw in another chunk of wood. Three hungry little girls would appear any second. Since breakfast would be cold cereal today, she wanted to make the room as warm as possible. She stood on tiptoe to reach the bowls that had gotten pushed back on the shelf and set them on the counter. The inability to reach high objects was the bane of being a short person.

As if on cue, three sets of footsteps shuffled toward the kitchen, bringing an end to her peaceful interlude. She set down her mug, turned, and opened her arms to her *dochders*. "So, what will it be this morning—cornflakes or raisin bran?"

~

They'd had a fun morning reading, coloring, and working on puzzles. After a quick noon meal of cold meats, cheese, bread, macaroni salad, and fruit, she hustled all three *kinner* off for a nap. Even Rhonda, who considered herself too old for a nap, decided to "take a rest."

A rest sounded like a fine idea to Amelia too, but she knew if she slept during the day, she would toss and turn all night. She dropped onto the rocking chair next to the living room woodstove and pulled her latest half-finished knitting project onto her lap. She rarely seemed to have time for knitting lately, and it was such a relaxing activity.

She usually used any spare time on weekdays to work on basket orders, but work was prohibited on the Lord's Day, so those projects would have to wait. She rocked and knitted and enjoyed the quiet time. When the girls awoke, she would take them for a walk with Meggie. They could all use a bit of fresh air and exercise.

Amelia had just settled into a rocking and knitting rhythm when she caught sight of a buggy rolling up her long gravel driveway. She had really wanted a day with her girls, but now it looked like she would have to forget that idea and play hostess to whoever decided to visit.

She stuffed her knitting back inside the canvas bag and tried to adjust her attitude. Now that the buggy had drawn closer, she could see that it was fairly bursting with occupants, but she couldn't imagine who they were. She hoped her girls wouldn't be too disappointed if they had to forego their hike and craft project.

"*Mamm*, there's a buggy in the driveway."

Amelia had been so intent on trying to determine who their visitors were that she hadn't heard Rhonda trot down the stairs. "You're awake already."

"I was only resting, not napping."

"Oh, that's right." Amelia struggled not to smile.

"I'm up too." Judith peeked out from behind her *schweschder*.

"So I see. I guess Joanna is still asleep?"

"*Jah*."

"*Nee.*" The smallest girl ran into the room and made a beeline for her *mudder.*

Amelia leaned over to scoop her youngest into her arms. "We might have to take our walk another day."

"Who is it?" Judith skittered toward the window, but Amelia snagged her arm to stop her.

"Let's not stare out the window. That isn't very polite. I thought it was Christina's horse at first, but I can't imagine who she would have with her." Amelia shifted Joanna to free one hand to smooth her hair into place.

"Let me look. I can tell you who's in the buggy." Rhonda was poised to race to the window.

"We'll find out in a minute, dear. Be patient. You girls go and get your shoes on in case you want to go out to play in a bit. Please bring me Joanna's shoes too."

The two older girls flew from the room and clomped up the steps. Maybe their excitement over visitors would assuage any disappointment over their change of plans.

Amelia hurried through the house to answer the knock at the back door. She unlocked it and opened it only enough to peek out in case she was mistaken about the visitor being Christina.

Shocked, she clutched Joanna tighter until the little girl squirmed in her arms. "Christina, what...?"

# Chapter Twenty-Seven

"Surprise!"

Noah stood beside Christina. There was nothing unusual about that, but the tall man behind them holding a *boppli* in one arm and clutching a little girl's hand with his free hand nearly caused Amelia's knees to buckle.

"May we *kumm* in?" Christina's eyes sparkled in amusement.

"Of course." Amelia opened the door wide and stepped back. She shot her *freind* a questioning glance.

"Look who I found outside playing when I drove by. When I asked if they would like to go for a buggy ride, they jumped at the chance."

"When you drove by? You live in the opposite direction." Amelia broke off at Christina's frown and slight head shake.

"Hello, Amelia. I hope we aren't intruding."

"Hi, Ryan and girls. You aren't intruding. You all know you are *wilkom* here any time."

"Daddy thought the buggy was fun. He said he liked it better than riding in a car." Gabby giggled. "I tried to tell him that before, but now he knows for himself."

Amelia smiled. "Is that right? Rhonda and Judith went to get their shoes on. You can go upstairs to find them if you want, Gabby."

The little girl didn't need any further encouragement. She dashed off toward the stairs seeking her playmates. Amelia lowered Joanna to the floor to join the others when she began squirming. "To what do I owe the pleasure of your company?" Amelia looked from one adult to the other.

"Noah and I were out for a drive when we spotted Ryan."

"Really?" Amelia found it hard to believe that Christina and Noah would be out alone in an enclosed buggy instead of an open courting buggy. She needed to take the girl aside and find out what she was up to.

"We decided to stop in to see you and the girls after we picked up Ryan and his little ones." Christina looked to Noah for affirmation and elbowed him when none was forthcoming.

Noah coughed. "Oh, right."

"I hope you didn't have plans." Ryan's concerned expression touched Amelia's heart.

"I had planned to take the girls for a walk to gather pine cones, leaves, and things for a craft project. That was my only plan."

"Great! We can tag along!" Christina clapped her hands. "Gabby would like that, wouldn't she, Ryan? And Noah and I like to walk."

Ryan nodded. "Gabby would be overjoyed. She likes to make things, and I'm afraid I'm not very good in the arts and crafts department."

"Fine. It should be fun." Amelia didn't know what else she could say. She certainly couldn't express how awkward she found this whole situation. She understood that Christina wanted to be helpful, but perhaps she had gone a bit overboard in matchmaking efforts she should not be undertaking. "If you want to go now, I'll need to tell the girls to grab their coats and bonnets."

"That's fine by me," Ryan confirmed. "The sun is still pretty bright, so it will be warmer now than if we wait until later."

"Christina, would you help me gather a few small snacks? I know little hikers can get hungry." Amelia nodded toward the kitchen.

"Sure." As soon as they crossed the threshold into the kitchen, Christina leaned close and spoke into Amelia's ear. "Please don't be mad. I really did see Ryan outside and acted on the spur of the moment."

"You and Noah were riding in—"

"*Nee.* It's not like that. I ran into Ryan first and then met Noah. He and I were going to go for a drive anyway. Since I had plenty of other people with me, I figured it would be fine if I picked him up instead of the other way around."

"Christina Brubacher, Ryan's house is not on your way to Noah's!"

"It is if I take the long route."

"You're incorrigible. And you're going to get us into trouble."

"We'll be fine. You and Ryan can serve as chaperones for Noah and me, and we'll serve as chaperones for you two."

"You're forgetting one thing. Ryan is not one of us."

"Yet."

"Are you recruiting? You know that isn't our way." Amelia began tossing oatmeal cookies and pretzels into small plastic bags.

"I'm merely being sociable."

"You're meddling."

"I prefer to think of it as helping. You and Ryan will never find out if you even want a relationship if you don't have a chance to be together."

"Shh!" Amelia's cheeks were hot enough to burst into flame.

Christina hugged her. "It will be all right. I promise."

"You sound like you want me to leave our community. You seem to be pushing me to make a leap I don't intend to make."

"Oh, Amelia, that's not it at all! I want you to stay, but I have a suspicion that Ryan is eager for a change."

"Lots of people want a change but don't plan to overhaul their whole way of life. That's what it would be like for him and his girls."

"We aren't so very different."

"Only as different as night and day."

Christina winked. "Maybe only as different as morning and afternoon. Maybe this little outing today will help you both determine if a change is possible."

Amelia wrinkled her nose and wagged her head.

"Don't give me that look."

"What look?"

"Like I suggested we fly to the moon."

"You might as well have done that. What you are scheming is about as likely as that."

"Not scheming, my dear. Simply providing an opportunity." She tugged on Amelia's arm. "Smile. This will be fun."

"That remains to be seen."

~

Her tension dissolved as Amelia romped through the woods with her *freinden*.

She'd decided to leave Meggie in the fenced-in backyard so she wouldn't scare off any wildlife they might be fortunate enough to encounter. Besides, she felt perfectly safe with other adults along. Her girls and Gabby skipped and laughed as if they were having the adventure of their lives. Jessie, strapped in a carrier on Ryan's back, pointed and giggled at the older girls.

Christina's knowledge of plants proved to be an asset indeed. She pointed out various shrubs and plants and told the *kinner* a little about each one. She told them which trees the pine cones they gathered and carefully placed in paper bags as if they were treasures had fallen from.

"Isn't that the running cedar you use for Christmas wreaths?" Ryan pointed to clumps of the fern-like plant.

"*Jah*. I'll gather some when I get ready to make wreaths. I'll use some sprigs of holly too." Amelia turned in each direction to survey the trees. "*Gut*. There are plenty of holly trees nearby too."

"*Kumm* quietly, girls, and look at the doe with her fawns." Christina pointed to a small clearing through the trees. Noah tiptoed closer with the girls right behind him.

Ryan scooted closer to Amelia and spoke so softly she almost had to hold her breath to hear him. "I wanted you to know that I did not mastermind this outing. I certainly did not object to it, but it was Christina's idea."

"I understand. Christina can get a bit carried away."

"I'm not unhappy about her plan at all. In fact, I'm grateful. This is exactly what I hoped we could do if you remember."

"I do remember." Amelia felt heat rise from her feet to her face. Her breath caught at Ryan's feather-light touch on her arm.

"I'm glad we could spend this time together. My being here on a social call shouldn't pose a problem for you, should it? I mean, we have chaperones."

Amelia's heart pounded at his nearness. "I-I don't know. I-I hope it will be all right—if anyone should hear of it."

"I wouldn't want to do anything to get you into trouble or to tarnish your reputation."

"Christina and Noah can vouch for me if necessary."

Ryan reached up to grab his hat that Jessie tried to pull from his head. "Leave it alone, you scamp." The little girl giggled and pulled at the hat again.

"Here, Jessie." Amelia bent to snatch a pine cone off the ground. "Look at this. Isn't it pretty?"

The *boppli* reached out for the offering and immediately gave up her attack on her dad's hat.

"I'll watch her to make sure she doesn't put the pine cone in her mouth, but she's usually very *gut* about that. I rarely need to grab something before it reaches her lips."

"You're so good with her, with all the girls."

"They are *wunderbaar kinner.* I love them all."

"It shows. Your care and your concern are obvious in everything you do or say. Even for me. I hope that's what I'm reading into your words and actions anyway."

Amelia ducked her head and hoped her black bonnet would conceal her flushed face.

"I didn't mean to embarrass you. I guess I'm hoping with all my heart that you care about me as I care about you. Even if you said you thought you *could* care about a big, bumbling man with two children, that would make me a happy person."

"Me! Me!"

Jessie's call for attention spared Amelia from needing to respond. The little girl held her arms out toward Amelia.

"Oh. I get it now. She's calling you." Ryan shook his head. "All this time when she's said that I thought she was talking about herself, but she means you."

"She can't quite get out Amelia, so she says 'me' instead." Amelia reached up to grasp one tiny hand. "Do you want me to take her?"

"You lug her around enough. I'll distract her." Ryan bounded around, making the little girl wobble and giggle until the others returned from watching the deer.

Amelia stepped back, putting space between them, but she laughed along with Jessie and Ryan. She didn't want to, and she tried not to, but she did care.

~

What would she have said if Jessie hadn't interrupted? Ryan had gotten the impression Amelia didn't only care about his children, but that she had some sort of feelings for him as well. but she was taking great care not to act on those feelings.  She carefully distanced herself from him as they walked. He could understand that. They did have a lot of onlookers.

He hoped he wasn't being too pushy. He certainly didn't want to scare her away. Her qualms were valid. He was not Old Order Mennonite. She was not of his community. He couldn't see her giving up her way of life. Would he change his?

If he wanted a chance with the woman who refused to abandon his thoughts and dreams, his family would have to make alterations. His daughters were young, and they adored Amelia. Change would be easy for them. But him? He glanced at the beautiful, petite woman almost within arm's reach. Yes. He could do anything for her.

Based on the information he'd gleaned from Noah and others in a roundabout way, his and Amelia's beliefs were basically the same, even if their customs differed. He'd been sure he hadn't fooled Noah at all with his casual questions. Noah had undoubtedly sensed Ryan's quandary, but he'd played along and actually been quite helpful. And he hadn't blabbed as far as Ryan could tell.

Ryan wouldn't have believed in a million years that he could be so crazy about someone again, but he was. Simply being in Amelia's presence caused his heart to beat in a strange, erratic rhythm. He thought about her almost constantly. He found himself wanting to do things for her and her girls. He wanted to make their lives easier and to help her as much as she had helped him. And he wanted to spoil her and treat her as the special woman she was.

He had been uneasy, to say the least, when Christina stopped and suggested this little outing. He wondered if Amelia would feel coerced and would refuse to participate. He feared she would be completely scared off and then he would lose all hope of winning her affection. But he'd taken the risk.

Amelia reached into the canvas bag slung across her shoulder and extracted an oatmeal cookie. She broke off a chunk and stepped closer to Ryan. "Here, let's trade." In one swift motion, she substituted the cookie for Jessie's pine cone. She stood on tiptoe to brush off his shoulder. "She was crumbling this poor pine cone all over you."

Ryan's heart stuttered at her nearness. Did she have any idea of the effect she had on him? "Thanks." Somehow he'd managed to croak out the single word.

"Now if you feel debris raining down on you, it will be cookie crumbs and not prickly pine cone fragments." She hesitated a moment before holding the remainder of the cookie to his lips. "A little nourishment?"

Her smile thrilled him. He had the insane desire to capture her hand and kiss her palm. Thank goodness common sense kicked in before he could act. His fingers brushed hers when he took the cookie, sending a tingle up his arm. "Mmm! Delicious!" He meant to glance at her only briefly, but he was held captive by her blue eyes. *You are not a schoolboy, Ryan Miller. Pull yourself together and act your age.*

~

For the umpteenth time during this walk, Amelia's cheeks burned. She had to pull herself from the depths of Ryan's dark eyes. Logic demanded she force herself to look away immediately. Her heart, she discovered, balked at submitting to rational thought. The rustle of dried leaves accomplished what her brain could not do.

Amelia tore her eyes away from the man who stared at her equally as intently and focused on the approaching little girls. She would have fanned her face to hasten the disappearance of the flush that undoubtedly spread across her cheeks, but she feared the action would have drawn even more attention to her plight.

"*Mamm! Mamm!* Did you see the deer?" Rhonda tore away from the other girls and raced to Amelia's side.

"I did. Weren't they beautiful?"

"I wish I could keep a little one as a pet."

Amelia laughed. "You are a true animal lover. You already have Meggie, Ruby, Mimi, and the horses. I think those are all the critters we can handle. Besides, the doe wouldn't be too happy if you took her *boppli*."

"I know, but the *bopplin* are so cute with their spots."

Judith and Gabby, each holding one of Joanna's hands, joined them. Amelia smiled. They all got along so well. Her girls treated Gabby and Jessie like *schweschders*. She glanced over the girls' heads and caught Ryan's smile and tender expression directed at the little ones. Her heart fluttered when he transferred that look to her.

A small brown rabbit hopped from one thicket to another, stealing the girls' attention.

"Let's see where he went!" Gabby cried. "Maybe we can find more bunnies."

That was all it took for the girls to set off on another exploration. They started off at a run, but Rhonda immediately slowed them down. "We need to be quiet, or we'll scare any bunnies away."

Amelia didn't have the heart to tell her the rabbit was probably long gone. The girls were having too much fun to spoil it with rationalizations.

It was a *wunderbaar* day! *Nee*, it had been a terrible day! Amelia was so mixed up. She could hug Christina for orchestrating this get-together one minute, and the next, she could throttle her. Every minute in Ryan's company made her crave more time with him. Her feelings had grown stronger in this short time together. She had enjoyed every second of the afternoon walk, which would make it so much harder to shelve it as a memory.

And that is exactly what Amelia needed to do. The day could only be a pleasant memory. It could not be the beginning of something that would continue forever. The thought of needing to end the budding relationship before it had a chance to blossom brought a physical pain as sharp as the emotional pain it caused. Life would have been so much simpler if Christina had not shown up at her house with Ryan and his girls. She would now have a much harder time keeping her feelings under control. She sighed.

"Are you all right?" Ryan looked worried.

Amelia nodded, unable to trust her voice not to crack.

"Are you getting too cold or too tired?"

The man's smile and concern would warm her if she was frozen solid. "I'm fine. We should probably go back to the house soon so the girls can make their projects before it gets too late."

"You're right, but I hate for the day to end."

"Me too." Amelia whispered the words, but a light squeeze on her arm told her Ryan had heard them.

# Chapter Twenty-Eight

They all laughed and talked on their trek back to the house. Noah pointed out different kinds of birds and tried to get the girls to whistle the tunes each bird sang. They giggled over their silly attempts. Ryan told them about the clouds floating over their heads—the thin, wispy ones and the fat, fluffy ones.

"The puffy ones look like cotton candy," Gabby said.

"Do you remember that?" Ryan turned to the adults. "We went to a carnival once. That sticky stuff must have made a big impression on her."

"I remember." Gabby licked her lips. "It was good."

"That makes me hungry." Rhonda sidled up to Amelia. "Can we have a snack?"

Amelia hugged her oldest *dochder*. "I was wondering when everyone's tummies would start rumbling." She fished through her canvas bag and produced the plastic baggie full of cookies.

"Cookies!" Judith squealed. "Are they oatmeal raisin?"

"They are." Amelia handed each girl and adult a cookie.

Joanna turned her cookie over and over in her hands without taking a bite.

"Aren't you hungry, little one?" Amelia immediately laid the back of her hand across Joanna's forehead. "It isn't like you to hesitate when a treat is offered."

"Tired."

"Oh. You're too tired to eat? I'll put your cookie away and save it for later, then."

"Carry? Then eat."

Amelia laughed. "So, you want me to carry you while you eat. That's so you can drop crumbs all over me, ain't so?" She chucked her *boppli* under the chin.

"We're all tired too." Gabby, Judith, and Rhonda all acted as if they couldn't take another step. They giggled and stumbled around.

"I think we have some tired girls here. It would be a shame to have to leave them here in the woods all night." Christina winked at Amelia over the girls' heads. "Finish your cookies, and we'll race to the clearing. Last one there is a monkey's *onkle*."

The girls giggled before stuffing their cookies in their mouths.

"Everyone chew and swallow," Noah admonished. "We don't need anyone choking."

Amelia stooped down so Joanna could climb onto her back.

"Hey, she doesn't have to run. Not fair! I could beat her!" Rhonda was big into fairness since she started school.

"That's okay, dear." Amelia patted her six-year-old's shoulder. "It will be a fairer race if she is not underfoot."

"Is everybody ready?" Christina reached for Judith's and Gabby's hands "Here, we'll help each other."

Noah grabbed Rhonda's hand. "Let's show them how fast we can run."

"On your mark. Get set. Go." Ryan made a noise like a starting gun.

Adults and children scrambled over stumps and sticks, racing toward the clearing. Joanna bounced on Amelia's back and shouted, "Go, *Mamm*!"

Jessie threw her head back and giggled when Ryan took off running. He had to remind her not to grab his neck in her excitement.

Noah and Christina ran at a fairly even pace, practically dragging the little girls they held onto. All of them gasped for breath by the time they reached the edge of the woods.

"It's a tie for first place!" Rhonda shouted as the five of them stopped at the same time.

Noah looked behind them. "It looks like a tie for last place too."

Gabby jumped up and down and clapped. "Two monkey's uncles!"

"Four!" Rhonda corrected her. "If you count Jessie and Joanna."

The girls shrieked and collapsed in a heap on the ground as they waited for Ryan and Amelia to catch up.

Amelia panted and squatted down to let Joanna slide off her back. "Ah, now I can take a deep breath. Okay, Joanna. It's your turn to carry me now."

"Too big!" Joanna's eyes grew huge as if she wondered how she'd ever manage that feat.

"Your *mamm* is a bitty, little thing. I'm sure a big girl like you could do the job. Why, I could probably carry her along with Jessie." Ryan stepped closer, pretending he planned to hoist Amelia into his arms.

She jumped back. "I don't think so!" She turned to Joanna. "Take my hand, little one, and we'll help each other."

All merriment died when the house and driveway came into the hikers' view and Meggie's frantic barking reached their ears. Amelia's heart pounded so hard that she feared it would burst right through her skin. Her stomach rolled over. "W-who could that be?" She stared at the black buggy parked behind Christina's.

"Were you expecting company?" Christina backpedaled until she stood right beside Amelia.

"*Nee.*"

"Everything will be all right." Christina patted Amelia's arm.

Easy for her to say. If the bishop popped in for an impromptu social call, Amelia was doomed. "Can you tell who it is?"

Christina squinted. "Not yet."

A man and a woman, both with red-orange hair hopped out of the buggy and strolled toward the backyard.

Amelia gasped. "Annie and Elam. I'm double doomed."

Christina snagged Amelia's hand and squeezed it. "It's okay. I'll take full responsibility for, uh, everything."

Somehow, Amelia doubted that would help. Why did she ever agree to this outing?

"There you are!" Annie's voice probably carried to the next county. "We checked the house earlier and decided to wait in the buggy for a while to see if you turned up."

Why didn't they leave when they found the house empty? Amelia certainly wouldn't have waited outside of someone's house. At least they hadn't been able to go inside since she had locked the door. She fingered the key on the braided string around her neck.

"Hi, Christina." Annie still yelled even though she had drawn closer. "I recognized your buggy and horse, so I thought I'd stop for a visit too."

"But we didn't know you had other company." Elam sounded angry.

Amelia bristled. What business was it of his if Amelia had company? It didn't concern him in the least.

"*Englisch* company." The red-haired man spat out the two words as if they were vile.

Amelia had told him time after time that Ryan was Mennonite. All he had to do was look at Ryan's attire or that of his little girls for Pete's sake. *Englischers* did not wear such clothes.

"Hello, Elam. Nice to see you again." At least Ryan showed *gut* manners.

Christina broke into the conversation before matters could get worse if that was possible. "Noah and I ran into Ryan and his girls and asked them to accompany us here."

"You ran into them?" Annie gazed through narrowed eyes.

"*Jah*, and the girls have had ever so much fun walking through the woods and learning about plants, birds, and clouds."

"Does the bishop know about this *gathering*?" Elam emphasized the last word.

Amelia instructed the four older girls to go into the backyard to play with Meggie. They didn't need to be privy to adult conversation. Besides, if they distracted Meggie, she might stop that infernal yipping.

"I don't know how things work in your community, Elam Wenger, but we are allowed to visit with *freinden*." Christina plunked her fists on her hips and fixed the big, red-haired man with a stern look.

"All kinds of *freinden*?"

"Of course. The bishop doesn't dictate who our *freinden* should be. One of my dear *freinden* is *Englisch*. She's a great person, and everyone in the community likes her."

"But *your freind* is a female."

"So? Ryan is a *freind* too," Noah added.

Amelia felt knee-high to an earthworm. "D-did you drop by for any special reason, Annie?" *Or were you simply being nosy?*

"Like I said, we happened to be in the area and spotted Christina's buggy. Elam has been wanting to visit folks, so we stopped, ain't so, cousin?" Annie elbowed the man, who simply nodded.

"Oh, well, uh..." Amelia struggled to organize her thoughts, but the only thing that came to mind was "go home," and she couldn't say that. She looked down when Judith tugged on her sleeve and pointed to the basket of leaves, acorns, and pine cones they had collected. Amelia brightened. Now she had a clear thought. "The girls were about to embark on an art project, and they're eager to begin. Please excuse us." Was she being rude to ignore the newest arrivals?

Ryan stepped a little closer and spoke softly. "Maybe we should leave now."

"That sounds like a *gut* idea." Although Elam muttered, his voice was loud enough to be easily heard.

Amelia saw red. She tried counting to ten but only got to four. "This is *my* home, Elam, and these are *my* guests. It is not your place to say they should leave. If you prefer not to associate with my *freinden*, please don't feel you need to stay." She grabbed Judith's hand. "Let's go work on your project." She only barely managed to walk away without stomping. That would not set the right example for the girls. She paused to call over her shoulder. "Ryan, please feel free to bring Jessie over. I'm sure we can find something for her to do too."

She had been able to glimpse the other adults' reactions from the corner of her eye. Elam stared after her with his mouth agape. Annie, too, stared dumbfounded. Christina appeared about ready to burst into laughter, and Noah coughed to cover a chuckle.

Ryan recovered first. "Okay, Amelia. Let's see what we can find to keep this little one's hands busy." He loped across the yard, bouncing Jessie on his back.

"Well, I never!" Annie's outburst sailed through the air. "We might as well leave, Elam, unless you want to do arts and crafts."

"I'll skip that."

"Christina, would you and Noah like to go visiting with Elam and me?"

Amelia strained to hear Christina's words. After all, she and Annie used to be best *freinden* until Annie had gotten the silly notion that Noah cared about her. What a difficult time that had been. The two young women had since resolved their problems, but their relationship did not appear to be as close as it had always been in the past.

"We're fine here, Annie. We did bring Ryan and his girls, you know, and I want them to make their project. In fact, I think I'll help them. It sounds like fun. You and Elam enjoy the rest of your afternoon though."

Amelia heard running feet and panting. Was Christina as put out with Annie and Elam as she was? Noah called out for her to wait up, that he would help with the project too.

Meggie ran around the girls, lapping up all the attention they showered on her. Jessie leaned over, trying to pet the fuzzy, brown hair, and nearly pulled Ryan off-balance. Amelia quickly righted the little girl and supported her *daed* for a moment.

"Well, that was an interesting visit," Christina whispered when she sidled up to Amelia.

"Strange, I'd call it."

"For sure."

"I hope I didn't *kumm* across as rude. I shouldn't have let him rile me."

"You were perfect!"

Amelia gazed at the four eager, little faces. "Whose fingers need to be warmed around a mug of hot chocolate before we begin working?"

"Me! Me!" Four wee voices spoke as one.

"Marshmallows too?" Gabby asked.

Amelia glanced at Ryan. "What do you think, *Daed*? Marshmallows or not?"

"I, for one, am a big fan of marshmallows floating in a chocolate sea."

Amelia smiled. His wink warmed her from her toes to her head. She ducked to hide the probable blush staining her cheeks. "Marshmallows, it is."

~

*I'm a big fan of yours too!* Ryan didn't dare voice that thought with Christina and Noah within earshot. He would have loved to say the words aloud, but he didn't want to cause her any further discomfort.

His heart had lurched when she called him *daed* the way any woman would refer to her husband around the children. What would it be like creating a new family with Amelia and her little ones? The girls already acted like sisters. He knew Amelia loved his daughters just as he loved hers. What about the two of them though? Could Amelia love him as he loved her? The admission of his feelings stunned him. Thank goodness no one could read his thoughts.

"All right, girls. Let's wash up before we sit at the table. You've been picking up dirty leaves and pine cones and petting the dog. I don't think you want a doggie-flavored snack, do you?" Amelia smiled at each child. They shook their heads and scampered off to the bathroom.

She was so good with them. She could get them to cooperate with a gentle request and a smile. She was smart, beautiful, and truly remarkable. "Huh?" He jumped when an elbow dug into his ribs.

"Where are you, man?" Noah smirked as if he knew exactly where Ryan's thoughts had wandered.

"I'm right here."

"Christina said she would take the *boppli* to clean her hands."

"Oh. Sure." Ryan had forgotten Jessie was still perched on his back since she had stopped tapping on his head. He turned so Christina could lift the little girl from the carrier. "Thank you."

"Cookie?" Joanna asked, racing back into the kitchen.

Amelia hugged her youngest. "I suppose you can have one. Is it okay for your girls to have another cookie, Ryan? I don't want to spoil their supper."

"Since there are no supper plans in the works at the moment, I don't think a couple of cookies will hurt anything. Besides, we need something to dunk into the hot chocolate, don't we?"

"My thoughts exactly." Noah reached for the carrier on Ryan's back. "Would you like me to help you out of this contraption?

"Sure." He spoke to Noah, but his gaze still followed Amelia, who had scooted over to glance out the window.

"They're gone," Christina whispered, but Ryan had read her lips. He saw Amelia's shoulders relax and heard her soft sigh. "Don't worry. I'm going to have a little talk with Annie."

Noah picked up the conversation. "I think it is Elam who needs talking to. What's up with that fellow?"

Amelia shrugged.

Christina wagged her head. "I believe it's time he headed home. Surely, he must have some sort of job to return to."

Ryan had wondered about that himself. And why didn't the man like him? Did Elam dislike everyone who was not an Old Order Mennonite? That didn't sound like a very Christian attitude to him. Or, even more disturbing, perhaps Elam hoped to win Amelia's affection and would be set against anyone who might be interested in her.

# Chapter Twenty-Nine

Amelia stowed all thoughts of Elam and Annie in a back corner of her brain and focused on helping the girls create their masterpieces. Joanna mainly liked playing in the glue, but Amelia finally persuaded her to arrange some leaves and small acorns on the white globs dotting her paper.

Christina held Jessie on her lap and let the little girl drop tiny bits of moss in the glue she had spread across a piece of blue construction paper. Gabby, Rhonda, and Judith concentrated hard on their projects, each creating a unique design.

Noah and Ryan took it upon themselves to take care of Amelia's necessary outdoor chores but seemed to be taking an inordinate amount of time doing the few things that needed to be done on a Sunday evening. Amelia wished she could listen in on the conversation between the two men.

"It's too bad I couldn't have strapped a hidden tape recorder on Meggie." Christina nodded toward the window.

Amelia looked up from Joanna's gooey mess and glanced out the window, where Meggie happily pranced along with the men. "You must have been reading my mind. They certainly seem to be taking a long time."

"I suppose they're having some kind of men's talk."

"About what?"

"Who knows? Crops or work or the weather." Christina smiled. "Or maybe Ryan has more questions about our ways."

"You're *narrisch*. He wouldn't be interested in pursuing a harder life than he already has."

"Change is not so crazy when you have someone you care about by your side."

"Now I know you've been reading Annie's books."

"I've only thumbed through a few. Annie mainly reads suspense. I'm thinking more along the line of romance."

Amelia tossed a balled-up paper towel at her *freind*. "You are completely delusional, unless you're thinking about your own romance."

Christina flushed. "My, uh, course is pretty well-set."

"Does that mean you'll be published soon?"

Christina lifted her shoulders to her ears and dropped them. "I'm thinking about you and a certain person."

"Don't waste your time on those thoughts. That is a two-some that will never be."

Christina swung Jessie to her other side to keep her hands from grabbing the glue bottle before fixing Amelia with a stern look. "Maybe you are in denial or you're trying to con-vince yourself otherwise, but I *know* there is something be-tween the two of you. I can see it in your faces and your actions. I can hear it in your voices."

"We need to get your eyes and ears checked."

"Very funny. I'm sure you know what I'm talking about. You must feel it in your heart, even if your brain tries to deny it."

"I never took you for a hopeless romantic before."

"I'm not, really. I'm a keen observer of people though, and I care a lot about my *freinden*."

"We've talked about this, Christina, and you are well aware of all the reasons why such a relationship would never work." Amelia glanced at each of the girls to ensure they were suitably occupied and not paying attention to the adult conversation floating above them. They all seemed oblivious and were probably confused by the mixture of *Englisch* and *Deutsch* languages the women were blending. They giggled as they glued their nature finds as well as bits of fabric and yarn onto heavy construction paper.

"I only see one hitch in the whole idea. Otherwise, you two seem very well-suited for one another."

"That one issue is not a minor consideration. It's huge. It's life-altering."

"All relationships are life-altering. My life will totally change whenever I marry. I'm used to running my own business, being my own boss. I'm not used to caring for my own home or accounting to someone."

"You help your *mudder* take care of the house and younger *kinner*. You've been accountable to your parents."

"True, but that's different. When I marry, I'll have to take someone else's needs and opinions into consideration. If I have *kinner*, they will have to take precedence over my business."

"Of course they will. But you can still run your store. Your *grossmammi* raised a family and helped with the grands while operating her business. You are very much like her."

"*Danki*, Amelia. I take that as a compliment. I've always admired my *grossmammi* more than probably anyone else I've ever known—but don't repeat that to my *mamm*." Christina laughed.

"I certainly meant it as a compliment. Your *grossmammi* was a remarkable woman, as is your *mudder*. You are following in their footsteps, so I know you will work things out when the time *kumms*. Noah is a very understanding, generous man from what I've observed."

"He is. And he wants me to keep The Green Thumb operating as usual. I might have to hire more help, though, if we are blessed with *kinner*."

"What about Annie?"

"She already helps when her *onkle* doesn't have enough work for her, but I don't think she's very suited to business. Her chatter can put people off."

"Maybe she'll go with Elam when he returns home."

"*If* he ever goes home."

Amelia giggled. "Exactly. I don't know what's with him. He occasionally tries to be nice and helpful, but then he reverts to being bossy, nosy, and opinionated."

"For sure." Christina tapped her mouth with the hand not clutching Jessie. "I shouldn't have said that."

Amelia smiled and patted her *freind's* arm. "You didn't say anything I haven't already thought."

"He's definitely a strange one, but somehow, I don't think he is your thief. He's annoying, for sure, but that doesn't make him a robber." Christina grabbed a wet paper towel from the pile in the middle of the table and wiped both of Jessie's sticky hands. "I believe your masterpiece is complete, little one."

Amelia wanted to ask Christina to explain her statement, but the girls were all finishing their projects. She carefully moved Jessie's paper to the kitchen counter to dry and told the other girls to add finishing touches to their creations so they could be moved.

"So, what are you going to do, Amelia?" Christina bounced Jessie on her knee.

"I'm going to clean up my kitchen table, send the artists to wash, and think about throwing supper together."

"That isn't what I meant, and you know it."

"There isn't anything I can do about the other matter, other than let it go. Our lives are different. We follow separate paths that only cross for babysitting needs."

"Hah!"

"That's the way it must be from here on out. I've enjoyed today way too much, which will make distancing harder, but I must do that."

"Don't be so quick to give up. All things are possible with the Lord *Gott*."

~

"What do you think?" Ryan studied the younger man's face so he could determine if his expression matched his words.

Noah rubbed a hand over his smooth jaw. "It wouldn't be easy, that's for sure and for certain."

"Most things worthwhile or important aren't easy to accomplish."

"True enough."

"Do you think it's possible?"

"Anything is possible if you believe in it."

"Has it ever been done before?"

"Do you mean has anyone who wasn't Old Order Mennonite become one?"

"Yes."

"I'm sure it's been done."

"Here?"

Noah's forehead puckered as if searching his memory caused discomfort. "I'm not sure." He snapped his fingers. "I do remember some of the older folks talking about a family who tried to join our group."

"Tried? Only tried? That doesn't bode well."

"I was young at the time, so I don't recall a lot about it. I believe it was a whole family. They were *Englisch*. They bought a farm and a horse and buggy. They gave up their cars and electric gadgets. They only stayed a few years. I remember my *mudder* saying she thought they were going to make it. She thought they had adapted, but they up and sold everything and returned to their old life."

"Hmm. But they were English. Converting must have been a huge change for them."

"I imagine. I would assume they had studied up on our way of life before taking that giant leap, but sometimes you don't really understand something until you get immersed in it."

Ryan snatched off his black felt hat, ran a hand through his hair, and plopped the hat back on his head. "It's bound to be easier for someone like me. I've practiced many of the same, or similar, customs all my life."

"But you would still have some major changes to make. Would you be able to give up your electric lights, air conditioning, and car that could take you the few miles to town by the time you hitched a horse to a buggy?"

"You make it sound like you all live in dark caves waiting for fire to be invented."

Noah burst out laughing. "We aren't that primitive."

"It isn't like I would have to sacrifice television, radio, or gadgets the way an Englisher would. I don't use those things either."

"True. You would have to learn another language to understand all the conversations. We all speak *Englisch*, of course, but we often converse among ourselves in *Deutsch*."

"Then I wouldn't know when someone was criticizing me or poking fun at me when I do things backward." Ryan chuckled. "That might be a good thing."

"*Gut.*"

"Huh?"

"*Gut*, not good."

"Oh, *jah*."

"I doubt anyone would make fun of you. We might laugh *with* you if you do something humorous, but everyone would do their best to help you."

"Would you be willing to teach me the language and how to care for horses and other necessary skills?"

"I could do that. But remember, the learning might be a whole lot easier than the doing and the feeling." Noah thumped his chest. "You have to feel in here that you are doing the right thing." Then he tapped his head. "And you have to believe in here that you can do it. Things are only possible if we believe and trust."

"Well said. I *believe* I am ready to make the change."

"What about your girls? They would have to make changes too."

Ryan chuckled. "I think they are way ahead of me. They mimic Amelia and her *kinner*. Gabby has already picked up some of the language. I wouldn't be surprised if Jessie's first real words were in *Deutsch*."

"You know you will have to discuss all of this with the bishop before I can help you, don't you?"

"Sure. I figured as much."

"I can tell you that his first question will probably be if you're making these changes for a woman. How will you answer that?"

Ryan rubbed his furrowed brow. "I can't deny that a woman is part of my decision, but it's not the entire reason I want to become a part of your community."

"I'm not trying to be nosy, but I want you to think and to have answers already in your head."

"I understand. I want to be as prepared as possible."

"Okay. Next, the bishop will ask why you want to join us."

Ryan considered for a moment. "I live right here in the midst of your community and am in contact with you folks every single day. My children's caregiver is Old Order. I see how happy my girls are and the values they are learning. I believe many of our beliefs are similar, and I would prefer to raise my children in the Old Order tradition." He paused for a breath. "Don't get me wrong. We have many wonderful people in my own church, but I fear our use of some modern conveniences might tempt my children to stray as they grow older. They are still very young, so change shouldn't be difficult for them. They have all their childhood ahead of them, and I want those years to be filled with the values and traditions of the Old Order Mennonite community."

"Great answer."

"Whew! That took a lot out of me. I want to say the right things, but I want the bishop to know I'm sincere in my pursuit."

"He is very astute and excellent at discerning a person's true character."

"That makes me a bit nervous. I don't have anything to hide, but it's rather unnerving to think a man can see clear through to my soul."

Noah chuckled. "It won't be that bad. Bishop Micah will act stern, but he is a fair man. If he asks if you would want to make the change if a woman was not involved, how would you answer?"

"I might not have made the decision this soon, but I'm confident I would still have the same desire."

"Fair enough."

"What else will I need to do?"

"I'm not sure if he will require you to attend baptismal classes as the young folks do before joining the church. He might meet with you privately for instruction."

"I can handle that."

"He'll probably want to know how you intend to modify your house and life to conform to our way."

"I'm assuming selling my vehicle and telling the electric company to cut the power won't suffice."

"Selling your vehicle would be right. You could use that money to purchase a buggy and a horse. I'm not certain, but you would probably have to redo your house."

"Do you mean remove the wiring?"

Noah shrugged.

"That would be a huge undertaking. It would probably be easier and less costly to purchase a different house!"

"I'm sure there are ways we can work together to get the job done more economically if that is even required. Bishop Micah would be the one to give you that information."

"Would you be available as a language tutor?"

"I could. Or you might want to ask a certain young lady." Noah gave him a sly smile.

"It wouldn't be appropriate for us to spend time alone together, would it?"

"Probably not, but Amelia could help you when you drop off and pick up your girls. I could fill in the gaps. When plowing season begins, I can show you how to do that with horses."

"You'd have to teach me how to hitch up and drive a team too."

"You'll catch on fast. Anyone who understands how to repair as many things as you do shouldn't have any difficulty picking up other manual skills."

"Do you think Henry Weaver would hire me in his shop if I needed to give up my present job? I do need to earn a living."

"That's possible. It's also possible you wouldn't have to change jobs. Have you thought what you will do if Bishop Micah denies your request?"

# Chapter Thirty

What a day it had turned out to be! All Amelia had planned on was a relaxing, fun day with her girls. Instead, the day had been filled with visitors—some pleasant and some not-so-pleasant—exploration, creation, and emotions that ran willy-nilly from one end of the spectrum to the other. Amelia was spent.

She collapsed in her favorite old rocking chair beside the living room stove when she should have simply crawled beneath the thick quilt on her bed. She would get there eventually. First, she wanted to think for a moment now that silence finally reigned in the house.

Christina's surprise visit had Amelia in turmoil. She was grateful her *freind* wanted her to be happy, but her actions had been unorthodox at best and downright risky, bordering on forbidden, at worst. She couldn't believe Christina would arrange such a meeting. Was Christina trying to force her to face emotions better left buried?

Amelia leaned her head against the high back of the chair, closed her eyes, and smiled. Ryan was such a nice man and a *gut daed*. His love for his girls was obvious. If she ever married again, she would want a man exactly like Ryan Miller. She would want it to *be* Ryan Miller.

She bolted upright. She should not even think such thoughts. Even if Christina had been right in her hunch that Ryan planned to join their community, Bishop Micah might not agree. Amelia could not allow herself to care and then have her hopes dashed by the bishop. What if Ryan couldn't go through with the change if the bishop did approve? Oh, why did she have to have feelings for the man?

She slumped back, banging her head on the chair. If only that would knock some sense into her silly head. She absolutely, positively could not care about Ryan. "Too late!" her heart whispered.

The bark outside the door sounded as loud as a gunshot. Amelia shivered. Had Noah and Ryan forgotten to secure the barn door and allowed Meggie to escape? She didn't think so. They knew how important it was to keep the animals safe. Once again, she would need to summon the courage to investigate.

She grabbed her shawl and flashlight and paused at the back door. She didn't want to go outside, but what choice did she have? She turned the lock and eased open the door. She felt to make sure the key still hung around her neck before slipping outside. *Here we go again. Won't I ever have another peaceful evening?* "What are you doing, Meggie?"

The dog pranced and panted as if trying to tell Amelia something. She ran down the steps and across the backyard. Amelia aimed the flashlight beam to follow Meggie's movement. The light traveled across the barn to a black space that should not have been there. She gasped and almost lost her grip on the light. Why had the barn door been flung wide open? Could someone be inside?

Fear for the animals' safety spurred her into action. Amelia hopped off the steps and jogged across the yard. "Did you open this door, Meggie?" Maybe Ryan and Noah hadn't properly latched it. She couldn't let fear paralyze her. She had to check the barn. She stepped closer and swept the flashlight's beam from one corner to another. Two bleary-eyed little pygmy goats bleated. The horses snorted and stomped. "I'm sorry to bother you. Is everyone all right?"

The fear in her voice probably did little to reassure the sensitive animals. She raised her voice. "Is anyone here?" She took one tentative step after another until she reached the goats' enclosure. Nothing appeared amiss. She checked each horse stall. Everything appeared normal, but something was not quite right. Goose bumps danced along her arms.

She yelped when the barn door banged closed. The flashlight flew from her hands when she spun around. Darkness enveloped her like a shroud. "M-Meggie?" Instantly, the little dog padded over and bumped against her leg. "What happened?" The wind had not been blowing hard enough to close the heavy door with such force. She needed to find that flashlight.

She dropped a hand to Meggie's head. Stroking the curly fur calmed her a bit. She stretched out one leg as far as possible and tapped around with her foot. She shuffled a few steps and repeated the process. Why did the flashlight have to go out when she dropped it? She felt around some more.

Had someone entered the barn and slammed the door behind them? Was she locked in here with the intruder? If so, the person must be holding his breath. She couldn't hear a thing. Had he merely locked her inside to scare her and then gone on his merry way? Why? She needed to get out of there and check on her girls.

Amelia tiptoed a few more inches away and tapped around for the light. She almost shouted with joy when her toe brushed against it. *Please don't be broken!* She crouched down to grasp the light and rose with her finger on the switch. She steeled herself to face whatever might be illuminated by the beam—if the bulb hadn't broken.

She held the flashlight steady and pointed it to where she believed the barn door was located and pressed the button.

Glorious light bounced off the far wall. Amelia blinked. She waved the light back and forth, startling the horses. No human faces appeared. Meggie did not bristle or growl. Had a sudden gust of wind blown the door closed after all?

She shuffled toward the door with Meggie glued to her side. She had to get out of the barn. She shushed the goats and horses as she passed them and laid a hand against the door. Even though Meggie was not a guard dog by any stretch of the imagination, Amelia was glad for her presence.

She shoved the door, but it didn't budge. She usually used both hands to open the heavy door, but that would mean she would have to lay down the light. She leaned into the door with a shoulder and cried out in pain. Still, the door did not open. She stooped to position the flashlight on the floor so that it shone on the stubborn door.

Using both hands, she pushed with all her might. Nothing happened. Who would have been prowling around in the dark and why lock her in the barn? Panic swelled. Maybe if she calmed down and tried again, the door would open. Meggie whined as Amelia grunted and flailed at the door.

Panic morphed into fear. Her *bopplin* were sound asleep in the house alone. She had to get to them. Surely, no one would break into her house and harm them. Was this merely another prank by the silly teens who set off the smoke bomb? Maybe they lurked outside the barn. Why didn't their parents keep better track of them? "Hello? Is anyone out there?"

Meggie's panting was the only sound Amelia detected. She cleared her throat and tried again. "Who's out there?"

Meggie whined and nudged Amelia's leg. Apparently, the dog sensed her distress. She patted the little brown head. "It's okay, girl. We'll figure this out." She said the words more to convince herself than to calm the dog. *Think, Amelia!*

How had she not heard anyone approach the barn door while she was inside? She never heard footsteps, the creaky door, or anything. Not until the door slammed closed, that is. The silence was almost as unnerving as her situation.

Amelia retrieved the flashlight and waved it around the barn. She stopped at the shuttered window. Unlike the door, the window's latch was on the inside. If she climbed onto something, she might be able to squeeze through and be free. She would try the door one more time before embarking on an acrobatic routine.

*Please let this door open, Lord Gott.* What if one of the girls awoke and couldn't find her? She couldn't let that happen. She laid the flashlight at her feet again, flexed her fingers, and drew in a deep breath. This attempt had to be successful.

But it wasn't. Amelia's heart pounded, and her breath came in gasps. She was truly trapped inside her own barn. She picked up the light and surveyed her surroundings for something she could climb on. It was too bad she stored the ladder in the shed. If she stacked a couple of hay bales, she might be able to reach the window. Long legs, which she did not have, would have been a blessing right about now.

She propped the flashlight and dragged one bale to rest beneath the window. She struggled to lift the second one to sit atop the first one, ignoring the scratches and pokes from the prickly hay. She hoped the two bales would give her the height she needed. Otherwise, she would have to wrestle with another bale.

She tossed the flashlight onto the top bale so it would be available when she needed it and scrambled up on the hay. Meggie hopped up with a little running leap. She hadn't figured on the dog trying to follow her. "I don't think you will be able to get out the window, pup. I'll *kumm* back for you. I promise."

Stretching as far as possible, Amelia could just reach the window. Would she be strong enough to hoist herself up and out? First, though, she had to turn the latch and push open the wooden shutter. She might have to go back for the third bale. Time was wasting. She had to get inside to her girls.

With a little jump, she batted the latch hard enough to make it turn. Another little leap allowed her to punch the shutter open. Great! She panted and waited for her racing heart to settle down. Cold air rushed through the open window, making Amelia wish she had grabbed a heavier cloak.

She eyeballed the distance between the window and where she stood with great trepidation. She doubted she could jump high enough to grasp the edge of the window, and she knew she couldn't scale the wall. Even a running start was not likely to help. But she also wasn't sure she had the strength to lift another bale of hay high enough to add a third tier to her tower.

All the same, she had to try to reach the window. She jumped over and over, trying to get higher with each leap. Tears of frustration filled her eyes. She blinked them away. She would make one last attempt and then she would drag another hay bale over. If only she had never entered the barn. *Wishing never accomplished a thing, Amelia. Give it another go. You can do this.*

She squatted and leaped. This time, her hands grabbed the edge of the window. Her arm muscles trembled. She begged them to be strong. With effort that could only have been an answer to prayer, she hoisted herself high enough to prop her elbows on the ledge. She resisted the urge to sob. She needed to concentrate on maneuvering herself up and out before her fingers grew numb with cold and she plummeted back down to the scratchy hay bales.

"Amelia!"

"Ahhh!" Startled, she relaxed her grip and crashed.

# Chapter Thirty-One

Taking the girls to the singing at church after their busy day had probably been a mistake. No, make that it *had* been a mistake. They were tired, and tired children turned into cranky children. And cranky they had been.

Ryan crept out of the church as quietly as an adult could with a child tucked under each arm. It wasn't that they misbehaved, but they had yawned, fidgeted, and wiggled continuously. He decided to remove them from the room before an all-out meltdown occurred.

"Where are we going, Daddy?"

Even Gabby's voice sounded exhausted. Poor little thing. They'd gone to church early that morning, as they did every Sunday. Their church did not have off Sundays like the Old Order church. They had attended Sunday School and then romped through the woods, played, and created their artwork. They'd had little more than a cat nap all day.

"We're going home, Gabby. I think you and Jessie are tuckered out." Ryan wasn't much better himself. The girls would probably fall asleep in the car. He prayed he wouldn't.

"Is the singing over?"

"Not quite."

"Can't we stay?"

Ryan chuckled. "You were falling asleep when you weren't squirming like a wiggle worm."

"No, I wasn't."

"What was the last song we sang?" It had been an easy one that all children learned in Sunday School.

"I don't know."

"Uh-huh." Ryan set Gabby on her feet when he reached the black SUV. Since all the members of his community drove dark cars, vans, or SUVs, he always had to double-check that he was trying to get into the right one. He wouldn't have that problem if he was Old Order. They all drove black buggies, but he would certainly recognize his own horse.

He opened the back door. "Can you climb in by yourself, Gabby, so I can buckle Jessie into her seat?"

"I can do it."

"That's my big girl." Ryan watched for a moment to make sure she didn't stumble before circling the vehicle to click Jessie into her seat. He reached across to make sure Gabby's seatbelt was secure before climbing behind the wheel.

He cranked the engine and flipped the switch for the heater. He wouldn't be able to do that in a buggy! But there were always blankets to snuggle beneath, and the cold was a good excuse to sit close to someone. He massaged his forehead. He was driving himself crazy with constant comparisons.

He thought about Amelia as he drove. How wonderful it would be to sit beside her in a buggy, to eat supper with her every night, and to work together to raise five little girls. He sensed she cared in the same way he did. He prayed she did.

A churning in his gut disturbed him. Something was wrong, but he couldn't put his finger on it. He'd drive past Amelia's house just to make sure everything was all right. A quick glance in the rearview mirror assured him the girls had fallen asleep, so he wouldn't need to explain their detour.

He slowed as he neared Amelia's property. He thought he saw a glow from the house, but it sat too far back from the road for him to tell if it was from a lamp inside. He turned onto the driveway and inched forward. He certainly didn't want to frighten her if she was simply reading or knitting in the living room.  Maybe he was being silly and should leave. But something wouldn't let him.

His eyes roved the yard and house as he drove closer. A light was shining from the living room. He angled his vehicle so the headlights highlighted the barn and outbuildings. Everything seemed to be in order. Wait! Were his eyes playing tricks on him, or was there a person in the barn window?

He threw the gearshift into park, cut the engine, reached beneath the seat for his flashlight, and jumped out. To be on the safe side, he locked the doors of the SUV. He raced to the barn, switching on the flashlight as he ran. He waved the light around to take in the ground and the structure. A person clung to the window ledge. "Amelia!"

He blinked and she was gone. Had he only imagined he'd seen her? A thump and a groan spurred him into action. He ran to the barn door and pulled, but nothing happened. How had it gotten latched on the outside if Amelia was inside? He fumbled with the lock. "Amelia! I'm coming!"

〜

Amelia lay flat on her back, too stunned to do anything except groan. She couldn't even shift off the loose, prickly pieces of hay poking her ribs. Meggie hovered over her like a *mudder* hen, alternately whining and nudging Amelia with her cold nose. Amelia attempted to raise up on her elbows when the dog swiped her rough tongue across her cheek. She turned her head away before Meggie could lick her again. "Ick! It's okay, girl."

She thought she was okay anyway. Various body parts throbbed, but Amelia didn't think she had broken any bones. She thought she had heard someone call her name, but she could have been delirious. She groaned. She needed to hoist her battered body up to the window again, but she didn't know if she had the strength to do so. *Give me strength, Lord. I have to get to my girls.*

"Amelia?"

She *had* heard a voice. This time, it was more muffled but still loud enough to be detected through the closed door. Was this someone she could trust, or was it the person who had locked her in here? The latch squeaked. She would find out in a few seconds.

She squinted when the flashlight's beam shone directly into her eyes. "Who's there?"

"Oh, I'm sorry."

The ray of light dropped from her face. Her eyes struggled to adjust. Did the voice truly belong to Ryan, or was it her wishful thinking?

"Amelia! What happened?" The big man crossed from the door to the bale of hay, where she still lay, in a few swift strides.

"I-I fell." She had the sudden urge to bawl like a *boppli*.

"Are you hurt?"

She tried to sit up all the way.

"Wait. You might have broken something."

A strong arm surrounded her. She wanted to lean her head on the sturdy shoulder and stay there forever, but she couldn't do any such thing. "I don't believe I did." She reached a sitting position with his assistance. "What are you doing here?"

"What are you doing here?" Ryan asked his question at the same time

Amelia swiped at the pesky tears that threatened to drip down her cheeks and attempted to right her lopsided *kapp*. "I got locked in."

"Why were you out here in the dark?"

"Oh my! I've got to get to my girls. Where are your *kinner?*"

"Asleep in the car."

"Are your doors locked?"

"Yes, but why? What's going on?"

"I have to get up." The world swirled around for a few seconds, but Amelia steeled herself against the dizziness.

"Let me help you, dear." Ryan practically lifted her off the bale. Meggie continued to hover. "It looks like you've had a good guard here." He patted the dog's head with his free hand. "Do you think you can walk?"

She swayed for a moment but regained her balance. "I have to check on my girls—and yours too." A pain stabbed her ankle when she bore weight on it, but Amelia couldn't be concerned about that right now.

"We will. Take it slow." Ryan kept an arm wrapped around her for support. "Is your door locked?"

"*Jah.*" She used the hand not tucked against Ryan's side to make sure she hadn't lost the key from around her neck.

Ryan leaned over to snatch her shawl off the floor and shook off bits of hay. "It's cold. You might want this on."

"I'm fine. Let's hurry." Amelia couldn't suppress a soft groan.

"You're hurt."

"I'm all right."

"You're limping. Is it your ankle?"

"My legs probably went to sleep." She limped again with her next step.

"I think it's more than the pins and needles of numbness wearing off."

"Please! I've got to get to my girls."

"Lean on me. I'll get you inside to them."

Amelia sucked in a sharp breath when the cold breeze slapped her cheeks at the open door. "I didn't close the barn window." She tried to control her shivering.

"I'll secure it later."

She tried to peer inside the SUV when they drew near. "We need to get them out." She would never forgive herself if something happened to Gabby and Jessie.

Ryan bent to look in the back window. "They're asleep. The doors are locked, and they have blankets. They will be fine while I take you in the house."

"*Nee!* Don't leave them here. Stay here with them. I'll check on my girls and be right back." Amelia pulled away from Ryan's side and instantly felt even colder. He grabbed her hand before she could limp out of range.

"What happened here tonight? How did you get locked in the barn?"

"I wish I knew." She didn't want to be rude, but she had to go to her *bopplin*.

Ryan must have read her mind. "Let me help you to the door and make sure you get inside okay. Then I'll sit on the step where I can keep an eye on my car until you come back out. I want to know what happened."

Amelia nodded and allowed him to assist her. Meggie trotted along beside them as if she needed to oversee the whole operation. Amelia slipped the cord holding the key over her head and unlocked the door. At least no one had tampered with the lock. "I'll hurry."

"Take your time. I'm not going anywhere."

She ignored the pain in her ankle and knee and hurried to the stairway. She must have banged her knee on the barn wall as she fell from the window. Thank goodness she landed on the bales of hay, or she could have had more se-vere injuries than bumps and bruises. She leaned heavily on the banister as she dragged herself up the stairs, praying her girls were safely sleeping.

She rushed into the bedroom across from her own where all three slept. She grabbed the flashlight off the dresser and switched it on, aiming it toward the floor so it wouldn't shine on their faces. The girls slumbered like little cherubs. Amelia crossed the room and lightly placed her hand on each chest to make sure it rose and fell as it was supposed to. *Danki, Lord, that my kinner are safe*. She tiptoed from the room, relieved no harm had befallen her *dochders*.

Amelia returned to the stairway and sank onto the top step with a gasp as realization struck her. Some devious person had deliberately lured her outside with the intent of harming her, or of scaring her at the very least. What had she done to deserve such treatment?

# Chapter Thirty-Two

"Amelia, is everything all right?" Ryan jumped up from his perch on the step and poked his head inside and whispered as loudly as he could. What could be taking her so long? He tried to calm his nerves. Maybe one of the girls woke up and needed to be soothed back to sleep. Maybe Amelia wanted to tend to injuries or wash up. He didn't dare call louder for fear of waking the children. He waited.

Desperation drove him to speak again. What if there had been someone in the house with evil intentions? He cleared his throat and called as loud as he dared. "Amelia?"

"Be right there."

He exhaled the breath he'd been holding and waited for his heart to stop hammering away at his ribs. The sight of her weary, but lovely, face brought immeasurable relief and joy. He wanted to run to her, wrap his arms around her, and never let her go. He wanted to promise to keep her safe and always take care of her. He couldn't do any of those things. Yet.

"Are Gabby and Jessie all right?"

Always thinking of others. That was his Amelia. He hoped she would one day be *his* Amelia. "They're still asleep. I've been keeping an eye on the car."

"They must be getting cold. Bring them inside."

"They have blankets. I checked and the car was still warm." That would not have been the case had he been driving a buggy instead of an automobile. He'd take happiness over heat any day though. "Will you please tell me what happened?"

"Let's sit. I'm too exhausted to stand much longer."

"Please grab a warmer coat. This shawl won't do the trick." He held out the shawl he had retrieved earlier.

Amelia took the shawl from his hands and shook it. "I'll have to pick all the hay off of this before I wash it." She tossed the shawl inside and grabbed a heavy cloak to wrap around her body before sitting on the top step.

He dropped down beside her, as close as he dared, and took her small, cool hand in his. Even though winter had not officially begun, the chill of the late autumn evenings often masqueraded as winter. "Are the children okay?"

"They're sound asleep."

"How is your ankle?"

"It will be fine. I must have banged my leg when I fell."

He wanted to fire off question after question but decided to give her a moment to collect her thoughts. She still seemed a little stunned. "Can you tell me what happened?"

~

Amelia had an almost overwhelming desire to lay her head against Ryan's shoulder and leave it there forever. Somehow, his very presence chased away all the terror she had experienced earlier. Meggie settled down on the step right beneath them and laid her head on Amelia's foot. "It looks like my protector is pretty worn out." She petted the curly, brown head.

"But I have a feeling she would stand at attention the moment anyone suspicious came near you. It appears she is a pretty good watchdog after all."

"She let me know something was amiss at the barn. That's for sure and for certain. Her barking alerted me."

"Was someone in your barn?"

"I didn't see anyone. I did look outside before I went out. I grabbed my shawl and a flashlight so I could find out why Meggie was at the back door. I knew you and Noah had cared for the animals and secured the barn earlier, so I was surprised to see her at the door. When I got close to the barn, I found the door wide open. I was afraid someone had messed with the animals. But then I thought someone might be playing a trick on me."

"You entered the barn? Alone?"

"What other choice did I have? I needed to make sure the animals were unharmed."

"Were they?"

"They were fine. The horses and goats were in their stalls where they belonged."

"Did you see anyone roaming around?"

"I did not."

"How did you get trapped inside the barn?"

Did Ryan realize he still held her hand? Amelia certainly had a keen awareness of that. She should withdraw her hand, but his touch brought such comfort and strength, she couldn't bring herself to move. "I-I'm not sure. I was so startled when the door slammed shut. At first, I thought someone closed it, but I guess the wind could have closed it."

"I don't believe the breeze has been that strong all evening, and unless I'm mistaken, the wind does not have hands to turn a lock."

Amelia couldn't contain the fit of giggles. Maybe she needed the emotional release. She couldn't stop laughing until she gasped for breath. Meggie sat up and stared as if

Amelia had lost her mind. "I'm sorry. For some reason, that struck me as hilarious."

"It makes me happy to hear you laugh."

"Laughing is better than crying, which is what I wanted to do earlier. I was scared and then angry and then frustrated that I had to climb a wall to escape from my own barn. And then concern for my girls overtook all those other emotions." Ryan squeezed her hand, sending a warm, tingly sensation throughout her body. "Do you think someone deliberately locked me in the barn?"

"That would be my guess."

"Who? Why?"

"That's exactly what I would like to know."

Amelia shivered. "I don't know what I would have done if you hadn't arrived when you did. I would have been stuck out there all night. The girls would have been so scared if they couldn't find me when they woke up. Oh, it would have been awful!"

"Knowing your determination, you would have scaled the wall until you wiggled out that window. And I'm sure you would have willed yourself to have landed on your feet when you leaped to the ground too."

Amelia elbowed him. "Are you trying to say I'm stubborn?"

"Um, I'd call it determined rather than stubborn. You are also a devoted mother who puts her children's needs ahead of her own. That's a very admirable thing." He squeezed her hand again. "You do know that I greatly admire you, don't you?"

Amelia's face heated. "I'm no different from any other *mudder.*"

"Oh yes, you are! You are very special. You are the bravest lady I know. Who else would have the courage to go out in the dark to investigate what was going on? And you had the common sense to figure out a way out of your situation.

I am concerned for your safety though. If someone was playing a trick, it was a very mean thing to do."

"I believe most people would have considered me foolish, but you're right. It was a very mean trick to play. I'm glad I had my trusty guard dog with me."

Ryan chuckled. "I'm not sure how much of a threat Meggie would be to someone, but at least she warned you of a problem."

"That she did. I think she might have just earned house dog status."

"I think that's a good idea, at least for now."

"She might not be an attack dog or anything like that, but she will make me feel a mite safer."

"I wish it could be me."

He had whispered the words, but Amelia heard them as loud as a shout. Her heart skipped a few beats, leaving her breathless.

Ryan cleared his throat. "Since I can't have the privilege of protecting you as I would like to do, is there someone who could stay with you again? Maybe Christina could come back, or even Jill, if that would be permissible."

"I wouldn't want to bother them. They have their own lives and work."

"I understand your hesitance. Most of us hate asking for help. Is there someone who would like a break from their usual routine?"

Amelia shook her head, even though Ryan probably couldn't see her. "With the holidays quickly approaching, people are busy getting their houses spruced up and their holiday projects and work completed." She glanced heavenward at the bright stars dotting the sky. A sudden thought occurred to her. "If you are fearful about Gabby and Jessie staying here, I can certainly understand."

"I have no qualms about that at all. There isn't anyone else I would rather have care for them. Why would I settle for someone else when I have the best?" He dropped her hand and wrapped his arm around her, tugging her a little closer.

"I mean, until we figure out what's going on." Amelia couldn't think clearly with Ryan so near. She should scoot over and put some distance between them, but she didn't want to leave the security his arm provided just yet.

"I don't want to change their routine, unless you don't want to watch them."

"Of course I want to watch them! I didn't want you to be concerned about their safety while you worked."

"I never worry about them with you."

She glanced toward the car. "They might be getting cold by now."

"I doubt it. They had heavy blankets piled on them. I know I should get them home and to bed, but I hate leaving you."

"I'll be fine." Amelia did her best to sound brave but feared she fell short.

"Do you think you should report what happened tonight to the police?"

"*Nee*. That's not our way. Besides, they will probably say it was those young folks pulling another prank."

"If that's the case, those parents need to be notified so they can keep their children in line. The police would need to know so they can inform the adults."

"You might be right, but I don't have any kind of evidence. There isn't any proof, and I would hate for the young folks to be blamed for something they didn't do."

Ryan shook his head. "If there had been any fingerprints or evidence, I'm sure I messed that up. I had my hands all over the latch and door. I wasn't thinking about preserving the scene. My only thought was to get to you."

Amelia patted his arm. "Don't worry about that. I'm just glad you decided to drive by my house tonight."

"Me too. I would still feel better if someone stayed here with you. Do you want me to stop by The Green Thumb tomorrow to ask Christina? I'm sure she wouldn't mind."

"Let me think about it." *Let me see how difficult it is to get through the rest of the night.*

"Okay. You can let me know in the morning. Are you sure you'll be all right tonight? I can stop by the Brubacher place on my way home."

"Oh, please don't disturb them. I'll be fine." Ryan gave her a little squeeze that made her want to latch onto him and beg him not to go.

"If you say so." He stood and pulled her to her feet. "I will stand right here until you go inside and lock the door. I'll listen for the click. Then I'll go to the barn to close that window and make sure everything is secure."

"*Danki.*" She turned toward the door, nudging Meggie ahead of her. She whirled around as a sudden inspiration struck her. "I just thought of something. Eleanore Gingrich might want a change of scenery for a few days."

"She's the bishop's sister, isn't she?"

"*Jah.* She lives with him, his *fraa,* and their *kinner.* She might want a little break from that routine. I'm sure she gets along fine with Nancy, but it must be difficult sharing a house and kitchen with a *schweschder*-in-law. She might not think spending a few days with three rambunctious girls is much of a trade-off though." Amelia laughed.

"I'd hardly call your children rowdy. They are very well-behaved. I have met your bishop a few times, by the way, and his family."

"You have?"

"Yes, and I plan to meet with him again, but that's a story for another day. I believe you might be right about Eleanore needing a break. Would you like me to stop by the school and talk with her tomorrow?"

"Maybe. I'll let you know."

～

Amelia hoped morning would arrive quickly. She doubted she would get a wink of sleep. She had made a bed for Meggie in the mudroom. If the tail-wagging was any indication, the pup couldn't be more delighted with her promotion to house pet. She sniffed her bed and turned around three times before plopping down to drop her head onto her paws and close her eyes.

"I'm glad one of us can snooze away the hours. But you earned your keep tonight, my little *freind*." Amelia patted the dog's head before checking the lock on the back door one more time and threading her way through the house. Having Meggie close by made her feel slightly more secure.

Bumps, bruises, and strained muscles throbbed with a vengeance as Amelia crept up the stairs while gripping the banister for support. She needed a shower to wash all her scrapes and scratches. The warm water would probably ease her tension and maybe even help her relax enough to fall asleep.

Nothing made sense about the evening. She didn't know why Meggie had run from the barn. She couldn't imagine who would have closed her inside and run off to leave her helpless. Robbery didn't appear to be a motive since nothing had been tampered with as far as she could tell. If someone took delight in frightening another person half out of their wits, then they should be having a great laugh now.

By the time she had dried off and donned her nightgown, she only had a few hours to wait for dawn. Whether she slept or not, whether she had energy or was exhausted, her girls would still need to be fed and chores would need to be done. And she needed to decide if she should ask Eleanore to stay with them. She groaned as she attempted to find a comfortable position. The new day ahead had to be better.

# Chapter Thirty-Three

Amelia had given up on sleep after an hour of tossing and turning and had wearily readied herself for the day and headed for the kitchen. Baking always soothed her and made her forget her troubles. She had relented and told Ryan he could stop by the school and talk to Eleanore on his way home. She would have spoken to Eleanore herself when she dropped items off at The Green Thumb, but she didn't want to interrupt her class.

Once she got the girls fed, Rhonda off to school, and the kitchen straightened up, she set out to deliver her treats. The fresh air should perk her up. The horse trotted lively as if he needed to wake up too. He had an interrupted night as well.

She stood with her back to the door as she arranged plastic-wrapped cookies, brownies, and cake slices on an empty shelf. It was a *gut* thing she had baked during the wee hours of the morning. Otherwise, Christina might not have any goodies for her customers. She glanced at Judith, Joanna, and Gabby as they entertained Jessie with their stuffed animals in a back corner of The Green Thumb. She jumped when the bells jingled, announcing a customer.

"I didn't mean to frighten you, Amelia." Naomi Brenneman hurried to Amelia's side.

"You startled me, that's all. How are you, Naomi?"

"I'm fine. I brought some treats to sell too, but I know mine aren't nearly as tasty as yours."

"I didn't know you baked for Christina."

"This is the first time. I thought I'd see if Christina could use a few more items to sell."

"Well, this shelf was empty before I started filling it, so she will probably be happy to have a few more things. What did you bring?"

"I only have cookies."

"I'm sure they will sell well. Would you like me to put them out, or do you want to speak to Christina first?"

Naomi stepped closer and laid a hand on Amelia's arm. "Would you like someone to stay with you for a while, I mean, until this prankster decides to give up tormenting you? I know Christina stayed with you a few times, but I certainly don't mind helping you out."

Sometimes Amelia wondered if everyone else knew her business before she did. "That's very sweet of you, Naomi, but I'm sure we'll be fine. You heard I got a dog, didn't you? She has done an excellent job of alerting me to problems."

"I did hear that, but another person could be such a comfort, and I don't mind one bit."

"*Danki*, dear, but I'm sure you must still have lots to catch up on after your trip."

Naomi waved her hand as if to dismiss that idea. "Pshaw! As I said before, I've been home for a few weeks now. I don't have a business to run or a fellow to visit with like Christina does." She smiled and winked.

"I believe I heard my name." Christina sailed in from the greenhouse where she'd been checking on some fall plants. "Nothing bad, I hope."

Naomi laughed. "Of course not. You certainly have a keen sense of hearing. I was telling Amelia I knew you had stayed with her previously and I'd be happy to take a turn."

"I thought—" Christina stopped abruptly as if she'd said something out of turn.

Amelia jumped in. She had mentioned to Christina her idea of asking Eleanore to visit but didn't want to put her on the spot with Naomi. "You didn't give me a chance to finish telling you that Eleanore may be visiting with us for a while. But I will definitely keep you in mind if she has a change of plans or if this craziness that has become my life doesn't stop by the time Eleanore has had enough of us." Amelia ended with a little chuckle.

"Oh. Okay. I'm sure Eleanore would like to get out from under Nancy's thumb. If those plans don't work out, please don't hesitate to give me a holler."

Amelia caught Christina's raised eyebrows and head shake. Naomi was never one to mince words or to keep her opinions to herself. "Sure thing, Naomi, and *danki* again." She finished arranging her treats while Naomi discussed leaving her own baked items at the store. Amelia hoped Eleanore would agree to help because she didn't think she'd care much for having Naomi share a living space with her. It wasn't that she didn't like Naomi. She simply didn't know the girl that well or think she would feel as comfortable with her as she would with Eleanore.

～

"Eleanore, it was so *gut* of you to *kumm* over."

"I'm happy to do so."

"I know you're busy with your teaching duties and everything else." Amelia's voice trailed off. She really wasn't sure what else Eleanore did besides teach. As far as she knew, she was not stepping out with anyone, and she certainly hadn't seemed interested in Elam Wenger.

It appeared the young woman had regained some of the weight she had lost during and immediately after her hospital stay, but she would not be considered fat, and she had such a lovely face with those big, brown eyes framed by dark lashes. Amelia hoped Eleanore's diabetes was under control.

"I generally spend my time working on lessons for my scholars and grading papers or helping Nancy tend to her *kinner* and the house. I can certainly do my schoolwork equally as well here as there."

"I hope Nancy doesn't mind doing without your help."

Eleanore laughed. "I'm thinking Nancy is relieved to be rid of me for a while. She won't have anyone trying to alter her food preparations."

"I'm sure she's grateful for all you do to help her."

"Hmm! She's not happy that I need to eat differently from the rest of the family. At any rate, a little change of routine will be *gut* for her and for me."

Exactly what Ryan had said. What an intuitive man! She added that to her mental list of his attributes. "I have a spare room, so you won't have to share with anyone."

"That wouldn't have been a problem. I would happily share a room with the *kinner*. They're such dear little girls, and Rhonda is doing remarkably well in first grade."

"I'm glad to hear that. Have you been feeling well? I wouldn't want to do anything to compromise your health."

"You won't do that." Eleanore patted her midsection. "As you can see, I found that weight I lost in the hospital. The doctor won't be at all pleased about that. I'm taking my medicine, but it's so hard to eat right when Nancy won't change her way of cooking." She sighed and shook her head. "That's not fair of me. It is her house and her kitchen, so she should not have to change things to accommodate me. I should be grateful she and Micah allow me to live with them."

"I'm sorry things are less than ideal and that food preparation is such a problem. Maybe Nancy doesn't understand your needs."

"I tried to get her to visit the diabetes educator with me, but she refused to go. I usually end up preparing something different to eat and ignoring her eye rolls."

Amelia smiled. "While you are here, please feel free to eat what and how you like. Or tell me the best way to prepare your food. I know a little about your diet since my *grossmammi* was diabetic, but I'm sure things have changed since I visited her as a girl."

"*Danki*, Amelia."

"I really appreciate your staying with us tonight."

"I'll stay as long as you want."

Amelia figured living in another woman's house must be very difficult for Eleanore. If she was like most women, she wanted her own home and family. She was such a nice person and so *gut* with the scholars. She would make an excellent *fraa* and *mudder*. "I hope you aren't allergic to dogs. I know most folks don't keep animals in the house, but Meggie's status has been raised to house pet for now. Somehow, I feel a little safer with her nearby."

"That's fine by me. I like animals. I simply can't imagine who would be bothering you of all people. You are kind to everyone and mind your own business. It does not make any sense." Eleanore clucked her tongue and shook her head.

"I can't figure it out either. I keep praying the problem will disappear as quickly as it began. *Kumm*, I'll show you where to put your belongings, and then I need to feed the girls."

"Lead the way. I'll drop off my things and help you with supper."

"We're having boiled potatoes and cabbage with leftover baked ham. I don't add butter or grease to my vegetables. Will this be all right for you, or should I prepare something different?"

"That will be great. I can eat most plain vegetables, especially cabbage, greens, and things like that."

"*Wunderbaar!* Everything is ready. I'll tell the girls to wash up." Amelia hoped she wouldn't need to interrupt Eleanore's life for long, but it might be fun to get to know her better.

~

Ryan set a plate of too-yellow macaroni and cheese made from a box and commercially canned green beans in front of Gabby. He scattered a few bite-sized pieces of green beans on Jessie's high chair tray while he spooned applesauce and the last jar of a baby food dinner onto a sectioned plastic plate.

The stuff didn't look especially appealing to him, but fortunately, his girls were not picky eaters. He would like to make healthy meals from scratch, but time and energy didn't allow for that. If he made the girls wait an hour while he prepared a proper meal, he would most likely have a serious mutiny on his hands. Stopping by the school to talk to Eleanore had thrown him off his usual schedule, but the delay had been worth it since the teacher was willing to stay with Amelia. So boxed and canned food it was.

Ryan dropped onto the sturdy oak chair next to Jessie with a grunt and began spooning food into her mouth. His mind was preoccupied with putting clues together to determine who kept bothering Amelia. But he didn't have much to go on.

"Where is your plate, Daddy?" Gabby spoke around the mushy beans in her mouth.

"Please swallow before you speak."

The little girl gulped and repeated her question.

Ryan hadn't even thought about food for himself. He had only been concerned with feeding the children. He knew he should have prepared a plate for himself to set a good example, but the thought of chewing those spongy noodles with their neon-yellow sauce did bad things to his stomach. "I'll get something in a minute. I wanted to tend to you and Jessie first."

"Aren't you hungry?"

He had been hungry an hour ago, but right now, his stomach warned him not to introduce those noodles and beans. He would look for a loaf of bread in a few minutes and spread some peanut butter between two slices. If he added a dollop of Amelia's strawberry jam, he would have a tasty meal. He'd top that off with an apple and be content until breakfast.

Breakfast. If supper was a rushed meal, breakfast was even more so. He tried to purchase the healthiest cold cereal he could find at the grocery store or those instant oatmeal packets, but he still felt like a terrible parent. He resolved to try to cook more on the weekends and make enough to heat up during the week. At least the girls had wholesome, home-cooked meals when they were with Amelia. He spooned another bite into Jessie's mouth.

His thoughts always seemed to work their way around to Amelia. No matter what else might be on his mind, images of Amelia always grounded him.

"Are you happy, Daddy?"

Ryan stared at his older daughter. "Why do you ask?"

"You're smiling. I smile when I'm happy."

His smile broadened. "Yes, you do. And yes, I am happy. I have two wonderful little girls. We have a nice house and food to eat. Who wouldn't be happy?"

"We're only missing one thing."

Jessie banged on her tray, obviously tired of waiting for her next bite of food. He scooped up another spoonful of applesauce and offered it to her. Now that she had teeth, he should probably offer her a bigger variety of food.

While Jessie licked her lips, Ryan jumped up to retrieve a loaf of bread, the peanut butter, the jam, a plate, and a knife.

He plopped back onto his chair, fed Jessie another bite, and began to make his sandwich.

"Aren't you going to ask me what we're missing?"

Right. He'd forgotten Gabby's comment. "I didn't mean to ignore you, sweetheart. What is it you need? More macaroni or milk?"

"No. I still have some. See?"

He spooned a few more green beans onto her plate.

"That's not it either." Gabby used her fork to push the beans away from the few neon noodles she hadn't yet eaten.

"Okay. I give up. What do you need?"

The little girl sighed as if she had to deal with a total dunce. He resisted the urge to laugh at her exasperation and offered her what he hoped was a serious expression. She laid her fork on her plate and stared into his eyes. "We need a mommy."

Ryan coughed and was glad he hadn't taken a bite of food or a sip of water before that pronouncement. "Wh-what makes you say that?"

"A mommy would cook our meals and sew for us. I got a tear. See?" Gabby twisted so Ryan could see the tiny tear in the seam of her dress. "A mommy would help us fix our hair and do the wash, and, well, all sorts of things."

"I don't do half bad at those tasks." He suddenly felt the need to justify himself to his four-year-old daughter.

"I know, but you have to work too."

"That's true, but I try to keep up with things. I know tonight's supper is not one of my best efforts, but I usually do better."

"This is okay."

Bless the child. Always so kindhearted. He prayed for the right words to say. "I'm sure you miss having a mommy, but I can't go out and buy one at the store, you know."

Gabby giggled. "You're silly, Daddy. You don't have to go to the store for one at all."

"Oh?"

"No. The perfect mommy is right here."

Ryan pretended to look under the table and around the room. He even glanced out the window. "Where? I don't see her."

Gabby giggled again. Jessie copied her big sister and laughed as she squashed the beans on her tray.

"Amelia would be the best mommy ever."

Ryan coughed harder this time. His eyes watered. Now what should he say?

"Do you want me to pat your back?"

Ryan shook his head. He reached for his glass and swigged down a gulp of water. He took a deep breath. "I'm fine. I swallowed wrong." His voice sounded strained, but at least sound came out. "Amelia has a home and children, dear."

"But her girls don't have a daddy. You could be their daddy."

"What makes you think they want a daddy? They seem perfectly happy to me."

"All children want a mommy and a daddy."

When had Gabby acquired such wisdom? "That's probably true, but sometimes things happen that leave children with only one parent. And that parent loves his or her children very much."

"Do you mean like Mommy dying?"

"Yes."

"Amelia's husband died too. You and she could get married and make a new family with all of us."

"You've got this all figured out, huh?" Ryan smiled a sad smile. He knew Gabby missed her mother. He also knew she loved Amelia and her girls. But would she be happy living with them forever?

"It sounds good to me."

"We would have to make a lot of changes, you know."

"Like what?" Gabby speared a bright noodle and popped it into her mouth.

Ryan grabbed napkins from the holder in the center of the table and wiped Jessie's hands after removing all the smashed beans. When he looked back at Gabby, the child still stared at him, waiting for an answer. "We do things differently. We ride in cars. They use buggies."

"I like riding in the buggy."

"We have electric lights and heat."

"Amelia has lights and a woodstove. Two of them."

"That's true, but someone needs to cut, stack, and carry wood. That's a lot of work."

"I've helped carry wood. I'm strong. See?" Gabby jumped up and lifted her chair a few inches off the floor.

"I do see. You are a very strong girl and a good helper. I'm not so sure you would like carrying or stacking wood every day. Please sit down now and finish your supper."

Gabby sat, picked up her fork, and shuffled the beans around on her plate. "Is that all?"

"What?" He had hoped the subject was done.

"What else is different?"

She obviously wasn't going to let him off the hook. He drummed his fingers on the table. "They often speak in the old language."

"I've been learning it. I can teach you."

"I'm sure you could." Ryan smiled and reached across the table to pat his daughter's hand. "And the biggest concern of all is that Amelia might not want to get married again."

"She'd marry you."

Ryan's heart stuttered. "What makes you think that?" He couldn't believe he was asking a little girl such a thing.

"She smiles whenever she sees you."

"Amelia smiles at you and Jessie and her girls too."

"Not the same way she smiles at you. Her eyes get all sparkly." Gabby fluttered her eyes.

Ryan laughed. "You're so silly."

"*Nee*, I'm right."
Was she? Oh, how he hoped so.

# Chapter Thirty-Four

Even though she had crawled into bed later than usual after staying up to chat with Eleanore, Amelia felt more rested than she had the previous few days. Her sore and stiff muscles had improved considerably as well.

She scrambled eggs in a pat of melted butter instead of bacon grease and stirred the plain oatmeal on the back burner. She'd let Eleanore add whatever she liked to the cereal. She had plenty of fresh fruit and whole wheat bread but wasn't sure what was allowed on her diet. If she could help Eleanore stick to her plan and even lose a little weight, she certainly wanted to do so.

Eleanore bustled into the kitchen carrying her canvas school bag as Amelia removed the cast-iron skillet from the burner. She deposited the bag near the door before offering to help with breakfast.

"If you would get down plates and bowls, that would be great."

"Sure. I hope you didn't get up so early because of me."

"I'm always up early. Ryan Miller drops his girls off pretty early." Why did her cheeks grow hot at the mere mention of the man's name? She ducked her head and reached for the long-handled wooden spoon to stir the oatmeal.

"What about your girls? Do they need help?"

"They're up and dressed. I only need to call them, and they'll troop down the stairs."

"I can take Rhonda to school today, so she won't need to catch the bus."

"She would probably love that idea."

"I'll call the girls if you're ready."

"Sure. I'll fix the plates. I'll let you get your own since I'm not sure of the portions you want."

"That's fine."

Amelia set the last plate and bowl on the table as the girls rushed into the kitchen laughing and jabbering. "Please sit down, girls. Eleanore and I will join you in a minute." Amelia covered the leftovers after the two women scooped out their eggs and oatmeal. "Gabby and Jessie are usually still hungry even if their *daed* already fed them."

"Poor man." Eleanore shook her head as she carried her plate and bowl to the table. "I'm sure it's hard for him to care for *kinner* and the house and to work full time. I hope he doesn't simply give them donuts for breakfast."

"I think he gives them cold cereal. He tries to give them healthy foods, but time is a big issue."

Eleanore chuckled. "Isn't it always? I rush around a lot too. At home, I always need to wait until Nancy is finished cooking before I can prepare something a wee bit healthier for myself."

Amelia patted her *freind's* shoulder. "Life isn't easy for you either."

"I make do. I have a roof over my head and a job I love, so all is well."

What a great attitude! Eleanore could have chosen to be bitter about her circumstances, but she chose happiness instead. She didn't yield to the temptation to dwell on the negative. If she ever felt sorry for herself, she did it in private.

Amelia reached over to wipe a glob of oatmeal from Joanna's chin before it dropped onto her lap. For a two-year-old, the little girl was remarkably independent, but she still needed help, whether she wanted to admit that fact or not.

Eleanore laid her fork down and stared out the window. "Does Ryan Miller arrive by buggy?"

"*Nee*, he drives a dark jeep-type vehicle. Why?"

"You must have other company, then."

Amelia raised up to peer outside and then slunk down. "Elam Wenger. Whatever could he want so early in the morning?"

"I think you're about to find out. He's walking toward the back door. Would you like for me to answer when he knocks?"

"I'll get it, but I might need you for backup." She smiled at her *freind*, who chuckled behind her napkin. Amelia rose as soon as he rapped on the door. "Give me strength," she mumbled.

She shuffled to the door, in no big hurry to speak with the man, but sensed that Eleanore was not far behind her. She opened the door a few inches. "*Gut mariye*, Elam. What brings you by so early?" She couldn't manage cheerful, but she could be polite.

"*Gut mariye*, Amelia. I needed to run an errand for my *onkle* and thought I would drop by to check on you and your girls."

"That's kind of you. We're fine. I'm trying to get them fed and get Rhonda ready for school." Would he take the hint and leave?

"Aren't you babysitting today?"

She clenched and unclenched her teeth. It was none of his business what she did, but she would answer anyway. "I expect I will. I usually do on weekdays."

"Have you had any more problems lately?"

"What sort of problems?" What did he know about the whole barn episode?

"You know, any intruders or things missing? My offer still stands to stay in your barn to keep watch at night."

"I'm sure that won't be necessary."

"You never know who you can trust. Someone you know and like could be trying to pull the wool over your eyes. You probably aren't used to deception."

Did he truly believe she was such a poor judge of character that she couldn't spot a charlatan when she encountered one? Was he hinting that she couldn't trust Ryan or one of her *freinden*? She fought to calm herself before she said something she would later regret. A hand on her shoulder surprised her. She jumped and gasped.

"I'm sorry," Eleanore whispered. The taller woman peeked over Amelia's head. "Hello, Elam."

"Oh, uh, hello." The big, red-haired man glanced at Eleanore for a split second and then refocused on Amelia. "I didn't know you had company."

"Eleanore is visiting for a while."

"Don't you live with your *bruder*, the bishop?"

"I do. Sometimes it's nice to have a little break from one's normal routine, ain't so? Why, look at you. You've been visiting here for quite some time now."

Amelia stifled a giggle. It must be the schoolteacher in her that allowed Eleanore to say such things so smoothly. She would never have been able to pull off such a speech.

Elam nodded. "I have been enjoying a nice, long visit with my family."

"I'm sure they have been happy to host you." Eleanore gave Amelia a little poke in the ribs. "Are you planning to stay until the holidays?"

Amelia coughed to cover the snort that almost escaped. Leave it to Eleanore to try to find out how long the annoying man intended to stay in Maryland without actually asking.

Elam cleared his throat and dropped his gaze. "I'm not sure how long I'll be staying."

"I see." Eleanore had donned her no-nonsense, teacher attitude. "I hope you've enjoyed your time here. Please excuse us. Rhonda and I need to get ready for school." She took hold of Amelia's arm and tugged her backward. "Close the door," she whispered.

Amelia obeyed as if she was one of Eleanore's scholars. "I don't believe what I just witnessed."

"What do you mean?"

"You dug for information and then put the man in his place in such a way that I doubt he was even aware of it."

"I think that's called being diplomatic. At least, I prefer that term to *sneaky* or *rude*."

"You were neither of those things. You were inquisitive but polite."

"I'm glad I didn't seem rude. It's too bad I couldn't find out how much longer he intended to stay though."

"By mentioning the holidays, you might have given him something to think about. Perhaps that will trigger a desire to go home."

"We can only hope."

The women laughed as they headed back to the kitchen to finish breakfast. Eleanore elbowed Amelia. "You don't care for the man a whole lot, do you?"

"I don't really know him, but I don't care to do so. I should be grateful he's concerned for our safety, but for some reason, Elam makes me nervous."

"Maybe that has something to do with his obvious obsession with you."

"Obsession? That sounds rather ominous."

"I only mean that he drops by whenever the mood strikes, he seems insistent that you allow him to protect you, and he wants you to think ill of people you like."

"People I like?"

"I'm assuming Elam was referring to Ryan Miller, and I'm assuming you and Ryan are *freinden* since you care for his girls, though I probably should not assume things."

"I, uh, I consider Ryan a *freind*. Elam has made negative comments about Ryan in the past, so your assumption is most likely correct."

Eleanore shook her head. "I don't understand the man. Do you think he got my subtle hint that it was time for him to go home?"

Amelia giggled. "I don't want to be mean, but I fear that went right over Elam's head." She glanced out the window. "Why is he driving so slowly down my driveway? I wish he would speed up, so he's gone before Ryan arrives." She willed him to move faster.

"Maybe he's unfamiliar with the horse and is taking it easy."

"You're probably right. I believe Annie mentioned he didn't like to take the buggy. I wonder if he purchased the bicycle she wanted him to get?"

"If Annie's *daed* needed him to pick up supplies from the hardware store or something, he probably wouldn't be able to carry them on a bike."

"True. I'd better check on the girls. I don't want to make you late for school." She faced the table where Joanna had oatmeal smeared all over her face and the table. "Oh dear!"

"It's still early. You tend to Joanna, and I can pack a lunch for Rhonda."

"I've already made sandwiches for you and Rhonda. If you don't mind, you can add cookies and fruit to hers and whatever you'd like for yourself." She grabbed a rag and began cleaning up the little girl and the table. "What happened, Joanna?"

Rhonda answered for her little *schweschder*. "She dropped the spoon and oatmeal went everywhere. Then she started using her hands to eat it. Ick!"

"*Danki* for that information, Rhonda. Hurry and finish so you won't be late. You are done, Joanna." She helped the two-year-old out of the chair. She spun around and gasped when she caught sight of Eleanore. The woman held a whole cookie in one hand and a cookie with a huge bite taken out of it in the other. "Eleanore?"

"Oops!" Eleanore swallowed. "Caught in the act." She laid down the intact cookie.

"Cookies aren't on your diet, are they?"

A sheepish grin crossed her face. "Everything in moderation."

Amelia chuckled. "Except Elam Wenger. Him—not at all!"

# Chapter Thirty-Five

Ordinarily, Ryan sang silly songs with the girls as they drove, or he told them stories. Today, he concentrated on his driving. Not only was he more tired than usual, but he was also running late. And he did not like being late. He would rather arrive someplace an hour early than be five minutes late. But when Gabby dumped her full bowl of cereal and milk all over herself and the floor, he had to practically start the entire day over again while dealing with a sobbing four-year-old. No matter how much he assured her the accident was not a big deal, she continued to sniffle.

Norman would be understanding, at least. Ryan couldn't ask for a kinder boss. He simply hated being late. He couldn't help that now though. He forced himself to relax a bit and joined in Gabby's song. He deliberately mixed up the words to hear her giggle. There was nothing like a child's laughter to bring a smile to a person's face.

Ryan's smile evaporated as he neared Amelia's house. Somehow, he knew the buggy leaving her driveway did not belong to Eleanore. He removed his foot from the accelerator and let the SUV coast. If he could turn back the other way, he would do so. The buggy didn't have to draw very near for him to see the other man's angry expression. He nodded at Elam as they passed one another but received only a stony glare in return.

Suddenly, the buggy stopped, and Elam hollered out at him. "Why are you always here?"

Ryan could have asked Elam the same thing, but he had neither the time nor the energy to get into a lengthy discussion with the man. "You know that Amelia watches my daughters while I work."

"Huh! You're here at other times too."

*Do not take the bait.* "I'm sorry, I can't talk right now. I'm running behind schedule. Have a good day." Jessie's whine from the back seat came at exactly the right time. "She's a little fussy today." He waved at Elam and drove off, leaving the man staring after him open-mouthed. He would give his baby an extra hug later for providing a way out of a difficult situation and for keeping him from saying something he might regret.

~

"Let me help you." Amelia rushed outside when she saw the SUV pull into the driveway. She reached for Jessie as soon as Ryan lifted her out of her car seat.

"Thank you, Amelia. It's been a tough morning."

"I don't doubt that." She nodded toward the road, but thankfully, the buggy had already driven out of sight.

"What's with that fellow?"

"I wish I knew. Eleanore and I were wondering if he would go home for the holidays." She shifted Jessie to one hip. "Here, I can take the diaper bag. I know you need to get to work."

Gabby hopped out of the vehicle and faced Amelia. Her lips trembled. "It's my fault."

"What is your fault, dear one?"

"That we're late. I spilled my whole bowl of cereal all over me and the floor. I had to change clothes." Tears welled in her eyes.

Amelia pushed the strap of the diaper bag up on her shoulder, so her hand was free to pat Gabby's back. "That's okay, sweetie. Accidents happen to everyone."

The little girl sniffed and blinked.

"I told her the same thing, but I don't think it sunk in." Ryan reached into the back seat again to extract Gabby's bag of toys she'd left behind in her haste to get out of the car.

"Do you know what I did one time when I was about your age?" Amelia asked.

The little girl wagged her head.

"I spilled the whole, full jug of milk on the floor. Milk splashed all over the place. I stood in the middle of the puddle and cried."

"What did your mommy do?"

Amelia smiled at the memory. "She tore off paper towels and made stepping stones. She tiptoed across them to hug me. And do you know what she said?"

"What?"

"She said if I wanted to wash the floor so badly, I should use the bucket and mop. Then she laughed and told me accidents happen."

"She wasn't mad at you?"

"Not at all. Your *daed* probably wasn't mad at you either, was he?"

"No. He hugged me and helped me clean up."

"There. You see? You don't have any reason to be sad. Grown-ups have accidents and spill things too. *Kumm.* Let's go inside and let your *daed* get to work."

Ryan smiled and mouthed his thanks over the little girl's head. Then his expression turned serious. "Was everything okay here last night?"

"We didn't have any problems. Don't worry about us today. We'll do some baking and keep ourselves plenty busy."

Ryan gave Gabby a quick hug and kissed Jessie's cheek. He gently squeezed Amelia's arm. "I really appreciate everything you do."

She ducked her head. She wasn't sure which burned more—her arm from his touch or her cheeks from embarrassment. She mumbled "Have a *gut* day" before taking the girls into the house. Lost in thought, she nearly collided with Eleanore, who was on her way out.

"Oops! Rhonda and I will be leaving now. The two little ones are looking at books in the living room."

"*Danki*, Eleanore. I hope we didn't make you late."

"Not at all." She lowered her voice. "I didn't take any more cookies." Red splotches dotted her cheeks.

Amelia patted her *freind's* arm. "Oh, Eleanore, I don't mind if you eat the cookies. I baked them to be eaten. In fact, we will probably bake more today. I just didn't know what you were allowed on your diet."

"Certainly not a jar full of cookies!" She attempted a chuckle, but tears filled her eyes.

"We'll talk later, *jah*?"

Eleanore nodded and sniffed. "Sure."

～

Thankfully, the day had been as uneventful as a day could be with four little girls to tend to, a house to clean, clothes to wash, and food to prepare. The girls helped cut out sugar cookies with assorted cookie cutters and especially enjoyed decorating them with sprinkles. They would have fun with the upcoming holiday baking.

Amelia worked on her decorative basket for an *Englisch* customer while the cookies cooled on wire racks and the girls napped. The design was a bit too fancy for Amelia's tastes, but the project was taking shape nicely. She had to quickly gather up her supplies a short time later when she heard little feet hit the floor over her head. Maybe Jessie would sleep longer if the others didn't wake her.

"*Mamm*, Jessie is awake too."

"*Danki*, Judith." So much for that idea. Amelia tucked her nearly finished basket into a safe place and hurried to bring Jessie downstairs.

"Cookie?" Joanna pulled her thumb out of her mouth long enough to utter the single word.

Amelia grabbed her hand before she could return to thumb-sucking. "You are too big a girl to suck your thumb. We'll have cookies when Rhonda gets home from school." Before grumbling could begin, she added, "Would you like to play outside for a few minutes while I get the clothes off the line?"

The three older girls couldn't put their shoes on fast enough.

Amelia bundled Jessie into her warm outerwear and called out to the others. "Get your coats on too. The wind was quite chilly when I hung the clothes out earlier."

Amelia shivered when she stepped outside. The girls didn't mind the cold as they ran and giggled and played with Meggie. Jessie laughed as she watched them from the bouncy seat Amelia brought outside for her. Amelia's gaze constantly darted from her task to the *kinner*. Would she ever feel safe in her own yard again?

They all paused to wave at Eleanore and Rhonda as the horse pulled the black buggy up the driveway. Amelia felt guilty for disrupting Eleanore's daily routine, but she had to admit she was relieved to have her here for another evening. Maybe after tonight, she would feel confident enough to be on her own again.

Amelia unpinned the last two dresses and dropped them into her basket. She turned to find Rhonda running toward her at full speed with arms opened wide. Amelia laughed, caught the little girl up in her arms, and swung her around. How *gut* it was to have her little family all together again! She would be so lost and lonely when all three attended school. Thank goodness she had a few more years before that happened. "Did you have a *gut* day?" she asked as she lowered Rhonda to the ground.

"*Jah.*"

"Where is your book bag?"

"In the buggy with my lunch box."

"You need to run get them, so Eleanore doesn't have to bring your things as well as her own."

Rhonda took off running but paused for a moment to call over her shoulder. "Did you make cookies?"

"We did."

Rhonda grinned and dashed away.

Amelia shook her head. *Kinner* were always in a hurry and always hungry for cookies.

Eleanore helped the girls shed their outerwear while Amelia washed up and set out snacks. She poured small cups of milk and laid paper napkins on the table. She would let each girl choose two cookies.

What could she offer Eleanore? Surely, the schoolteacher was as much in need of a snack as the *kinner* were. After talking all day and probably playing with the scholars at recess, Eleanore was most likely as hungry and thirsty as Rhonda. "Would you like a snack, Eleanore?" Amelia looked up from placing a cookie on Joanna's napkin. "Please help yourself to whatever you like."

Eleanore laughed. "I'd *like* a cookie. They look scrumptious and are so pretty. But I will behave myself and have some carrots if you have any."

"I do. There should be carrots, celery, and cauliflower in the refrigerator as well as fruit." Amelia finished doling out cookies and returned the tin to the counter. She smiled at Eleanore, who bit into a stalk of celery as if she were angry with it. "I suppose after looking at cookies, that celery has all the appeal of—"

"A bale of hay!"

Amelia laughed. "What can I do to help you? I can prepare food however you like."

Tears sprang into Eleanore's big, green eyes. "It's so sweet of you to offer. You're the only one who has besides the medical people." She swiped at her eyes. "But I don't want to inconvenience you at all."

"You aren't in the least. You've provided a break in my routine. *I* am the one who has inconvenienced *you*. I've totally disrupted your life by asking you to babysit me and the girls."

"Nonsense! You provided a nice break for me. Please don't change your habits or your meals for me. I will adjust however I need to."

"Have you?"

"Have I what?"

"Adjusted."

"To my life with my *bruder* and his family? Living with them might not be my first choice. But I love them all and can get along adequately there."

"Have you adjusted to your illness?"

"Oh." Eleanore turned to look out the window over the kitchen sink. "I-it's so unfair. I'm not a bad person. I'm not hugely overweight. And yet, I still got this disease."

Amelia squeezed her *freind's* arm. "Of course you aren't a bad person. You are a very *gut* person. And you are not that overweight at all. Sometimes unfortunate things happen to *gut* people."

Eleanore nodded. "I know that in here." She tapped her head. "But some little two-year-old inside me wants to jump up and down and chant, 'Not fair! Not fair!' "

Amelia laughed. "We all have those imps inside of us."

"Really? Do you?"

"Sure, but I have to keep it quashed or my three real, live imps will join the fray."

Eleanore smiled. "I guess you've been questioning why strange things have been happening to you."

"I did at first. Now, I'm trying to keep my wits about me and not panic. I try to focus on keeping my *dochders* safe. And I pray a lot."

"I've prayed without ceasing, as the Bible says."

"What have you prayed for?"

"I've prayed the Lord *Gott* would make me well, but that prayer hasn't been answered."

"I'm certainly not an authority, but maybe you should pray for acceptance instead. It could be that the Lord is using this disease to make you stronger."

"You mean I should ask Him to help me accept the fact that I have diabetes that is not going away?"

"Perhaps. I have a feeling we need to accept things before we can deal with them and move on."

"That's interesting. I'll think about it."

"And I'd better think about getting five girls away from the table and cleaned up before Ryan Miller gets here." She glanced outside to make sure he hadn't already arrived. "I wonder where Meggie is. She plopped down in the sun after romping with the girls. She usually stays near the house."

"Maybe she got cold and went inside the barn. I'll check if you like."

"You don't have to go back outside. I'll check on her after I get the girls busy with something other than eating cookies."

"I'll just poke my head out for a quick look."

"She will probably beg you for a handout, so be prepared."

Eleanore unlocked the door and eased it open. "I don't see her."

"That's odd."

"Amelia, why are your little goats wandering down the driveway?"

# Chapter Thirty-Six

"What? How did they get out? They were in the pasture with the horses." Amelia raced toward the door. She peeked around the larger woman. "*Ach!* The silly animals are heading toward the road. I have to get them. Why didn't Meggie bark?" She snatched the shawl off the hook next to the door.

"I'll help you." Eleanore snatched up the cloak she'd taken off only moments earlier.

"I should be able to get them. Please stay with the girls, if you don't mind."

"Sure."

Amelia dashed down the driveway, thankful that the soreness in her leg had eased a bit. She slowed her pace when she neared the wayward animals so she wouldn't frighten them. "*Kumm,* Mimi. *Kumm,* Ruby." She kept her voice soft and even.

The spoiled goats eagerly trotted toward Amelia as if expecting a treat. "That's it, girls. Let's go back to the barn so I can get you a treat." As soon as they were within reach, she grabbed their collars and began leading them to the barn. She crooned to them the whole way.

"How did you two get out?" She glanced at the pasture where the horses still chomped on whatever grass they could find. At least she didn't have to chase them down. She would examine the fence for holes as soon as she secured the two rascals in the barn. Where in the world was Meggie?

"Now, you two stay put." Amelia shook her finger at the goats. She gave them each a treat and patted their heads. "You will need to stay inside now." She might as well bring the horses in, too, before she checked the fence. She whistled for Meggie as she exited the barn, but the dog did not appear. She bent to retrieve a scrap of paper off the ground and turned it over. A label. From a package of mints. How did that get outside her barn? She shoved it inside a pocket to discard later.

The horses whinnied as she neared the pasture. "I hear you. You would probably like to stay out longer, but we're going inside now. I'll find a treat for you too." She scanned the fence but didn't see any obvious damage. The gate was still fastened. "I don't understand it." She led the horses to the barn. "It's too bad you can't tell me what happened."

Amelia searched for Meggie after she secured the horses. The girls would be heartbroken if something had happened to the curly-haired dog. Truth be told, she would be upset too.

Eleanore looked relieved when Amelia stepped into the kitchen. She stopped pacing the floor with Jessie. "I was beginning to worry."

"I decided to tuck all the animals in for the night while I was out there."

"Great idea." Eleanore glanced toward the table where the older girls sat coloring and mouthed one word. "Dog?"

Amelia whispered. "Not a sign of her. I'll look again later."

Eleanore peered out the window. "I wonder where she is. Oh, I believe Ryan Miller is here, unless you are expecting someone else."

"I'm not." Amelia was also not expecting another problem, but as she had told Eleanore, some things were out of a person's control. Could she accept being the target of a phantom thief and prankster and deal with it?

~

This had been one of those days he would be glad to put behind him. After Gabby's early morning mishap that got him off to a late start, Ryan had been playing catch up ever since. It didn't help that he'd sprouted eight more thumbs and fumbled with nearly everything he touched. Norman had shot him sympathetic looks all day, but the kind man had never once voiced a complaint or criticism. Ryan promised he would do better the next day.

Now he was late to retrieve his children. He was only fifteen minutes late, but late was late. Perhaps an early bedtime for him and the girls was in order. A little extra sleep could only improve his brain's functioning. The care package Sarah had sent home with him again meant he didn't have to spend time preparing supper. That should give him a few extra minutes to get other evening chores done early. He had learned that nothing was predictable with little ones though.

He noticed the animals had already been taken in for the evening as he drove up to Amelia's house. He threw a panic-stricken glance at the dashboard clock. Was he later than he'd thought? Not really. She must have taken care of outside tasks earlier than usual.

Ryan parked as close to the back door as possible so he could hustle the girls out quickly. Weariness loomed large. He took a deep breath and hopped out of the SUV, surprised Meggie hadn't been right there to greet him. Maybe Amelia had taken the dog inside.

"Gabby, your *daed* is here!" Amelia called over her shoulder as she opened the door to admit him.

"I'm sorry I'm late. It seems I've been late all day."

"You're fine. The girls have been playing and coloring. Jessie has been zooming around in her walker. I'm guessing she'll be walking before we know it."

"I'm not sure I'm ready for that."

Amelia laughed. "Ready or not, the time is upon us."

He loved the sound of her laugh. If he had a way to capture the sound, he would listen to it over and over again. He hoped one day to be able to hear it every day and night.

"I'll get Jessie ready to go."

Ryan grasped her arm, stopping her. "Is everything okay? You took the animals in early."

She offered a small, shaky smile. "I had to nab two escaped goats, so I put all of the critters in early."

"How did they get loose?"

"I don't know. The gate was closed, and I didn't see any gaps in the fence."

"I can take a look for you."

"That isn't necessary. It's getting dark now. I'll ask one of the men who stops by with wood to check."

Ryan longed to be the man who provided for Amelia's needs. He smiled down at her. "I truly don't mind checking."

"I know. You are very kind, and I appreciate that."

"You're easy to be kind to." He cleared his throat. He needed to steer the conversation in a different direction. "Do you have Meggie inside tonight?"

She lowered her voice. "I-I don't know where Meggie is." Her big, blue eyes shimmered with tears.

"What happened?"

"I don't know. Eleanore didn't see the dog when she and Rhonda got home. I thought for sure Meggie would help me bring in the goats, but she didn't appear. I whistled for her and looked around but couldn't find her. I haven't told the girls, but they will start asking about her soon."

"That's odd. Has she ever run off before?"

"Never. She's always right here by the back door or in the barn." She pulled a crumpled paper from her pocket and handed it to him. "I found this by the barn. I don't eat these mints or buy them, and Eleanore hasn't been near the barn."

"How did the paper get outside your barn? Maybe one of your customers dropped it and the wind blew it there."

"I suppose that's possible."

"But not very likely, huh? I think I'll go out and look around for the dog."

"Please don't trouble yourself. You have a lot to do. I'm sure she'll turn up soon." Amelia sniffed. "I hope she does."

"I'm going to make a quick search before it gets any darker." When Amelia began to protest again, he put an index finger to her lips. "Shh! I don't mind, and I'll only be a minute or two." She nodded, and he reluctantly moved his hand. He really wanted to enfold her in his arms and assure her that everything would be all right. Instead, he gnawed his tongue and slipped out the door.

Would it be wrong to pray that the little dog would run to meet him with a bark and a wagging tail? He didn't think so. Besides, didn't thinking it make it a prayer already?

Ryan waited until he got a short distance from the house before whistling and calling for Meggie in case one of the girls sat near a window and would hear him. He jogged all the way out to the tree line, pausing to call, whistle, and listen. What could have become of the dog? Had someone deliberately let the goats out and then taken Meggie? The children would be devastated. He almost wished he'd never brought her here. He hoped she hadn't ventured into the woods and gotten injured.

That early bedtime he had longed for would not likely occur. He didn't care though. Helping Amelia was more important. He couldn't bear the thought of the children's tears if something had happened to their dog. He had to find Meggie!

He plunged into the nearly dark woods and called again. He stopped walking among the crackly, dried leaves periodically to listen. Surely Meggie would bark or run out of a thicket if she was close by. Unless she was hurt. He strained to hear any yip, bark, or whimper, but he heard nothing. Daylight was nearly gone, and he would have to abandon his search soon.

He paused one last time to listen. How was he going to tell Amelia and the girls he hadn't found their pet? A strange scratching noise grabbed his attention. He hoped whatever animal made that sound was moving away from him and not toward him. Since the wind had grown stronger, maybe the sound was a tree branch scraping against an adjacent tree.

"Psst! Here!"

Ryan shook his head as if cobwebs filled it. He thought he had heard a whisper, but it must have been the wind. Were his ears playing tricks on him?

Without a flashlight, searching deeper in the woods would be futile, and possibly dangerous, since he couldn't see tree roots or debris. Besides, his children would be famished by this time, and he didn't want Amelia to have to provide another meal for them.

He should quicken his pace once he emerged from the woods, but he didn't know how to break the news that his search had been unsuccessful. *Please, Lord, give me the right words to say and help Amelia and her girls to accept the disappointment.*

He tapped on the back door, not comfortable with simply walking inside and announcing himself. His spirits plummeted even further when he caught sight of Amelia's hopeful expression. He'd rather be anywhere than standing in the doorway of her home at this moment about to give her bad news.

"You didn't see any sign of her?"

"I'm afraid not. I'm sorry, Amelia."

"It isn't your fault at all. I appreciate your looking for her."

Ryan didn't know how she did it, but the amazing woman even managed to give him a smile. A genuine smile because there was nothing phony about Amelia Stauffer.

"I haven't said anything to the girls yet, but I'll tell them we can still be hopeful. Since you didn't see any sign that she had been injured, we can hope she simply wandered off and will return when she has finished exploring. And we'll pray. I don't think the Lord *Gott* will mind that."

It was amazing how her sentiments echoed his own. That had to be another indication they were right for each other.

"Why are you looking at me like that?"

"Like what?"

"Like I've said either the most profound or the most ridiculous thing in the world."

Ryan chuckled. "Profound. You astound me with your perception, your wisdom, and your faith."

"You're going to make me blush. I am not special in any way."

"Oh, but you are. Very special."

Amelia stared at her shoes. He knew he had embarrassed her, but the words flew right out of his mouth with his heart attached to them.

Eleanore's call from the kitchen saved him from blurting out more of his feelings. "Amelia, a buggy is driving up. Are you expecting someone?"

# Chapter Thirty-Seven

"*Nee*. I can't imagine who would be visiting at supper time."

"I need to grab my two girls and leave so you can see to your guests."

"You're fine. If you'd like to stay for a bite to eat, you are certainly *wilkom* to do so." What was wrong with her? She should have let him go, and here she practically begged him to stay. Her heart and head kept getting all twisted around each other. Hoping for something that could never be would only cause pain. It was more likely that Meggie would return home than it was for her and Ryan to have a relationship. Yet some part of her hoped for both.

"Daddy, I'm hungry. I think Jessie is too."

"Okay, Gabby. We're going home right now."

"Can't we eat here?" Her pitiful wail was almost comical.

"We've been through this before, Gabby. It is not polite to invite yourself to dinner or to whine. Sarah sent us a nice casserole, so you won't have to wait long to eat."

Amelia hesitated, not wanting to interfere, but knowing the girls probably were quite hungry by now. "I have plenty. I don't—"

A knock at the door interrupted her. Her heart pounded, but at least she had other adults in the house with her. Pranksters and thieves didn't knock on their victims' doors though, did they?

"Do you want me to answer it?" Ryan asked.

"I'll get it." It would never do for him to answer her door. What if the visitor was Bishop Micah or one of the ministers? "It's probably Christina dropping off a payment." Amelia attempted a smile.

"Wouldn't she have gone home long ago?"

Amelia shrugged. "Maybe she had a late customer."

"She occasionally does," Eleanore agreed. "But that's usually during planting season."

Amelia strode to the door with a confidence she did not feel. She dragged in a deep breath before turning the lock. She opened the door only far enough to peek out and was surprised to discover a shock of red hair sticking out from under a straw hat.

"Elam! What are you doing here?" A yip made her glance down. "Meggie! You're back!" She stepped outside and bent down to hug the little dog. "Where have you been?" Ryan trailed outside behind her as if to offer moral support.

She plucked a few dried leaves from the curly brown fur and hugged the pup again. "It looks like you've been romping through the woods. It's not like you to run off." She straightened and searched Elam's face. "Why do you have my dog?"

"I found her. Don't look at me as if I stole her. I would never do such a thing."

"Where was she? She has never wandered off before."

"It's hard to tell what a stray dog will do, ain't so?" He glared at Ryan.

"She's not a stray. She was given to us. She's a *wunderbaar* pet. She is gentle and loves my girls as much as they love her, and she's a great watchdog."

"Huh!"

"I'm glad you found her and brought her home. I've been worried about her." Amelia would be grateful, even if she didn't like the man's attitude.

"Happy to help. We all try to look out for our own. Best to stay clear of outsiders though." He shot Ryan another mean look.

Amelia sensed Ryan's rising anger. She opened her mouth to try to defuse the tension, but Ryan spoke before she could utter a sound.

"Where did you say you found the dog, Elam?"

"I didn't say. What are you, an *Englisch* detective?"

Amelia wanted to wipe the smirk off Elam's face. Why did he act so self-righteous? The man had a real attitude problem. She wanted to take him to task in the worst way. Thankfully, Ryan responded before she could voice any of her thoughts.

"I don't have any desire to be a detective, but it would be helpful to know where you found the dog. If by some odd chance she disappeared again, we'd have an idea where to look for her."

"*We?*" Elam looked from Ryan to Amelia.

Things were rapidly spiraling out of control. Amelia forced a smile. "I certainly appreciate your bringing Meggie home, Elam. I am so thankful she wasn't hurt. I would like to know how far she wandered though."

"I found her trotting along the road."

"Oh my!" Amelia patted her racing heart. "She could have been struck by a car. Was she all the way over near the Wengers' place?"

"Uh, *nee*. I was on my way out and spotted her."

"She must have traveled through the woods part of the way to pick up the leaves and pine needles." Amelia reached down to brush more debris from the brown fur. Meggie immediately swiped her rough tongue across Amelia's hand. Amelia smiled. "I should scold you, you mischievous puppy, but I'm so glad you're safe that I can't bear to do it." She leaned a little closer to hug the dog yet again. "And you need a bath. What is that smell?" She jumped back, almost crashing into Ryan, who put out a hand to steady her.

Elam's frown morphed into a scowl. He looked as if he planned to physically remove Ryan's hand from Amelia's shoulder. She took a baby step forward as Ryan lowered his arm. "I'm sorry, Ryan. I didn't mean to bump into you." She hoped her comment made it perfectly clear to Elam that Ryan's touch had been purely a protective instinct.

"I'm fine."

"Say, don't you have little *kinner* to get home?" Elam focused on Ryan. "I can help Amelia tie up this bad dog so you can go ahead home."

Amelia gasped. "I don't tie her up." She patted Meggie's head. "She stays in the barn or in the house. And she is a very *gut* dog, not a bad one."

Elam quirked an eyebrow. "Hmm. If she always stayed in the barn or house, I wouldn't have found her wandering. Where do you want to confine her? I'll put her away for you."

"*Danki*, but I'll take care of her later. I want to feed and bathe her."

Elam shrugged. "If you say so, but my advice is to pin her up or chain her to a tree or something."

Amelia shuddered. "I'll handle this in my own way."

"Hello, everyone." Eleanore poked her head out the door and smiled. "I wondered what had happened to you, Amelia. Oh my! Meggie is back! I'm so glad." She clapped her hands. "What a pleasant surprise. Amelia, dear, do you want me to continue to hold supper for you?"

Leave it to Eleanore to intervene so diplomatically. She could probably settle squabbles between scholars in a matter of seconds and have them playing together as if nothing had ever happened. Amelia faced her in time to catch Eleanore's little wink. "I'm sure the girls are getting hungry."

Eleanore chuckled. "They have been asking if they are going to get supper tonight."

"I need to gather up my two and take them home." Ryan headed for the door.

"*Jah*, you should."

Eleanore planted her fists on her hips and glared at the red-haired man. "Elam Wenger, that was totally uncalled for. Why, if you were one of my scholars, I would make you apologize and then sit in the corner to ponder your rude behavior."

Amelia bit her lip to keep from giggling. At least Elam had the sense to look ashamed.

"I'm sure Amelia is grateful you brought her dog home, but it's probably best that you leave now, so she can tend to her girls."

Amelia wanted to hug her *freind*. Only Eleanore could get away with such a speech.

Elam muttered something unintelligible and stalked off.

Ryan paused before entering the house to call out to the retreating man. "Say, Elam, you wouldn't happen to know anything about escaped goats, would you?"

The big man swung back around. His angry glare was evident, even in the dim light shining from the open door. "Why would I know anything about goats? I don't mess with other people's animals or belongings. And I don't like being suspected of doing so." With that, he stalked off to his borrowed buggy.

Surely, Ryan didn't think Elam let out her goats or stole her dog. Maybe she

was naïve, but she couldn't believe even Elam would stoop that low. Amelia called out her gratitude one more time. "*Danki* again for returning Meggie, Elam." She barely heard his grunt.

Amelia hugged Eleanore. "You were *wunderbaar*! I think you might be a better guard than Meggie."

Eleanore laughed. "Years of teaching school tend to make a person sort of take charge. Once again, I hope I didn't sound mean or bossy."

"Not at all. You sounded like a schoolteacher who expects proper behavior and will accept nothing less."

Ryan snorted. "I rather enjoyed that scene. I'm sorry if I stirred the pot there at the end, Amelia."

"Why did you ask Elam about the goats?"

Ryan shrugged. "Just curious."

"You don't think he was behind the goats' escape and Meggie's disappearance, do you?"

"I can't believe a grown man would do such a thing, but I don't really know Elam well. I think I've caused enough trouble. I need to get my girls and leave you ladies to your supper."

"You might as well stay for supper. Otherwise, you will have very cranky *kinner* by the time you get home. You can save Sarah's casserole for tomorrow."

"I feel like I impose on you way too much as it is."

"Nonsense. I love the girls as my own. I have plenty of food, so you are *wilkom* to stay."

"*Danki*. I appreciate it."

Amelia whipped around to look up into his face. "You used our word."

He smiled and winked. "I'm learning."

Amelia's heart hiccupped. She smiled back. Was he truly learning more of the Old Order ways because he wanted to pursue a relationship with her? Did she dare hope? Meggie tried to sneak inside before Amelia could ponder that idea further. "You need a bath first." She blocked the dog's entrance. "You smell strange."

"Sort of spicy," Ryan said. "Almost like aftershave combined with doggie odor."

Amelia laughed. "Exactly."

"Interesting."

⁓

Ryan was plagued with guilt throughout the entire meal. He should not be adding to Amelia's burden this evening. She had more than enough to do without his adding three more people to her table. If they were married, he would feel different because he would be providing for the family and helping Amelia in every way possible. Now, he felt like a hindrance rather than a help.

Of course, Amelia tried to put him at ease, and Eleanore kept a lively conversation going with tales from school. Ryan tried to relax and enjoy the pleasant company and delicious food. His girls certainly seemed at home here. Poor tykes appeared exhausted. They probably would have created quite a ruckus if he had made them wait to eat.

Ryan wiped Jessie's face and hands when she began to play with her food. "You're finished." He handed her a toy to play with while Gabby finished eating. "I'll help you clean up, Amelia, and then get these girls out of your way—at least for a few hours."

"They are never in my way, and you do not have to help clean up."

"It's the least I can do."

"I won't hear of it. I'm going to clean the kitchen and bathe that smelly dog if Eleanore will read to the girls."

"You'll need help with that job, I daresay. I can do the dog wash for you." He wanted to check out the dog again anyway. Some little niggling idea tickled his brain.

"I have bathed her before, so I'm sure I can do it again. I will need to do it inside, though, so she doesn't get too chilled. Then she can have her supper."

As if she knew she'd been the topic of conversation, the little dog barked at the back door. Ryan crossed the kitchen in several long strides. "I'll peek out and make sure she's all right." He noticed Amelia's concerned expression, so did a quick check and hurried back to the kitchen to assure her the dog was fine and only wanted attention.

Amelia laughed. "She might not like the kind of attention she's going to get."

"That's why I want to help you. You're tired. The dog is hungry. Together, we can accomplish the task quickly. Don't you think?"

"I have an idea." Eleanore lifted Jessie from the high chair and bounced her on one hip. "If you are both agreeable, I will get all five girls ready for bed while you two tackle the dog bath. I was thinking you might as well let the girls sleep here, Ryan, since you'll be bringing them right back in a few hours anyway."

Ryan shook his head. "I couldn't put you both to all that trouble." Besides, that would mean he would have to face an empty, tomb-like house.

"That's a great idea, Eleanore, if you want to undertake such a job."

"Pshaw! I handle a roomful of *kinner* every day. Tending to these sweet little girls will be as easy as pie."

"I don't know." Ryan hesitated. The idea made perfect sense, but he enjoyed his evenings with his little ones.

"It's up to you, Ryan," Amelia said.

He looked at Gabby's heavy eyelids. Jessie had already leaned her head against Eleanore's shoulder. "I suppose that makes sense. I can drop off some clothes for them in the morning."

"Great! Let's go girls." Eleanore ushered them out of the kitchen. "I'll wash dishes when I'm finished, Amelia. I'm sure these girls will be sound asleep in a flash."

Ryan smiled down into the sweetest face he'd ever seen. "Are you ready to tackle a smelly dog?" He snapped his fingers. "I believe I know where I've smelled that scent before."

# Chapter Thirty-Eight

"What scent?" Amelia's mind had already shifted to the items she needed to gather to bathe the dog. She would have waited until tomorrow to perform the task since she was already exhausted, but she wanted to keep Meggie inside tonight. And she couldn't let a dog with leaves, pine needles, and dirt embedded in her fur and smelling like a mixture of spices, damp earth, and doggie odor stay in the house.

"Meggie's scent."

Amelia laughed. "Which one? The dirty dog smell or the earth smell?"

"The spice smell."

"I can't imagine where she picked that up. She certainly is filthy. She must have been rolling in leaves and dirt. Why would she run off?" She paused for a breath. "I'm rambling. I'm sorry. Where have you detected that spicy scent before?"

"Elam. Didn't you notice when you were talking to him?"

"I was too focused on the dog."

"I was as well, but I guess that smell stuck in my brain. It's some sort of aftershave or cologne or something."

"I suppose Meggie's fur would absorb some of the scent from sitting near Elam in the buggy, ain't so?"

"Unless your dog uses aftershave."

Amelia laughed. "We don't have any of that here."

Ryan chuckled. "Are you ready to bathe the beast? Where is the washtub? I'll fill it for you."

~

Amelia toweled off the soaking wet dog and quickly jumped out of the way before Meggie shook herself and sent water droplets flying in every direction. "I suppose she'll dry soon enough once she's in the warm kitchen. I appreciate your help, Ryan."

"It was rather fun. Doing anything with you is enjoyable, even washing a dog."

Amelia's face burned all the way to her scalp. He always said the nicest things. She coughed to clear her throat and divert attention from her face. "I'll spread an old blanket or towel on the floor near the stove and hope she'll lay on it."

Ryan chuckled. "You dote on the dog the same as you do on your *kinner* Did I say the word correctly?"

"You did. You're picking up the language quite well."

"It doesn't come to me as easily as it does to Gabby."

"She's around it all day here. Besides, I think it's easier for little ones to learn new things than it is for us older folks."

"Older folks? You're all of what—twenty-six or twenty-seven?"

"I'm twenty-eight."

Ryan gasped and thumped his chest. "That old?"

Amelia giggled and swatted his arm. "Sometimes I feel a whole lot older."

"Don't we all! There are days I am sure I'm a lot older than thirty."

Amelia stood on tiptoe to reach a stack of old towels on a high shelf in the washroom. If she jumped, she could reach them a lot easier.

Ryan placed his hands on her shoulders to prevent her from jumping. "I can get whatever you need, so you don't need to leap up on a shelf like a cat."

His hands were strong but gentle. His touch sent a jolt of current throughout her entire body. Her heart pounded as her breath stalled. "I, uh, was going to grab a couple of those towels." Her voice quivered. She needed to put some space between them, no matter how much she enjoyed his nearness.

A voice from the other side of the washroom door sent Amelia crashing back to reality. She hopped away from Ryan with a quickness and pointed to the towels she wanted right as Eleanore poked her head inside the room.

"The girls are ready for bed now."

"*Danki*, Eleanore. We'll be right there."

~

Guilt pummeled Ryan once again as he drove home in silence. No singing. No jabbering. No clapping. No childish sounds reached him from the back seat. He felt lonely. And guilty. He'd never left the girls anywhere overnight before, and he wasn't at all sure he liked doing it now. He knew they were well cared for. Amelia and Eleanore both adored children. But he still felt odd.

He should be excited to have some time to himself, but he wasn't. He should be happy to be able to read for a while and then crawl into bed without having to get two wiggly little girls bathed, calmed, and settled for the night. But he already missed them. He heaved a troubled sigh.

He hoped Amelia's prankster did not return. He didn't fear for his girls, but he worried that Amelia would try to confront the person again and get hurt more seriously than she'd been in the barn. Who would torment a widow and her children? Who would have let her goats and dog wander free? Did Meggie really smell like spicy aftershave because she had been in the buggy with Elam for a few minutes? Was that long enough to absorb the smell from him, or had she been with him longer than that?

And what about that whisper he'd heard in the woods? Had it been the breeze rustling the remaining leaves on the trees, or had his imagination simply been working overtime? Perhaps fatigue and lack of sleep did strange things to a person's mind.

He wished he could fit all the puzzle pieces together so Amelia could have some peace of mind. She was brave and intelligent, and her faith in the Lord was strong, but she couldn't hide the concern in her eyes. He wanted nothing more than to gather Amelia and her children into his arms and shield them from all harm, but it was not his place to do so—yet.

*Kinner*, not children. He had better start thinking in *Deutsch*. Not an easy task for a brain that had functioned only in English his whole life. He'd heard a smattering of the language throughout his life, but he had grown up in a home where only English had been spoken. He didn't know when his people had stopped using the old language, but he vowed to learn it as quickly as he could.

~

Amelia tiptoed through the silent house, checking the doors and windows for a third time. She stopped beside the woodstove to pet Meggie's head. "You're all dry now, but I will still let you stay inside so you don't get chilled and so you don't wander off again." The dog thumped her tail against the floor. Amelia was sure Meggie smiled at her.

She wished the dog could talk and tell her if someone had come onto the property to let the goats out and to take her away. Elam had a knack for showing up after strange occurrences, but Amelia still couldn't believe the man had been responsible for each of them. He might be odd, but he wasn't evil.

She sighed. Eleanore had gone to bed shortly after the girls. She would need as much rest as she could get to deal with her scholars the next day. Amelia should have followed her, but her thoughts still churned a mile a minute. She climbed the stairs with only the flashlight beam to guide her steps and tiptoed to the girls' room to check on them a final time.

All of them slept like little angels. They were such sweet girls. Caring for Gabby and Jessie had turned out to be so much more than a job. She dearly loved the girls, and to her dismay, she had fallen in love with their *daed* too.

She pulled the quilt back over Joanna, who had a habit of kicking off her covers and later whining because she'd gotten cold. She patted her youngest to soothe her when she moaned softly and then crept from the room.

Once she'd drawn her own quilt up beneath her chin, Amelia squeezed her eyes shut and willed sleep to claim her. But as she'd learned over the past few years, sleep could not be ordered like a hamburger at a fast-food restaurant. It showed up when and if it wanted to, according to its own agenda.

She rolled onto her side and snuggled further beneath the covers. Sleep still refused to accept her invitation, regardless of how much she begged. She might as well try to sort out some of her troubling thoughts and hope that would give her some peace.

First, she needed to admit to being more than attracted to Ryan. She cared for him very much. Maybe too much to allow him to change his entire life for her. Joining her community would be a huge upheaval for him and his girls. It wouldn't be fair for him to sacrifice everything for her. What if he was later sorry and resented her?

Maybe it would be easier for her to learn to use modern gadgets and to drive a car. The gadgets might be all right, but the very thought of driving gave her chills. She liked the leisurely pace of the horse and buggy and watching the changing scenery as she passed. In a car, everything whizzed by in a dizzying blur. And what about her community? Her relationships with old *freinden* would forever change. Could she adapt? Could her girls adapt?

Amelia flipped over onto her back, raised up on her elbows, and pushed herself to a sitting position. Since sleep would not be paying her a visit any time soon, she might as well abandon the effort. She repositioned the pillow to cushion her back as she leaned against the cherry headboard. Was it possible she was reading Ryan's cues all wrong?

The words "marriage" and "love" had never even been whispered, though they had been hinted at. At least she thought so. The memory of the tenderness and concern in Ryan's expressive brown eyes made her smile. His touch, no matter how casual, had always raised goose bumps up and down her limbs. He had often mentioned his desire to care for and protect her and her girls. But she didn't think protection was his only concern. *Ach!* It was all so confusing.

Her sigh bore the weight of the world. *How do you feel, Amelia? What do you want?* "What I want and what I need are two entirely different things," she whispered to the night. "I need someone to give me a stern talking to. And the sooner, the better."

What she wanted, though, was to love and be loved. She wanted more than anything for them all to be a family. But she would not encourage him or ask him to give up his ways to embrace the Old Order way of life. That was a matter between him and the Lord *Gott,* and she would not interfere. She was glad he was talking with Noah Zimmerman and Bishop Micah and getting his questions answered, but she would not try to sway his decision.

The girls would all be ecstatic though. Her little ones missed having a *daed,* and his missed having a *mudder.* They already behaved like siblings, so a transition, if one indeed occurred, should be fairly easy. There were bound to be bumps in the road, as in any change, but they could smooth those out. She could only hope and pray and leave the outcome to the Lord.

Admitting her feelings to herself drained her emotionally and physically. She scooted down in the bed, ready now to embrace slumber.

A thump followed by a muffled groan dragged her back to a state of high alert. She bolted upright with her heart pounding. Who or what made that noise?

# Chapter Thirty-Nine

Meggie would have barked if someone entered or tried to enter a downstairs door or window. The noise must have been from something or someone upstairs. Maybe Gabby awoke and was frightened in a different bed. Even though she napped in that same room every day, things could look scary in the dark.

Amelia flung off her covers and slipped out of bed. She thrust her arms into the sleeves of her robe and padded barefoot down the hall to check on the girls. She swung around with a gasp when one of the stairs creaked. She wished she had grabbed the flashlight off her dresser.

Her girls never wandered the house at night. Would Gabby have been brave enough to go downstairs alone? Amelia shored up her courage and followed the fading footsteps. It couldn't have been a stranger prowling about or Meggie would have growled or barked.

Amelia crept down the stairs. "Gabby?" If clouds hadn't obscured the moon, she would at least have had a dim shaft of light shining in the uncovered window. "Ahh!" One hand flew to her mouth to stifle a scream when she bumped into a body. A hand grabbed her upper arm, keeping her steady on her feet.

"Amelia?"

"Oh." The single word whooshed out on another gasp. Amelia patted her chest where her heart pounded like a jack-hammer. "Eleanore! Oh my! I forgot you spent the night." She paused to suck in oxygen. "I thought an intruder had done something to keep Meggie from barking." How had she forgotten she had a houseguest?

"I am so sorry. I must have scared you worse than you scared me." Suddenly, she started giggling and couldn't stop.

"What's so funny?"

Eleanore tried to stop laughing but hiccupped instead, sending Amelia into a fit of giggles. "Look at us. Two grown women sneaking around in the dark and scaring each other." She snorted and giggled again.

Amelia recovered first. "I was only sneaking because I thought you were my prankster or a robber or something."

"And I was sneaking because I was trying not to awaken anyone to witness my kitchen raid."

"Your what?"

"*Ach*, Amelia! I confess. That gnawing I sometimes get in my stomach drove me from my comfortable bed as it does more often than I care to admit. I had hoped to find a little snack to tide me over until morning. I'm such a failure at this whole diet thing."

Amelia took her *freind's* hand and squeezed it. "You are not a failure. Any change is difficult, especially at the beginning. Maybe you aren't eating enough to sustain yourself. Fruits and vegetables are low calorie, so perhaps you need to add more food to your diet."

Eleanore smiled. "Nice try to make me feel better, dear, but what I really need is a big dose of willpower. I'm never going to get a handle on this disease if I can't control my-self."

"I think you're too hard on yourself. Give yourself a little more time and pray for guidance."

"I've been praying. I've begged the Lord *Gott* to heal me, to take away this disease, or to take away my desire to eat."

"You need to eat to function. How would you teach all day if you ate nothing?"

"Maybe I could starve away the pounds and the disease."

"I'm afraid you would only make yourself sicker. Have you tried praying for acceptance?"

"I don't know." Eleanore heaved a heavy sigh. "I've prayed so much I don't even remember what all I've prayed for."

"*Kumm.*" Amelia tugged on the larger woman's hand. "Let's go to the kitchen and find a healthy snack for you."

"*Nee, nee.* I don't want to keep you up any later, Amelia. I'll get a glass of water and go back to bed."

"To listen to your belly grumble the rest of the night?"

"There isn't that much time left until the day officially begins."

"Several hours. That's too long to be miserable. I have apples, if that's okay for your diet, or raw vegetables. I also have peanut butter you can spread on crackers. Will any of those things work?"

Eleanore tried to pull her hand from Amelia's grasp. "Don't worry about me. I'll get some water. I can wait until breakfast to eat."

"What will happen if your blood sugar drops too low? Maybe your body is trying to warn you. At least take a look and see if something appeals to you."

"Oh, all right." Eleanore followed Amelia into the kitchen. She snatched a flashlight off the counter. "Don't bother with the lamp. I don't need that much light to grab a few crackers and the jar of peanut butter. A little bit of protein should tide me over until breakfast."

"Are you sure that will be enough?" Amelia dropped Eleanore's hand and shuffled to the pantry to pull out the food.

"I can take care of this, Amelia. Please go back to bed. I'm so sorry I woke you up."

"You didn't. I hadn't fallen asleep yet."

"Why not? You must have been exhausted."

"Maybe too tired to sleep. Or else my mind was too busy to give me peace."

"I can understand that. Is there something troubling you? Besides all the shenanigans going on, that is. I'm a great listener. And I promise not to blab."

Amelia laughed. "I didn't think you would. I, uh, was trying to figure out how my animals got loose."

"Hmm." Eleanore crunched on a cracker. "I have a feeling there is more than your animals disturbing your sleep. Perhaps a certain person—a certain male person—is invading your thoughts as well."

Amelia was glad the room was so dimly lit. Her face must be tomato red. "I'm sure I don't know what you mean."

"And I'm sure you do. The man I'm referring to appears to be a very nice, caring person and a devoted parent. He also appears to be very taken with you."

Amelia gasped. "You could tell that in only a few minutes in his presence?"

"I'm very astute and quite a *gut* judge of character. Not that I would ever judge anyone, mind you. It seems to me that Ryan Miller has all the right qualities. Plus, he is quite pleasing to look at."

"He has all the right qualities for a woman in his community."

"Perhaps I'm not the only one who needs to pray for acceptance."

"Acceptance of what?"

"Of *Gott's* will. Perhaps change is part of His plan."

~

Ryan wrinkled his nose and swallowed fast. He had intended to brew his morning coffee a little stronger. He hadn't intended to make it strong enough to curl his hair and cross his eyes. If he downed the whole cup, he would surely be jittery all day. He poured a cup of orange juice and dumped the remaining coffee down the sink. *That stuff should clear any clogs out of the pipes.*

He had packed a bag with clothes and diapers last night since he couldn't sleep or even concentrate on a book. The silent house was too oppressive. He was used to noise. He missed the chatter and giggles of little girls. He knew Gabby and Jessie were fine with Amelia, but he'd missed them even more than he thought he would.

Poor Amelia. She had to be so frustrated and frightened by all the strange happenings. He dropped onto a kitchen chair with a granola bar in his hand. He absentmindedly tore the paper and bit off a chunk. If the perpetrator was merely a prankster, he'd played enough tricks. Why keep hassling a kind, young woman?

Ryan leaned against the jacket he'd flung across the chair the previous night and heard a crinkly sound. He slipped a hand into the pocket and extracted the source of the noise. He flattened the paper on the table. Who would have dropped a mint wrapper outside Amelia's barn? Even if she'd had English customers for her baskets, they would not have been near her barn.

He chomped on another bite of the granola bar, scarcely registering that it was half stale and tasted like sawdust. This was certainly not a breakfast he would ever feed his children. He laid the rest of the tasteless thing aside and focused on the wrapper. He supposed the paper could have blown from a car parked near the house. That was the only logical explanation, but even that didn't seem too likely. He wasn't sure why, but he jammed the wrapper back into his jacket pocket to contemplate again later.

He tossed the remainder of the granola bar into the trash, vowing never to purchase such items again, and swigged down the rest of his juice. He needed to get moving so he could drop the bag off with Amelia and arrive on time for work. He wanted to solve the mystery of the mint wrapper, but that would have to wait. He had a slew of other issues vying for his attention.

Noah promised to meet with him again at lunchtime, and Bishop Micah planned to visit in the evening. Ryan made a quick survey of the house on his way out the door. The place didn't look too bad, especially since the girls had not been home to mess up what he had tried to straighten the night before. He had Sarah's casserole to heat for supper, so the kitchen wouldn't become too dirty. He was as prepared for tonight as he could be.

~

Acceptance. Change. Accept change. The words reverberated through the chambers of Amelia's mind. She hadn't expected Eleanore to toss her words back at her. *So, it's fine for Eleanore to accept changes, but not you, huh?* But Eleanore's life depended on her accepting change. If her diabetes got more out of control, it could cause serious harm. Why, her very life could be in jeopardy if she didn't change her lifestyle and diet.

Amelia, on the other hand, did not have to make a change. She had made enough of them in the past few years to last a lifetime. She had gone from a girl to a married woman to a *mudder* to a widow so fast that she still reeled from all the twists and turns her life had taken. Her health did not depend on her making a change. She could be perfectly happy continuing as she was.

*Do you want to be alone for the rest of your life?* She laughed aloud at that thought. She had three young *dochders* who kept her plenty busy. Once they grew up and married, they would have little ones who would visit often and fill her heart and life.

*What about at night when everyone returns to their own homes, leaving you alone with the creaks and groans of an old house for company?* Amelia couldn't answer that question, but she suddenly felt sad. It would be difficult to be alone, but she would adjust. Wouldn't she? She could make a lot of baskets to sell and do all the knitting and quilting she wanted. And if she no longer had Meggie, she would acquire a cat or small dog. She'd read that pets make excellent companions.

Did she want to spend her older years with a dog or cat? *Ach!* She needed a strong cup of *kaffi* to drown out the annoying voices in her head. She wasn't likely to get any sleep with her brain whirring a mile a minute.

She dragged herself from the rocking chair next to the woodstove, where she had been sitting for at least an hour after a few fitful minutes of sleep, and padded to the kitchen. Wisps of steam rose from the spout of the copper tea kettle she'd set on the burner earlier. Since the water was already hot, she might as well have tea, even though it would not provide the jolt of energy that *kaffi* would.

Change. The word continued to plague her. Change for whom? Surely, Eleanore and Christina weren't encouraging her to leave their community. They would never do such a thing. They must be referring to accepting a different change, perhaps remarriage. Even the bishop encouraged that whenever he got the opportunity, but she was sure he meant for her to consider one of their own men.

If Ryan did join them, she would be happy, but would he? Would the bishop approve his membership? More importantly, would the bishop approve a marriage between the two of them? But if they were both members of the same community, they would be free to pursue a relationship. She absently unwrapped a tea bag and dropped it into a mug. She sloshed boiling water over it and stirred in a spoonful of sugar. She pulled out a chair and sat at the table, still pondering the situation.

She already loved Gabby and Jessie. No matter how much she tried to deny it, she already loved their *daed* too. Her words to Eleanore haunted her. Accept change. Embrace change. She prayed her dreams and desires were the same as the ones the Lord *Gott* planned for her. She took a sip of tea. She could always hope.

# Chapter Forty

The bright spot in his otherwise bleary morning had been seeing Amelia and his girls. He'd given Gabby and Jessie bear hugs and told them how very much he had missed them. His arms had ached to hug Amelia too. The Lord willing, he would be able to do exactly that one day soon.

Amelia had looked as lovely as ever, but Ryan couldn't miss the shadows beneath her big, blue eyes. He hoped he hadn't been the cause of her sleeplessness. Most likely, though, she had still been puzzling over Meggie's disappearance and sudden reappearance along with all the other strange events. Somehow, he had to get to the bottom of this whole thing for everyone's peace of mind. He patted the pocket with the crinkly label. He *would* put the clues together.

The scrumptious blueberry muffins Amelia had packed for him, along with the travel mug of good coffee, got him through the morning just fine. Since his schedule had been thrown off the previous evening, he'd forgotten to pack his lunch. He would have to grab something when he met Noah. It seemed he needed his girls to keep him on task. At least he was meeting Noah at The Green Thumb. He could always purchase homemade zucchini bread or a basket of apples.

~

"You will get the hang of it." Christine smiled at him a short time later. She had been helping Noah with the language instruction.

Ryan rubbed a hand across his eyes. He took a bite of the meatloaf sandwich Christina assured him she didn't plan to eat and washed it down with a swig of water. "I don't know. Don't they say you can't teach an old dog new tricks?"

Noah clapped him on the back. "You aren't exactly ancient, my *freind.*"

"Sometimes, I wonder. I'm sure the language is much easier for children to learn."

"Who?" Christina quizzed him.

"*Kinner.*"

"See, you remembered. You know a lot more than you think you do. I'm sure you've picked up many words from being around Amelia and the rest of us. They are probably all stored in your brain somewhere."

"Now, that could present a problem. I was so befuddled last night and this morning that I didn't even pack my lunch box. I'm sure any words in my brain are totally mixed up."

Christina laughed. "Don't be so hard on yourself. You're progressing well. Sometimes, the more you push, the harder a thing becomes."

Ryan nodded and polished off the last of the sandwich. "Delicious."

"*Applendisch*, not delicious. And I'll tell *Mamm* you enjoyed her meatloaf."

Ryan wiped his mouth and pulled the scrap of paper out of his pocket. "Say, do either of you eat these mints?"

Christina studied the label. "Not me. Why do you ask?"

Noah peeked over her shoulder. "I don't eat them either."

Ryan tucked the paper away. "Amelia found this near her barn. She hadn't seen it before her goats got loose and the dog went missing yesterday. She doesn't eat them either."

"Oh my!" Christina cried. "Did all the animals return home?"

"The goats were still in the driveway, so she was able to lead them to the barn. Elam brought Meggie home."

"Elam!" Christina's sip of water dribbled down her chin. "Oops!"

Ryan chuckled. "I gather you don't care much for the man."

"I care about him as I would care about any of the Lord *Gott's* creatures." She lowered her voice. "I'm not sure how much I trust him though."

Ryan swiveled his gaze to Noah, who nodded in agreement. "He's a different sort, I'll say that. But I don't know him well."

Ryan kept his voice soft too. "Is it a bit strange for a fellow to visit for so long without needing to get back to work?"

Noah got up, strode to the back door, opened it, and hurled his apple core into the woods behind the shop. "It does seem unusual. Most men have jobs or farms or some kind of work that keeps them busy. This isn't a terribly busy time of year if he only farms, but there are always animals and chores to tend to. Maybe he lives with family. I never asked."

Ryan rubbed his chin, debating whether he should voice his thoughts. He trusted Christina and Noah, so why not say what was on his mind? "I wonder if Elam eats those mints."

Christina hopped off her stool. "Do you think Elam was the one who let Amelia's animals out? Do you think he's the one who has been messing around her barn?"

Ryan sighed. "Surely, he wouldn't do such things. He would have no reason to frighten Amelia. He acts like he cares about her. At least, he certainly hates that I'm at her house so often. And he claims he would never hurt anyone or take something that didn't belong to him."

Christina drummed her fingers on the counter. Ryan could tell she was trying to piece things together. He could practically see the gears turning in her brain. If anyone could help solve a mystery, it would be Christina.

"Those mints have a strong scent. I've never smelled them when I've been around Elam, but it could be that he simply wasn't eating any at the time."

Ryan chuckled. "All I smelled yesterday was that aftershave. He must have wallowed in it. I had to help Amelia give the dog a bath."

Christina laughed. "Amelia is as sensitive to smells as I am. I can see her scrubbing Meggie." She drummed some more. "I might have to pay Annie a little visit. She'll know if her cousin has a penchant for those mints."

Noah squeezed Christina's arm and gave her a loving smile. "Uh-oh. The sleuth is at work. Don't go getting yourself in trouble again."

She shook a finger at him. "I didn't get myself into trouble before. It found me all by itself."

~

Amelia flipped the basket around and around and smiled. It turned out rather nice if she did say so herself. It was a bit fancy for her taste, but she had followed the *Englisch* customer's specifications. She had even added a few extra flourishes, small ones. She hoped they suited her customer.

The girls had all been extra tired since they'd gone to bed later than usual the previous night. They had almost been eager for their naps. Despite her own weariness, she wanted to take advantage of every opportunity she could get to work on her basket orders. The holidays were rapidly approaching.

Amelia yawned as she pushed to her feet. She twisted from side to side to loosen muscles that had grown taut as she worked. If she didn't get a breath of fresh air soon, she might very well drift off to sleep herself. She decided to bring in the clothes that had been blowing on the clothesline. That would wake her up.

Meggie zoomed across the yard to meet her as soon as she opened the back door. Amelia fastened her jacket before bending to pet the little brown head. "*Gut.* I see you are still clean.  How did you get so dirty yesterday, and why did you wander off? Were you chasing a rabbit or a squirrel?"  Amelia wished the pup could tell her how the goats got loose and why she had run off.

Amelia could scarcely take a step without the dog moving right beside her. Meggie followed her all the way down the clothesline. "What's the matter, girl? Did something scare you yesterday?" The dog gave one short bark. Amelia chuckled. "I believe you would talk to me if you could." She patted the dog again. "Brr! It's cold. Let's go."

Meggie waited for Amelia to hoist the full laundry basket to her hip and then trotted along beside her to the door. "I suppose you want a treat since you've been such a fine helper." Amelia juggled the basket so she could open the door. "I'm so happy you're back that I will gladly give you a treat."

"Who are you talking to, Mamm?"

Amelia jumped and grabbed the basket to keep the clean clothes from spilling to the ground. "You scared me, Judith. I didn't think anyone would be awake yet."

"Just me. I'm first. Hi, Meggie." The little girl bent down to receive a doggie kiss.

"I was talking to Meggie when you heard me. I promised her a treat."

"Me too?"

"Do you want a doggie treat?"

"A girl treat."

Amelia smiled. "You may have a snack when everyone else wakes up." She glanced over her shoulder a final time to make sure she hadn't dropped anything. "What's that?" She squinted. "I must have dropped something, and the wind blew it out near the woods." It had been quite windy. She set the basket inside the mudroom. "I'll be right back, Judith. Let me go fetch whatever I lost out there."

She ran across the yard to retrieve the wayward piece of laundry. "It's not clothing. It's a handkerchief." A pretty handkerchief with embroidered flowers. Amelia didn't own such a thing, but some of the other ladies made them and used them. She hadn't seen it when she pinned the laundry to the line earlier. Nor had she spotted it the previous evening, but she had been preoccupied. Where had it *kumm* from?

⁓

As the day drew to a close, Ryan found himself more and more eager to see his girls. He hadn't been able to spend much time with them when he dropped off fresh clothes earlier, and he missed them.

He pushed his fatigue aside as he drove the few miles to Amelia's house. Any chance to rest was hours away. He would need to feed and bathe the girls once they got home, read to them, pray with them, and tuck them into bed. Then he had the meeting with Bishop Micah. The outcome of that conversation would determine the amount of sleep he could hope to get that night.

Ryan couldn't help but smile when Amelia opened the door to admit him into her home. She could make the darkest day bright and chase away weariness simply by being herself. It took all his willpower not to wrap his arms around her in a gigantic hug. He settled for lifting Jessie from Amelia's arms and hugging his little girl.

Not wanting to be excluded, Gabby raced to his side and latched onto his leg. Rhonda, Judith, and Joanna followed but hung back as if unsure if they should venture closer. Ryan's heart went out to the children. He balanced Jessie on one hip and leaned down to give all the older girls a hug. He glanced up in time to catch Amelia swiping a hand across her eyes. Was she wiping away a tear?

A pot lid clanged in the kitchen, so Ryan assumed Eleanore had returned for the evening. Good. It eased his mind a little to know Amelia wouldn't be here alone with the children—*kinner*. He had to adjust his vocabulary. Would he ever be able to think in a different language, or would he always have to think in English and translate the words in his head before speaking?

"Jessie took five steps today!" Amelia announced.

"No! Really?" Ryan hugged his baby. Amelia looked as excited and proud as any mother would at her child's accomplishment. She truly loved his daughters. Might she love him as well?

"She really did, Daed. And she hardly wobbled at all." Amelia's cheeks flushed a delicate shade of rose. Was it because she called him *daed* as if they were married? That thought brought heat into his own face.

He stood Jessie on the floor. "Let's see you walk, big girl!"

"It might have been a one-time thing, Ryan," Amelia reminded him. "You know little ones can't always repeat something they've done only once."

"I know. We'll just try one time, and then I'll take my two *kinner* home. You must be aching for a break about now."

She smiled. "You remembered the word! I am not in need of a break. I'm used to three little ones all the time, so what are two more? Especially when they are as sweet as your girls." She squatted down and held out her arms. "Jessie, *kumm* here, please."

The tot peeked up at her dad and then focused on Amelia. She bounced twice as if working up her courage before toddling eight steps into Amelia's waiting arms. She squealed, obviously pleased at her accomplishment.

Amelia scooped up the little girl and hugged her. She stood and twirled around. "You did it, Jessie! You can walk!"

Ryan's eyes watered. He had to sniff and blink to keep the tears at bay. His baby was growing up. He hurried to embrace the child and the woman holding her. "She did it! Thank you, Amelia."

Amelia laughed. "I didn't do anything. It was all your *dochder's* doing."

"I'm sure you worked with her and encouraged her. She knows you love her, and she feels safe here to try new skills. I appreciate all you do." Ryan's throat tightened. He figured he'd better stop talking before he started blubbering like a baby, uh, *boppli*. He coughed to clear his throat. "Go gather your things, Gabby. We need to go home and get supper so Amelia's family can eat theirs."

The four-year-old started to obey but turned back. "Can we eat here?"

"We will not impose again. Besides, I have company coming over later." Ryan winked at Amelia and whispered, "Your bishop."

Amelia gasped. Her lips formed an O, but no sound came from her mouth.

Eleanore stepped around the corner waving a cloth. "Were you going to tell him about this, Amelia?"

# Chapter Forty-One

Amelia's face blanched as white as the fabric square she took from Eleanore's hand. "I don't think it belongs to him."

"What is it?" Ryan held out a hand.

Amelia unfolded the material. "A handkerchief. I'm sure you don't carry anything like this, and I doubt it belongs to Gabby."

"No, I can't say that I've ever used a woman's handkerchief. Where did it come from?"

"I found it near the woods when I was removing laundry from the line. I didn't see it when I hung the clothes out, and I didn't see it yesterday when I led the animals to the barn, but I wasn't really looking in that area. Did you see it last night?"

"No, but it was growing dark, and I was focused on looking for a wayward pup. Could a basket customer have dropped it?"

"They don't go near my barn, but I suppose the wind could have blown it."

"Maybe, but we've been ascribing a lot of things to the wind lately." What were the chances that the wind had blown a candy wrapper and a handkerchief from who knows where? He didn't reveal his doubt to avoid upsetting Amelia. Now he had another clue to the crazy puzzle that had become Amelia's life and no time to ponder the matter this evening. Perhaps after the bishop left and the house was quiet, he could try to sort things out.

He managed to get the girls home and fed, but they did not want to settle down to go to sleep. He'd had to read three books before their eyelids drooped. Then he'd had to race around to restore order to the kitchen and had barely finished that chore when a knock sounded at the front door. Right on time. Bishop Micah was prompt. That was for sure. Ryan took a deep breath and strode through the living room. *Please, Lord, let the man be gracious and agreeable. Please don't let me make a mess of this meeting.*

Amelia could scarcely concentrate on Eleanore's elaborate tale of her day at school. She dropped more knitting stitches than she could count and finally decided she should put the project away before she did irreparable damage to it.

"It will be all right, you know."

Amelia jumped when Eleanore patted her knee. "What? I'm sorry. What did you say? My mind wandered a million miles away."

"I daresay it only traveled a few miles."

Amelia pretended she didn't understand Eleanore's words, but her *freind's* implication came through loud and clear. Her cheeks burned. "What do you mean?"

"I remember Ryan said Micah planned to visit him tonight. I'm sure you wish you could be a fly on the wall in that house."

Amelia shrugged. "It's Ryan's business."

Eleanore tapped Amelia's knee again. "Business that could very well affect you."

"Not necessarily."

Eleanore frowned. "I am neither blind nor deaf."

"What is that supposed to mean?" Amelia jabbed her knitting needles into the ball of navy-blue yarn. Her stitches had gone from bad to worse. She needed to give up on the whole project for now.

"It means, my dear girl, that I am nearly one-hundred-percent sure that the outcome of tonight's meeting could very possibly determine your future."

Amelia couldn't comment. Anything she said could be misconstrued as agreement with Eleanore's previous observations. She would continue to silently hope for a favorable outcome to that meeting. In the meantime, she sought a change of topic. "Where do you think that handkerchief came from?"

"I can't imagine, but maybe whoever dropped it is responsible for letting the goats out and luring Meggie away."

"That would mean the perpetrator is a woman. That was definitely a woman's handkerchief."

"True, but that doesn't mean a man couldn't have acquired it from a woman."

"Do you know any women who use these embroidered hankies?"

"I've seen some of the older ladies with them. Some of the women used to embroider them to sell. I can't think right off hand who I've seen use them."

"I have seen them too. A vague memory keeps trying to creep in, but I can't quite grasp it. I believe I've seen younger women use them as well, not that there is anything wrong with that. They are useful, necessary items and only embellished with flowers or colorful trim." Amelia tapped her head. "I hope I can reel that memory in."

"Don't stress over it. As I said, a man could have borrowed his *mudder's* or *fraa's* handkerchief and stuffed it in a pocket. Whoever it belongs to must not have noticed that it fell out while they were here."

"Hmm. So you don't think Meggie simply wandered off or got interested in chasing a squirrel and got lost."

"Possible, but not likely. That dog would be too afraid she would miss a treat or a pat on the head. She's completely devoted to you and the girls. If I didn't know better, I would say she had been specifically trained to guard you."

Amelia chuckled. "She is loyal, and she's never ventured far away before."

"That dog would sleep in your bed if you let her. I'm sure she's laughing to herself right now that she maneuvered her way indoors tonight."

"You're probably right. You've grown pretty fond of her yourself, it seems to me."

Eleanore hung her head. "Guilty. She is a *gut* pup, and if you feel safer with her in the house, then she is exactly where she should be."

"I'm concerned she might become too comfortable inside and not want to be outdoors at night anymore, but I suppose that should be the least of my worries."

"Cast your worries on the Lord *Gott*. That's what the Bible says."

"I know, but that isn't always easy. I think it's human nature to want to be in control."

"Don't I know it!" A rumble punctuated her comment. Eleanore patted her belly. "See what I mean? I think I can control my body, but it lets me know I'm not in charge."

"It must be telling you that you need a bedtime snack."

Eleanore wagged her head and clucked her tongue. "How am I ever going to lose weight if my belly keeps calling for a snack?"

"If you choose something small and something allowed on your diet, you should be fine, ain't so?"

Eleanore frowned. "You had to go and stick that 'something allowable' in there, didn't you? I was thinking more along the lines of a small cookie."

"You're incorrigible. Go get a *healthy* snack, or do I need to fix one for you?"

Eleanore poked out her tongue. "Meanie." She pushed herself out of her chair with a grunt. "I can handle the job myself. I will get a couple of crackers with a mere smear of peanut butter to stick to my ribs through the night. How is that?"

"That sounds like a better idea than a cookie. I won't tell your scholars you made a face at me." She yawned and watched her *freind* shuffle to the kitchen. She should go to bed, but it was so toasty next to the stove.

"Don't you want to supervise?" Eleanore flung over her shoulder.

"I trust you."

Trust. She needed to trust the Lord that everything would work out well. He had a plan. Was it wrong to hope His plan for her included Ryan Miller and an end to all the annoying pranks?

~

Amelia had been up since well before daylight to bake. This was her day to provide treats to be sold at The Green Thumb. Christna would stop by on her way to the store to pick them up. Amelia had always enjoyed baking for the store. She liked experimenting with recipes and concocting new treats.

Today, she'd made tiny shoefly tartlets and chocolate chip whoopie pies to go along with the old faithful banana bread and zucchini bread. She'd had extra time to experiment this morning since she'd crawled out of bed so early and Ryan would be later bringing the girls because they had checkups at the doctor's office first thing. The downside of his late arrival was she would have to wait longer to see him and hear how his meeting went with Bishop Micah.

Eleanore left early to prepare some work in her classroom before the scholars arrived and took Rhonda along with her. Amelia only had to occupy Judith and Joanna with some toys on the living room floor so she could package her baked goods. Everything had to be sealed in individual plastic bags or wrap in order for Christina to sell them, and that was easier done without little ones underfoot.

Amelia hummed as she worked to try to take her mind off the possible turns Ryan's meeting with the bishop could have taken. Had it gone favorably? Would Ryan be allowed to take instruction for baptism into their church? Or would Bishop Micah flat-out refuse Ryan's request and admonish him to take more time to pray about the whole matter?

Eleanore had hit the nail on the head. The outcome of that meeting could directly affect Amelia's future. She might have to abandon all hopes for a relationship with Ryan, other than the working one they now had. Her breath caught at her next thought. Would Bishop Micah forbid Ryan to bring Gabby and Jessie here to cut off all contact with her?

Tears clouded her vision. She couldn't bear the idea of not being able to see and hug those precious little girls. Surely, the bishop wouldn't cause such an upheaval in the *kinner's* lives. They had been through so much already in the few short years they'd been on earth. She couldn't see the man doing that. He was not cruel, just stern.

Amelia sniffed. The humming had not helped. Her mind refused to be diverted from the path it had been following since yesterday. She looked down and groaned. She'd wrapped a tartlet upside down. Now she would have to remove the plastic wrap very carefully and rearrange it so people could see the top of the pastry instead of the bottom. She vowed to pay closer attention to the few remaining treats.

She had just added a wrapped treat to the bag when a knock sounded at the back door. It was too bad her visitors couldn't simply pop in as they had done not so long ago before she started keeping the place locked up tight. She stowed treats she was saving for Ryan in a cabinet before hurrying to the door.

"*Gut mariye*, Amelia."

"Hi, Christina. You certainly are bright and cheery this morning."

"It's a beautiful, crisp morning. The sun is shining. *Gott* is in His heaven, and all is right with the world." Christina laughed. "I heard that somewhere. I didn't make it up. But it sounds nice."

Amelia smiled. Maybe everything was fine in Christina's world. Her own was tilted out of kilter at the moment. "*Kumm* inside. I have everything almost ready to go."

"Whoa!" Christina grabbed the side of the door and did a quick sidestep as Meggie shot toward the opening at top speed. Christina barely managed to close the door enough to prevent the dog from slipping through. Amelia had let her out in the backyard earlier.

"Meggie! What's wrong with you? You know better." Amelia shook her finger at the dog, who did not look at all penitent. She tried to peek outside over Christina's head but was too short to see much.

"Do you want her in or out?"

"In, please."

Christina closed the door all the way and locked it.

Amelia stared at Meggie. "Something isn't right."

"With you or with the dog?" Christina looked from the animal to the woman.

"Maybe both of us. But I'm concerned about Meggie. She has never behaved like that before."

"Do you mean she's never tried to run over someone to get into the house?"

"*Jah*. Look at her. She seems nervous or afraid." The little dog had jumped into the basket Amelia had fixed as a bed for her and laid her head on her paws. She raised big, brown eyes to search Amelia's face. "What's the matter, girl?"

When Amelia reached down to pet the dog, her arm brushed against a shelf, sending a white cloth fluttering to the floor.

Immediately, Meggie bristled and leaped to her feet. Her little body shook in agitation. She growled and barked. Amelia jumped back. "What is it?"

"It's that cloth." Christina pointed. "It seems that Meggie doesn't like it."

"That's the handkerchief I found near the woods. I don't have any idea who dropped it there."

"I think Meggie must know. And she doesn't seem to like the owner too well. Has she ever acted like this around anyone?"

"Never."

Meggie inched closer to the offensive item, sniffed it, and barked again. Amelia snatched it off the floor and returned it to the shelf, pushing it out of sight. She spoke soothingly to the dog until Meggie calmed down and trotted back to her bed.

"How odd!" Christina shook her head. "I wonder what it all means."

Both women jumped at the loud rap on the door. Amelia patted her chest. "It can't be Ryan yet. His girls had doctor's appointments and surely can't be finished this soon." She started for the door.

"Don't you want to find out who it is before you open the door?"

"I can't do that without opening the door. I wasn't sure it was you when I answered your knock."

"But you were expecting me. Are you expecting someone else?"

"Not at this time." Amelia stepped closer to the door with Christina on her heels. She unlocked it and opened it a crack. She barely suppressed a groan.

"What does he want?" Christina whispered in her ear.

Amelia shrugged. "Elam. What can I do for you?"

The big man removed his hat, ran a hand through his red hair, and slapped the hat back on his head. The spicy scent of his aftershave swirled around him. "I wanted to check to make sure you were all right."

*Not again!* "Why wouldn't I be?" Before she could say anything else, Meggie hopped up and barked.

"You remember me, don't you? I brought you home?" Elam stepped back but kept his eyes on Meggie. "What's wrong with your mutt?"

"You tell us!" Christina snapped.

Elam frowned, and his face turned crimson. "How should I know what's wrong with the mean mongrel? This is the thanks I get for rescuing her?"

"Meggie is not mean. She's a *gut* dog." Amelia defended her pet as she would one of her *kinner.* "She's obviously frightened of you."

"I can't imagine why. *I* tried to help her by bringing her home."

Christina had stepped backward for a moment but then lurched forward, waving the handkerchief at Elam. "Do you recognize this?"

A puzzled expression crossed Elam's face. "It looks like a lady's handkerchief, but I don't have a clue who it belongs to. Why should I? You two should know which of the women in the community uses such things."

Meggie barked at the handkerchief before scurrying behind Amelia. The dog had never cowered before. What was going on? Amelia reached back to give the dog's head a pat. "Meggie seems afraid of you and of this handkerchief. Do you know why?"

Elam sputtered. "I came over here to be charitable, not to be accused of upsetting a dog and owning some frilly, dainty rag. I am not some common criminal, and I resent being thought of as one." He backed up and threw out his arms to keep from tumbling off the steps.

Amelia reached for his arm to keep him on his feet. "I'm sorry, Elam. I'm not accusing you of anything. I'm only trying to figure things out."

"Well, you've been figuring all wrong."

Christina was not willing to let the matter drop. "So you didn't borrow this handkerchief from someone and drop it here when you let the goats out and took Meggie?"

"You're *narrisch*! Why would I let goats out? And for the last time, I brought the dog home. I didn't remove her from the place. I'm leaving." He stormed off before Christina could say another word.

She shook her head. "That didn't go very well, did it? I'm sorry I got a little carried away, Amelia. I thought I could force him into an admission."

"He might be a pest who can't take no for an answer, but I don't believe he's the culprit." Amelia stepped back inside and closed the door.

"Do you think he knows who is at fault?"

"I'm not sure, Christina. He seemed genuinely perplexed."

"So we're back to square one."

"I guess so."

Christina studied the handkerchief. "I'm going to keep an eye out for whoever uses handkerchiefs like this."

Amelia nodded. "I guess that's all we can do at this point. Let me finish packing up the treats so you can be on your way. I know you like to open the store on time."

"It looks like your charges have arrived." Christina pointed to the window.

Ryan's dark SUV crept up the driveway. Amelia tried to calm her nerves and her enthusiasm. "Let me help him get the girls inside. I'll be right back."

"Take your time, dear. It's still early."

Amelia hurried to the vehicle and opened the back door as soon as it stopped. "Hello, girls." She unfastened the strap on the infant seat and lifted Jessie into her arms. "How did the appointment go?"

Ryan helped Gabby out and ran to catch up with Amelia. "Here, let me take her. You'll be lugging her around all day. At least let me carry her now."

"I'm used to carrying much heavier loads than this little girl."

"I know, but let me give you a break."

Gabby skipped up the steps ahead of the adults and entered the house, calling out to Judith and Joanna.

"Did their appointments go well?" She really wanted to ask about the meeting with the bishop but didn't dare do so with the girls and Christina within hearing distance.

"They are as healthy as horses."

"Splendid. I figured everything would be fine. They are always so bright and alert. I believe I would have picked up on anything amiss."

"I'm sure you would have. You are a *wunderbaar mudder.*"

She smiled at his words. "You're learning fast."

"I'm working on it." He smiled and winked.

Amelia's cheeks blazed. She hoped Christina didn't witness that display. But when she entered the kitchen with Ryan following close behind, she found Christina wrapping treats and licking her lips.

"I didn't pilfer a treat," she offered. "A big crumb fell on the counter and begged me to eat it."

Amelia laughed. "I'm sure it did."

"Hello, Ryan." Christina tucked the wrapped treats inside a plastic bag. "These tarts will be a big hit if my little sample is any indication. I might have to buy them myself." She picked up her full bags. "I'd better get going or I'll be late opening the store."

"I have to get to work too," Ryan said. "I didn't want to miss too much time. I don't want Norman to fire me." He chuckled. "I'll talk to you later, Amelia."

She nodded. She knew he didn't want to discuss Bishop Micah's visit in front of Christina either. She would simply have to wait and wonder a little longer. Ryan and Christina walked out together, leaving Amelia to busy herself with the girls and with never-ending chores.

She fed the girls a small snack since she assumed Gabby and Jessie hadn't had time for a proper breakfast. She wiped down the kitchen counters and washed dishes while the girls played in the living room. "Oh no!" Christina had forgotten the whole bag full of whoopie pies and a loaf of zucchini bread. She would never have enough goodies to sell without them.

"Girls!" Amelia peeked into the living room where they busily erected a block tower. "We will need to take some things to The Green Thumb. Christina forgot some of her treats."

From their cheers and squeals, she knew they didn't mind the trip. They loved going to Christina's shop. Amelia would make sure she left nothing in her buggy today that could be stolen.

# Chapter Forty-Two

Amelia tethered the horse and helped the older girls out of the buggy. She threw the lap blankets over her shoulder, hung the bag of treats on her wrist, and hoisted Jessie to perch on a hip. "We won't stay long, girls. You didn't leave any of your toys in the buggy, did you?"

"*Nee.*" Gabby held up the bag of small toys. Judith held up her books.

"*Gut.* Let's go inside." Amelia led the girls around the three cars parked in the lot and to the front door.

Christina opened the door for an *Englisch* customer, who had her hands full, and held it for Amelia and the girls. "My, my! Didn't I just see you ladies?" She lifted Gabby from Amelia's arms and tickled the little girl.

"Did you notice that you forgot something?" Amelia held up the arm from which the bag dangled.

"I thought I should have had more things to put on the shelf. How silly of me. But at least I get to see you all again." She nodded at the blankets and smiled. "Are you planning to spend the night?"

"I didn't want to leave anything in the buggy."

"Oh. I understand."

"Let me take Gabby so you can help your customers. Girls, please go behind the counter to play with your toys." Amelia held her hands out for the *boppli*.

"Here are my favorite girls. I can watch them while you put out your treats, Amelia, and Christina helps her customers." Annie scurried across the room.

"Annie! I didn't see your buggy out there." Amelia was sure her buggy was the only one in the parking lot unless Annie had parked around back. She cast a wary glance around the shop.

Annie giggled. "Don't worry. Elam isn't with me. I rode my bike and left it around back."

"Oh. It's *gut* to see you."

"*Gut* to see me alone, you mean."

Amelia felt the flush crawl up her neck and across her cheeks. "I didn't say that, Annie."

"It's all right, Amelia. I know you have a heart of gold and don't mean any harm. Let me see what these little ones have brought with them. Give me the *boppli*, too, so you can work."

"You don't have to do that. I can hold her and do things. I do that all the time."

"Then you need a break. I really do like *kinner*, you know. It doesn't look like I'll ever have any of my own, so humor me and let me have fun with these girls." She sighed dramatically.

"Oh, Annie. You'll have your own family. I'm sure of it."

"I don't know about that. Time is slipping away."

"You certainly aren't ancient, dear. Be patient a little longer. The right fellow will *kumm* along when you least expect him."

"I hope you're right." Annie lifted Jessie from Amelia's arms. "Shoo! I've got this."

Amelia sent Christina a questioning look. Annie was a sweet girl, but she didn't always volunteer such assistance.

Amelia began unloading her treats and placing them on the shelves.

Christina sidled up to Amelia on her way to the greenhouse to help a customer with some fall plants. "She's at loose ends since her uncle doesn't need her help at his produce stand right now, and I think she's tired of Elam."

Amelia swallowed a chuckle and nodded. She peeked over her shoulder when the chimes rang as the shop's front door flew open. She smiled. "Hi, Naomi."

"Oh! Uh, hello, Amelia. I didn't expect to see you here. Where is your buggy?"

Panic seized her. Had her entire buggy been taken now? She dropped the bag of snacks and ran to the door. "It was right there to the side of the store where I always park. Didn't you park beside it?"

Naomi grabbed Amelia's arm. "I didn't bring my buggy. I rode my bike and left it behind the store. I walked around the opposite side to enter, so I didn't see the hitching post at all. I only saw another bicycle."

Amelia patted her pounding chest. "Oh my! You scared me for a minute. I thought the whole thing had been taken this time. I'm just going to take a quick peek." She stepped outside and walked around far enough to ensure her horse still happily munched on the few available sprigs of the grass and the buggy was still intact.

Relieved, she returned to her task but wondered why Naomi had seemed so shocked or panicked to see her in the store. Maybe she had simply been surprised. But the color had certainly drained from her face. Amelia repositioned herself slightly so she could see the other woman in her peripheral vision. Naomi's jerky movements made Amelia a bit jittery herself. "I brought fresh treats if you want one." Perhaps Naomi had had a rough start to her day and a little something sweet would cheer her up.

"I'm fine. I don't need any food right now."

"Hi, Naomi. I'm down here on the floor." Annie waved a hand in the air. "That was my bike you saw."

"My! It seems like a reunion." Naomi's chuckle sounded strained, forced. "Are you, uh, alone?" Her gaze swept the store.

"Elam isn't here if that's what you mean. He certainly has a strange effect on folks, doesn't he?"

Naomi coughed. "I didn't mean anything, uh, I mean, it's just that you two are usually together. I, uh, I'll just look around a bit." She pushed a brown curl under her *kapp* where it belonged, gave a wide berth as she stepped around Amelia, and rushed down the first aisle.

Amelia caught Christina's eye and sent her a silent question.

Christina shrugged almost imperceptibly and called after the retreating young woman. "Can I help you find anything, Naomi?"

"Uh, *nee*, I know what I'm after."

"Okay. Take your time." Christina hurried behind the counter to check out the remaining *Englisch* customer.

Amelia straightened up and gave her lower back a little massage before stepping back to observe the display with a critical eye. She trounced right across Naomi's toes. "Oops! I'm sorry, Naomi. You were so quiet I didn't realize you had moved behind me." She laughed, but Naomi did not join in.

Naomi had jumped so violently that her purse flew from her hand along with the packet of straight pins and embroidery thread she'd been holding. Thank goodness the pins were in a sealed package, or they would need to crawl around to find them all.

"Let me help you gather your things, dear."

"Nee, I'll get it."

"It's my fault you dropped everything. The least I can do is pick it up." The contents of the handbag trickled out of the open top when Amelia lifted it off the floor.

"Oh my! I'm making a bigger mess. I'm sorry. What's this?" Amelia couldn't keep from gasping. She held up an embroidered square of material.

Naomi jerked it out of Amelia's hand. "It's a handkerchief. I'm sure you've seen them before." She snatched her purse away and stuffed the handkerchief inside.

"We've seen one exactly like that, haven't we, Amelia?" Christina peeked over Amelia's shoulder.

Naomi gathered up the pins and thread and thrust them into Christina's hands. "Here. You can put them back. I have to go."

Amelia laid a hand on Naomi's arm. "Were you at my house the other night?"

"You would have known if I'd visited, don't you think?"

"Maybe not at my house, but at my barn?"

"Why would I possibly go to your barn?" Naomi pulled away and stomped toward the door.

"To let my goats out and to take my dog."

Naomi didn't turn around. "Amelia, you're *narrisch*. Why would I do such a thing?" Her voice quivered slightly.

Christina stepped forward. "Why don't you tell us?"

"There is nothing to tell." Naomi reached for the doorknob but suddenly burst into tears.

Amelia rushed forward. "What is it, dear? You can tell us." When Naomi threw her hands over her face and sobbed harder, Amelia embraced her. "Can you tell me something about all the strange happenings and thefts that have occurred?"

"I-it's a-all m-my f-fault. I'm a horrible person." She cried harder.

"You are not a terrible person. Were you the person who let the goats out?"

Naomi nodded against Amelia's shoulder.

Christina's voice was not as gentle as Amelia's. "Did you take the dog, steal Amelia's blanket, quilt, and basket, and lock her in the barn?"

Annie whistled behind the counter and mumbled, "Oh dear!"

"I-I did." Naomi sniffed hard.

Amelia felt near to tears herself. "Why? What did I do to upset you so much?"

"Nothing. You didn't do anything. It was what I was afraid you would do."

"I don't understand." She led the distraught young woman to one of the stools. "Sit down."

Annie jumped to her feet and pushed a stool out from behind the counter. "I'd like to hear this too, Naomi. Why did you do all those things and make it look like my cousin was to blame? Elam might be annoying at times, but he is not a bad person."

Fresh tears coursed down Naomi's cheeks. "I never said he was a bad person." She swiped at the tears. "But he never paid any attention to me. He acted like he wanted to court Amelia. I had to make her not like him so he would leave her alone. I didn't mean to cause any harm."

"My animals could have been hurt or lost. My girls were upset over the loss of their special blanket. We lived in fear that someone would try to harm us." Amelia paused for a breath. "How did you get Meggie to leave the property?"

"That was the hardest thing. She didn't want to *kumm* with me. I had an old leash I attached to her collar and tugged her down in the woods. Then I thought someone was approaching. I guess that was Eleanore. The dog broke free. I whispered as loud as I dared to call her back, but she wouldn't *kumm*. So I ran. I hope she made it home okay."

"Elam found her and brought her home." Amelia shook her head, trying to make sense of everything. Elam had been truthful. He really hadn't had anything to do with all the mischief.

Christina shook a finger at Naomi. "Amelia could have been badly hurt when she tried to get out of the locked barn in the dark. She had to climb on hay bales, and she even fell."

"I didn't want anyone to get hurt. Honest. I was, well, I wasn't thinking right. I was upset. None of the men in Indiana took any notice of me. When I came home and found Elam visiting Annie's family, I thought what a nice man he was. Only he acted like I didn't exist."

Annie snapped her fingers. "I wasted all that effort trying to get Amelia and Elam together, even though Amelia clearly wasn't interested, when all along I could have steered him in Naomi's direction."

"Annie!" Amelia and Christina cried together.

Amelia rubbed her eyes. A pain had formed in her forehead and extended behind her eyes. "What possessed you to play matchmaker, Annie? That almost never works out."

"So I discovered." Annie sighed. "I'm sorry, Amelia. I'm a lot like Naomi. I want to find a special *freind*, and I knew Elam wanted to as well. I thought I could help him out since I couldn't seem to help myself." She looked at Naomi. "If I'd known of your interest in him, I would have tried to help. Maybe I can still—"

"*Nee!*" Naomi cried. "I am not worthy of anyone's affection. I went about everything all wrong."

Amelia was inclined to agree but held onto that thought. If Naomi had tried to gain the attention of a fellow in Indiana in the same manner, it was no wonder she returned home depressed and unattached. "Now, now, Naomi. Don't throw in the towel. We all do things that are a little silly sometimes." She caught herself before she said "foolish." The girl already felt bad enough about herself. There was no use heaping coals on her head.

"Why aren't you angry with me, Amelia? I was horrible. I scared you and made your life miserable. I *stole* from you." Fresh tears cascaded down her cheeks.

"What use would anger be? I'm sorry you resorted to such tactics, but I'm thankful my family and animals weren't harmed. And I believe you've learned a lesson."

Christina seemed not so willing to let things go. "Did you make and set off the smoke bombs too? That was a very dangerous thing to do."

Naomi's jaw dropped. "Smoke bombs? I don't even know what they are. I wouldn't begin to know how to make them or use them."

"I believe you." Amelia didn't think Naomi could fake the horror and surprise that crossed her face.

"You're too nice, Amelia. You should be furious. I don't deserve your kindness, and I don't deserve such a fine man."

"Elam?" Amelia, Christina, and Annie all exclaimed at the same time. The three women exchanged incredulous glances.

Amelia recovered first. Never one to malign another person, she sought to be positive. "Elam would probably be flattered to discover you were interested in getting to know him better."

Naomi sniffed and swiped at her eyes. "Do you really think so?" Her brief hopeful expression wilted, and her shoulders slumped a few seconds later. "He'd run the other direction if he knew everything I've done."

"Who would run where?" The voice boomed from the doorway.

All three women and even the little girls shrieked. Why hadn't the bells jangled the moment the door opened?

"Hey, Elam. What did you do to the bells over the door?" Annie found her voice first and was the only one of them who would be so blunt.

"Why does everyone always assume I've done something wrong? I can never get a break." His hangdog demeanor was almost pitiful.

Amelia suddenly felt sorry for the big, red-haired man. She also felt remorse for her erroneous opinion of him.

"I-it wasn't Elam." Naomi hastily rubbed away the remnants of her earlier tears. "The little bell thingy flew off when I entered. I grabbed it and laid it over there." She pointed to a shelf. "I'm sorry, Christina. I should have told you when I first arrived. I can't seem to do anything right these days."

Christina waved off the apology. "Think nothing of it. I'll get my stepladder and hang it back up later."

Elam crossed the aisle in two giant steps. "Don't bother doing that. I'm tall enough to easily reach the top of the door to reattach the bells without the ladder." He grabbed the bells and scooted over to rehang them. "You're Naomi, ain't so?"

She nodded as if she'd suddenly become mute.

"You aren't the only one who feels like you do everything wrong. I've felt like that a lot in my life, especially since I've been here. But you know what?" He waited for her to nod again. "We all do the best we can, and that's all we can do. To tell you the truth though—" He paused to smile. "—I'm still pretty rough around the edges. I'm working on smoothing things out.'

They all laughed, but Amelia thought the man's speech was quite profound. "You're right about striving to do our best, Elam. We are all works in progress, and we all make mistakes. Thankfully, we can all forgive." She looked at Naomi and smiled.

"*Danki*," Naomi whispered.

"Where are all of Amelia's things?" Annie, never one for subtlety, blurted out.

Amelia cringed. She wouldn't have dreamed of embarrassing Naomi in front of Elam.

"What things?" Elam fluttered the bells to make sure they were secure. "Is something else missing, Amelia?"

"*Nee*, not at all," Amelia was quick to assure him. "We were only talking about, uh, about—"

"About what lousy tricks I played." Naomi stepped forward. "I appreciate your trying to protect me, Amelia, but I need to own up to my mistakes."

"Annie, would you take the girls to see the flowers?" Annie's frown told Amelia she was not happy about missing any of the action, but Amelia believed the girls had heard enough. Even though the women had been conversing in *Englisch* so Amelia's little ones wouldn't understand, Gabby would have made sense of some of the conversation. Amelia hoped the *kinner* had been too absorbed in their playing to take notice of the adults.

Annie sighed. "Sure, Amelia. Okay, girls. Let's take a walk."

Amelia smiled. "*Danki*, Annie." She turned back to Naomi. "You really don't have to air your dirty laundry, Naomi. All is forgiven, and we can move forward."

Naomi peeked at Elam and then stared at the floor. "I at least owe Elam an explanation and an apology."

"You don't owe me anything." Elam's forehead wrinkled in obvious confusion.

"Let me tell you why I do, and then I need to ask your forgiveness too. Please hear me out."

Elam nodded. "I'm listening."

Naomi repeated her story about playing pranks with the hope that Amelia would blame Elam and want to keep her distance from him. Her face turned ten shades of red when she explained why she wanted to hinder any relationship between them, and Elam's cheeks bloomed brighter than Naomi's. "So you see, Elam, I am a terrible person who could have caused a lot of harm."

"But you didn't!" Amelia interjected. She hated for the woman to have such a low opinion of herself.

Naomi ignored Amelia's remark and focused on Elam. "I humbly beg your forgiveness, Elam. I am truly sorry for casting you in a bad light. I will no longer try to *kumm* between you and Amelia."

"Wait!" Elam and Amelia protested at the same time.

"Amelia is not interested in me, Naomi, and she never has been. I was a bit overbearing, I'm afraid, but I really did want to protect you, Amelia. I figured since I didn't have to rush off to a job, I would have been better able to stand guard than the other men. I went about everything all wrong, and it took a while for me to get it through my thick head that we could only be *freinden,* if I hadn't ruined that chance too. So I need to ask for forgiveness for my sometimes-boorish behavior and for trying to cast Ryan Miller in a bad light. I need to work on my mistrust of strangers, I'm afraid."

"But you were a stranger to us!" Christina interjected.

"True, but since I'm Old Order, I figured I was the same as one of you."

*Sometimes*-boorish behavior? A *bit* overbearing? Amelia let those objections slide. "I don't hold any grudges. I'm sure Ryan won't hold any grudges either. I am happy to have the whole mess cleared up."

"You can stop living in fear," Christina said.

"And poor Eleanore can return to her home."

Christina chuckled. "I'm sure she considered staying with you a vacation."

"I will bring your belongings to you later if that's all right with you, Amelia."

"You needn't rush." They had done without them for so long that another few days wouldn't make a difference. "I'm going to check on the girls."

"I'll go with you." Christina linked arms with Amelia, and the two headed for the greenhouse. At the doorway, she leaned close to whisper, "Do you think Elam and Naomi will hit it off?"

"Stranger things have happened. Elam certainly seemed flattered that Naomi went to such great lengths to keep us apart. If she had only asked, I would have told her I did not have any kind of interest in the man." She couldn't resist a

little shiver, even though she no longer considered Elam as obnoxious as she once
did.

# Chapter Forty-Three

"I am going to miss you all." Eleanore's eyes watered when Amelia told her about Naomi's confession.

Amelia hugged the schoolteacher. "I will miss having you here. Please stay tonight. We'll enjoy the evening together. You know that you are *wilkom* here any time, don't you? You don't need an invitation. Any time you need a break or want to visit, please drop in. I know it can't be easy living with your *bruder* and *schweschder*-in-law."

"You're right. It isn't, but I try to make the best of it."

"One day soon, I believe, you will have a home of your own."

Eleanore laughed. "I like your dreams." She glanced toward the window. "It looks like the subject of your dreams has arrived."

Amelia followed Eleanore's gaze to rest on the dark SUV creeping up the driveway. She playfully swatted her *freind's* arm. "Not so."

"I disagree. I'm going to take the girls outside so the two of you can have a private conversation. I know you are eager to learn how Ryan's visit with Micah went."

Amelia wanted to know but was afraid to find out. "You don't have to leave."

"You can't have privacy with all our listening ears around. Please talk things out. I believe you have a lot to say to each other." She turned and clapped her hands like the schoolteacher that she was. "Who wants to go outside one more time before it gets dark?"

Ryan smiled at the conclusion of Amelia's tale. He wanted to hug her but didn't dare. "I'm so glad you don't have to be afraid any longer. It's sad Naomi believed she needed to go to such extremes, but I'm happy to know all your belongings will be returned and you no longer need to glance over your shoulder every time you step outside your house."

"So am I. It is such a relief. Naomi will return all our belongings. The girls will be glad to have their special quilt back, but I think we will go ahead and make our new one too." She dropped her gaze to the floor and wrung her hands.

Ryan knew she wanted to ask him about his meeting the previous evening. He wanted to share the news with her but feared she wouldn't be as elated as he was. What if he had read her all wrong? If so, he might be heartbroken as well as embarrassed. He had to take the chance. "I wanted to tell you about my visit with your bishop last night."

"*Jah?*" She twisted her fingers more.

Ryan reached for her tiny hands. "I'm afraid you'll snap the bones."

Amelia laughed. "It's a silly habit I resort to subconsciously when I'm nervous."

"Are you nervous now?"

"I am. I'm eager to hear what Bishop Micah said but also a bit afraid."

"Let me put your mind at ease. He said I could join your church. I won't need to take full instruction since our faiths are similar but can meet privately with him. I will need to renounce my 'worldly' ways, which I will happily do." He watched as Amelia's eyes grew larger and brighter. Her smile made his heart sing and his spirit soar.

"I'm happy for you, if you are sure this is what you want."

"I couldn't be more sure. There is only one thing I want more than joining your community."

"What is that?"

"To have a life with you. Do you think that is a possibility?" Ryan held his breath. If she said it was not even remotely possible, he might collapse into a heap of misery.

"Are you sure you want to live without electricity, a car, and a telephone?"

"I'm sure I can live without those things, just as I'm sure I *can't* live without you, dear Amelia."

"Then I think a life together is very possible."

"You do? Truly? For sure?"

Amelia laughed. "For sure. Truly. I do."

He lifted the petite young woman and twirled around with her until they both laughed and gasped for breath. He set her down, brushed his lips across hers, and gazed into her eyes. "Do you think we could have a short courtship because I am already certain that I love you."

"I-I love you too."

Ryan wrapped his arms around her and pulled her close. He liked the way her head fit right below his chin. "I will tell the bishop I am a fast learner so he can speed up whatever instructional sessions I need to have. We are starting tonight, by the way. Then we can discuss future plans with him. Does that sound *gut* to you?"

She smiled. "*Jah.* It sounds perfect."

They drew apart at the pitter-patter of multiple pairs of feet approaching. "We'll have to be crafty to find alone time," Ryan whispered. He couldn't resist kissing her again when she smiled and blushed such a delicate pink color.

Four little girls appeared in the doorway, followed by Eleanore who carried Jessie. "I tried to keep them away longer, but it was growing chilly and dark."

"Oh my!" Amelia looked out the window. "Where did the time go? I'm sure everyone is getting hungry for supper."

"Gather up your belongings, Gabby, so we can go home." Ryan reached to take Jessie from Eleanore's arms.

Gabby hung her head. Her lip poked out in a pout. "I hoped we could stay."

Amelia wrapped her arm around the little girl. "We will have lots of suppers together, dear one, but your *daed* has some things to do at home this evening. I will see you bright and early in the morning, and we will bake more cookies after chores. How does that sound?"

"What kind of cookies?"

"I was thinking about making iced gingersnaps and leaf-shaped sugar cookies."

"Can we decorate them?"

"Of course."

Gabby jumped up and down. "I can't wait. Okay, Daddy. Let's go so we can hurry and come back."

The adults laughed.

Eleanore took Gabby's hand. "I will help you gather your things." She led the little girl to the living room. Not to be left out of anything, Amelia's three girls followed.

Ryan stepped closer to Amelia and spoke softly. "We'll tell them when we can all sit down together. Does that sound all right to you?"

"That sounds fine." A tear trickled down her cheek.

Ryan wiped the tear away with his free hand. "I hope this is a happy tear."

"Very happy."

~

Amelia hummed as she scrubbed the soup pot. She had already bathed the girls, read to them, prayed with them, and tucked them into bed. She'd had a hard time not telling them her news but didn't want them to become too excited to sleep. And she knew they would be happy. They loved Ryan, and they already treated Gabby and Jessie as *schweschders*. Besides, it would be better for her and Ryan to tell all the *kinner* together.

"I take it everything went well with Ryan's meeting with Micah?" Eleanore picked up a bowl from the dish drainer and began drying it.

"It did." Amelia scrubbed harder. She looked up when Eleanore elbowed her. "What?"

"You are about to wear a hole in the bottom of that pot if you keep abusing it. Would you happen to have some special news?" Eleanore gave her a sly smile.

"I do have very *gut* news. Ryan is going to take instruction to join our church."

Eleanore clapped her hands. "I knew it! And then..."

"Then what?"

"You tell me."

Amelia's cheeks heated. She swiped at a tendril of hair with her arm. "We plan to have a serious discussion with the girls."

"Does this mean what I think it means?"

Amelia blinked back tears and nodded. "You were right."

"See. The Lord *Gott* does work everything out for *gut*. We only need to trust Him, not that that is always easy to do."

"I know everything will work out for *gut* for you too, my *freind.*"

"I'm happy seeing you so happy. And I'm so glad all that nonsense with Naomi is over. You know, she might be the perfect person for Elam."

Amelia laughed. "You could be right. There is a right person for you too, Eleanore. I feel it in my heart."

Eleanore smiled. "Perhaps we will all have a happily ever after."

# Epilogue

Amelia studied the artwork on the wall and smiled. Some of the first graders had mostly scribbled and barely stayed within the printed lines of the coloring page. Others had drawn and colored their own creations. Rhonda was a member of the latter group. She possessed quite an artistic talent and had created a lovely farm scene, complete with horses, goats, and a dog resembling Meggie. Amelia hoped that little artistic flair didn't cause a problem somewhere down the line. She couldn't see that occurring though. Rhonda was such an agreeable, obedient little girl.

The holiday gathering at the school mere days before Christmas was festive and joyful. The scholars had outdone themselves. They performed their recitations and re-enactment of the Christmas story with only minimal prompting from Eleanore. Amelia knew she should not be prideful, but she couldn't help that teensy bit of pride that crept in when Rhonda recited her lines flawlessly. Goodness knows she had rehearsed her part so often her younger *schweschders* could probably have spoken the lines with her.

Christina, who stood next to her, nudged her with an elbow. "What are you smiling at?"

"The scholars. Didn't they do a splendid job this evening? I will have to make sure I tell Eleanore how *wunderbaar* the whole program was."

"Everything did seem to go off without a hitch." Christina nodded to the display right in front of them. "Let me guess. That picture is Rhonda's, ain't so?"

Amelia laughed. "Surely her name printed in the lower corner didn't give you a clue."

Christina chuckled. "I didn't even see the name, smarty pants. But I have seen Rhonda's artwork when she sat coloring at The Green Thumb. Maybe I should see about purchasing some of her masterpieces to hang on the walls of my shop."

Amelia poked her *freind*. "Silly! Don't go telling her things that will go to her head. It wouldn't do for her to feel pride."

"Even though you do."

"Shh! I'm her *mudder*. I'm allowed to rejoice in my *dochder's* skill, but I intend to keep that to myself."

Christina glanced around the schoolroom. "It looks like the whole community turned out for the school Christmas program again this year, except for the few shut-ins."

"*Jah*. It's so nice to see everyone together. Eleanore said some of the older scholars were going to take treats to those who could not attend. Isn't that a great idea?"

Christina nodded. "Eleanore is so caring. She always finds a way to get her scholars involved in the community." She lowered her voice. "Psst! Look to your left at the couple pretending not to be a couple."

Amelia peeked over her shoulder to discover Naomi shuffling along beside Elam. "I had heard that Elam returned. I guess Naomi's visit to his hometown went well."

"Apparently. From the looks of things, I'm thinking an announcement might be forthcoming."

"Wouldn't that be something! Here Naomi thought she would be ostracized for her behavior, but she had exactly the effect she had hoped for. She managed to gain Elam's interest, and the feeling certainly appears mutual." Amelia dropped her voice to a mere whisper. "But she didn't have to worry about me being attracted to the man. He is not my cup of tea. It's great that the two of them hit it off so quickly though. Do you think Naomi will move to Pennsylvania?"

"I'm sure she will if they do indeed marry. I was surprised to learn that Elam owned a farm and ran a successful blacksmith business  Who'd have thought?"

"I know. He seemed so content to while away his time here as if he didn't have any responsibilities. I hope they will be happy." Amelia glanced toward the table where her little ones sat munching cookies with some older girls before letting her gaze wander the room.

"You wouldn't be looking for someone in particular, would you?"

"I'm not looking for anyone at all."

"And Christmas doesn't come in December."

"I was simply checking on my *kinner.*" Amelia's cheeks grew warm.

"They are over that way." Christina pointed in the opposite direction. "But I do believe I see some almost members of our community here tonight. Isn't that grand?"

"*Jah.*" Amelia's single word came out as a whispered squeak.

Christina lowered her voice. "I'm so happy for you, Amelia. I'm glad things have worked out just right. You and Ryan are perfect for each other."

"Shh!" Amelia placed a finger to her lips. "We haven't announced anything."

"That's only a formality that will be remedied soon. No one who looks at you can miss the way your faces light up when you see each other."

Amelia's face couldn't possibly get any hotter without bursting into flame. She needed to turn the conversation in a different direction. "It's remarkable how everyone has already accepted him even though he hasn't officially joined the church yet."

"But most people already knew him and liked him. He has been well-respected ever since he moved to the area. He fits in well and should transition just fine. Noah said Ryan has caught onto our ways very quickly."

"I'm sure he would be happy to hear that."

"And you're not?"

"Of course, I am. He has been working hard."

"Who has been working hard?"

The deep male voice caused little shivers to race up and down Amelia's spine. She looked up into the brown eyes she would never tire of gazing into. For a moment, she was speechless. She couldn't even form a coherent thought.

"We were saying what a *gut* scholar you have been." Christina broke the silence.

"*Danki.* See, even the words are rolling off my tongue a bit quicker." He chuckled, and the women laughed with him. He stepped closer to the wall to point out colors on the scholars' drawings to Jessie, who wiggled in his arms.

Christina tapped Amelia's arm. "I see Annie over there alone. I know she is glad to be home. She wasn't thrilled that she had to travel with Elam and Naomi as a chaperone. She had hoped to meet some of the young folks there and maybe find a special *freind* of her own, but she ended up following Elam and Naomi around. She looks a little sad, so I'll go try to cheer her up."

Amelia nodded. "She does seem blue. I'm sure she will find someone when she least expects it." She leaned closer to Christina and whispered, "Like we did."

Christina laughed. "I hope so. She's pretty tired of working for her *onkle.* It would be nice if she found some special talent that would bring her joy."

"We'll have to help her discover one."

Christina sighed. "Would that we could. I'll catch up with you later."

Amelia watched Ryan set his wiggly little girl down. Jessie had celebrated her first birthday a few weeks ago and had become so adept at walking that she disliked being held for very long. She toddled toward Amelia with outstretched arms.

Ryan tried to capture her, but she reached for Amelia again. "Amelia has to carry you around day after day, little one. Let's give her a break."

"I don't mind taking her at all, Ryan." Amelia leaned down and held out her hands to the *boppli*, who giggled and lunged forward. Jessie threw one arm around Amelia's neck and planted a slobbery kiss on her cheek. "Aren't you a sweet girl!" Amelia hugged her and patted her back.

"*Mamm.*"

Amelia's heart skipped a beat. She looked from Jessie to Ryan. What was she supposed to say?

Ryan squeezed Amelia's arm and mouthed, "I hope so. Very soon." He leaped away to chase Jessie, who apparently wanted to practice her walking skills.

Amelia's face felt as scorched as it did after working in the garden on a hot, humid, mid-July day. She needed to look away from the man and *boppli*.

Christina, who had been walking back in their direction, smiled and winked at her. She sidled up to Amelia and whispered directly into her ear. "Maybe we will both be married and expecting little ones by next Christmas."

Now Amelia wished the floor would split apart and swallow her. She hoped Ryan had been too far away to hear that comment. She elbowed her *freind*. "Hush! You'll start rumors."

"They can't be rumors if they end up being true."

"You have strange logic." Amelia stared at the floor to give her cheeks a chance to return to normal color. She sensed another presence and dared to lift her eyes. "Eleanore! Your scholars did such a fine job. You must be pleased with them."

"They are very bright *kinner* and always eager to do their best."

"Well, it's obvious they adore you, and you are so *wunderbaar* with them."

"I love teaching." She chuckled. "It's a *gut* thing I do since I'll probably be doing it all my life."

"I'm sure you will have a family of your own, dear. Just give it time."

Eleanore laughed. "Don't hold your breath. But I love my job, so I'm okay with it if I don't find someone special."

"Like we told Annie, don't give up hope." Christina patted the woman's arm. "Excuse me, please. I see Noah, so I believe I'll mosey in his direction." She reached up to smooth her hair.

"You look as lovely as always, Christina, but I have a feeling Noah wouldn't care if you wore a sack over your head," Eleanore teased.

Amelia smiled as she watched Christina head toward her beau. Both their faces lit up as their eyes connected. If she and Ryan exhibited the same reaction, their feelings for one another would not be a secret. She tore her gaze from the couple and focused on Eleanore. "I appreciate the nights you spent with me and the girls. I hope you've adjusted to being back home."

Eleanore sighed. "As much as I can. I really shouldn't complain. I have a place to live, and it's great spending time with my nieces and nephews."

"Have you been feeling well? You're looking well."

"Oh, the diet is still a challenge. Those chocolate brownies over there on the table have been calling to me, but I will continue to ignore them."

"*Gut* for you! You can conquer those cravings. I know you can."

Eleanore squeezed Amelia's arm. "*Danki* for your confidence in me. You have more faith in me than I have in myself. I'd better go greet a few parents I haven't spoken with yet."

Amelia watched the schoolteacher saunter off. She jumped when a hand tapped her shoulder from behind.

"I finally have you to myself." Ryan spoke softly. "Well, as much as possible in a room full of people and with a little one in tow."

"There certainly are a lot of people here. The Christmas program is quite an event." Amelia lifted Jessie from his arms. The little girl finally seemed tuckered out. "Someone is growing tired."

"It's about time. I've been chasing her everywhere." He lowered his voice even more. "Maybe next year we will attend the program together as a family."

Amelia's heart skipped a beat. "That would be nice."

"I'm almost finished with my instruction. Bishop Micah and Noah have been very helpful with all the practical aspects of my new life, but I'm afraid I will still need your help with some things."

"That's what couples do. They work together and help each other."

"*Couple* is such a nice word, don't you think?"

Amelia gasped when she gazed into his eyes. She felt as if he could see right into her heart and soul. No one else existed at the moment, not even the little girl who had laid her head on Amelia's shoulder. Had the whole world stopped? When Ryan took her arm and led her to a far corner of the room, she followed as if in a daze.

"I can't wait any longer, dear Amelia."

"Wait for what?"

"I know we have spoken about our intentions, but I want to formally ask you. Will you do me the honor of becoming my *fraa*? I love you more than life itself, and I love your girls as my own. Are you sure you could take on two more little ones and their *daed*? If you need to reconsider everything, I truly understand." He shuffled his feet and stared at the floor.

"I don't need time, and I don't need to reconsider a thing. I love you, Ryan Miller, and I love Gabby and Jessie."

Ignoring anyone who might be looking in their direction, he wrapped an arm around her in a brief hug. "You have made me the happiest man alive. And I promise to give you a proper hug later."

Amelia smiled. "I'll hold you to that promise." A tug on her skirt finally drew her attention away from the man who had stolen her heart. Four little girls with cookie crumbs lining their lips stared at their parents. She smiled at them as Ryan stretched to wrap his arms around all of them.

"I love all of my girls," he whispered.

Amelia blinked hard to keep the tears from falling. The Lord *Gott* had indeed blessed her with this *wunderbaar* man. She now knew beyond the shadow of a doubt that she was following the path He had outlined for her. Her hopes and dreams were about to be realized. *Gut* things did *kumm* to those who waited.

Across the room, Christina smiled and nodded at her. She made an okay sign with her thumb and forefinger. But life was so much more than merely okay. It was grand.

Together, Ryan and Amelia and their girls walked outside toward the legion of black buggies. Snowflakes fell like silent crystals around them, promising a white Christmas this year.

Amelia stood outside the buggy, waiting for her three girls to settle themselves on the buggy seat. She covered them with their favorite old quilt with the brown-and-white dog, tabby cat, bluebird, and black-faced sheep embroidered in the corners that Naomi had returned with all the other belongings she had taken. The new version of the quilt was on the quilting frame, but Amelia decided to add three more animals as soon as Ryan and his girls decided on their favorites.

Ryan had already tucked his girls into his new buggy and slipped over to take Amelia into his arms. "I promised a proper hug."

"So you did." She hugged him back as fat snowflakes drifted onto their shoulders.

He bent to capture her lips with his own before whispering, "Merry Christmas, my *lieb*."

"And Happy New Year." Amelia stroked his cheek and gazed into the blue eyes she loved.

"The happiest."

# Eleanore's Wish

## Plain Paths, Book Three

Eleanore Gingrich loves teaching school in her old Order Amish community in Southern Maryland. In fact, teaching is the joy of her life. Her parents' tragic deaths after an accident two years ago required her to move from the only home she had ever known. Now she lives with her brother—the bishop—and his wife and four children. She loves her family but often feels like she gets in their way. Secretly, she wishes for a home and family of her own.

She wishes even more that she did not have diabetes and high cholesterol. She has not been able to come to terms with her health conditions and struggles to follow her doctor's orders. In her eyes, having chronic illnesses and being slightly pudgy don't exactly make her prime marriage material. Thank goodness she enjoys teaching her scholars!

She is surprised and confused when small gifts suddenly begin appearing in unexpected places. Is someone playing tricks on her, or does Eleanore have a secret admirer?

# Acknowledgments

Thank you to my daughters, Rachel and Holly, for your encouragement and support, not to mention all the promotional and technical help. (Rachel, you've sent notices every time the library acquired one of my books! Holly, I wouldn't have a website or newsletter without you!)

Thank you to my fantastic, loyal readers, who eagerly read books, post reviews, and send me messages of encouragement. It's always wonderful to know that my stories have touched a heart or brought a smile.

Thank you to my mother, who read every poem, essay, and story I wrote while growing up. I wish you were here to read my books now, but I know you are celebrating my accomplishments in heaven.

Thank you to Dana Russell for all your support and for providing opportunities for book signings every time I release a new book.

Thank you to my Mennonite friends, Greta and Ida, for all the stories and information you have shared with me.

Thank you to my editor, Kimberly Steinke, for polishing my story.

Above all, thank you to God who blessed me with dreams, ideas, and stories. Without Him, I can do nothing. With Him, all things are possible.

# About the Author

USA Today Bestselling Author Susan Lantz Simpson has been writing stories and poetry ever since she penned her first poem at the age of six. She has always loved the magic of words and how they can entertain and enlighten others.

Susan's love of words and books led her to earn a degree in English/Education. She has taught students from prekindergarten to high school and has also worked as an editor for the federal government. She also holds a degree in nursing and has worked in hospitals and in community health.

She writes inspirational stories of love and faith and has published a middle-grade novel (*Ginger and the Bully*) in addition to her inspirational romances (Plainly Maryland Series and Southern Maryland Amish Romances Series). Her novella, *The Christmas Fudge Miracle,* is included in the USA Today Bestseller Amish Christmas Miracles Collection. She was a finalist in the OCW Cascade fiction contest. She is a member of ACFW. She lives in Maryland and is the mother of two wonderful daughters. When she isn't writing, she enjoys reading, walking, and doing needlework.

# Dear Reader

If you enjoyed reading the fourth book in Amelia's Hope, I would appreciate it if you would help others enjoy this book, too. Here are some of the ways you can help spread the word:

**Lend it**. This book is lending enabled so please share it with a friend.

**Recommend it.** Help other readers find this book by recommending it to friends, readers' groups, book clubs, and discussion forums.

**Share it.** Let other readers know you've read the book by posting a note to your social media account and/or your Goodreads account.

**Review it**. Please tell others why you liked this book by reviewing it on your favorite retailer.

Everything you do to help others learn about my book is greatly appreciated!

Susan Lartz Simpson

# Other Titles by Susan Lantz Simpson

Plainly Maryland Series
*Plain Haven*
*Plain Discovery*
*Plain Truth*

Southern Maryland Amish Romance Series
*The Promise*
*The Mending*
*The Reconciliation*
*Rosanna's Gift*
*Lizzie's Heart*
*Samuel's Return*

Plain Paths Series
*Christina's Courage*
*Amelia's Hope*

*The Christmas Fudge Miracle*
in the Amish Christmas Miracles Collection

*The Sweetest Gift*
in the More Amish Christmas Miracles Collection

*The Healing Season*
in the Amish Across America Collection